D0763350

A Trick of the Light

David Ashton was born in Greenock in 1941. He studied at Central Drama School in London from 1964 to 1967, starring in *The Voyage of Charles Darwin*, *Brass*, *Hamish Macbeth* and *Waking the Dead*. His most recent performance was in *The Last King of Scotland*.

David started writing for film, television, theatre and radio in 1984 and has seen many of his plays and TV adaptations broadcast; he wrote early episodes of *EastEnders*, *Casualty*, *Dalziel and Pascoe*, a film for Channel 4 starring Minnie Driver and Bill Paterson called *God on the Rocks*, six *McLevy* series starring Brian Cox for BBC Radio 4 plus a pilot for a new series, *Doctor Johnson's Dictionary of Crime*.

This is his third McLevy novel, *The Shadow of the Serpent* (2006) and *Fall from Grace* (2007) being the other two.

ALSO BY DAVID ASHTON
The McLevy Mysteries:
Fall from Grace
The Shadow of the Serpent

A Trick of the Light

An Inspector McLevy Mystery

DAVID ASHTON

To Stan + Meredith

Best wishes David

Polygon

First published in Great Britain in 2009 by
Polygon, an imprint of Birlinn Ltd
West Newington House
10 Newington Road
Edinburgh EH9 1QS

www.birlinn.co.uk

Copyright © David Ashton 2009

10 9 8 7 6 5 4 3 2 1

The right of David Ashton to be identified as the author of
this work has been asserted by him in accordance with the
Copyright, Designs and Patents Act, 1988.

All rights reserved. No part of this publication may be
reproduced, stored, or transmitted in any form, or by any
means electronic, mechanical or photocopying, recording
or otherwise, without the express written permission of the
publisher.

ISBN: 978 1 84697 091 7

British Library Cataloguing-in-Publication data
A catalogue record for this book is available
on request from the British Library.

Typeset in Great Britain by SJC
Printed and bound in Bungay, Suffolk by
Clays Ltd, St Ives plc

TO
SONJA

1

One of my cousins, long ago,
A little thing, the mirror said,
Was carried to a couch to show,
Whether a man was really dead.

JAMES THOMSON, 'In the Room'

Leith Docks, Edinburgh, 1864

The man had been running for his life. A shaft of light from one of the creaking ships moored in the harbour caught his face like a lover's hand and tilted it to the side as he came to a juddering halt in one of the narrow wynds; the stone passages that spread like broken veins from the main artery of the Old Docks.

Breath jagged in his throat, heart jumping as he listened. Nothing. Good. He had lost them.

The face was almost petulant, a drooping full lower lip somewhat redeemed by the bony hooked nose and flecked hazel eyes. He had lost his hat in the chase and his golden hair glinted treacherously like a beacon in the stray beam of light. It flopped over one eye in a manner some might describe as affectation but his wife thought most becoming. Like a true plantation owner. A shadow in the sugar cane.

A bitter smile crossed the man's face. His name was Jonathen Sinclair. He was an officer in the Confederate Army and a measure out of his depth as a clandestine agent beyond the battlefield.

And his wife? She was far away. Lost in a dream.

The silence was profound; just the soft hissing of the rain, hardly audible, a saturating, insidious blanket of moisture that seeped into his very bones.

Melissa. Sweet Melissa. They had married with the approaching Civil War as best man. Since then, only snatched moments of marital bliss where the grim spread of death and blood did not stain her pretty dress nor lessen the desire that her husband must acquit himself a hero.

1

Her passion gripped and ringed him round. . . A wilful heat, a passion-ate certainty. The South must triumph.

But that was before Cemetery Ridge, and before the Alabama was sunk in Cherbourg breakwater with thousands howling on the shore as the ship went down. How many men swam under the sea that day? How many brave sailor boys? What songs were they singing?

Jonathen Sinclair realised – approaching midnight in the Leith docks, in a foreign land, in a damp, dank climate where the sun seemed to grudge each moment in the sky – that he was not a hero. Not by a long travail. He was capable of heroic deeds most certainly, but he could not hammer through the long pain. A real hero endures.

And when he dies, angels lead him to heaven where a white house stands upon the hill with a woman looking out the window. A farmer's girl. Her face always the same. Loving and full of welcome. Waiting for him.

He almost burst out in a reflex of laughter but that small moment of release was strangled by a sound somewhere in the dark empty space that unrolled in all directions before him; one of which was out past the nudging ships and into the blank pitiless ocean.

Footsteps. Certain in pursuit. The fixed betrothed, coming for her rav-aged bridegroom.

A sudden shriek on high and he clapped his hand over his own mouth to forestall startled response.

As if he had divided into two parts; one the grim guardian who had watched his own men, under the merciless hail of Union artillery, splinter into the sky, grey uniforms spouting red. And the other?

A young officer stands looking at himself in the mirror, slouch hat firm-ly upon his head, cord with acorn tassels stitched in place, travelling cape over his shoulders. A handsome dandy.

It was a seagull. No more. Damned bird. Screeching like a lost soul in the black sky above.

And the footsteps had stopped. Perhaps they had never existed. A fig-ment of his guilty conscience.

Sinclair removed a hand from lips that had tasted forbidden fruits and puffed out a short breath.

He had learned the value of stillness, waiting in the reeds by the river to surprise a Union munitions column; arms so badly needed that they might justify the inglorious action about to be taken. Early morning, the sun new-risen, clouds like cotton, as if the world has just been born.

> 'When I was young I us'd to wait
> On Massa and hand him up his plate;
> Pass down the bottle when he got dry,
> And brush away de blue-tailed fly.'

Abe Lincoln's favourite song they said. A minstrel song. A slave's song. Of revenge.

A large horsefly with a blue-black belly had landed on the back of his hand where he gripped the revolver. It was searching out blood and stung through just as the ragged volley of shots rang out and the dark uniformed Union soldiers fell from their horses into the yellow waters.

His own soldier boys whooped and screamed as they waded out, bayonets fixed, knives in hand, to finish off the few survivors. The blade driven deep, cut and drown rather than waste a bullet, savages in threadbare Confederate grey; the war had turned them all into barbarians.

As they hauled the plunging horses with their precious cargo back towards the riverbank one of the floating bodies suddenly sprang to life and a terrified young Union soldier ran towards what he hoped might yet be safety amongst the long rushes, not seeing in his blind panic the still figure of the officer standing there.

Then he did. Halted. His mouth opened as if to say something in explanation before the back of his head exploded and he toppled to lie in the shallow water, fragments of bone and blood swirling forlornly around Sinclair's muddy boots.

Corporal John Findhorn, who had fired the shot and would die of his wounds on the long retreat to Virginia after, like Sinclair, surviving the slaughter of Gettysburg, looked down at the corpse and shook his head. 'That man should have stayed dead,' he pronounced.

Findhorn, a Baptist from Arkansas, tended to the laconic. Sinclair found him a great relief. Most people, including himself, talked too damned much.

He sucked the back of his hand where the insect had drawn blood and spat it out to join the rusty streaks in the yellow water.

He and the corporal looked across and read death in the other's eyes. Then Sinclair gazed up to where the sun burned with fierce indignation above in the powder blue sky.

The South had no base from which to build. Their only ironclad, the CSS Virginia, had been scuttled to prevent capture. No ships or guns; the Confederates could only steal or buy and the Union naval blockade was strangling them like an anaconda.

The blockade must be broken.

A sound jerked him back to the present. In front of his retreat, ships creaked quietly in the harbour like docile beasts of burden. Behind though. Surely he had not been outflanked? He turned slowly, hand sliding into the folds of a thick coat where his revolver had its resting place.

He had but three bullets remaining.

His eye caught a flicker of movement in the darkness. Low down. A crouched shape. Too small for a man, too large for an outcast dog.

Sinclair lunged with his free hand, the other gripped to his gun, and his clawed fingers found purchase on hair. Human hair. He hauled up, backwards to the faint light and looked into the feral, terrified face of a young boy.

'Don't mark me, sir,' the captive whimpered, face crunched up in pain. 'I'm no' harmful.'

'What are you doing here, eh?' Sinclair spoke softly and dragged the boy close by to muffle the exchange, only too aware that more dangerous foes might lurk in the shadows.

'Where I sleep,' replied the other with muted indignation. 'A' right for some.'

This pallid show of gumption brought a brief smile to Sinclair's lips.

He chose his words carefully. *The Scots valued consonants more than vowels at times and he had mitigated his accent accordingly.*

Light and clear. Keep it so.

'What is your name?'

'Samuel Grant.'

'Not Ulysses S.?' he asked with a bitter smile, reminded of the Union General who was a thorn in the flesh of the South and had driven the Johnny Rebs from Tennessee to open a route through Atlanta into the heart of the Confederacy.

'Ulysses?' The other screwed up his face at the unfamiliar name. 'That's foreign.'

Sinclair laughed softly and a glint of animal cunning showed in the boy's eyes as if he thought there might be some advantage to be taken.

'I've seen you, sir,' he whispered.

'Where?'

'At the Happy Land.'

The man's own eyes hardened. *Lie down with dogs, you get up with fleas.* It was indeed true that after dark the streets of Edinburgh and Glasgow were littered with the poverty-stricken discards of society but some

4

were thieves, some were dishonest whores and many took the guise of help-less victim. And then struck.

Sinclair realised that his fingers were still entwined in the boy's greasy hair. He spread and released them, then stood back a little to fish in his pocket, producing a coin held up before him. Forbidden fruits.

'How would you like to earn this?' he whispered.

'Whit do I have to do?'

'Close your eyes – and open your mouth.'

A look of sullen resignation came over Samuel's face and he swallowed hard before performing as commanded.

Sinclair grasped him by the back of the neck then popped the coin in and jammed the jaws shut as the boy's eyes shot open in surprise.

'Now leave and forget me,' said Sinclair, coldly. 'Before I cut your throat and feed you to the buzzards.'

The coin was almost gulped down at this but then spat out into the hand and Samuel Grant fled silently into the darkness of the nether wynds as if the hounds of hell were on his trail.

Sinclair took his pocket watch from a high waistcoat pocket where it exchanged beats with his heart, and squinted in the faint light.

Quarter before midnight. His grandfather's gold timepiece rarely lied.

Rendezvous was the hour itself. Now or never.

He took a deep breath, replaced the watch and sauntered out into the docks like a man without a care in the world.

It only took a dozen steps. Enough for him to observe the sailing ships close by with a few small steamers beyond not at all suitable for blockade running, not enough speed and backbone; the ladies he desired, iron-pad-dled, schooner-rigged, the Emily, the Charlotte, the Caroline, were already built or being so back in Glasgow.

But that city had become infested with Federal agents of the Union and so he must transact commerce where the power lay. Every lady has her price. And a respectable pimp to boot.

Brothers of the Gusset.

Edinburgh, He had spent a week here in sober negotiation and opposite pursuits. Now, it all must end.

While these thoughts ran through his mind, his senses had been pre-ternaturally tuned to the surroundings. There was a dense, muffled quality to the air as if everything was held in suspension, but nothing behind. No footsteps.

He whistled a tune under his breath. Devil take the blue-tailed fly.

Then a figure detached itself from the shadows up ahead and stood directly in Sinclair's path.

At least his equal in height, the face hidden, shrouded in a black oilskin cape which fell to ankle length; like a deadly shade the figure waited for a reckoning.

Sinclair had twisted and turned in vain; he knew both the identity and intention of his adversary.

A dull glint of metal showed as the man raised his arm to point directly at the target. Sinclair gazed down with regret at his own hand where all that glinted was a thin gold wedding ring; he would never get to his revolver in time and would die like a dog for a vanquished cause.

The South was doomed. And he was no kind of hero.

A dull explosion and then the bullet smashed into his body. Jonathen Sinclair fell back and then lay still, fair hair spilled over the one hidden eye.

No angels came to take him away to a house on the hill.

For him at least the war was over.

2

Warped and woven there spun we
Arms and legs and flaming hair,
Like a whirlwind on the sea.

WILLIAM BELL SCOTT, 'The Witch's Ballad'

Leith, Edinburgh, 1882

James McLevy awoke with a snort of fear, hair standing on end as he shot bolt upright in his lumpy bed. Of late his dreams had been giving him hell and this was no exception.

Now was he truly out of the Land of Nod? As a policeman he would demand of his senses proof. Pain. Pain is a great indicator of the conscious state. A pin. A pin would be irrefutable, stuck into the back of the hand, but where do you find a pin in the pitch dark?

He scrabbled for a phosphorous match, struck it up and lit a squat dismal candle that had its place by his bed on a small rickety table. As the candle coughed its way towards a feeble luminosity, McLevy regarded the still burning match.

Caught yet by the wild fancy of the dream, what followed made perfect sense to him. He extended his thumb and wafted it over the flame. A howl of pain followed, the match was blown out, and the inspector then stuck the fleshly digit into his mouth to suck upon it like a distraught child.

A foul nightmare. Buried alive.

He had found himself in a cavernous long passage that wriggled ahead like a worm, having been led there by a female form that he might only observe from the back; the presence was shrouded in a long scarlet cloak with the hood pulled up as to obliterate all recognition.

How he'd got there he had no idea but it was surely connected to a previous fantastick episode where he'd been dancing naked round a fire; no, not naked, not him, he was in coat and low-brimmed bowler, in his heavy boots, the rest were naked or damned adjacent – *female* naked.

Was Jean Brash one of them? Surely not. She was a bawdy-hoose keeper with a fine taste in coffee, not one of these loose-lipped, loose-limbed wanton creatures capering round the flames. Their bosoms bounced with no regard for modest gravity and their rounded bellies heaved and shone through the draped shreds of discoloured linen that shook in ribald accompaniment to all this gallivantation.

The inspector should have arrested the sprawl where they pranced but what was he doing dancing in tune?

Then it was as if someone had drawn a curtain and the scene was blacked out.

And he was in the narrow tunnel, following the Red Figure – was it fatal? Had Edgar Allan Poe, a man McLevy found close to his own dark imagination, not penned *The Masque of the Red Death*?

The effigy did not look back and the passage became even more confined, with a glutinous creamy scum hanging from the curved walls.

This doesnae look good.

He remembered thinking that at the time and then the figure vanished from sight and he was left to stumble alone into the uncharted murky orifice insinuating onwards.

McLevy found himself upon his hands and knees, crawling like a Jerusalem traveller, the roof pressing down, the surface below a dismal brown claylike substance that clogged and sucked as he squelched forward. The creamy scum wasn't much help either and some instinct told him that if any of that landed upon bare skin, it would scald a hole like hot fat through a stretched membrane.

His lungs were shuddering from lack of air as if a clawed hand were reaching through the wall of his chest and an impulse flashed into his head that he'd better get to hell out of this rat's nest.

At the end of the passage was a small chink of light where an egg-shaped hole, too meagre for a man of his bulk to negotiate, indicated a possible source of succour. But how was he to squeeze through?

He jammed his arm and head in but that was as far as he could get, no chance of his big backside following suit and anyway he could now see that the beckoning light had its origin from a lantern held by the Red Figure, who had popped up into view once more.

She stood by a small jetty. A rowing boat was moored in the still night-blue water where a spectral oarsman, black garbed and hunched over, rested with his back to the proceedings.

Not a promising sight, but then his attention was usurped by the slender white hand emerging from the folds of the red cloak to move towards the hood that still obscured the figure's countenance.

For once in his life Inspector James McLevy abandoned the consuming curiosity of his natural bent, because he knew in his bones that once he saw that face the game was over.

He reached down into the depths of his being, where all this turbulence was wreaking havoc, and *wrenched* himself up and out of it into a shocked salvation.

Witness him bolt upright, hair aghast, thumb wedged between his lips, with the beginnings of a snottery nose.

He removed the singed digit, wiped the seeping organ with the cuff of his crumpled nightshirt and swung out of bed, feet landing with a thump on the cold floorboards of his attic room.

McLevy flapped his nightshirt over bare calves to create a welcome draught of cold air coursing up and over his clammy skin, then took a deep breath.

He was still alive, conscious of crime before it even stirred in the womb of Iniquity, a renowned thief-taker in his own city, feared by lawbreakers high and low, prone to violence when necessary and sometimes just for the hell of it, a great drinker of coffee, a sharp splinter in the rump of authority. He had survived bullets, knives, strangulation by a servant of the Crown and a drug-crazed thuggee, drowning even though he could not swim a stroke, at least two lethal women and ten times that number of murderous bastard men – one of whom had tried to spatter out his brains with hobnailed boot and viciously executed downward stamp.

The inspector realised he was muttering all this to himself: the sign of a disorderly mind.

A charred and dented coffee pot of discoloured metal stood on a stone ledge beside the hearth, where the dead ashes of last night's fire lay scattered. He picked it up, shook it gently to and fro with his head cocked to the one side, then poured out the thick sludgy brew into an equally discoloured cup and sifted the mixture through his teeth.

The liquid hit the pit of his stomach like a falling stone and almost at once provoked his bowels into subdued commotion, but it did the trick.

He was himself again. James McLevy. Inspector of police. A solid, save for the bowels, proposition.

With measured tread he retraced his steps to the bed and shoved his feet into a shapeless pair of old socks. This action he followed by solemnly donning a nightcap with a dangling wee toorie – a birthday gift courtesy of his landlady, Mrs MacPherson, who knew well the prevailing chills of her attic rooms – and then made his way towards the large draughty window, which overlooked his beloved Edinburgh.

En route he stopped to regard himself in a mildewed oval mirror, bought from a toothless female hawker in Leith Market who had obviously no interest in further vanity. The glass was laid at an angle against a pile of his literary and scientific books. It reflected McLevy in all his glory.

He saw a distorted version of Wee Willie Winkie.

A man of some bulk. Curiously dainty hands; the one holding the cup raised a pinkie in elegant acknowledgement of his own image. Sturdy enough calves, from being on the saunter so long in the streets of Leith, a barrel-shaped corpus tending to a wee bit too much heft round the stomach, the broad shoulders sloping deceptively.

And then the face. It was on top of the body. That much you could say for certain.

The light from the candle threw a fragile arc round the room that rimmed him at the neck so McLevy craned forward, peering down to confirm what he already knew.

White parchment skin, pitted and creviced, full lips with a curious pout like the ornamental fish of Jean Brash's new garden pond in the Just Land, a slightly spread nose from keeking hard up against too many windows, tufts of salt-and-pepper hair sticking out from the nightcap, and, below a gloomy brow, the eyes. Slate-grey. Lupine. Not friendly.

Seen too much.

McLevy turned away abruptly. Like the hawker he had no use for further vanity but had bought the damned reflector because of a recent incident at the Leith station.

He had entered full of autumnal relish but became aware of sniggering amongst the morning shift of half-witted young constables. His own right-hand man, Constable Mulholland, hiding the amusement in his blue eyes, stooped down from a great height and informed the inspector that the dishcloth stuffed round the neck that morning to avoid the spilling content of a yolky egg at breakfast upon his whitish shirt, had failed to be removed and was hanging down his front like a dog's tongue.

McLevy had lost face. To know that folk had laughed behind his back. A childhood memory of similar humiliation had surfaced. It cut him to the bone.

A gang of boys following him through the wynds, howling names, spittle and stones showering his back.

His mother had cut her throat, mad auld bitch. Jamie McLevy would be next. Mad for certain sure.

Thank God that Lieutenant Roach, his superior in rank if not in merit, had failed to witness the incident of the overlooked dishcloth.

Ergo the purchase. Every morning, before setting forth, McLevy surveyed his façade in the glass, before twisting over a shoulder to make also sure the back of his thick coat held no trace of a careless repast, or the inadvertent detritus of a solitary life.

This weakness angered him. Why should he give a damn how people thought or what he looked like? It was a recent personal tremor, a self-conscious frailty.

Why should he give a damn? But, he did.

He set his cup down on the spindly-legged table in front of the window, where he read and penned such thoughts as struck him worth the trouble into his diary, pulled back the faded brown curtains and gazed out over his city.

Auld Reekie. The sky was dark as would befit the time of year, trails of street lamps on the main thoroughfares paid homage to the correlated straight lines of planned logic but off all of this mathematical probity ran crooked wynds, narrow deviating slits of passage, and sly conniving side streets – his hunting ground.

The night was silent. But McLevy fancied he could hear the ticking of a thousand clocks, the sighs of a thousand sleepers; men, women and children all sharing the peaceful slumber denied to him.

So be it.

The city was like a huge beast, flanks heaving as it slept in the darkness, and McLevy felt his breath shift in rhythm to that deep motion.

A movement on the roof to the side and he caught from the corner of his eye a slinking form padding with swift sure steps on the oily slates.

Bathsheba. A cat that often visited but not now. She had something in her jaws. He focused his eyes; was that a tail hanging from her mouth?

McLevy's long sight was exemplary, though from short up the edges blurred with increasing incidence; he tapped upon the window pane and the cat halted and turned, her yellow eyes gleaming in the sooty blackness of an Edinburgh night.

Aye. Right enough. It was a long tail. Even had a vestige of life, looping round with the cat's swivelling turn of the head. But the rest of the body told a different story. Dead as a doornail, the jaws clamped shut around.

From the feline point of view Bathsheba observed a disembodied bulbous white shape gawking through the window, so she slipped behind a chimney stack to enjoy the fruits of her labour in peace.

A nearby church clock tolled out its verdict on the state of Scotland.

Four o'clock. A distance from dawn. The Witching Hour.

It might have been a trick of the light from the flickering street lamps but it struck the inspector that the holy spires sticking piously up into the sky to remind God that they were aye on parsimonious and pious duty, were listing somewhat to the side; slanted, as if some insidious force were magnetising them from the straight and upright.

However. It was only a trick of the light.

October had almost gone, the dark half of the year approaching. Halloween. The old legends had it that evil spirits were abroad and it were best to be in disguise lest they steal your very soul; but all good Christians would be well protected, buttressed by faith, wrapped tight by rectitude, sin-proofed to Satan's three-pronged attack.

Only those with a spotted conscience need be concerned. The likes of James McLevy. Marked by madness. Or worse.

The inspector's thoughts returned to his dream.

And what of these naked females, cavorting round the flames? Try as he might he could not recall their precise features, just a general impression of libidinous ecstasy.

McLevy realised that his feet were freezing, even in the woolly socks. There was no point in going back to bed, however, not with a troupe of sleekit females lurking under the covers. He let out a grunt of amusement at that notion but could not rid himself of a feeling of foreboding.

Who was the figure in the red cloak and why did she put such fear into his heart?

Perhaps he might coax some flame from the ashes with judicious blowing plus a few tinder stalks, then a wee bit of coal, and rustle up another pot of coffee?

Yet he did not move from the window.

Perhaps they were all uncanny wraiths from the primitive depths of vanquished time, to be dismissed or at the very least taken into custody.

Naked as sin.

Just as well he'd had his hat and overcoat on.

Yet what was he doing dancing in tune?

3

I could not get the ring without the finger.

THOMAS MIDDLETON, *Master-Constable*

To see the two women in the Princes Street tearoom, it would never have occurred to the ignorant or unwary that they might have in mind a desire to rend tooth and nail the flesh that held the opposite's very skeleton in place.

One was unassuming in her dress, respectable and neat as a maiden aunt, frills forbidden, small-boned and dowdy almost, a heart-shaped face, tiny almost claw-like hands, the nails a little longer than custom might prefer. Her eyes – dark, beady, like a restless bird's – darted here and there under the lowered lids.

Her nose was narrow, as if it had been sucked by some inner force to press up against the cartilage in order to accentuate the cheekbones on each side. The mouth in contrast was wide, small milky teeth lurking behind wet lips as she sipped the scented tea.

The other was dressed in the height of fashion; a gown of vivid aquamarine brought out the colour of her green eyes and the red hair, swept up save for some cunning tendrils that had escaped to call attention to the contours of her neck, contrasted with the porcelain skin of her face. A mocking twist to the lush, slightly parted lips below a delicate nose completed the picture.

A pretty female, perhaps a little empty-headed even, the observer might have concluded. Flighty. Not like the sober wee soul opposite.

Both women had taken great care in how they would present themselves one to the other.

The bird of paradise and the sparrow.

Neither, of course, might be what she seemed.

Deadly rivals they most certainly were.

The dowdy woman was known only as the Countess and the vision in aquamarine, Jean Brash.

They shared the same profession, that of a bawdy-hoose keeper.

While Edinburgh matrons discussed the relative merits of French cakes, mesmeric influence and petticoat tails, the Countess poured out more tea with a steady hand.

'Darjeeling. I always find the fragrance so. . .soothing, don't you?' she remarked, in an accent that more than hinted at some passing acquaintance with the Balkans.

'I'm more of a coffee hand,' said Jean. 'Black.'

'You prefer stimulation?'

'I like to keep busy. Welcome all comers.'

The Countess sighed as if this statement carried hidden undertones, which indeed it did.

'I have asked you here, Jean Brash,' she murmured, 'so that we may not quarrel.'

The other took a sip of her coffee and made a face.

'Bitter,' she said. 'I don't like bitter.'

The older woman smiled in sympathy and then a look of concern came upon her face, as if she had just remembered something of vexation. She straightened up and her restless eyes became fixed on Jean.

'You have taken two of my girls,' she announced.

'They came running.'

The Countess put the provocation of this statement down to the bitterness of the coffee.

'One of them, Simone, *ma petite demi-mondaine*, she is highly skilled, supple to the double joint, and represents a large investment.'

'I doubt she will return,' Jean announced, looking into the cup as if it might improve the flavour somehow.

'Why not, if I may make so bold?'

'Simone told me pain had begun to outweigh pleasure in her . . .obligations.'

The Countess smiled in polite disagreement. 'Pleasure begins when pain completes itself. Sometimes the Tiger needs a little . . .blood.'

'I've seen the stripes,' said Jean flatly.

Indeed, the girl, who obviously specialised in waiflike crushed-flower creatures – what Hannah Semple, the keeper of the keys of the Just Land, would call *one o' thae lily pads* – had shown Jean the livid marks a certain ship-owner had quirted on her lower back and buttocks. There was an element of seduction in the display and Jean was reserving judgement on Simone, the French aye being a tricky proposition, but one thing was for sure – the skin did not lie.

'Part of the profession,' replied the Countess.

'Not in my house. Not my girls. Justice for all.'

The older woman laughed as if genuinely amused, her eyes glittering with a sudden merriment.

'But my dear Mistress Brash, your house is like a market place where everything is laid out like a flesher's slab. In my hotel, the client may indulge himself in total privacy to the furthest extent of his wishes. I attract the most distinguished of men for that very reason.'

Jean had lost two judges, the aforementioned ship-owner and, at the last count, at least three High Churchmen to the Countess. All with money to burn. It rankled greatly. She had stuck to her principles but it still stung like hell.

Accordingly, she'd been delighted when the two magpies had flown over to the Just Land. And no-one was going to escape the consequences of comparing her immaculate bawdy-hoose to a flesher's slab.

'Simone tells me that a deal of your tigers are so old, they must bring medical support. And the reason they have to inflict pain is because they're incapable of anything else.'

Stick that up your moth-eaten drawers, she thought.

The Countess carefully replaced her cup and tapped her nails on the rim of the saucer.

There was a sudden hush in the tea house as the door swung open and a tall elegant young woman slipped in, accompanied by a large imposing man who sported a curling moustache of splendid proportion and whose dark magnetic eyes swept over the assembled matrons, pausing fractionally to register Jean's cool gaze before sweeping on.

The woman had the bleached, almost translucent quality of

someone who rarely saw the light of day, her eyes lidded as if the brightness of assorted bone china and white tablecloths were blinding her where she stood.

The man seated her with a courtly gesture, removing his soft wide-brimmed felt hat, which sported a small dark green feather in the band. This action revealed a shock of black unruly hair, carrying more length than fashion would dictate, a lion's mane.

He shook it from side to side as if revelling in the attention the pair were attracting from all quarters. When he smiled, his teeth were large and white, a picture of health.

The woman's own hair was ash blonde, *lint white*, as the Scots might say, neatly swept under a grey buckram hat with a small crown that perched equally neatly upon her head.

Her skin was pale, almost that of an albino, and when the eyes suddenly snapped open, they were of a dark violet hue, searing against the white skin.

For a moment the eyes rested on Jean and, despite herself, the bird of paradise flinched slightly in reaction.

Then the woman bent over the menu card, which listed a plethora of delectation for the Midlothian sweet of tooth, and the moment passed. The tea room breathed again, gossip recommenced, and the Countess leant forward so that her face was in close proximity.

There was a scent of cloves from her skin and for some reason it reminded Jean of the plague.

'An exotic coupling.' The Countess smiled, the small teeth tucked behind stretched lips. 'Do you know them?'

'Not personally,' replied Jean wrinkling her nose.

'Sophia Adler and Magnus Bannerman. From the American shore. I have heard him speak. He is magnificent.'

'What does he talk about?'

'Events beyond the grave.'

'I leave that to the minister. Reverend Snoddy. He's awfy severe on the sinful.'

The Countess smiled once more with a hint of condescension and Jean wondered if the woman believed the one before her to be as simple and shallow as presented; that would be more than useful.

Of course she well knew that the couple had been doing the

rounds of high society in Edinburgh, Magnus Bannerman preaching the possibilities of an 'Unseen World' and Sophia Adler a trumpeted conduit to the same. They had not as of yet seen fit to visit their talents upon the Just Land.

Perhaps the incorporeal nature of their calling was incompatible with a bawdy-hoose but Mister Bannerman seemed certainly to be a man of parts.

She would place him about forty-five years but in prime condition. A fine specimen.

The Countess was now so close to her that Jean could discern a faint straggle of hair just below the thin nose as she spoke.

'The woman is a *sensitive*. A bridge to the future.'

'The future?' Jean looked dubious. 'I have enough mischief in the present.'

'Indeed you do,' said the Countess and the beady eyes found purchase, hooking into the green gaze opposite.

'The French girl. I want her back.'

'That is not possible.'

This uncompromising retort was accompanied by a dazzling smile and nod of the head as if they had reached an agreeable solution.

'She's settled in nicely and they're all cosied up.'

'Cosy?'

'Her and Francine.'

'Francine?'

'She's French as well. They're all over the place.'

Jean let out a silvery peal of affected laughter, which would have appalled anyone of her intimate acquaintance, one police inspector in particular.

'Francine dishes it out though. There's not a tiger born can match her stripes.'

Before she might confide further titbits from the boudoir of applied as opposed to received flagellation, the Countess reached across and laid her hand upon the back of Jean's, nails resting lightly upon the other's bare flesh.

There was something invasive in the gesture, penetrating, as if it contained the seeds of violence, and Jean felt a shiver run up her arm like the electric current of a primitive defence mechanism.

She had wanted to meet this woman face to face to gauge the opposition. Well, she had gauged and there was something evil behind the unassuming façade that could not be ignored or underestimated.

An enemy. Lethal, equal and opposite. For Jean Brash was also a dark and dangerous creature. And the shiver was as much in recognition of her own propensity for visceral and bloody conflict.

Nor had the woman been fooled by the vacuous act. Jean could read it in her face.

'I want the French girl back.'

'That is not possible.'

Almost identical statements, but this time the claws were unsheathed on both sides; Jean calmly removed her hand from under that of the Countess and rested it some inches away.

'I never force people against their will,' she remarked, quietly. 'It just brings grief.'

'Don't make an enemy of me, Jean.'

'I hope you enjoyed the tea,' came the response. 'That coffee was a disgrace.'

The Countess laughed and leant back to gather her possessions as if accepting dismissal. As she did so, she spoke almost casually, drawing on a pair of black leather gloves, which encased the small hands like another skin.

'But of course I know your history,' she murmured as she prepared to rise. 'For you everything must be a fight. You dragged yourself from the gutter, and the habit remains. To provoke, antagonise. From the gutter. How sad.'

'You'd best depart,' said Jean. 'Before I burst into tears.'

The Countess stood, fished in her handbag to find a small purse from which she extracted some coins and then laid them carefully on the table.

'For your trouble,' she remarked.

Then she waited for a moment, gazing thoughtfully down at the seated woman.

'I have always considered,' she said finally, her eyes resting on the contours of Jean's gown, 'the show of colour to be somewhat vulgar.'

'I like to be noticed,' was the retort.

18

A shake of the head as if taste was a subject wasted on the garish, then the Countess's face once more set itself in concerned sympathy.

'Don't go beyond your class, my dear,' she announced gravely, 'especially if you wish to avoid pain.'

And then she was gone.

As Jean sat alone toying with her teaspoon, stirring the coffee to see if it might alter the taste, a woman who had been sitting at a distant table walked across, dainty cup and saucer in a stubby-fingered hand, to seat herself heavily in the chair previously occupied by the Countess. Her name was Hannah Semple. The keeper of the keys of the aforesaid Just Land, loyal to her mistress unto death.

The death of others, that is. Hannah had a cut-throat razor and it was her boast that she rarely snapped it open without drawing blood.

Not in a Princes Street tea room, of course.

The clothes of respectability sat somewhat uneasily on her solid frame. By her own admission Hannah Semple was no beauty; a squashed pug-like physiognomy contained round deep-set eyes to echo the canine theme. Broken veins, which age and bitter experience had etched into her cheeks, added to the fine mix.

She reached across and munched into an untouched slice of Dundee cake. Jean said nothing. Hannah munched on.

Neither had noticed a small portly man who had slipped out from a table near the window and followed the Countess as she made her dignified exit. He had not paid his bill but that was not unusual for Alfred Binnie; his function was more a matter of exacting what was due and punitive.

He had paid keen attention to Jean Brash, weighing her up with dispassion as a poulterer would a live chicken.

Calculating which way the feathers would fly.

Upwards usually, as the blade came down.

Binnie left unseen. His speciality.

'No' bad cake,' pronounced Hannah, sending a few crumbs flying to scatter like birdseed on the table. 'Too dry, though. Lacks moisture.'

She knew her mistress well. Jean Brash had that *broody* look upon her face. Things had not gone to plan.

'I am afraid, Hannah,' said Jean, 'that the Countess and I did not find a measure of agreement.'

'Over that wee French trollop?'

'A bruised and innocent lamb.'

'She hasnae the pox, right enough,' replied Hannah, helping herself to another slice. 'The doctor confirmed same. Clean as a whistle. I meant tae tell you.'

'I am glad to hear it.'

'She'll be useful, no doubt,' was the stolid summation. 'Innocence is aye useful.'

'The Countess wants her back.'

'Uhuh?'

'I intend to keep her.'

Hannah shook her head gloomily. She had a bad feeling about all this; mind you she had a bad feeling about most things most mornings.

'Did ye offer payment?'

'Did I hell.'

That took care of that then. Trouble would ensue. For certain sure. Sharpen up the cut-throat.

'The other yin's a menace.'

'Jessie?'

'None other. Lippy. A menace.'

'She has a deal to say for herself,' agreed Jean. 'But we may knock her into shape.'

Jessie Nairn, a pert wee magpie who had found her way over from Paisley to the Countess's establishment, had also flown the coop. Her reasons were not scored so deep and Jean suspected a restless temperament allied to an eye for the better chance, the Countess being allegedly mean of payment and disposition. Jean had seen many such types as Jessie pass through her hands, but the girl had spirit.

Besides she had arrived with Simone. Justice for all.

'She stays as well?' muttered Hannah.

'She does.'

'Your decision, mistress.'

'It is indeed.'

There was a gleam in Jean's eye Hannah recognised. A fancy name for it would be *the light of battle*. Looking for a face tae punch would be another.

Jean's own nose had been out of joint since the Countess had opened up a rival establishment in Leith and the fact that the boy Cupid had not been hanging round her skirts of late did not help.

Ah well, whit's fur ye will no' go by ye, Hannah resolved, *even if it's warfare and violence.*

She joined her silence to that of her mistress.

They made an odd pairing: a dumpy thickset creature and the refined woman of fashion.

Both were warriors.

However, what was coming would be a cruel reminder that no-one is as strong as they hoodwink themselves to be.

A universal truth. Rarely realised.

For Sophia Adler, across the room, waiting patiently for a slow-witted local lassie to emerge from the depths of the kitchen with a pot of *your finest Scottish brew* as Magnus had commanded, it was a different contemplation.

She had been content to watch her companion wreak havoc amongst the plump pigeons of the tea room with his hawk-like demeanour, but then her attention had been drawn towards the two women sitting diagonally opposite.

One was beautiful, one was not.

Sophia had the fleeting image of a dark shape shifting between them. Death perhaps. It was much on her mind.

Of course – the moment was broken by the thud of the teapot as it landed on the table, spilling some brown liquid out of the spout to stain the white covering like dirty blood on an altar cloth – of course, and her lips twisted in a smile of wry amusement as she watched the scared waitress scuttle back to the safety of the kitchen, it could have just been. . .a trick of the light.

Now you see it. Now you don't.

4

I think for my part one half of the nation is mad – And
the other not very sound.

TOBIAS SMOLLETT, *The Adventures of Sir Launcelot Greaves*

Lieutenant Robert Roach clove easily to moral indignation, long
upper lip swirling in ethical distaste as he heaped scorn upon the
luckless Constable Ballantyne.

He had found the young man in the small cubbyhole of a
room set aside for the lesser beings of the station to store their
spare boots, waterproof capes and whatever other paraphernalia
made up the office of constable; a room that Roach rarely ventured within, it being subject to the unwholesome odour of a
leaky water closet and the fetid smell of discarded footwear; a
room that should not have contained the spectacle of a policeman gazing earnestly at his own image in the cracked mirror and
waving his hands in what he imagined to be a gamut of spell-
binding gestures.

Mulholland watched with some sympathy as the strawberry
birthmark that spread from Ballantyne's neck to at least half way
up one side of the face, pulsed with shame.

The constable himself, none other, in his own identity, had
once been caught by Roach staring into that very same cracked
mirror, but he had been in love at the time and that made it, to
his mind, a slightly less heinous misdemeanour.

The fact of that once precious love being now dust in the
wind, and his prospects of making sergeant blown to hell along
with it, seemed to be of no concern to his superiors.

Roach had buried the matter like a bad drive in a bunker and
McLevy, a man for whom Mulholland had risked life and limb on
more than one occasion, had the cheek to look aggrieved when
recently informed that he, the inspector, was making an eejit out
of himself by reason of hanging a tea towel round his neck like a
washing line.

A bitter residue still lingered in Mulholland's heart from that unlucky time of lost emotion. He had been unjustly castigated for inadvertently causing the father of his budding beloved, Emily Forbes, to hang himself by the neck with a pulley rope as a bychance of trying to solve a case all on his own and therefore gain promotion with the welcome addition of a blushing bride; something any red-blooded young fellow would surely attempt. Surely.

But it put somewhat of a damper on the wedding prospect because, as McLevy had remarked at the time, *it is difficult for a father to give away the bride with his neck at a funny angle and his tongue hingin' oot.*

Hilarious.

Anyhow, it was a bitter residue.

And not his fault.

The welter of self-justification has ensnared many a stalwart man but Mulholland was sprung like Perseus from the labyrinth when Roach turned and asked, 'Well constable – and what is your opinion?'

Mulholland had drifted away on the tide and so missed the previous part of Roach's diatribe but he had enough on hand to take refuge in ancestral wisdom.

'Terrible, terrible, sir,' he avowed. 'My Aunt Katie always says that a man who looks into his own face overly much often, is looking at catastrophe.'

'Does she indeed?' muttered Roach, who considered Mulholland's Aunt Katie an Irish myth whose effect was not unlike the sea haar that descended on a clearly defined golf course and fogged up a perfectly decent approach.

He turned his baleful gaze back onto Ballantyne who, in truth, was a harmless, innocent soul and totally unfitted to be a policeman.

'I will not have mesmeric conjuration within the legal boundaries of the Leith police station,' Roach thundered like some prophet from the Old Testament. 'I will ask you once more, constable. Was there, at any given moment, demonic intention in your mind?'

The young constable blushed anew and struggled for words, which were never his friends at the best of times.

'It wisnae the devil, sir.'

'Then whom were you regarding?'

'Me. Jist me.'

'And the gesturing of your own appendages?'

Ballantyne looked down at his hands, the long and finely tapered fingers at odds with rest of his awkward body, as if they might supply an answer.

'Have a life of their own sometimes, sir.'

'And *what* was in your mind?'

Ballantyne bit his lip and almost swallowed the words rather than let them see the light of day.

'Jist – hocus-pocus.'

'Hocus-pocus?'

Roach let out a baffled growl and Mulholland who, in truth, was wondering why the lieutenant was getting himself into such a twist over a piece of daft behaviour, decided to bring some much needed intelligence into the situation.

'This mesmerism stuff is all over the city now, is it not constable?' he asked with a friendly smile.

Ballantyne cheered up at the encouragement, little suspecting what might be behind the façade; the boy was, as has been noted, too trusting for his chosen profession.

'Aye. Everybody's talking.'

'And you thought to have a pass, eh?'

'Aye.'

'A bit of innocent fun?'

'Uhuh.'

'Not a thought in your mind.'

'No' really.'

A hesitation, and the interrogator in Mulholland was onto it like a flash; it is astounding how often humanity begins with apparent intent to assist the afflicted and ends up screwing down the coffin lid.

'But there was something, eh? Some little thing. What was it now?'

Roach watched in silence, instinctively sensing that Mulholland was close to something. The tall constable flicked a glance his way as if to acknowledge the subtle interplay between them.

Neither of these prescient beings noticed a figure slip in at the back and rest up against the wall.

Softly does it, thought Mulholland, *not hammering in like a certain abject personage.*

'What was that little thing?'

Ballantyne hesitated once more, then looked up into the blue Irish eyes of his fellow constable and blurted out the pitifully painful truth of the matter.

'They say it can make things disappear.'

'So you looked in the mirror to put the 'fluence on and do a vanishing act?'

'That's right.'

'And what would you want to make disappear?'

This was the moment when the lieutenant might re-evaluate his promotion prospects if Mulholland displayed a continuing talent for such fine-milled investigation.

Ballantyne fell silent.

They waited. Hounds on the trail.

One of Ballantyne's hands, which indeed had a life of its own, crept unconsciously up to touch the livid birthmark that disfigured his face.

It was as if something had kicked Mulholland hard in the pit of his stomach; in the name of his own cleverness, showing off in front of his lieutenant he had humiliated a fellow constable, a fellow human being, and if the ground had swallowed him up like another vanishing act, he would have accepted it as part of his just desserts.

Lieutenant Roach though was made of sterner stuff. He searched in his mind for a phrase to indicate that whatever mitigation of physical defect, he, as premier authority in the Leith Police station, could not allow mystic influences of any kind access to a cracked mirror.

Strangely enough, nothing much came to mind.

Out of the ether, however, a voice sounded forth.

'Away ye go, constable,' said James McLevy. 'And tidy up your desk, it looks like a midden.'

As the grateful Ballantyne quit the scene, the lieutenant reflected, not for the first time, how his obstreperous, noisy subordinate had the ability to ghost up out of nowhere.

At the most inopportune moments.

McLevy shot the shamefaced Mulholland a look to blister tar-macadam, and then turned to gaze enquiringly at Roach.

The lieutenant found he had an obscure need to defend his actions, but why should he? He was the superior and he had no need to vindicate his conduct.

'I caught Ballantyne in the act of gazing wilfully into his own personal likeness,' he vindicated, nevertheless.

'I gathered that,' was the terse response.

'Mesmerism has no place in my station!'

'It's all the rage,' said McLevy, annoyingly. 'I'm sure Mrs Roach is intrigued, is she not?'

'It is superstitious drivel,' Roach retorted, but was aware of the ground underneath his feet shifting as 'twere in a sandy bunker at the mention of his wife who was, in truth, intent upon dragging him shortly to some society cabal on the subject. For some reason arguing with his inspector often had this effect; the man instinctively perceived a weak point and then poked it with a sharp stick.

McLevy adopted a mild, even more irritating tone.

'There is a measure of scientific doubt, sir. And while science doubts, we must all hold our breath.'

'I shall hold my breath for no-one. The pernicious influence of spiritism is creeping round this city like a pestilence. Like some sort of. . .Catholic plot.'

'Oh, you blame the Pope, do you?'

'I would not be surprised,' expostulated Roach, who suspected his inspector of ultramontanist leanings; no-one knew where McLevy worshipped, if he did so at all, and the man was known to whistle seditious Jacobite airs to boot.

'I had no idea.'

'Had not of what?' asked Roach, who was beginning to lose the thread.

'That the Spider of Rome was weaving this web.'

Roach took a deep breath.

'Our country is founded upon the decent God-fearing bedrock of Protestant Christianity, McLevy. Undermine that, and anything can happen.'

'So, in the defence of your realm,' said McLevy, his tone changing of a sudden to reflect the angry contempt he felt within, 'you would hammer in upon a glaikit wee boy who seeks to rid himself of the brand our deeply compassionate Lord has seen fit to burn upon his face?'

For the second time that day Mulholland felt the ground swallow him up but, strangely enough, though a muted hiss escaped from Roach's lips, he did not respond in a fashion the constable would have anticipated.

'It is not our task to question the ways of the Deity, inspector,' he replied firmly. 'And, I would remind you, *thou shalt not take the name of the Lord thy God in vain.*'

'That's between him and me,' was the equally obdurate response.

Roach, in his lieutenant's garb, was an immaculate assembly of straight lines and knife-edge creases. He had a long snout of a nose, dry skin and irregular snaggled teeth that were the bane of his life.

A crocodile in uniform.

He was half a head taller than his inspector who, despite the mild late-October weather, was muffled up in his heavy coat looking like some bad-tempered winter animal newly emerged from its lair.

Just leave it, Mulholland begged silently of McLevy. *While you're still at the races.*

But no. Too much to hope.

'If Ballantyne chooses to delude himself that some mysterious magnetism can change the workings of his body cells and leave him with a skin to match the purity of his innocent intentions, then good luck tae him.'

For a moment McLevy's voice thickened and Mulholland guessed the cause to be either bile or sentiment. He hoped sincerely it was bile; the idea of his inspector having finer feelings was an alarming one.

'It's *his* delusion,' went on McLevy, his eyes shifting to where Ballantyne sat disconsolately at his desk, trying to impose order onto what indeed was an irredeemable mess. 'His delusion, and he is welcome to it.'

Roach narrowed his slightly bloodshot eyes.

'What the Lord lays upon us, we may not avoid. His mercy is infinite. His burden is heavy.'

McLevy sniffed, and then, with a mercurial change of mood, grinned savagely as a random thought struck home.

'Anyway, ye should have let him finish the job.'

'And why, pray?'

'Because had he done so to no effect, it would have proved that the forces of the occult could hold no sway with the malediction of a Presbyterian Almighty.'

The inspector let out a wild whoop of laughter.

'Now Ballantyne will be in doubt for the rest of his life. You have created the opposite of your intent. Jist like God.'

What Mulholland found bewildering was the way these two went from one level to another.

'That is close to sacrilege, James,' said Roach quietly. 'The pagan in you rises.'

'It's near Halloween,' came the reply. 'I'll be dancing at the bonfire.'

Before Roach could muster a response to this profane assertion, there was an altercation of sorts at the station desk and, having had little satisfaction from Sergeant Murdoch who had his inert domain there, a young man strode towards them.

He was almost as tall as Mulholland but broader of frame, wearing what looked like an old sailor's coat with brass buttons; he wore a naval cap of sorts, set at a rakish angle tipped to the back of his head. The fellow was fresh complexioned, open faced, with a thick walrus moustache, obviously an attempt to add gravitas to the twenty-two-year-old countenance chosen for its domicile. His eyes protruded slightly, almost fish-like, pale blue, but they had a fierce directness of purpose.

He committed himself to Roach, totally ignoring McLevy who stood aside in mock deference, a gleam of amusement in his eyes. Indeed there was something childlike and disarming about the whole presentation before them, a brash young boy caught inside a giant's body.

'Are you in charge here, sir?' he asked, the voice a little higher-pitched than the frame would warrant.

'There may be some who would dispute such,' replied Roach, dryly, 'but that would seem to be my function.'

The young man blinked a little at this, and looked round all three policemen as if they were in disguise.

'I am here to report a crime,' he announced finally.

'You've come to the right place then,' said McLevy.

'No denyin' that,' added Mulholland.

Roach, of course, at this point, should have handed the case to McLevy and walked off to gaze at the portrait of Queen Victoria that hung in his office, comforting himself with the thought that both his sovereign and the Supreme Chief Constable in heaven would find no fault with their loyal servant, but some imp of perversity seized him and so he stood there as a member of the silent trinity.

It is the habit of policemen when they are in any way uneasy – as Mulholland was with the roasting he was expecting from his inspector, Roach with the realisation that the persecution of Ballantyne had unearthed a streak of cruel intolerance in his nature that he had himself suffered from greatly under the rigid edicts of his long dead father, and McLevy with inappropriate ribald images still surfacing from his dream – that they will displace the emotion in accusative form upon the first member of the general public unfortunate enough to swim within the murky depths of their oceanic authority.

And so they stood. Not one regarding the other, all focused on a stranger in their midst.

'Whit's that in your poche?' said McLevy out of the blue. He had noticed a suspicious bulge to the right side of the stranger's reefer jacket. 'No' a revolver I hope?'

The young man looked down at the pocket and frowned; this encounter was not turning out the way he had seen it in his heroic imagination. He plunged his hand into the deep recess of the garment and brought out the suspicious shape.

'A cricket ball,' he declared.

'Ye indulge at the cricket?' asked McLevy, as if it was a sign of anarchist leanings.

'I play cricket, football, hockey, swimming and rugby,' was the proud response.

'What about golf?' queried Roach.

'A splendid pastime.'

Roach nodded approvingly but McLevy was not yet finished with his line of enquiry.

'I'll wager ye also try your skill at boxing?'

A look of surprise flashed into the stranger's eyes.

'I do.'

'Last night I'll be bound.'

'Indeed.'

The young man hesitated but curiosity got the better of him as the inspector knew it would.

'What draws you to that conclusion?'

'The skin on the knuckles of your right hand is somewhat abraded,' McLevy remarked. 'Of course ye could have received such chasing a ball, but there is also a bruised discolouration indicating impact and I also note the marking of a mouse under your left eye.'

The inspector pursed his lips and assumed the manner of a discriminating deductor.

'It is therefore my premise that your opponent had a hard head and got lucky wi' a swipe or two.'

Mulholland and Roach exchanged perplexed glances; this was not McLevy's usual mode of speech or behaviour. The young man, however, let out a burst of spirited laughter.

'By God you are right, sir. He did indeed have a frontal skull bone fit for a granite quarry. And I made the error of aiming down.'

'Ye should aye punch up,' said McLevy. 'More leverage.'

He was enjoying the looks of bafflement on the faces of his lieutenant and constable so decided to put another dent in their brainpans.

'I also surmise,' he pontificated, 'that such a wealth of sporting activity and the leisure time available to pursue such, can only point to one vocation – that of a university student.'

This time when the young man laughed the face expressed merriment and humour but no sound emerged, as if the laughter was choked at source.

'Almost exactly so, sir, except,' and here he stepped up before McLevy with some purpose, almost as if he was about to engage him in a bout of fisticuffs, 'that I have not long before attained my degree.'

'In medicine, no doubt,' the inspector punched up as his opponent towered over him. 'Ye have the natural arrogance necessary to the medical profession but not enough brains tae disport yourself in the legal.

'Besides,' he continued, as the young man let out a puff of air as if slightly winded, 'you would seem tae me to lack the requisite treachery to succeed in law.'

'You represent the law,' came the shrewd response.

'And I am *steeped* in perfidy,' the inspector replied urbanely. 'You, on the other hand, are jist beginning.'

A blink of the eye showed the blow to have gone home and McLevy decided that was enough deductive intuition for the moment.

'Ye came to report a crime, I believe?'

'Yes. A friend of my mother's. Her home.'

'Up in flames?'

'Broken into and robbed.'

'In Leith?'

'No other place.'

'Indeed there is not,' said McLevy with a fierce smile, as if mortally offended. 'It is a well known fact that we are the centre of the universe, here.'

The young man looked at Roach and Mulholland to see if this statement contained a trace element of irony but the lieutenant's long upper lip gave no hint of such, and the constable's blue eyes and fresh complexion told of nothing but unperceived insignificance.

Which brought his attention back to the inspector, who regarded him with what seemed dark suspicion.

'Ye can put the cricket ball away,' he said.

The young man did so.

'Whit is the precise address in Leith?'

'42 Bonnington Road.'

'And the victim of this criminal depredation?'

'Mistress Muriel Grierson.'

A small bell rang in Roach's head but he decided to hold his counsel. Best to keep his own wife out of it, she had a habit of creeping into just about everything.

'And *your* name?' McLevy asked in official tones.

'Doyle,' said the young man who felt that he had just lost a round and been punching air. 'Arthur Conan Doyle.'

'Well, Mister Doyle,' said his elusive combatant. 'I am James McLevy, inspector of police. Let us go and investigate criminality thegither.'

5

I tell you what I dreamed last night
It was not dark, it was not light,
Cold dews had drenched my plenteous hair
Through clay; you came to seek me there
And 'Do you dream of me?' you said.

CHRISTINA ROSSETTI, *The Convent Threshold*

Magnus Bannerman whistled cheerfully to himself as he laid out the cards.

Two pack solitaire, shuffle and deal. Forty Thieves. Otherwise known as *Napoleon at St Helena*, it being the pastime with which the defeated Emperor beguiled himself on his last and lonely exile.

Magnus enjoyed the idea of himself and the little Corsican reading the *tableau* and making their plans.

The Frenchman dreaming of a lost empire and he on rich pickings in a foreign land.

As in many other solitaires, kings were a drawback. Took space, were hard to move. You had to build up foundation from the aces. Royalty gummed up the works.

Careful planning. You saw a space; the first impulse would be to fill it up, but then a vital link might be lost for it was necessary at some point to dig into the covered *talon* of cards; the past must be resurrected.

It was all a matter of recovery.

And careful planning.

His large spade-shaped fingers were surprisingly dexterous as he twisted the cards over to lay them face up.

Now he was left with the pack of the pasteboards held over, sixty-four in total. *The hand.* Face down in a solid rectangle. You may only turn them once.

If they had no place, thence to the *talon.*

Before he began, Magnus surveyed the spread. It had possibilities but would depend on the order of what ensued from the pack.

Now if he was a true sensitive he might intuit what was to come. But he was merely a gambler with a gift of the gab.

Before he made his first move, Magnus snapped open a small silver case and extracted a slim cheroot, which he lit up to puff out a thin spurt of smoke, eyes closed in tobacco heaven. Some preached against the leaf but they had no idea what it added to the pleasures of the flesh.

He opened his eyes once more and gazed round the well-appointed hotel room. Yes indeed, the lap of luxury, who would have thought a riverboat gambler down on his luck could have found such a sweet little ace in the hole?

His eyes flicked to the side door behind which Sophia was enclosed.

His own quarters were out across the hall for propriety's sake but the woman shared her bed now and then if she had an itch to scratch.

Not presently though. Something in the tea house had set her mind inwards and Sophia had retreated to the separate small side room in her quarters she always insisted on possessing no matter where they had their lodgings.

And it had to have a lock. What she did in there was anyone's guess; commune with the spirits?

Another mystery was the small leather suitcase she carried by herself everywhere they travelled. That case Sophia kept in the side room as well and when he had made the mistake one day of trying to spring the catch in a London hotel lobby, the Langham no less, while she was powdering her pudenda, the damned woman somehow knew and in a white fury warned him that if he wanted to keep his procreative means intact, he'd best contain his curiosity.

Or his testicles would pay the price.

She hadn't exactly phrased it in such blunt fashion but Magnus had got the message. Yes, indeedy.

And the other message received was that of the milk cow. These fine young teats of hers, with a tug here and a tug there, brought forth rich reward.

But it was *her* milk. She provided. He merely managed the liquid flow. That was his talent.

Magnus had always been a showman, a gambler, a handsome

brute, a lady's man; he hid his card manipulations behind a ready smile and friendly, open face.

He was also blessed with a fine baritone voice and eloquent sincerity of speech; he could have been an actor or nostrum salesman but Lady Luck had claimed him as her own.

For a while.

Then the damned Civil War had blown the steamboats out of the water; not that he had taken sides, a gambler never takes sides so he cursed Abe Lincoln and Jefferson Davis in equal measure.

Between them, however, they had wrecked the fine currents that Magnus plied his trade in, and if that were not enough, then came the railroads.

No romance to the iron horse.

Where was the full moon shining on the Mississippi water, where a man might wander up to a pilgrim who had made a killing in some cattle deal, had money to burn, whisky on his breath, leaning against the rail dreaming of some woman who was never in a million years his wife, and offer up a friendly game of cards?

The air would smell of river blossom; some mulatto girl, barelegged, with long slender arms, slowly washing clothes by the bank, a traveller's mind wandering to some tryst with such a succulent creature, and in that splendid state of priapic suggestibility he would be a lamb to the slaughter.

A secluded cabin, a whisky bottle on the table, perhaps some other travelling men, a fresh deck of cards and that sweet thrill when the deal went down.

No such delight upon a train. Conductors, railway detectives and sour-faced women keeping an eye on their sad-faced husbands.

In the long years after the war, his luck had gone to hell even with the calculated skill he could bring to bear. He gambled now in saloons where the pilgrims were sharp-eyed and quick tempered.

Ended up in San Francisco, down by the docks, lost all his money in a game of poker. Some dewy-eyed kid turned over a full house and cleaned the table.

Magnus walked out of that bar with a five-dollar bill in his shoe, court of the last resort. He was over forty years and running out of luck.

Somewhere off to the side he could hear a bunch of heathen Chinee squabbling over a game of mah-jong on one of the junk ships. A crescent moon above hooked into the sky, and it seemed as if he was the last man left alive as he walked along the creaking waterfront.

How long he had wandered, he'd lost count of that. Hours, days, nights, his head was full of dark thoughts: damned Irish stock, Bannerman, a name for someone who carried the flag at the front and died first in battle.

Found himself, like something in a dream, in front of a tall building that stood alone, composed of slatted wood, weathered by the salt currents of the sea. By the door were pinned cards advertising the wares of various flowers of the night who promised innocence and satisfaction.

Penetrate the one to achieve the other.

Then, almost in keeping with the exotic macabre feel of the occasion, a melancholy pulsation as if it was his last moment alive, his attention was caught by a newly tacked-up piece of thin white vellum amongst the promised joys.

The paper was already curling up, as if recoiling from the company it kept, and on impulse he ripped it from the nail and held it out under the light to reread the words he had already registered.

What is your future? said the message.

Magnus came back to the present. A hotel in Edinburgh. Turned over a card. It was the jack of diamonds.

He knew that future now.

The side door opened and Sophia Adler slipped through, locking it behind. She had changed into a simple pale green gown that fell softly round her uncorseted body in seductive folds and for a moment Magnus felt a carnal urge to leap across at her like some natural animal. But then he observed she had that distracted air and slewed, swivelling motion to her eyes; as if she had been floating in a fluid universe and was still immersed in some opalescent reverie.

Accordingly he returned to the cards, turning them over slowly while she walked to the window and looked from the hotel onto the sober thoroughfare of George Street spread out below, not yet echoing the busier parallel of Princes Street a few roads further down.

The weather was mild but the distrustful citizens paid no heed to the possibility of clemency; heads down, hunched as if suffering a driving rain, they shuffled and darted in the gloomy afternoon amidst carriages and sundry vehicles like denizens at the bottom of the deep, half-blind, anxious to avoid contact lest it contaminate.

At least that is how it appeared to Sophia. So much of her time when alone was spent in a world of shifting shapes and snatches of voices on the wind, that she was sometimes unsure where one world ended and the other commenced.

But she had worshipped at the shrine and cleansed her soul. Now it was almost time to begin.

Vengeance.

She was nineteen years old and had waited long enough. This was the city. Sophia had made her plans. Now it was time. Magnus snapped over a card and muttered in annoyance at the result. Then he suddenly laughed; it was one of his most attractive features, a sound that seemed to come from low in his belly and fill the room with genuine physical pleasure.

'*What is your future?*' he said, sliding one more unsuccessful card into the overlapping *talon*.

She smiled, remembering the way the flimsy door had creaked open in San Francisco and she had clutched a small derringer under the table in case her intuition had deceived, but no – a man stood there, liquor on his breath, a wild, desperate look to his eye. Caged inside himself.

The chosen one.

An empty space that she could fill.

It would take time but she had the power. He was the instrument.

'How much did you charge that night?' Magnus asked.

'Five dollars. It was all you had,' she answered from the window, watching a vagrant dog barely escape the wheels of a hurtling carriage, the coachman whipping the horse on in brutish fashion.

As the vehicle plunged off, the barking dog was joined by another, a yellow cur, slinking, less brave, the weaker of the two animals.

But strong enough to kill a rat.

Magnus laughed once more and puffed out a last thin column of smoke before stubbing out the cheroot. She liked that smell on his breath, it brought back memories.

Good before they became otherwise.

Her mother's eyes looking into hers. Dilated, wild and wanton.

The broad back of a man. A man she recognised only too well.

She pulled herself back from memory. The hotel room was a pale peach colour, which she found restful and untainted by previous association: the place newly converted from three buildings meshed together.

The Spiritualist Society of Edinburgh, though not the main thrust of the organisation, had done them proud. It was the end of a long tour of Victoria's kingdom and Sophia had insisted Magnus arrange that it end here. They had travelled all the main cities, word of mouth creating a hunger for what they had to offer. Another world. Where the dead spoke.

But not all of them. Some stayed hidden. Waiting for a sign. Waiting for vengeance.

She shivered with a hunger of her own and crossed back to lay her hand upon his shoulder. Corporeal comfort.

Magnus was halfway through the game. Finely poised.

'You think it can be solved?' he asked.

'How would I know?' she replied.

Something in her tone stilled his restless fingers and he remembered the moment when he had pushed open the door and entered that dirty little airless room to find a figure sat facing him in the shadows, face and hair concealed behind a white veil like a bride's, one hand under the table, one palm upwards pointing towards him.

Like any good gambler he had established the ante, slid over his last five dollars, and waited for his future to be told. No crystal ball to look within.

The figure spoke and asked his name. He gave it. She had a soft accent, Southern hint perhaps, hard to tell.

His own had no trace of a family of ten, in Pittsburgh's fair city, grinding poverty and empty guts.

His father all the way from Armagh found a German woman

to his liking and set about recreating the very reason he had left Ireland in the first damned place.

A big man. Big hands. Michael Bannerman. Worked in the steel mills on the south side as a puddler. Magnus was the oldest. He got the knuckle first. His privilege.

Truth be told, he was probably an evil brute to have around, big like his father, violent in temperament, and, from an early age, slippery with the stair-head girls.

The breaking point had come when his devout mother Marta, back early from kissing the Pope's backside, discovered her own first born bare-arse naked with the wife of her husband's best friend, Sonny, who worked down the docks with an iron hook instead of a right hand.

Turned out the damned priest had keeled over, a heart attack, hence Marta back at the wrong time, hence her scream to see a decent neighbour and wife spread-eagled up against the cellar wall, hence her wastrel son hauling up his pants and rabbit-footing out of there never to look back.

Magnus sometimes wondered what had happened to the wife, Maria, Spanish blood she had running in her veins, hot to touch. Then he thought of that hook.

Spanish blood.

He was fifteen. After that, on his own.

Took on another identity. Clever with cards, words, took on another voice, buried the stink of a ferrety existence, buried the times when his father's fist had smashed him to the floor, buried all his dark violence deep behind a smile, down forgotten deep to the entrails.

Buried the beast.

That was the past. Another life.

'Put your hands in mine,' the voice had said.

The figure extended both of hers, palms up, across the table and he covered the white fingers with his own great paws. He felt a jolt of sorts run up his arm and the shape opposite shuddered as if lightning had struck her down the very middle.

She whipped her hands back and regarded him through the veil. The silence brought out anger, as if she was intruding into a secret, like someone at a circus peering in a cage.

At the hidden violent animal.

'I have paid you five dollars,' he growled, as a bear might. 'I demand to know my prospects.'

There was a sound behind the veil that might have been smothered laughter, then the gauze was lifted and he looked into a pair of violet eyes that pierced him to the bone.

'You're a dead man,' she said, pale skin glowing in the dark. 'You've run out of time. You have no prospects.'

He knew this to be the truth.

She was young, he could see that now. Might be no more than seventeen years. Or seven thousand.

That damned superstitious Irish blood; it infected him with wild belief.

He had switched away from the eyes. Down to the mouth. The lips were rosebud pink, sensuous. Forming words.

'You have but a single chance,' they said. 'The only future left . . .is the one you have with me.'

That's where it had started.

All this had flashed through his mind as recollection froze him in front of the spread deck.

Sophia reached forward and in a sudden movement, smashed all the cards together, *foundation* aces, kings, queens, treacherous one-eyed jacks, she destroyed their various citadels, then pulled his head round so that he was looking up at her.

'The only future left,' she said.

After such a declaration, her eyes crossed focus, a comical phenomenon that happened when she had been in the fierce grip of the other world or as a harbinger of sexual passion.

Either way, it always made him laugh. But then he delved deep into her body and the power was like nothing he had ever known.

And then he forgot the world.

6

Oh! What a snug little island,
A right little tight little island.

THOMAS DIBDEN, *The Snug Little Island*

Muriel Grierson lived in fear of her husband, Andrew. The fact that he was dead in no way lessened the anxiety she felt at his house being desecrated by the removal of its most valuable contents while she and the maid Ellen were out shopping for provisional salvation at Leith market.

Of course this expedition had been at Andrew's posthumous behest, for he frowned upon money wasted over vegetables or meat – *the cheapest cuts simmert lang, taste aye as guid as hutheron veal* was his oft-repeated dictum.

Although it was nigh on two years since he had last glowered at her over such a repast bolstered religiously by the root vegetables in season – *mair time buriet, mair flavour tae be found* – she could not rid herself of the parsimonious habit of picking over the stalls that offered wrinkled provender.

So, when she returned with the laden Ellen trailing behind after such a frugal foray, her first response on opening the front door to find the furniture agley then going into the drawing room to discover drawers pulled out, contents scattered, was to look up in horror at the portrait of her husband, draped in black crêpe, that scowled accusingly down at her; her second action was to scream.

The sound still echoed in her ears, to a certain extent numbing her against the awful aftermath of finding her few pieces of jewellery gone; most galling of all a diamond brooch that Mamma had bequeathed her, being an especial sad loss, a mother-of-pearl music box that played 'Flow Gently, Sweet Afton' – a wedding present from Andrew's employees at the funeral parlour – and a large amount of cash she had foolishly not lodged into her British Linen Company savings account when she had discovered it recently, hidden in a locked bottom drawer in Andrew's desk in the study.

The desk had also been hastily ransacked, the papers strewn over.

All this in varying degrees of accuracy, detail, and emotional heat she reported to McLevy as he stood like a block of wood amid the carnage of the rifled drawing room.

The inspector noted it all down while covertly observing the way Muriel rested upon the manly arm of young Arthur. He, of course, was unaware that dependence has its own tendrils but in the inspector's experience when a woman leant upon you, it was always a good idea not to lean back.

Tempting, but not a good idea.

The wifie had an oval-shaped face and was pretty enough in a china doll fashion but McLevy sensed a restlessness of sorts. As if she had spent her life striving for something just out of reach.

Not an uncommon condition for the female; women often dream of a better life in another universe.

He evidenced her age at near forty, though she dressed younger, and guessed there were no children.

Funeral parlours do not encourage procreation. Roach, his own lieutenant, had undertaker's blood running in his veins, and he was also childless.

McLevy and his constable had snuffled round the house, outside and in, to discover a few things that the inspector was keeping to himself for the moment.

Mulholland was presently closeted with the now unburdened Ellen; the constable was good with maids and this one, short and dumpy, with a face that would never threaten Helen of Troy, was tailor-made for his Irish charm.

The inspector just frightened dumpy women.

'Arthur has been a tower of strength,' declared Muriel, 'with my own poor husband dead and buried.'

McLevy, as soon as he'd seen the portrait, had recognised Andrew Grierson, a miserable bugger who aye looked as if sizing you up for an imminent wooden box.

'I'm sure Arthur has been,' he muttered, 'and will be ever more, but whit was he doing here?'

'I beg your pardon?' said Muriel, who was beginning to form

a dislike of this uncouth creature. Could he not see her distress, her demonstrable lack of jewellery?

Arthur, who had been conscious of her hand tightening on his arm, sending a palpable tremor through the limb, sensed insinuation of some kind in the inspector's words and hastened to defend the fragile form beside him.

But he did so with some care, because Mister Doyle, despite headstrong ways and occasional rush to judgement, was no-one's fool.

He had observed that McLevy unsettled people. The inspector had done it at the station to his colleagues, to Arthur himself, and was doing it again.

To the unsuspecting Muriel.

Doyle recognised the technique himself from the rugby scrum. It was all a matter of equipoise. Keep the opponent off balance, the feet slipping under, limbs splayed, then apply the pressure.

And hammer him down.

'I happened here by chance,' he offered. 'I was delivering a note from my mother to Mistress Grierson.'

'Mistress Doyle and I are old friends,' added Muriel, 'and were to meet this evening.'

'The note was to confirm a time,' Conan Doyle said firmly. 'A little later than planned.'

'But I may now have to postpone,' said Muriel, 'with this dreadful loss of property. This. . .catastrophe!'

McLevy had a fine ear for the tonal nuances of respectable Edinburgh and this seemed to be quite a song and dance from her, as if something was being concealed, but he nodded as if it all made sense.

'On a cursory examination, there appears no sign of forced entry,' he announced, shoving his notebook deep into his coat pocket. 'All windows front and back apparently intact, no boiler hammer crashing through the panels of your door, no jemmying of the outside locks.'

While stating the obvious, he had one ear cocked to the other room out by the hall where Mulholland was no doubt beguiling the stolid wee Ellen, his hair neatly parted, blue eyes shining as if butter would not melt in his mouth.

But it would. Butter.

That hornbeam stick of his had cracked open many a criminal pate and had the man not looked up at the suicidal revolving feet of his once potential father-in-law?

The constable had been down many dark alleys and was as near to insidious and shifty as McLevy himself in the onerous pursuit of justice at all costs.

He also had an innocent face that invited female confidence, which he would have then no scruple in abusing.

But since McLevy had not heard any wild self-incriminating cries, he must assume that Ellen was holding also to her story.

A'body sticking to their guns.

'Ye left the house after a bite tae eat at half past one o'clock in the afternoon,' he stated pedantically. 'And returned at three o'clock, that same day. An interval of one and a half hours. Doesnae leave long.'

Conan Doyle nodded a mature agreement.

'I would concur with you, inspector,' he stated, as if indeed they were investigating the crime as equals. 'And it leads me to an inescapable conclusion.'

'Whit might that be?'

'Mistress Grierson assures me that the front door has a spring mechanism that locks automatically upon closing; I myself, on finding larceny, examined the outside back locks and windows before searching out authority.'

'Authority,' the inspector scratched his head as if puzzled by something. 'That would be me?'

'Exactly!' beamed the young man, as if the slower student had caught the current. 'I agree with you, sir, no sign of a break-in.'

'Apparently.'

'Definitely! What do we then conclude?'

'Oh, you go first,' was the shy response.

Doyle drew himself to his full height under Muriel's admiring gaze.

'Examining the known facts I can only therefore deduce someone has procured a copy of the house keys.'

For a moment a shadow crossed the woman's face and then she let out something very close to a wail.

'Oh, say not so, Arthur!'

The young man tried to soften the severity of his supposition.

'No-one is blaming you, Muriel –'

'I *never* let them out of my possession.'

'Whit about Ellen?' grunted the inspector. 'Does she have a set?'

'Ellen has been with me for nearly ten years, I would trust her with my life!'

But could ye trust her wi' your jewellery? was the thought in McLevy's distrustful mind.

'Whit about your husband's keys?'

'They were buried with him. Alongside his measuring stick for the deceased and his wedding ring still upon the finger. It was stipulated so in his will.'

While McLevy mulled over that strange request, Doyle put his hand to his chin in a manner that suggested deep contemplation.

'So, we have two possible sources, both of which would seem –'

'Three!' McLevy, who had endured quite enough of this high-falutin elucidation, marched out into the hall followed, after a second, by the others, Muriel letting go her vicelike grip on Arthur's arm to squeeze her skirts through the door. The inspector walked rapidly up to the front entrance and pulled aside the draught excluder curtain to disclose a bunch of keys hanging from a nail.

'Oh dear,' said Muriel feebly. 'I forgot. The spare set. They've been hanging there since the beginning of time. Andrew always kept them by the door in case of –'

'Catastrophe?'

Conan Doyle paid no heed to the sardonic tone in the remark.

'Of course. Now the solution is obvious!' he cried.

'Is it?'

Nothing in McLevy's experience was ever obvious. All things had, lurking within them, a subtle subversion.

'Remove the keys,' said the young man eagerly. 'Press them into soft wax, imprint both sides, replace, then make a metal copy from the imprint and no-one is any the wiser.'

The inspector put on what Mulholland would have recognised as his *daftie* face where he let his jaw drop and eyes widen; it served him well in that the more folk felt obliged to elaborate, the more they gave away.

He did not necessarily suspect the fellow before him of mal-feasance but somebody somewhere had something up the sleeve, up their jooks, a secret thought, a notion withheld.

'Who would do all that?' he asked.

'Anyone who knew of the location.'

'And who might that be?'

'Someone who was often in the house.'

'Such as who?'

This stopped the train of deduction in its tracks because the one person present who might qualify for that possibility was Doyle himself. However Muriel, who had been, for her, strange-ly silent since the revelation of the twitched curtain, suddenly launched forth like someone with a story to tell.

'Of course, when Andrew died the house was *invaded* by trades-people; the reception of the coffin, the mourners, the relatives, it all needed to be catered for.'

'Aye. Nothing like a deid body tae provoke appetite.'

Muriel nodded vigorous agreement.

'Ellen and I were rushed off our feet; I had to employ extra staff, provide food, whisky – the amount of whisky consumed at a funeral is nothing short of scandalous – and I distraught with grief. That would surely be the time and opportunity.'

Conan Doyle had moved out of the limelight and now watched from the side. Although he had a highly developed sense of chiv-alry towards the frail vessel of womanhood, he was also trained to observe.

And it struck him with some force that the inspector was play-ing Muriel like a hooked fish.

Had he, Conan Doyle, man of medicine, acute of sensibility, a student of the great Joseph Bell who taught him to be on con-stant alert against the assumptions of a lazy mind, to take the contraposition to implication and only deduce from known facts – had he also been played like a fish? For a moment he caught a glimpse of himself in a long mirror that hung by the side of the coat stand in the hall, and with his protruding eyes and droopy moustache, he might well have been mistaken for a large cod.

With an effort he shook off this unflattering comparison to hear the inspector cast another query.

'But your husband died two years ago. Why wait until now to utilise this presumed copy. What has changed?'

McLevy hauled his notebook out and licked his lips, turning pages, peering down as if to refresh his memory.

'Ye found a sum of money in his desk. Notes of the realm. Near a hundred pounds, ye said?'

A nod in answer.

Silence is golden.

'Approximately two weeks ago, ye said?'

Another nod.

'A deal of money. Ye should have banked it. Bankers aye like to see money coming in at the door.'

'I didn't like to. . .handle such.'

'Was it tainted?'

'It was – Andrew's.'

'Well, it's gone now. A fierce amount. What use would he have had for it?'

'I do not know.'

The garrulous Muriel had suddenly clammed up like a clabby-dhu.

A door further up the hall opened quietly and Mulholland slipped out. McLevy had positioned himself so as to have the vantage, looking out past the other two down the corridor.

The constable shook his head to signal that Ellen had tucked in her elbows and given away nothing.

Conan Doyle cleared his throat. His features had altered from cod-like, more towards that of a Chinese Mandarin.

'Is it your contention, inspector,' he announced gravely, 'that there is a connection between the discovery of the cache of money and the larceny?'

'Possible. Possible. All things are possible.'

This cryptic response galvanised the policeman into sudden action as if what he had just said had unleashed a font of energy in his own being.

'Who else did ye tell about this treasure trove, eh?' he demanded fiercely.

'Only Ellen, of course,' replied the startled Muriel, 'And –'

'Arthur, of course,' said McLevy. 'Naebody else?'

A moment, then she shook her head.

A moment. But McLevy registered such slices of time.

He suddenly smacked his hands together, which sounded like a gunshot in the stillness.

'You'd be surprised the number of folk who leave their spare keys on a nail by the door and anyone who knows the working of a household bereft o' common sense would, as I did, check their whereabouts.

'Now!'

He almost jumped up into the air, and Mulholland, who had witnessed this explosion of energy before, often with violent consequences, hoped that nothing untoward was about to happen to Big Arthur and wee Muriel.

'I examined the keys for traces of wax but found none,' McLevy continued. 'That means damn all. They could have been cleaned, and it is my contention they played a part in all this but not in the way, Mister Doyle, that you would have me believe.'

'I would not have you believe *anything*, inspector,' replied Conan Doyle stiffly. 'I merely suggested a possible mode of deduction.'

'Deduction?' McLevy gave another little jump. 'Deduction depends on experience, sir. And experience is hard-earnt!'

Having delivered that pithy aphorism, he strode past, heading towards the rear outside quarters of the house; as they trailed after him, the others were taken aback to see the bold Mulholland looming in the narrow space as if he had materialised out of nowhere.

The constable nodded politely but did not follow. He moved instead towards a small window at the hinder part of the premises and took up his station there as a silent jerk of the head from a passing McLevy had so instructed.

Left alone for a moment, the constable felt a strange lightness enter his being and whipped out his hornbeam stick to brandish it in the air in the manner of *The Count of Monte Cristo*. He thrust it forward into an imaginary opponent's guts, a man who bore a marked resemblance to his own inspector, and was about to eviscerate a dead ringer for Lieutenant Roach when a dry cough brought him round to face the maid Ellen.

She must have emerged behind him as silently as he had accomplished earlier and regarded him with wary eyes.

'I'll away and make some tea,' she announced.

7

Swerve to the left, son Roger, he said,
When you catch his eyes through the helmet-slit,
Swerve to the left, then out at his head,
And the Lord God give you joy of it.

WILLIAM MORRIS, 'The Judgement of God'

The inspector was out in the garden looking at the back wall of the house by the time Doyle and Muriel caught up with him and he gestured all around as if to say, *whit do you make of this?*

Truth to tell the place was not a verdant proposition; a despondent lawn of sorts, some wilting blooms that had shot their autumnal bolt and various gorse bushes that no doubt longed for a wild highland hillside.

Perhaps this emaciated Eden might have served as metaphor to the state of joyless marital rectitude within, as the vibrant growth of Jean Brash's fauna and flora at the Just Land testified to the luxuriant and fertile nature of sin, but the inspector's attention was fixed upon an area of earth just below a small high window.

The large leaves of some yellowed ornamental brassica of sorts obscured the patch but when McLevy knelt to separate the leaves, the part print of a shoe was revealed.

'Whit d'ye make of that?' he asked of Doyle.

'It is very small.'

'Uhuh? A dwarf maybe?'

This was unfair to a certain extent, since McLevy and Mulholland had already more or less worked out the *modus operandi* of the break-in before the inspector had decided to wreak further havoc in the despoiled household.

A normal tactic for McLevy, who considered that in burglarious activity the crime from outside usually had its counterpart within.

Yet why he chose to involve Conan Doyle in the process was a mystery, except that there was something about the young man; his mixture of bumptiousness and sensitivity, arrogant belief in his own acuity allied to a vulnerable awkwardness that irritated and intrigued McLevy at one and the same moment.

Who else could he possibly know that might fit such a description?

Having displayed the dwarfish concavity, the inspector then indicated a part of the wall below the small window.

Doyle peered keenly at the house bricks and noticed some faint scrapes on the stone. This he reported to his mentor, who then asked for a conclusion.

'An animal of sorts?' Doyle responded somewhat weakly.

'I'll show ye a trick,' said McLevy. 'Mulholland!'

In answer to this bellow, the small window high above suddenly flew open with a wrenching shove and Mulholland's long nose poked out, followed by the rest of his face.

'It is a simple matter,' McLevy declared to the bemused Muriel and the young deductor. 'If you examine the wood of the window frame you will see it bears the mark of a thin forcing tool, low down. I would imagine it has aye been hard to shove open and pull shut, swollen wi' weather nae doubt.'

'Yes,' offered Muriel, anxious to make a contribution. 'It has never functioned to proper office, I was forever saying to Andrew –'

'Aye, well, Andrew is no longer extant,' said McLevy callously. 'I take it to have been jammed shut but not fastened secure. Neither flesh nor fowl.'

'Yes.'

Muriel swayed slightly but Arthur did not offer the steadying arm she desired. He was on the case.

McLevy now spoke quietly, almost disinterested.

'Your movements are watched. There is a side lane runs along where ye leave your bins out for the scaffie men and as soon as you depart, two of the thieves scale the wall into your garden. Quick tae the back part of the house, one on the other's shoulders, lever open the window and then –'

'But the size of the aperture!' Doyle could not forbear interrupting.

'No' for the likes of you and me Mister Doyle.'

'A *dwarf?*'

'A snakesman,' said McLevy.

Conan Doyle's mind entertained the sudden picture of a creature, half man, half reptile, slithering up the wall.

'A small boy,' Mulholland said loftily, 'on the back of an accomplice, wriggles in at the window.'

McLevy resumed the tale.

'To the front door, keys from the nail, unlocks. The accomplice, dressed perhaps as an honest tradesman, has knocked upon the front door, it is opened as if by the maid, he steps inside. To any onlooker a normal procedure. The criminals make a heavy lift, wedge the high window back shut, keys replaced on the nail, out the door, close it fast, spring lock jumps into place. All is – as was.'

Mulholland watched from the aforementioned window as his inspector spread his arms like a man about to perform an illusion.

'Hey presto: the mystery of the locked room!'

After a short squeezed bark of laughter, McLevy dropped his arms to scrutinise the man and woman before him.

'All this jiggery-pokery is not unusual for the criminal fraternity; they are a devious crew, indeed it has aye struck me that if they applied such intelligence to lawful pursuits they would rule the Empire – no that is not unusual – but it leaves some questions hangin' in the breeze.'

He ignored Conan Doyle and fixed his gaze upon Muriel.

'Assuming, as I think it just to do so, that the money found was the felonious motive, how did the criminals know this? How did they know about the jammed window? How did they know the location of the keys?'

The mistress of the house made no reply; her fingers which, like her mind, had not been still this whole time, curled into her palms to make two small fists.

At this moment, Ellen the maid, a stoical wee soul, born and bred in the locality, came wandering out the back door from the kitchen, her demeanour showing no trace that she had witnessed a police constable attempt to skewer two of his superiors where they stood.

'I've made a pot o' tea, mistress,' she announced. 'Can I tidy the drawing room and lay out the cups and saucers?'

Muriel looked at McLevy, who nodded permission; he had made severe examination and gleaned all there was to hand.

'I shall now make some enquiries amongst your neighbours as regards tradesmen at your entrance,' he announced to Muriel. 'But respectable folk are remarkably unobservant and I'm not hopeful.'

'I'll wedge the window tight,' Mulholland said helpfully. 'But you need to get a decent joiner in and a strong catch new-fixed.'

So saying, he popped back out of sight like a jack-in-the box and the window was duly pulled shut.

There was another moment's silence. McLevy stood completely immobile, as a stone statue.

A bird sang. Short, staccato notes, like a warning.

'Would ye no' have a wee cup of tea, inspector?' asked Ellen out of the blue. She might indeed be dumpy but showed no sign of fear.

He looked into her eyes. They reminded him of his Aunt Jean's, brown, steadfast under scrutiny, and it was to his everlasting shame that he might suspect this honest maid of having a lover on the sly and tipping the transgressor off about a bottom-drawer bonanza.

He could hear his aunt's voice.

Jamie McLevy, is there nothing in this wide warld that ye don't hold in deep misdoubt?

Muriel and Conan Doyle were somewhat taken aback to see a warm smile light up the inspector's face as he inclined his head respectfully towards Ellen's chunky form.

'No thank you, miss,' he said. 'I have business on hand. A policeman aye has business on hand.'

She smiled in return and for a moment he was reminded of someone from childhood, then he turned towards the others and pointed down to the earth below the window.

'Don't touch the soil. I shall send a man round to make a cast of the footmark, though to my eyes it is a common shoe, nondescript amongst its fellows.'

He had not removed his low-brimmed bowler during all this time but now tapped twice as if to wedge it on his head before stepping up close to Muriel.

'Mistress Grierson,' he began and for a moment her heart thudded against the tight confining corsetry.

Her thoughts ran wild. What if he suddenly said, *I arrest you for the murder of your husband Andrew that you have poisoned tae death wi' rancid meat and buriet vegetables, and I suspect you also of fondling the flesh masculine* – what if he knew her guilty secret?

But he said nothing of the sort, though his face was solemn, grey eyes piercing, seeking a trace of culpability in her own.

'Once more I am brought back tae the question; who knew of the discovery in the desk, the located spare keys, the jammed window? Somebody did. And used that knowledge.'

Her chin came up slightly.

'In that I cannot help you, inspector. I have lost a great deal that is precious to me. I believe it is your task to find it.'

Once more she grasped onto Arthur's arm. This time in a firm taking.

'And I have disclosed nothing to a living soul!'

McLevy's face was impassive at this vigorous denial.

'I shall make enquiries in the usual quarters for your purloined valuables, but you can kiss the money goodbye.'

A brusque nod and he was out of sight.

The bird sang once more. A sharp, piercing note.

Muriel avoided Ellen's eyes.

'I'll awa' an' lay out the tea then,' said Ellen, but at the doorway she suddenly stopped.

'My mother knew him,' she remarked.

'I beg your pardon?' Muriel asked.

'McLevy. The thieftaker.'

'Is he noteworthy?' Doyle said with sudden interest.

'Aye. In Leith especial. A'body kens him. And fears as well. High and low. No mercy.'

For a moment Ellen's eyes narrowed as if she had some personal experience of such to relate but then she resumed her theme.

'Anyhow, my mother knew him. The inspector. Her family lived in the same cobbly square as him and his auntie. When he was a wee thing.'

'What was he like?' Conan Doyle enquired eagerly.

'Hammered,' was the succinct response. 'The big boys battered hell out of him every day.'

'Why?' he pursued.

52

'Jist devilment, I suppose. Then one day it stopped.'

'For what reason?'

'Nobody knew. But my mother was playing that time. She saw the leader o' the gang. A big shamble of a laddie. On his hands and knees, crawling, bleeding like a pig. Spewing like his bones were broken. Jamie McLevy was half his size. Watching on. Tackety boots. His auntie must have bought them. Iron at the toe. Brand new upon his feet.'

These were the most consecutive sentences Muriel had ever heard the maid utter in her life.

'I think I can draw an inference there,' murmured Doyle.

'My mother said when she looked intae his eyes it was like a wolf on the trail. A wild beastie.'

Ellen passed on into the house.

Muriel wondered if it was worth her while to become tremulous but Arthur had a faraway look in his eye.

Meanwhile outside, McLevy and Mulholland walked slowly in silence to put a little distance between them and the persecuted front door of 42 Bonnington Road.

'What do you think to all this?' asked the constable.

'That wifie is hiding something,' replied the inspector, scowling at the innocent pavement. 'And I will find it out.'

'Something between her and Big Arthur?'

'I doubt it. On his side certainly not.'

Then they stopped and looked at the houses surrounding, each with the shut-faced prim expression of a spinster at a wedding.

'I don't fancy our chances,' said the constable.

'Neither do I,' grunted McLevy. 'But it has tae be done. You take even this side, I'll take the odd opposite.'

And yet neither of them moved.

Since Conan Doyle had approached them at the station, this was the first moment of a guarded privacy they normally enjoyed day in day out.

On the saunter.

Each with his thoughts but an understanding forged by bitter experience of the dark side of humanity. Mulholland still immune with a young man's vitality, McLevy only too aware that everything gathered during the years was no protection against his own transitory nature.

As is the habit of men they spoke about such things rarely if at all, but something had changed.

Or was changing.

'Ye made a right show of yourself wi' Ballantyne,' McLevy said grumpily

'I was only trying to help,' came the huffy response.

'Ye were sookin' up tae the lieutenant. The boy is afflictit, an easy mark.'

Mulholland flushed in anger and shame.

He bit his lip to restrain a riposte of how the affliction did not stop the inspector tearing lumps out of Ballantyne if he banjaxed a case procedure.

At that moment a call turned them both round and Conan Doyle came striding up towards them, the picture of health and certainty.

'Inspector McLevy!' he cried breezily, as if the two had just met by chance. 'I wonder if I might beg a favour?'

McLevy made no response. Favours were not his speciality.

'I dabble a touch in the writing of stories. Adventures. Tales of mystery. Haunted houses.'

Doyle roared with laughter, as if recognising the ludicrousness of a hale and hearty fellow like himself having truck with such pastime.

'But I have great interest in detection. In-vestigation. And I wonder if I might accompany you at such.'

'I don't detect ghosts,' said McLevy.

'You can't get the restrainers on them,' Mulholland added somewhat stiffly.

'Of course not.'

Having agreed this, Doyle's face took on a serious mien and he spoke quietly, soberly, a different man entirely.

'But does not the function of policeman and doctor bear similarity? We analyse, we observe symptoms, eruptions on the body and mind, you of guilt, me of malady? Identify the offender, cure the contagion. Protect the innocent.'

McLevy scratched his nose. It had begun to itch.

'Crime,' he remarked tersely, 'is certainly contagious.'

'Yet we all desire to catch it, do we not?'

'Indeed we do.'

A glint of humour came into McLevy's face. There was a shrewdness to this young man that belied his bluff manner.

From Doyle's point of view, he was intrigued by a similar incongruity of overt behaviour and subtle thought.

'I would consider it a great honour. . .' Doyle's voice lowered in tone, 'if I might attend your. . .casebook of enquiry?'

The inspector's lips quirked at such portentous description as regards some of his more mundane 'enquiries', for instance, the time he and Mulholland had trawled the back-yards of Leith to find half a dozen abducted hens, solving the mystery through the deformity of one which, though plucked of all its feathers, still lacked the one eye and one leg it had lost during a life of adversity.

However, he had also witnessed bodies hacked to pieces, and on one particular occasion a face blown so far apart that it looked like a spilt bowl of stewed rhubarb.

'I'll bear it in mind,' said he. 'But it cannot be these present shenanigans; you have too personal a connection and it's no' enough challenge.'

'You will solve this case?'

'Never all of such. There's aye a loose thread. It's only in books everything is remedied.'

McLevy looked up at the sky, which was unremittingly overcast, and pursed his lips.

'I'll try tae find ye a ghost or two wi' murder thrown in.'

'Good man!' exclaimed Doyle, as if all were done and dusted and he had not perceived the sardonic tone. 'I shall await your pleasure, sir.'

With that he nodded to the silent Mulholland and then strode on up the street, scattering a few pedestrians in his wake like the liner *Oceanic*.

'Did ye no' wait for your cup of tea?' McLevy called after.

'I have to get back to mother,' came the unabashed reply. 'Family comes first!'

McLevy watched the young man until he turned the corner and disappeared.

The inspector became aware of his constable's critical scrutiny and wondered what expression had been on his face.

Whatever shape taken, it was vanished now.

'All right,' he said as if all so far had been an everyday occurrence. 'You take the even, I'll take the odd.

8

An' when Massa rode in the arternoon,
I'd follow wid a hickory broom;
De poney being berry shy,
When bitten by de blue-tailed fly.

TRADITIONAL, 'The Blue-tailed Fly'

Glasgow, 1864.

My Dearest Melissa,

I have little idea if this letter will ever reach you and I can offer no kind of address to which you may reply should that eventuality occur.

I have been mightily sick crossing the Atlantic Ocean to reach this god-forsaken place. I call it so because I am staying in lodgings down by the docks and what I see from my window does not induce the notion that any kind of decent God-fearing people exist in these parts.

Rather I watch the Devil in all his many guises and humanity so wretched and base as near defies description.

Possibly I am seeing all this through jaundiced eyes. I disembarked but two nights ago, was smuggled in like a plague carrier and have been kept out of sight ever since.

The only time I ventured forth was last evening in the darkness when the streets were awash with a tide of men and women spilled out from the taverns. The Scotch are in the main a small race and damned ugly.

How did I come to this pass?

The night I spent in your sweet arms still lingers with me but directly after came horror one hundredfold.

Gettysburg.

The battle lost.

After the defeat, it was a nightmare journey, the wounded groaning their lives away, dragged on wagons, calling for a mercy we could not grant them.

We were attacked on all sides by the Bluebellies, a heavy rain beat down on us as if the Almighty himself was on the Union side. The screams and shrieks of the dying haunt my sleep and burn images indelibly in my mind to this day.

There is little glory in war that I can see.

We took refuge in the town of Williamsport and had not Jeb Stuart and Fitzhugh Lee arrived in time with their troops, it would have been all up with us. The Confederate Army would have been no more.

General Robert E. Lee would have broken his sword.

But they came. And so the war continues.

We made it through to Virginia although the Potomac River was swollen to flood by the rain and there. . .there I am afraid. . .I forswore my reason. Fell into a fever.

How long I cannot say. Time lost meaning.

When I recovered, I was told that I might serve my country in another capacity. I was then taken to a rendezvous with Secretary Mallory, a heavyset man with a thin rim of beard and shrewd in the eyes.

I was given orders, papers I must deliver in person.

I will seal this letter now, the messenger is due to leave by the Evelyn; Curious how many ships bear names of the gentler sex. I pray he will make it through to Galveston and see this delivered.

As for me, I wait for further orders. I am still a soldier though at present I discharge the duties of a secret Confederate agent.

Bonded to stealth.

I miss your sweet face.

But love seems to have little purchase in this world.

Let us hope the South wins, and that we may all find peace.

Your husband,

Jonathen

9

Thou rascal beadle, hold thy bloody hand!
Why dost thou lash that whore? Strip thine own back:
Thou hotly lust'st to use her in that kind
For which thou whip'st her.

WILLIAM SHAKESPEARE, King Lear

The chattering magpies of the Just Land had descended on Leith market like tidings of such birds.

In their gay bonnets, bright colours and fashionable outdoor coats, parasols twirling, daintily avoiding the muck below lest it cling to their shiny black halfway-laced boots, they moved from one glittering bauble to the next with little cries of joy and excitement, displaying such innocence that the onlooker would have been hard-pressed to guess their chosen profession.

Perhaps a boldness in the gaze, a candid assessment of the males before them, either passing respectable or the cocksure peddler at his stall, that weighed such men in the balance and found the exact avoirdupois and possible cost of their carnal inclinations. Perhaps that might have tipped the wink.

The peddlers looked them straight in the eye; the passing respectable if they had previous acquaintance and a wife to hand craved invisibility, as if they were on the other side of a thick veil.

Or if no previous acquaintance enjoined, they clenched buttocks in distaste as golden opinion does when confronted by noxious depravity.

It is difficult to walk in such a state and the motion often resembles a bad case of haemorrhoids; yet virtue surely thus contained must be its own reward.

A distance aside from the main party, Francine and the Countess's Simone rattled away to each other in quick-fire French, much to the chagrin of Lily Baxter who was accustomed to being Francine's light of love. Of course she could not give utterance to her annoyance, being a deaf mute, but her face, which was by nature sunny, was set in sulky lines. Beneath curly tousled hair, the childlike open countenance bore witness to the unhappy thoughts that ran in her mind.

Lily and Francine had been lovers and followed their craft for nigh on two years. They had stretched, scourged, thistled, and inflicted requisite degrees of pain upon the supplicatory clients of the Just Land, sending them home milked dry of deviation to their wives who would have, in the words of Hannah Semple, *died wi' their leg up*, had they known of their husbands' compulsive drive for subjugation. Francine's speciality.

The Frenchwoman ran the show: severe, leather-clad in the manner of an Egyptian princess, her chalk-white beautiful face gazing with dispassion at the hopeful mounds of flesh spread-eagled below; like a cartographer plotting out proposed lines of mortification.

Lily darted here and there around the Berkley Horse, a piece of equipment that had set Jean Brash back a pretty penny but was worth its considerable weight in gold, giving access – fore, aft, over and under – to the quivering recipient.

At the altar of agony, in the cellar of the Just Land, Lily was the acolyte, bearing the instruments of salvation with an innocent fervour, only the occasional grin letting show the mischief in her mental process.

Now and again she popped her head up above the straps and buckles of the horse like a jockey who had just won the race. A wicked flash to her lover, then out of sight.

Two of a kind.

But that had all changed since the arrival of Simone.

Both women were from Paris, but while Francine was of an educated background, a sophisticate whose artistic bent for painting had been sidetracked into stripes of a different kind, the other was a guttersnipe whose assumed airs and graces fooled most, but not Francine who knew the real thing, or Lily who could smell the fake a mile away.

However it amused the Frenchwoman as she watched Simone change shape like a chameleon to attract and seduce.

Francine was attracted for certain but the other verb had yet to come into play.

Now that Francine spoke constantly in her native tongue her voice had dropped in tone, the French vowels and gutturals sliding into ancestral cadence, the language a warm, sensual flowing stream, no longer shot through with Anglo-Saxon ambiguity, and Lily, who could not hear all this in any case, was left out in the cold.

A touch on the elbow brought her round. It was the other girl from the Countess, Jessie Nairn. She was also from the streets – Paisley, the west of Scotland – and the harshness of her life showed in the eyes. Whatever good deeds done or witnessed were lost in the mists of time.

Jessie spoke slowly, forming the words with her lips; she had already learned how to communicate with Lily.

'Have ye lost your big rub-a-dub then?' she asked.

Lily's eyes narrowed.

'I'd help ye out,' said Jessie. 'But I like the hairy men. Bigger the better.'

She roared in most unladylike laughter while her eyes appraised Lily with cool calculation.

The mute turned her head away and looked over to where Francine was standing with Simone, the tall woman wearing a dark mannish jacket that accentuated the slim lines of her figure. She jutted out one hip and Simone laughed at some remark. Very Gallic. Very gamine. Very droll.

I hope she burns in hell, thought Lily, the jealousy rising in her throat as a fear of loss, a fear of the love that made her tremble in the moist night never being hers again, never filling her eyes with tears, never catching her breath away, never...

This time the touch on her elbow was more like a sharp punch.

'Ye must be desperate,' Jessie asserted. 'The woman's nothing but skin and bones.'

The image of Francine as a skeleton in leather caught Lily's fancy and her eyes lit up in sudden humour. She punched Jessie back in the muscle of the arm and stuck up her small fists in the parody of a prize-fighter.

'C'mon,' said the Paisley girl. 'We'll buy you a scarlet ribbon.'

The market was still crowded, though some of the barrows were being wheeled away. While Big Annie Drummond, who was supposed to be keeping an eye on the assorted magpies as senior heaviest member, was distracted by a cream cake stall and two of the barrows had crashed wheels with vituperative results, a small portly man stepped out from one of the crooked wynds that fed into the square.

Simone had found a pretty embroidered handkerchief and was holding it up to the light admiringly while Francine impaled the hawker with a glare as he tried to charge her an extortionate price for a miniature wooden figurine.

God knows how it had ended up in Leith but it was of African origin with a rounded belly and tapered breasts, the shape of which reminded her of Lily's.

Her recollection jolted, Francine looked up to see her lover staring at her from across the square while Jessie rummaged amongst a tangle of cheap ribbon.

The Frenchwoman smiled but Lily's face did not move a muscle and while all were thus engaged, Alfred Binnie, the portly man, uncorked a small phial of liquid and, as he passed behind Simone, poured it delicately high on her back.

For a moment it was as if time suspended, everyone frozen in the scene except Binnie who passed through like something in a sleight of hand; then came the acrid smell of burnt clothing as the powerful acid found its way through the thin outdoor coat, inwards into the crinoline folds of the dress, burrowing further like an incendiary worm to the epidermal layers. And there it found a place to feast.

A piercing scream from Simone rent the air and all except Lily stopped in their tracks to look around for the source of such howled disturbance.

From the deaf mute's point of view she watched her rival's mouth open and close in silent agony as her body shuddered in pain; then Francine ripped off the back of the coat with her powerful hands and further ripped the layers of respectable apparel off the body like an impatient lover until white skin was revealed.

A livid mark ran down parallel with the backbone and the revealed naked flesh in a crowded market place might have put Francine in mind of some morality depiction from the middle ages, had she not been otherwise occupied.

One of the market folk, an old man who sold posies and

blooms, cut, lifted and stolen from reputable Leith flower-beds by his own grandchildren, grabbed a cheap linen tablecloth from an indignant fellow hawker, dunked it into a bucket of water and threw the dripping material to Francine who caught it like a matador and pressed it up against the smouldering skin.

Simone's body arched and she fell limply backwards so that her head rested upon Francine's shoulder.

The rest of the magpies, with Big Annie in the vanguard and showing a remarkable turn of pace for one of her tonnage, hurtled towards the pair, feet churning up the mud, their faces contorted with concern.

Again from Lily's vantage, it was like a shadow play for children where the grotesque shapes collide and spin around each other but no harm is done.

The only other person who had not moved in all of this was Jessie Nairn, who stood beside Lily with a thin piece of scarlet ribbon dangling from her fingers.

She was calculating her chances of survival. One way or the other.

10

> Many a carcase they left to be carrion,
> Many a livid one, many a sallow-skin –
> Left for the white-tail'd eagle to tear it, and
> Left for the horny-nibbed raven to rend it.
> ALFRED, LORD TENNYSON, *Battle of Brunanburh*

Jean Brash in a fury was a fearsome proposition. Her green eyes were ablaze with wrathful animosity as she leaned over the balustrade and looked down at the policeman below who, from her vantage, was an unwelcome foreshortened intruder.

'What the hell do you want, McLevy?' she almost spat, having emerged from an upstairs bedroom.

Big Annie Drummond, who had puffed her way up the stairs to deliver the news of the inspector's arrival, now made better weather of the descent while the man himself gazed up at her mistress with a bland expression of general goodwill.

'I hear one of your girls had a wee contretemps,' he remarked, standing in the ornate hall festooned with décor arabesque and fancy mirrors designed to flatter the clients into thinking they might be Pashas rampant and incarnate should they glance at themselves before ducking into the doorways of sin.

McLevy furnished an odd reflection in his low-brimmed bowler and it is to the mirrors' credit that they withstood the burden of this adverse radiation without cracking into lines of distressed complaint.

'What's it to do with you?' came her terse response.

Big Annie before she disappeared into the main salon shot the inspector a look as if to warn, *hold onto your hat.*

'It would appear as if,' he offered mildly, 'there may have been some criminal intent involved.'

'*Intent?*'

'Criminal. I investigate such. That is my profession.'

There was a silence as they measured each other up.

To be truthful McLevy when he heard about some stramash in the market had jumped at the chance to abandon Mulholland in bootless pursuit round the pawnbroking fraternity for trace of stolen jewellery. The inspector's opinion being that whoever had committed the theft was too long in the tooth to pledge the articles in such an obvious slot.

They would be fenced after the heat had died down and reappear in Aberdeen or some other far-flung outpost.

So he had left his umbrageous constable in the lurch and headed for the Just Land in the hope of a cup of Jean's excellent coffee while 'deducting', as young Arthur would have it. Plus the fact that he was nosy by inclination.

'Ye better come up,' said Jean finally. 'For sure I'll never get rid of you if I leave it to natural causes.'

So, he did. Come up.

Simone lay face down in the bed, inert and silent. Her bandaged back, high up near the shoulder blade, provided a stark contrast to the lacy confines of a room more usually reserved for clients who had a yen to re-experience the warm glow of infancy.

Everywhere McLevy glanced he saw babyish frills; the coloured friezes on the wall depicted various nursery rhyme characters, one in particular, Little Bo Peep, eminently prominent, shepherd's crook clasped firmly in one hand while she scanned the horizon for absent mutton.

For some reason, the inspector found this disconcerting so he concentrated hard upon the body in the bed.

'She appears peaceful enough,' he volunteered.

'Laudanum.'

'That would explain it.'

'The doctor put a salve on her but he is of the opinion that the scar trace may remain.'

'Scar?'

'Acid. Poured down her back.'

'Dearie me. Who would do such a thing?'

Jean did not answer. McLevy tried again.

'Did anyone witness the culprit?'

'*Culprit?*'

This seemed a feeble word to describe someone capable of such a vicious attack but Jean was also aware that McLevy was a subtle swine, especially when on a case, and might well have used the word to provoke an unwise reaction. So she held to silence.

'Wrongdoer, then. Assailant. Nasty piece of work.'

'Not a thing. Nobody saw a damned thing.'

'Man or woman?'

'Not even that.'

'Dearie me.'

It looked as if his chances of scrounging a cup of coffee were somewhat slim, but McLevy was wondering whether to believe Jean's assertion of this mysteriously invisible spectre who poured acid onto folks' hinterlands because, if she did know who had done this, the person concerned would suffer a swift reprisal that had nothing to do with the law unless in the Old Testament connotation.

An eye for an eye.

Bugger the coffee, he went for blood.

'This is your own fault, Jean,' he said bluntly.

'How so?'

'The streets are hoachin' with two things. One is the advent of mesmerism in our fair city and the other is that yourself and a certain *arriviste* have been spoiling for a rammy since she opened her doors.'

'*Arriviste?*'

'Don't keep repeating whit I say. The Countess. The word is a certain French lassie broke ranks. This on the bed wouldnae be the girl by any chance?'

Jean's face betrayed nothing but she cursed the fact that there was not a dark happening in Leith that did not reach McLevy's ears. He had a nest of informants second only to her own, but where she garnered intelligence by understated influence of favours granted, dispensed over and under the counter like drugs in an apothecary shop, the inspector ruled by fear.

No mercy.

If he asked, you answered and many were the craven souls who sought to gain what they mistakenly hoped to be protective cover should they ever stray from the path of righteousness.

It is a human trait to lick the leather boots of power and it never gets you anything but a sore tongue.

'What if it *is* the girl?' she replied coolly.

'You tell me,' McLevy retorted; he had suddenly spotted the whereabouts of the sheep. They were hunched together in another frieze at a corner of the room and unless he was visually deluded, one of them, a ram no doubt, was tupping an anxious looking ewe.

'Why should I do your job?'

But having said such, Jean proceeded to perform this very function.

'The hand that poured the acid might not be witnessed but I believe you know the one responsible.'

'Do I?'

The inspector's eyes widened. Now they had changed places. She the prosecutor, he the defendant.

'A vicious creature. Long nails. Cowardly.'

'Tae strike from ahent, ye mean?'

'Exactly. A dirty stinking coward.'

'These foreign types, eh?'

'The lowest scum. Worse than policemen.'

'That bad?'

'And you know the person. You know the name.'

'And so do you,' said James McLevy, the game over. 'It is your contrivance this happened.'

Jean's lips thinned but he continued apace, having spotted three ships a-sailing over the recumbent form of Simone on the far wall, so making use of nautical metaphor.

'Ye have received a shot across your bows. A warning. The message is – give the girl back.'

'Not a hope in hell.'

'Then it will be war between you.'

'I didnae start it.'

'As always, you are the innocent party.'

'The history of my life.'

Simone whimpered in the bed and her feet scrabbled under the covers as an animal might do when dreaming.

McLevy stared at Jean's beautiful but impenitent face and wondered how sin left no mark on the human countenance.

'Now, here is another warning. Ye have no proof that the Countess was behind this event and if I catch you either in the act itself or instigating attempted vengeance upon the woman, I shall have no option but throw you into the cells and thence to the Perth penitentiary.'

This provoked severe indignation and Little Bo Peep frowned as Jean muttered an expletive under her breath while the inspector walked towards the door.

'And whit about *her*? How come she escapes your vile clutches?'

'Proof,' came the stern response. 'If I find proof then justice will prevail.'

'*Justice?*'

'Don't keep repeating what I say!'

As they glared at each other the door flung open and Hannah Semple burst in like an avenging angel.

She had a page of paper grasped in her mottled fingers and did not remark McLevy who had nearly been knocked over backwards by the outflung portal.

'Mistress!' Hannah cried. 'See whit I've got. Lily Baxter pressed it in my hand, a decent wee soul for a' she doesnae speak a word and witness the way Francine and that Simone on the bed there have been slaverin' round one tae the other – but see what Lily gave me!'

These were a lot of words for Hannah who tended to deal them out with care lest she find herself short on occasion, but the keeper of the keys was unaccustomed to excitement of this sort and she brandished the paper.

'She's a good wee drawer. Acted it all out for me. A creepy bugger at the back o' Simone, pouring out, passing by, and here's his likeness!'

Hannah stopped suddenly. Jean had made no move to take the paper. Her eyes seemed focused beyond as if a malignant presence was lurking.

Then a hand reached out from behind and magicked the image out of her hand.

'If I may be so bold,' said a voice.

McLevy held the paper to his eyes and wondered for the umpteenth time if he should risk a visit to an ocular shop.

In focus finally, he saw a figure of a fat podgy body with a huge head out of proportion, which he assumed Lily had created to augment the possibilities of identification.

The face was round, pouch-eyed, a small pouting mouth like a mole, no nose to speak of, the chin weak and the hat above this unattractive assembly a full-blown bowler unlike his low-brimmed affair.

Francine may have been the artist but Lily Baxter had a gift for caricature, no doubt about such.

'Not a pretty sight,' he said. 'How high does he ascend towards heaven?'

Hannah now knew why Jean had looked like a cow stuck in a dank bog. She reluctantly raised a hand about four inches above her own stature of five feet to indicate height.

'According to Lily,' she muttered.

McLevy turned the page round so that Jean might share in the pictorial exhibition.

'Recognise this sconeface?' he asked.

'No.'

Hannah thought to offer something but caught a glint in Jean's eye and sniffed loudly instead.

'Ugly bugger, eh?' she said.

'I don't know him either,' McLevy remarked. 'So his ill favour is not of the parish. But I'll find him if he stays above ground.'

Simone let out a small awakening groan from the bed and McLevy suddenly shot back to her side and stuck the picture before her dilated eyes.

'D'ye recognise this malefactor?' he asked loudly.

She squinted, and then shook her head slowly.

'Not a visiting randie-boy to the Countess?'

'They're all creaking bones,' said Jean disdainfully.

Simone shook her head once more, then her eyelids drooped and she slid back into the dream that offered a velvet cushion against inflicted agony.

The inspector gave up, shoved the paper into his coat pocket and walked back to the door where he paused for a moment like an actor about to deliver the curtain line.

'I don't want any dead bodies of this description found on the streets or floating in the docks.'

He pointed to yet another nursery character that had caught his attention. Fat and egg-shaped.

'You leave Humpty Dumpty tae me.'

The door closed and he was out of sight.

In the silence, the black outline of a bird flew past the window outside and cast a shadow on the veiled curtains.

'I'm sorry, mistress,' Hannah muttered. 'I didnae know and I didnae see ahent the door. The man's a bloody menace.'

Jean's face was thoughtful. She was beginning to map out the lines of strategy.

'Get Lily to make another drawing,' she said finally. 'In fact, if we make use of carbon paper and keep her at it, we may have enough and to spare.'

'For what?'

'Handing out to my people. I wish to find this dirty wee gutterblood.'

Hannah nodded. Jean fixed her with a glance.

'Earlier. You had something to say?'

'No' certain sure mind, but. . .in the teashop. At one of the tables. It might have been him.'

'And I didn't notice,' Jean stated with an edge of annoyance. 'Because I was too fixed upon the Countess.'

'She's a tricky customer.'

'So is James McLevy,' said Jean, while a fluted snore from the bed sounded as if in agreement.

Indeed, the man himself was walking through the gardens of the Just Land with much on his deceptive mind.

Despite his warning to the contrary the inspector was convinced that Jean Brash and the Countess would fight tooth and nail until one or other had the last word at the graveside of her rival.

Either woman could kill two roosters in the one second.

For a moment an image from his dream, the cloaked red figure, sprang into his senses and he glanced around swiftly lest the spectre be lurking in the shrubbery, but nothing was manifest. Yet why was his waking thought being harassed by a nightly vision?

He could not answer that, so returned to contemplation.

So be it. Then while they fought like Oberon and Titania over the changeling, he might take them both.

If they broke the law, and there was no doubt they had in the past and would in the future, a habit exacerbated by the coming conflict, if they did, he would get his chance.

A curious melancholy came upon him. For the Countess he did not give a damn but Jean Brash was a different matter.

Where would he find another decent cup of coffee?

He covered a multitude of feeling with that sentence and stopped to look into the big fishpond that Jean had recently caused to be gouged out of the harmless earth.

Women were aye *making* something. Never content.

Great wodges of thick, dark green ornamental leaves moved gently on the surface of the water, with some large lily pads of an uneasy yellow coloration spreading their empire like Victoria Regina.

Beneath all that vegetation lurked some – to his eyes – bloated exotic fish that had never done a hand's turn in their life.

Sluggish, pale gold, bilious green, scarlet fins like blood in water, they cruised and nudged below the leaves.

The inspector frowned. It would be his advice to put a net of sorts over the pond to guard against the advent of a marauding heron. These fat layabouts were an easy mark.

But good advice is seldom heeded.

Why had the Countess made such a provocative move?

Who was Humpty Dumpty?

A harsh cry overhead came from a passing crow, warning anyone below: *Get ready tae dree yer weird.*

Suffer your fate. Complaint gets you nowhere.

McLevy moved off towards the iron gates of the Just Land and disappeared into the evening mist like a wisp of the imagination.

Now you see him, now you don't.

11

> Behold I shew you a mystery;
> We shall not all sleep
> but we shall all be changed.
>
> THE BIBLE, Corinthians

In the silence of the darkened room a distant grandfather clock chimed seven times. Possibly in another venue at the modest quarters of the Edinburgh Spiritualist Society, a ghost or two had gathered to witness the whirr of a mechanical universe and the striking result of chronological certainty but in the main salon there was so far only corporeal presence and a hushed silence.

The gas burners had been dimmed to a peep so that a pale sickly light caught the occasional white shirt front or brightly pleated dress collar of the latest fashion, but the rest was subdued garmentation, gloomy and overcast as the sky had been all day.

Lieutenant Roach sat bleakly beside his rapt, attentive wife and regretted for the hundredth time that he had partaken so heartily of onions at supper. He had a weakness for fried liver, bacon and the pungent bulb of the lily family; Mrs Roach had instructed the cook accordingly because she wished to flatter his stomach into accepting what his mind would most certainly reject.

A visit to an otherworld where unseen influence held sway and ethereal spirits did not indulge themselves in offshoots of the *Allium cepa*.

Now he was reaping a digestive whirlwind in the form of repetitive gaseous eruptions that insisted on bursting from whichever conduit might yield to pressure.

The audience, of which he was an unwilling and uncomfortable participant, was seated in rows with a centre aisle facing onto a small stage where a single figure sat in a chair, illuminated from each side by a large honey-coloured candle on a simple holder.

The silence stretched.

The figure did not move.

The lieutenant smothered an inconvenient upsurge and blinked his eyes.

Surely the woman would have some kind of visitation shortly? Not that Roach would believe it for a moment but at least it would get the ball rolling towards the hole.

Three places to the rear, in fact the back row, where his massive frame would incommode no watcher behind, Conan Doyle sat between his mother Mary and Muriel Grierson. The young man was conscious of a certain emanation from Muriel's direction that seemed somewhat odorously provocative.

A perfume most certainly but not a clean sharp cologne to bring a chap to his senses, more of a musky offering like a delicate crooked finger from a shadowed doorway.

He took a deep breath but kept his eyes fixed on Sophia Adler, whose ash-blonde hair shone behind the white veil in the candlelight like a signal to the spirits.

Magnus Bannerman had spoken first and spoken well of the *gravitatio universalis*, the universal fluid that linked all creatures of the cosmos and flowed through the human body, an unseen magnetic force that might connect us to these unknown worlds.

He painted a picture of a parallel existence where the departed spirits floated in suspension, desperately waiting to be conjoined with those left behind. Waiting for a call, a hand to be stretched across the great divide.

The American even found a modicum of humour. He, Magnus, was not that hand. He held his own up in the air and waggled the fingers. There was a sharp burst of laughter but Sophia, who at that moment was sitting at the side, bowed her head and Magnus quickly returned to serious mode.

Only belief could sustain contact. The credence of those watching and the intense divination of the sensitive.

From us to them. The natural. A sublime interpreter.

Doyle was impressed, but not overly so, by the spiel. He had read deeply of the spiritual world with its phenomenal possibilities and this man reminded a little of a fairground huckster. Yet he could not dismiss the fellow because he sensed that under the delivery, and it did not escape his notice that Magnus's magnetic power might have part source in his handsome features and flashing eyes – for the women, of course, men are not so easily swayed – under the smooth hypnotic flow of words, there seemed a core of true belief.

Almost in spite of the man himself, as if Magnus was being called to witness a more powerful force than his own being; he a mere mouthpiece who might only express itself in this somewhat florid fashion.

Or was the fellow merely a skilful actor hinting at a reality that did not exist, as actors are wont to do?

Make-believe.

Or indeed was Doyle, jealous of the man's ability, projecting all this ambivalence upon a screen of shadows?

Because there was no doubt that Bannerman transfixed the audience when he abandoned the eloquent modulations to speak simply at the end of his address.

'I do not ask you to give your credence lightly,' he announced in a soft drawl. 'There are compulsions beyond us. Beyond our mortal understanding. If we abuse them, they may take vengeance upon us.'

Here he had stopped abruptly and looked over at the quietly seated Sophia.

Conan Doyle at that moment understood where Bannerman received his ballast and belief. It was from the woman.

Everything comes from the woman. Good or bad.

Or is it all an act?

'If we honour them,' Bannerman ended his thought, 'we may be blessed.'

With that he extended his hand towards Sophia and assisted her to mount the stage.

Magnus then took her place at the side, while she sat without fuss and arranged her pale blue dress, a simple cotton affair, accentuating her appearance of innocence and vulnerability.

Her arms were bare and the veil was held in place by a circlet of silver. She looked like something from a fairy tale. A princess waiting for a gallant knight.

All this had happened in the past.

Now, in the present, it seemed there was only Sophia Adler and Arthur Conan Doyle.

He felt a pull from inside as if some force was moving him towards the fragile being on the stage.

As if the complex inner being sheltered behind his massive frame had found harmony of response.

His mother Mary glanced at him from the corner of her eye. She knew her son and his passionate search for a meaning to life. They had both renounced the Catholic faith, the faith of a morbid alcoholic husband and father who now resided in an institution for such lost souls.

But it left an empty space.

And nature abhors a vacuum.

Mrs Roach, meanwhile, laid her dainty cat's paw upon the dry saurian skin of her husband's hand and murmured.

'Robert. Do you not feel the spirits around us?'

Roach closed his eyes as if sensing the afterlife but in reality he was trying to control a knot of oniony wind that had gathered in his lower depths and was whipping about inside like a fireball looking for an exit.

Luckily at that moment Sophia began to utter softly and the attention of all became fixed upon her while Roach gave thanks to whatever spirit had answered his pressing need.

Many of the audience were ready to believe or already converted and some had even experienced séance phenomena.

Ghostly shapes flitting in the dark, raps on the table, musical instruments sounding in their ears, though never a trombone, raising of ponderable bodies, objects falling from the ceiling including lumps of ice, fresh flowers and fruit, which might indicate that the spirits were somewhat eclectic in their shopping;

all these events dubious in origin and dependent upon the eyes being distracted or deceived.

Sophia Adler was none of these things.

For a start there were no manifestations; nothing appeared, not even ectoplasm, no oozing smoke from an obliging orifice that writhed into deceitful shapes while the female medium slumped erotically, limbs splayed.

No. That was not on show.

It was merely voices.

Sounds from her throat, soft at first, disjointed, rising and falling in pitch, not even words decipherable, as if filtered through a mesh of static interference.

They tumbled from her mouth and distorted the surface of the veil as if struggling to get free.

At one point she almost toppled from the chair, slowly lurching to the side like a newly felled tree but Bannerman leapt nimbly upon the stage and gently brought her to an upright position where she remained in better balance.

Now words began to form. Phrases. Random, questing, plaintive messages, some of which began to strike home amongst certain of the watching conscious throng.

A child searched for her mother. A wailing lost soul that had died of the fever. A woman called out in pain from the audience. It was her daughter. She named the wraith and there was an agonised exchange of sorts. Tears streamed down the woman's face. This was not an act. Not for her.

The child vanished, others took her place; some found no recognition in the watchers and were elbowed aside by clamouring rivals; behind the veil Sophia's face contorted further and it seemed to Conan Doyle as if these sounds were being wrenched out of her, as if she was giving birth.

Birth of any kind is a painful proposition. He had witnessed such with women as part of his studies and found it a terrifying process; indeed he was anything but sure whether men, medical or not, should be anywhere near the event. It was a dark and bloody passage.

He would write about it someday.

At times Sophia was like an animal growling; guttural, then yelping as if chased by the very hounds of Hell, then through the gibberish a sudden clarity as if a curtain had parted. A man's voice sounded; his wife was not to concern herself, she was to marry again and live a happy life. He had died at sea when the ship went down.

An old woman closed her eyes and smiled bitterly to herself. *Fine advice, my buckie, but a wee bit on the late side.*

These were not necessarily happy visitations but as full of ambiguity and sorrow as life itself.

Which made them all the more real.

The force field inside the small room was charged with a raw intensity beyond the meagre experience of the diminished reality doled out to us as life.

The atmosphere was thick with untold stories and no-one dared meet another's eye lest they see the naked emotion of a heart stricken with regrets.

For do not we all hide these feelings as if they were unwanted children, pale ghosts that follow us through existence?

Even Robert Roach had a momentary fear that he might hear his father's admonishing tones cataloguing the many parental disappointments in an ungainly son, but the lieutenant pulled himself together and awkwardly attempted to calm his wife who was fluttering like moth to candle as she waited to recognise a dead ancestor that had departed with no warning and might return in the same fashion.

Her family specialised in sudden death.

As Roach searched in the little chamber of his emotions for a rarely expressed affection that might assuage his wife's palpitations, another disbelieving member of the audience received a lightning bolt of sorts.

His name was Gilbert Morrison, one of two brothers in the shipping business. A dry stick with a cruel streak, it was an accident of sorts that he had found himself in these quarters.

Accidents do happen.

He had been walking along George Street when struck by a poster outside the hall that housed the Spiritualist Society.

An image of Sophia Adler met his narrow gaze, with fulsome tribute in words below as to her abilities in the realm of cryptaesthesia. Her face was partly in shadow, the eyes hidden, but it had a susceptible, waiflike air that provoked a whiplash sentiment in Mister Morrison normally expressed in very different surroundings.

On an impulse, Gilbert, this rare occasion, let his darker compulsion influence the public persona.

Fate works that way sometimes.

Yet before that he was intercepted, as all the attendance including an irritated Roach had been, by a gaunt figure with long white hair who stood at the entrance of the hall with a placard raised high.

The message was succinct enough. *This is against God!*

The man's name was Jupiter Carlisle. He was to be found in front of most theatres in Edinburgh most nights railing against the sins of the flesh as depicted by lewd actresses and seemed to have transferred his implacable hatred of evil over to mesmerism for this evening.

Jupiter was haggard with rectitude and fixed Gilbert with pale blue, washed-out eyes gleaming with a zealot's fire. There was an unhinged quality to the man, and though he was mocked and reviled by the very folk he sought to save from sin, he inspired a strange trepidation. No-one wanted him too close lest lunacy contaminate.

The Ancient Mariner.

His voice was high-pitched and parched as if he were drying up inside.

Thus he addressed Gilbert.

'Enter into this place,' he pronounced, 'and you enter a palace of iniquity where the Lord dwelleth not.'

Gilbert pushed past but Jupiter persisted.

'Only the Lord raises the dead. This woman Sophia Adler is against Christ and must suffer consequence.'

As Gilbert went through the door and was nodded past by a sleepy old gateman, the judgement followed.

'He will strike her down. The Lord anoints, the Lord provides. This mesmerism is of Satan's making and you will lose your soul, sir. The flesh is aye weak and you are of the flesh!'

A confused message to which Gilbert had paid no attention, the very essence of spiritualism being a lack of corporeal form; however in this case flesh was his motivating force, his darker compulsion.

So perhaps Jupiter had a point.

Gilbert had been one of the last to enter and so found a seat at the end of Conan Doyle's row on the extremity just by the door, closed behind by an obliging usher.

There was a stronger light by this portal and so the maritime merchant was picked out by the downward shaft as if illuminated by doom or destiny.

It illustrated a long hatchet of a face with deep-set eyes, high cheekbones and a mouth that invited the inserted envelope.

None of the strange auditory happenings had made much impression upon Gilbert.

He was distant by nature, worshipping two forces – power and money – both of which he now possessed in quantity sufficient to justify the vicious greed that had driven him from one act of treachery to another.

Morrison was a ruthless man. Predatory. He gave thanks to the Almighty on Sunday and the rest of the week was his own; exemplifying the Presbyterian edict that a grim heart leads to God.

Indeed the idea of a voluptuous or delicious deity would have sent him scurrying to a hole in the ground.

As Sophia writhed in her chair, his thoughts were not of a spiritual nature but more to indulge the dark wish that put an image in his mind of acquiescent supine surrender.

Therefore it was a great surprise to Gilbert when the woman suddenly whipped her head round and stared wildly, it would seem, straight to where he was sitting, surrounded by a halo of light.

Slowly one bare arm, flesh that he had been regarding with detached relish, rose from the body and pointed an index finger towards him.

For a moment her mouth opened and closed but no words emerged, then she let out a stifled shriek and fell abruptly back in the chair exposing a flash of white throat as if to a lover's kiss.

Or bite.

The stirring in Gilbert's loins was matched by an agitated rustle in the audience but Magnus Bannerman announced softly that they must compose themselves, this was a delicate moment, anything might happen, the sensitive must be left to replenish her vital sources, otherwise she might be torn to pieces by the spirits.

And so they fell silent. And waited.

Then with a shocking crash the door burst open with a sound like a thunderclap and two howling figures ran inside to chase each other dementedly round the room.

One was a devil, the other a ghost, and they emitted high-pitched screeches and cursing as they moved like will o' the wisps in the gloom.

Two young well-to-do louts in costume, who were anticipating Halloween by some days, had crept into the halls past the dozing caretaker and thought it a great diversion to join the whirling spirits in satanic caper.

To add to the mayhem, Sophia's head snapped up, the veil fell aside, and her white face shone in the darkness.

At the same time the nonplussed Muriel heard a ghostly voice echo in her ears. *Jezebel!* was the message from the other world. And then for good measure, repeated once more. *Jezebel!*

In fact this was a distant malediction from the departing Jupiter Carlisle, out in the street, which had floated in the still air and wafted through a partly opened small high window below which she sat at the back of the hall.

In a state of susceptibility, Muriel received the arrow of accusation straight into her guilty heart and what had made it worse was that the reedy, querulous quality of Carlisle's voice bore an uncanny resemblance to that of her dead husband.

Jezebel!

Meanwhile the devil and ghost had skipped nimbly under the unavailing grab of the ushers but then ran into the governance of Conan Doyle who had recovered from his surprise, having wrenched his arm away from Muriel's panicked grip, and proceeded to exercise a rugby-honed ability to take the slippery customer in tight embrace.

He tucked the cursing, fractious hooligans, one under each arm, strode out to the street and deposited them on the cobblestones with a hefty boot in the backside to speed them on their way.

From a far point down the street Jupiter Carlisle howled some words at the scene, dismissing them all as heathens who merited burning in the fires of Hell.

As Doyle walked back inside, brushing his hands in satisfaction, because nothing pleases a man more than to mete out summary punishment, he crossed paths with a tall thin person who brushed past without acknowledgement but was recognisable as the target of Sophia's pointed finger.

And he had met the fellow not long before when the University had put on a rowing competition, which Arthur's boat had won.

Various shipping merchants had been invited in the vain hope that they might contribute something to the club's coffers and this thin man and his fat brother had attended, eaten the food, drunk the beer but given damn all.

'Good evening, Mister Morrison,' Doyle said to the man's back and received a mumbled, belated response.

Perhaps he was embarrassed. In truth Conan Doyle would not have placed the merchant as a seeker after truth.

When Arthur returned to the hall, the chair on stage was empty and Magnus Bannerman was soothing the startled spiritual questors who were milling around like a shoal of confused herring.

'We shall meet again,' he assured them. 'There will be other times. If you have received a message from the unseen world, count it your fortune; if not, then be of good cheer and cultivate patience. Your time will come.'

He shook his mane of dark hair as if in wonder at what he had witnessed and walked with great dignity to disappear through a door behind the small stage.

Roach, attempting to hustle his excitable spouse away from the scene in unobtrusive fashion, found himself face to face with the hero of the hour and muttered a greeting of sorts to Doyle before taking his wife and indigestion home.

Arthur walked up to where the small formidable figure of his mother stood amongst the distracted crowd who were being gently guided to the door by members of the Society.

'Well, Mam?' he demanded with a twinkle in his eye. 'What do you think to all that?'

Mary Doyle nodded solemnly. She had raised this great oak from an acorn and filled his thought with chivalric purpose to shield them both from the terrible strains of a bleak reality; scrimping every penny to keep the home from breaking apart as her husband Charles slid inexorably from a gentle artistic man to a bitter alcoholic wreck.

The Catholic clergy had taken the male side, advising her to bear and suffer, for that was her lot in life. And so she created a sword in her mind then cut fiercely through the thin cord that bound her to Romanism.

Her children were everything. Especially Arthur.

In common with the Camelot king, he aspired to noble deeds and though no-one's fool in terms of the pragmatism of daily life and the vicious twists of humanity, yet he yearned to soar like an eagle above the grinding banality of everyday existence.

The idea of spiritualism chimed mightily with these high-flown idealities.

A higher plane. And in the case of Sophia Adler, a striking beauty to light the way.

Mary's lips quirked in amusement but held a trace of concern. The Anglican Church might attract her in the future but it would not do for Arthur.

He had an inbuilt resistance to the authorities, except perhaps the sporting ones, because they spawned injustice of which he was a ferocious, implacable opponent.

All this had flashed through her brain as she gazed from her small stature up at his giant frame.

Her knight in shining armour.

She had created him so.

And now he was his own creation.

Mary realised that she still had not answered his question, and so like many an intelligent woman, took refuge in Shakespeare.

'*There are more things in heaven and earth, Horatio –*' she began.

'*Than are dreamt of in your philosophy,*' he ended.

Although both of a questing, combative nature, they knew enough of each other to leave it there for the nonce and turned of one accord to regard the shaken Muriel.

'I shall never again attend to one of these events,' she declared. 'The language was deplorable.'

Conan Doyle burst out into a loud guffaw and Mary tried in vain to hide a smile.

'I don't think the bad language came from the spirits, Muriel,' she remarked equably. 'More from a badly raised pair of mislearnit young brutes.'

Muriel bit her lip. She had wondered whether to present her-self after the day so far and now wished she had stayed put. The others had convinced her that it might take her mind away from things but the opposite had occurred.

The whole world was laughing at her.

Ravaged by burglars, accused by voices in the dark.

Luckily the shaft of *Jezebel* that she had felt aimed so precisely at her blameworthy core seemed not to have been heard by her companions.

She turned to Conan Doyle but he was no longer on hand. Dis-appeared into thin air.

This stuff was catching.

12

What in the midst lay but the Tower itself?
The round squat turret, blind as the fool's heart.
ROBERT BROWNING, 'Childe Roland to the Dark Tower Came'

Magnus Bannerman carefully poured out a measure of whisky into a large tumbler and sniffed in appreciation before downing half the liquid in a fiery gulp.

It had taken him a time to accustom his Pittsburgh taste buds to liquor other than bourbon, but malt whisky slid down a subtle treat and had a kick like a mule.

By God he needed the drink. It was nerve-shredding when Sophia went off on these excursions into a shipwrecked sea of souls; to this day Magnus did not know whether she was just a brilliant operator who could deliver generalities, then hone them as reaction from the audience dictated, or had some genuine con-nection to the supernatural.

But he had recognised her talent for connecting with people and the curious enchantment she could lay upon them. Magnus had poured all his energy into promoting that talent and they had become successful in an amazingly short time.

All due to his efforts.

It is thus we take credit for filling our own emptiness with another's ability.

What had never occurred to Magnus, however, was the fact that since their meeting in San Francisco, Sophia had used him, not the other way around.

It is often so with men and women.

As Magnus lifted his glass he noted that so far Sophia had not said a word and seemed disturbed by manifestations of this night; though that was not unusual, these 'trips' to the other world were a rocky ride.

Either that or, like a finely tuned actress, she was exhausted by the performance.

He never knew. That was half the fun. The other half was yet to come because after exhaustion, appetite ensued.

Carnal hunger. But not right now.

She was standing, staring out of the window at a brick wall that surrounded the stone yard to the rear of the hall.

Yes siree. A brick wall.

He sank the rest of the whisky, lit up a cheroot and laughed quietly.

'That was hell on wheels when these two godforsaken ghosts came shooting through the door.'

Sophia made no response.

'Hell on wheels,' he agreed with himself, pouring out a smaller shot.

A restrained tap at the door signalled the advent of the members of the Society no doubt, with a discreet payment to pass over for the guided tour.

'Enter!' he called commandingly, sliding the glass a modest distance away as if it was still untouched.

But it was not one of the shrivelled, serious folk who made up the committee. This was a fellow as large as Magnus himself, who filled the doorway like a bear in a cave.

Of course. The behemoth that had scooped up those two little bastards and marched them out into the darkness.

Magnus laid down his cigar and stood up, all civility and gallant as hell.

'I thank you, sir, for your assistance with these low types. Whom do I have the honour of addressing?'

'My name is Arthur Conan Doyle,' said the man, while Magnus could now see that he was young and impressionable, an easy dupe at cards. . . Pity there wasn't a pack to hand.

Just a stage-door Johnnie.

'Well, thank you again, sir,' said Magnus, not introducing himself since he had done so earlier on a general scale. 'Is there something more I can do for your good self?'

In other words, my friend, close the door quietly and the spirits be with you in your absence.

Bannerman realised that Doyle was staring past him as if he, a man of some substance, did not exist.

He turned to see that Sophia had swivelled round from the window and was looking directly at their visitor. She had now completely detached the veil and her pale face glowed in the dimness of the room. The violet eyes, pupils enlarged, were fixed upon the intruder.

'I was most impressed by your. . .abilities, Miss Adler.'

This gauche observation from a gawking hulk in Bannerman's estimation deserved little in response but Sophia surprised him by nodding gravely. Usually she had no time for stage-door Johnnies, their appellation for various male admirers who were caught between psychic appreciation and unrequited urges.

'It is a gift, Mister Doyle,' she said. 'A great responsibility. I did not seek it. But I am responsible.'

Doyle had not remarked her soft lilting Southern accent during the evening's events but found it remarkably pleasing to his rather large pink ears.

His usual mode with young women was a joshing badinage where heavy-handed raillery took the place of finer feelings but it had no application here and he found himself in all senses of the phrase, tongue-tied.

'I was – as a matter of fact – wondering,' he blurted out, cursing himself internally for a blockhead and bemused by the force that had driven him to abruptly quit his mother and Muriel's presence to head for the door through which Magnus had disappeared. 'If we might discuss. . .spiritual matters. At some juncture. As it were, at your convenience. Of course.'

All during this Sophia, who had disturbing and deeper thoughts in her mind, found it strangely difficult to take her eyes from his as if some bond was forming between them.

The attraction was not necessarily physical. Magnus more than met her needs and Doyle though of imposing stature was not someone who so far stirred her sensual juices, yet there was something she could not define.

A depth. A darkness. A fear. As iron eats into the bone, something gnawing. She could sense a procession of figures waiting to take possession.

It drew her. A power of sorts.

From Doyle's point of view, as well as the myriad forces that hurtled him towards this woman he was conscious also of an emanation from the Muse.

Could Sophia Adler inspire creation?

'Miss Adler has many demands upon her time,' Magnus Bannerman interposed easily in the silence. 'If she responded to every invitation then her more important work might suffer.'

The words were smooth but Sophia could sense something else.

Jealous. He was jealous. How ridiculous men are.

'Leave your card, Mister Doyle,' she said quietly. 'I promise nothing. Promises are cheap.'

Doyle's brow furrowed. He did not have a card. Medical students rarely do.

Then he remembered that he had scratched some words out for a joke to impress his brother Innes as regards his new station in life. It was on a dog-eared rectangle of cardboard he had fashioned from an offcut sewing pattern of his mother's.

A fumble in the pocket produced the object, which he handed to Bannerman as intermediary.

The American read it with some difficulty; the handwriting was deliberately ornate and flowery to amuse the young reader.

'Arthur Conan Doyle. Doctor of Diagnosis,' Magnus said flatly.

'Well, I will be one day,' Doyle grinned suddenly, to all appearances like a young man without a care in the world. 'That is my intention.'

'I am sure you will succeed,' remarked Sophia, dryly.

Doyle made a little circular motion of his forefinger to Bannerman who was holding the card as if had just busted a promising flush.

'The address is on the back,' offered Doyle. Innes had insisted upon that.

How can you be a doctor, without a proper spot for consultation?, the lad had scornfully pronounced.

Memory made Doyle smile.

His little brother.

Bannerman said nothing.

Sophia made no move and the young man realised he had outstayed his welcome.

Yet he could not leave without one question.

'At the end. . .' he said. 'Why did you scream?'

'Did I?' replied Sophia. 'Or was it someone else?'

She dipped her head to signal goodbye and Doyle bowed somewhat jerkily then exited, crashing the door behind.

Magnus laughed; loud enough that someone might hear had they lingered outside.

'Dime a dozen,' he announced, crumpling the card between his fingers to throw carelessly on the ground.

'Pick it up,' she said.

Magnus laughed incredulously.

'Pick it up.'

Finally he did so, making a great production out of teasing out the thin, creased cardboard and handing it over to her with a little bow.

Sophia put it away carefully into a pocket of her dress. He noticed that her hand was trembling.

'Never seen you do that before,' he remarked idly.

'Do what?'

'Scream. Fill your lungs and let rip.'

He'd had to think quickly and stall for time while she sprawled akimbo, but he was good at that. Yet still he did not know what was real and what was not with this woman.

One thing for sure. She put a strange dread into him. Along with desire. One fed upon the other.

Sophia smiled and he began to relax. Not long now and he would be the master while she wriggled like a catfish.

No doctor had a cure like his.

He moved closer, not too close, just enough to let her feel the heat emanating from a vigorous man.

'What did you see?' he asked softly.

'What do you mean?'

'To let it rip like that.'

She passed her tongue over those little rosebud lips like a child.

'A face I recognised.'

'From when?'

'Not long ago. Not long at all.'

A few days past she had disappeared into the depths of the city and would tell him nothing on return.

This was, like the scream, unusual to be sure.

Magnus was suddenly surprised by a shaft of panic. As if the world was spinning out of control.

Why had he made such a play over Doyle? Sure, he was a big hulk but he was no threat, just a kid. And yet he, Magnus, had reacted as if under attack.

Or was it nothing to do with Doyle?

Deeper.

Of late he had been suffering blackouts. Time vanished and he could not remember what had happened. And always when he came out of it, Sophia was leaning over him. She told him he had slept like a dead man. Afterwards he was under the spell of a blinding headache.

Sophia watched the thoughts pass behind his eyes like clouds. As for her, the decision was made.

Surely as a sign from above.

Vengeance.

'Shall we return to the hotel?' she said. 'I have sore need of privacy.'

She reached out her hand to run it down the side of his neck, the nails scratching lightly on his skin. Magnus Bannerman had known many women but no-one to set his blood aflame like this one. Her body wrapped around and he forgot everything but his desire.

He pulled her in, tight and fierce, as if he might crush her, bones and all.

Sophia closed her eyes. That was what she wanted. That was what she hungered for. All the way back to a day in the hot sun when she had turned fifteen.

A day in the sun.

When her mother betrayed the memory of a good man.

But now it was October in Edinburgh and time for a reckoning.

There was one voice still to hear.

She had waited all her life for that voice. Now she would bring it forth.

Time for a reckoning.

13

And when night
Darkens the street, then wander forth the sons
Of Belial, flown with insolence and wine.

JOHN MILTON, *Paradise Lost*

That night a series of events took place to put a smile on Satan's countenance.

Each was connected to the other by intangible lines, as if a spider's web of violence and deceit were being spun over the city, where a movement such as that of a fly twirling itself into sticky oblivion as struggle created its own winding sheet, provoked another action in response.

Two card-trumpers sat in the Rustie Nail tavern down by the docks and schooled their features not to reflect an inner malicious glee as they watched the mark once more take the bait.

They had lured him in with a common enough ruse; the simple ones are oft the best.

One pretended to be drunk, quarrelsome but with money to burn, the other amused, good-natured, not even wishing to take this fool's gold as he dealt the cards in an alcove.

It was hidden from the main maelstrom of vagabond whores who had flocked to the place because a ship had just docked from Holland and the tarry breeks also had money to burn. Wild women and cheap whisky make a jolly Jack Tar.

The sharpers called themselves Mister Evans and Mister Todd.

The game was *vingt et un*, where the object was to add your card values as near to twenty-one as possible without going *squandered*. A fancy name for over and bust.

The nearest to twenty-one was the winner, unless a *natural* took place: that is, an ace plus ten or court card.

Easy rules.

Any child could play.

The *banker* dealt the cards. That was the good-natured Mister Evans. The drunken Mister Todd bet against.

Both took the part of cattle merchants who had sold their beasts for strong profit at market and were whiling away the time in rough surroundings before heading back to their respectable lodgings, thence, next morning, to the Borders where their rustic wives waited to herd them once more into the pen of domesticity.

The odds of the game were in favour of the *banker* because if the scores tied he won, but Mister Todd did not seem to recognise this fact, protesting noisily at his continuing ill fortune.

Mister Evans shook his head as Mister Todd, whose two cards totalled fifteen, called up for another twist and went spectacularly *squandered* as a jack of spades turned over.

As designed, this attracted the attention of a small portly man who was standing nearby, observing the larger more raucous *belles de nuit* with a certain hunger.

The man wore a bowler hat and had a completely forgettable face with small beady eyes, which glittered as he watched the cavorting melée.

But he did not relish such rough company it would seem, so when Mister Evans caught his eye to smile his apology for his companion's membership of the bad loser's club the portly man came over to observe matters.

After two further defeated hands, Mister Todd went to relieve himself on the misty late-night cobblestones and Mister Evans suggested that the gentleman might like to join in the fun.

His friend needed to be taught a lesson. There might even have been the slightest suggestion of envy on Mister Evans's part as he described the absent micturator having a larger farm, the result of a bovine inheritance from a providential marriage.

A greedy glint in the small ratlike eyes as the first bait was taken.

To begin, Mister Smith, as the mark so named himself, did very well indeed. Then the wagers increased. The bank changed hands as Mister Todd, puffed up with irritation and his own importance insisted that it should, over to him.

But his cards stayed the same, worsened by bad decisions and a stubborn refusal to acknowledge the laws of gambling probability.

Mister Todd then demanded a doubling of stakes as was his banker's lien, and the other two were happy to comply.

But suddenly, as if night had changed to day, the accepted order was reversed and Mister Todd began to enjoy the most incredible run of luck.

He drew five to a count of sixteen; *naturals* and court cards followed him like obedient sheep and as the other two strained to recoup their losses, the stakes were doubled yet again. Good money after bad.

The pocketbook of Mister Smith, a previously bulging receptacle, which clever Mister Evans had noted as he stood beside him at the bar while the little man paid for his beer, complaining that it stood no comparison with good London ale, began to shrink like a punctured bladder.

Mister Todd defied the odds of gambling and gravity as he swayed over the table to collect his winnings, face apparently red with alcohol, clumsy with the cards; *surely it was only a matter of time?*

A silent message the apologetic Mister Evans signalled as they pushed their stakes into the middle. All his money in the little man's case; but this hand he sat proud on twenty, the cards face down, hidden to all but Mister Smith.

Mister Evans went bust. *Squandered.* Sadly.

The *banker* turned over thirteen, an unlucky number. The next card up was four. Seventeen. Not enough to vanquish the two face-down cards. But of course, the *banker* did not know the value of the hidden hand. Twist or stand?

If he stood pat, Mister Smith would win. For a moment the man hesitated and then with a careless sweep of the hand turned over the next card.

It was a four again. Twenty-one. A boozy roar of triumph from the *banker* and an exasperated sigh of annoyance from the nice Mister Evans.

Mister Smith turned away abruptly as if he could not bear to look at the loss and, at that moment, the sharpers made a fatal error.

One winked at the other, confident that the man's back had no eyes to see. But there was a dirty cracked mirror in the opposite empty booth to reflect this collusion.

Yet when Mister Smith turned back, nothing in his face indicated what, if anything, he had seen.

His hand however, slid down the side of one plump little leg, while his face screwed up in puzzlement as if he could not believe what had just happened with the cards.

Mister Evans opened his mouth to compose words of consolation; he himself had lost as well and who could believe that this uncouth fellow might stumble upon such a change of fortune?

Who could believe?

The words never passed his lips.

The little man made a sweeping gesture under the table and both men seated on the other side froze as if an icy hand had been laid upon them.

The money was scooped swiftly up and then some words were finally uttered.

'Thank you, gents.'

Having said this, Alfred Binnie turned and made his unhurried way through the swirling smoke and heaving bodies of the Rustie Nail.

The paralysis of their nether abdomens being sliced through by a razor-edged knife that might disembowel an ox, held the two sharpers in suspension for what seemed like an eternity.

Both looked down and saw the blood seeping out of the deep cut in their lower bellies through the thick material of the tweed trousers worn to support the pretence that they were from the outlands of Jedburgh or the like.

Then the pain bit in and their groans mingled with the frenzied whoops of the tavern throng as two of the mariners burst into an impromptu hornpipe.

One of them reeled backwards and crashed into the alcove.

He apologised in Dutch. His native language.

14

And so I lie with her and she with me,
And in our faults by lies we flattered be.

WILLIAM SHAKESPEARE, Sonnets

Muriel's small bedroom overlooked the side lane and a crack upon her window brought her awake with a start of fear.

The breath caught in her throat – she had been dreaming but of nothing she could easily remember, vague feelings of shame, and accusing voices in her mind.

For a moment she lay quite still. Unable to tell what had disturbed her sleep.

Another crack of pebble on glass solved the mystery.

She shifted eyes to the window, the counterpane pulled up just under her nose like a frightened child or old maid in a country cottage.

But she was neither.

Muriel Grierson was a respectable widow. Or was she?

She slipped out of bed and padded with an oddly feline gait, bare feet upon a lush carpet, to the glass where she looked out into the lane.

He was standing where she knew he would be; silver hair flattened a little by the evening damp, shining wetly in the faint gleam that spilled down the narrow track from the streetlight.

Samuel Grant. Her lover.

The man she had met by chance in the street when a cab driver had splashed her skirts with his carriage wheel and when she taxed him, the fellow had responded in a most impolite fashion. A passer-by then berated the miscreant until the brute apologised.

The passer-by. A well-set man with silver hair.

From this accidental beginning he had courted her but of course most discreetly; it would not be proper for Muriel to be seen enjoying such company.

How could one put it? She was yet, though decked no longer in widow's weeds, carrying the indefinable marks of grief and he was somewhat. . .not quite of the same class.

Well mannered to be sure, a trifle flamboyant in his dress, stocky of frame, in age perhaps some years less than her but. . .how can one put it?

In fact there were more years between them than she realised but ignorance is often bliss as regards age in love. And so Muriel mused on regardless.

He was a little short of grace. Not coarse exactly, just lacking a certain refinement. But she liked that. An uncomplicated, unconfined vitality. She liked that.

They had met, therefore, in secret in areas of the city where she was not known and the clandestine nature had brought a certain spice as if she were having an *affaire de coeur*.

Then one night when her maid Ellen was having her regular evening away with her family, Muriel had permitted Samuel the house. It was dark enough that no-one might notice from the street and so she had allowed him in. And then she had allowed him quite a lot.

She had never enjoyed the act of love, it was something to be endured, like an affliction. Her husband Andrew had approached it as if measuring out a corpse.

A grim undertaking.

But Samuel Grant enjoyed what he termed *rough and tumble* and, to her surprise, she found that the act was not divorced from a certain. . .pleasure.

Besides Ellen's regular absences, she encouraged the woman to vacate the premises on other evenings and Muriel was worried that her maid smelled a rat.

Yet she grew more reckless; sexual pleasure does have that effect. Rules the roost.

They pulled the curtains shut and Samuel had the run of the house. The master bedroom where the marital rites had been grindingly performed was abandoned in summary fashion and, pleading melancholic memories, Muriel had shifted to a smaller *bouncier* mattress in a more compact room. With no family portraits looming above.

This space she decorated in bright, vibrant colours, indulged in feminine frills and boudoir fripperies that would have given her late husband a heart attack had he not been already deceased from exactly that.

And it was from this chamber of guilty excess that she looked down upon the cause.

Samuel waved up cheerily. She had warned him previously that even though Ellen had her evening off, a long-standing social engagement must be fulfilled this night.

No matter, declared bluff Sam. He'd come late or he wouldn't come at all. This was his style.

And she liked that.

But this time when she opened the front door and he slid in fast to embrace her in manly fashion, she retracted from desire in order to tell him the terrible events of the day.

Samuel's eyes widened and he let out a small whistle of surprise.

'That's a lift tae lose,' he announced.

'I want my mother's brooch. I was fond of the music box. The rest is not important.'

'What about the money?'

'I do not mourn it especially.'

Muriel shook her head to emphasise such and stepped back. A light from the hall lamp outlined her body through the thin nightgown and Samuel's mind, never a strong, fixed point at the best of times, wandered.

But a lustful lunge might be misinterpreted as a cavalier attitude and there was no telling where this conversation might lead.

'As I told you, I suspected Andrew had kept the money hidden for a reason.'

'Some things are best paid for in cash.'

'Such as?' she asked sharply.

Whores for one, came into his mind but he kept his expression bland and open; it had served him well with many women to act the child in man.

They suffered the flinty exactitudes of matrimony and flowered like cherry blossom at a friendly face and joyful rumpling of the bed sheets.

Muriel was such a woman.

Cherry blossom.

But not at the moment. At the moment she regarded him with a wary questioning stare.

'I showed you where that money was kept.'

'You did, my dear.'

'And now it's gone.'

'It has. For certain sure.'

'As if the thieves knew exactly where to find it.'

He nodded as if she had made an irrefutably wise assertion but cursed his big mouth because putting two and two in summation, a boastful whisky speech in the Foul Anchor tavern to a certain Seth Moxey might yet come back to haunt him.

Samuel had a round, pleasant face with a little goatee beard and radiated a kind of damaged innocence, as if life's tribulations had left a mark but the spirit was undaunted.

He was known to his acquaintances as Silver Sam both because of his hair, which had prematurely attained this hue and gave him a gravitas far beyond his actual age, and the fact that he enjoyed personal artefacts of the precious metal. Watch and chain, silver ring, tiepin, take your pick.

He enjoyed the glitter; however, this was not the time for outward show.

Muriel was not directly accusing but harboured suspicions that she longed to be disproved because women, despite their innate mistrust of men, always hope to meet an improved specimen somewhere along the line.

Yet Samuel knew that protesting innocence too loudly might imply a feeling of guilt. A man's excuses never quite ring true.

'I will make enquiries,' he said.

'So will Inspector McLevy,' she replied.

Samuel winced internally. That was not a name he wished to hear. No-one of the fraternity wanted that bugger on his trail.

'Yet he is a policeman, my love. Certain doors may be closed against him.'

'Unlike my own, which seems to be open to all comers.'

A bitter riposte. They trembled on the edge of their very first quarrel.

We all begin with such high hopes, do we not?

She knew that he was a dabbler on the fringes of respectable society, *a buyer and seller of this and that*, as he was wont to say, and it added to her relish of cocking a snoot at accepted custom.

But witnessing that unlicensed, licentious freedom was the grim effigy of her husband who looked down from the various portraits in the house that she dared not remove for fear of adverse comment.

Perhaps Andrew was correct. She was cheap. Besmirched. This was no better than she deserved.

A deep breath then out with it.

'Give me your word,' she said.

'For what, Moumou?'

His pet name for her brought no softening to her face.

'Swear that you are not compromised by this theft.'

He placed his hand solemnly over the heart area, or as near as he could, given that his pocketbook resided there.

'I swear upon my mother's grave.'

The mother that had thrown him out as a young boy to make his living on the streets of Leith by whatever his wits might conjure up. Samuel had pimped, lied, stolen, been abused and defiled many times one way or the other but had somehow managed to haul himself out of the mire.

And he was never going back.

Not if he could help it.

Muriel looked into his eyes. They did not flinch. He had learned this at an early stage. Steadfast mendacity.

'Upon her grave,' he repeated.

A long silence where he noticed that there were some thin lines from the sides of her eyes as if a crow had walked past in the snow. Age withers us all.

'I believe you,' she finally declared.

He bowed his head to hide a relieved smile.

'And I shall strain every nerve to find your jewels,' he murmured.

Later in the bouncy bed, having tested the springs with vigorous consummation, they lay side by side.

She was snoring. Lightly. Ladylike. But snoring.

He watched her with some fondness but not enough to alter the train of his thought.

95

Seth Moxey was a dirty dog. And he, Samuel Grant, was a bletherskite.

A liar and a buffoon. But still alive.

What a bugger that McLevy was involved.

Muriel came awake with a jolt and looked down at an admittedly naked breast, the nipple of which was like a sentry at attention under his absent-minded caress.

'Jezebel,' she announced to the ceiling.

'Who might that be?' he asked cautiously.

'A wicked woman who was trampled by horses and eaten by dogs. In the Bible.'

Samuel blinked. His knowledge of scripture was not vast but it sounded like one of those punishments from on high. He was not a follower of that sort of retribution, in fact religion struck him as attracting stiff-necked folk who then dished out God's will to make up for what they lacked.

He was more for live and let live.

'She must have been wicked, right enough,' he offered, transferring his thumb to the other nipple in the interests of equality.

'Andrew was forever talking about evil women in the Bible. It seemed to fascinate him.'

Muriel shook her head, troubled by pleasure's close connection to guilt, for instance in the case of papillary stimulation and worried memories.

'I was called by such a name tonight.'

'By whom?' he demanded with indignation. 'I'll punch their nose aside!'

Muriel thought of trying to explain that the nose in question might not be materialised, finding its physical expression through a sensitive's visage behind a veil, but decided to leave things be.

Yet the timbre of the spirit voice had sounded weirdly like her dead husband and *Jezebel* had been his crushing verdict on any woman who wore trace of cosmetic covering or flaunted an improvement upon what nature had provided.

What if he'd been watching them all this time?

What if he were watching them now?

Muriel was not someone who liked to delve into the dark crevices of the mind and regretted most bitterly that she had agreed to accompany Mary Doyle and her son to the Spiritualist Society, but Mary was an old friend, Muriel had welcomed the distraction, and Arthur was. . .well, shameful to admit such, but in her new-found sense of fragrant release, she was attracted to his courtly manners and massive frame.

Plus vibrant innocence.

Innocence always attracts the opposite.

Was she depraved, or merely *awakened*?

'What if he's watching us?' she whispered.

'Who?'

'Andrew. His ghost.'

Samuel glanced around somewhat uneasily but then his essential practicality came to the fore.

'Well if he is,' he said, 'he'll just have to thole it. We're alive and he's departed. Life is hard.'

It was not the only thing.

Muriel had been trying to keep her mind focused on the dark events that seemed to presently lurk in her life but found that her hand, not unlike herself, had strayed into temptation.

And provoked the risen Adam.

A creature of sensation.

She wheeled over suddenly and straddled him, the first time she had performed such an action.

If Andrew was watching he might as well get his money's worth.

'Do you think I am wicked?' she demanded of Samuel.

'Only when you smile,' he answered.

And they rolled down the hill into love's oblivion.

15

'Tis not what once it was, the world,
But a rude heap together hurled.
                        ANDREW MARVELL, 'Upon Appleton House'

When Jean Brash approached the gates of the Just Land she was astonished to see all the lights ablaze and three extremely drunk young men roaring fit to burst upon the verdant lawn – for Jean had green fingers.

Facing the men was an indignant Jessie Nairn; she seemed to have taken the place of the ex-blacksmith Angus, who doubled as Jean's coachman, doorman and keeper of order in the Just Land. He was out in the streets with a paper likeness of the acid-pourer clutched in his meaty fist and woe betide the little swine if he was found.

Jean Brash and Hannah Semple had been closeted in a safe house in Laurie Street not far from the Leith Links, one of Jean's many mansions. There they had met with various street-Arabs and keelies, a substratum of criminality but invaluable for reconnaissance. Her *people*.

It would not be wise to have so many visitors to the bawdy hoose, so therefore the safe house.

Now the hunt was on. But with no success so far. A reported knifing in one of the taverns, two sharpers cut savage deep and a man answering the description of the quarry. But he had disappeared out into the night.

A watch was also being kept on the Countess's 'hotel' but nothing to report except various respectable pillars of the community ducking in for illicit pleasure, one of whom, Gilbert Morrison, had been politely screened from the delights of the Just Land due to a predilection for inflicting punishment and was indeed the very man who had left the welts on the *derrière* of Simone.

Which had provoked her to leave the Countess.

Which was the cause of this war with Jean.

Casus belli.

Cherchez la femme.

There had been a violent run-in in the back wynds of the Tolbooth with one Patrick Fraser, who was a bully-boy for the Countess and had gathered a crew of like-minded thugs around him. During the fracas Patrick had received a sharp reminder from wee Donnie Toms that size is not always the point at issue. Donnie had kicked up a storm.

Blood had been spilled, bones broken.

The streets were hotting up. Various *guisers* on a Halloween approach were also on the randan; imps of hell, witches, satanic figures in livid finery roamed the byways, startling the carriage horses with ghostly apparition.

The city was seething with disquiet and everywhere there was a feeling of things breaking apart, as if the earth was moving under the scrabbling feet of Edinburgh gentlefolk.

Nowhere more apparent than within her own grounds, Jean observed. For a moment she was tempted to plunge headlong into the rammy, because it had become so itchy-scratchy in the safe house waiting for news to break that she had left Hannah Semple to run the operation and walked briskly back through the streets praying that she might bump into a man answering the likeness of Lily Baxter's sketch.

No such luck.

However, she would not take her grievance out on other folk but employ a stately approach.

Like Victoria Regina.

So Jean walked softly.

As for the roaring boys on the lawn?

Logan Galloway was a contemptible young snotter whose father had made a fortune exporting horses to France where they were no doubt cooked and eaten, hooves and all.

He was a skinny runt, nebby by nature, temper not improved by an earlier incident that evening when he and a companion had thought it great high jinks to don Halloween disguise and terrorise a meeting of the Spiritualist Society, in the certain knowledge that none of the impotent attendance would be able to lay a glove upon them.

They had been unpleasantly surprised to find themselves

picked up by the scruff of the neck and booted out by a man mountain that Galloway vaguely recognised as a rugby player for the University.

Then they had been pursued through the streets by a madman brandishing a placard.

After giving him the slip, they had met with a similarly inclined young lout, drunk like sand-beds in the tavern, and presented themselves at the door of the Just Land for further recreation.

But something had gone agley.

As Jean slipped up by the shadows, the combatants were well into their stride.

'You little hure!' screamed Galloway, face flushed and eyes glazed. 'You stole my money!'

'I stole nothing,' said Jessie. 'Ye spent it.'

'You're a liar!'

'And you're mortal fou,' said Jessie, a hint of insolence creeping into her tone.

A few catcalls from the lighted windows added to the fun and Jessie played up to the watching magpies.

'Ye spent your money, ye had your pleasure. Now, away an' cock yer feathers on the dunghill.'

More laughter from the windows.

Galloway's countenance, which was not unlike some of the wretched horses his father shipped across the Channel, in that it was long, bony, and swivel-eyed, near sundered itself in wrathful umbrage.

'How dare you address me so, ye little bitch,' he almost foamed at the mouth. 'I'll split your insolent face!'

Galloway unexpectedly, for Jessie had him pegged as a wee bag of wind, threw out a haphazard fist and hit a glancing blow on the shoulder that tumbled her to the ground.

Flushed with this triumph and the sudden silence of the jeering magpies, though this may have been in part due to something else they had just noticed, Galloway lifted his hand to swipe the impudent wee *hure* flat across her mouth.

He then found an odd event to transpire.

As if by unseen force his expensive jacket was sliced open from side pocket all the way up to the armpit.

As he gazed, violent act arrested, at this rent in his fashionable attire, as if by magic a female form appeared before him. The apparition had green eyes and red hair.

'You may leave us now,' said Jean Brash, who had abandoned her stately approach through force of necessity.

Galloway staggered back but then recovered his nerve as he realised Jean was on her own. No Hannah Semple, no Angus the enforcer, just a single woman.

With a straight gleaming blade in her hand, but that might be overcome.

He signalled to his cronies and they began to close in. Now there were no more threatening oaths but the danger was more real. Jessie scrambled on her hands and knees further back towards the house and stifled shrieks came from the watching magpies.

Jean remained calm but it was one thing to cut lumps out of a swankie young halfwit's jacket and another to inflict physical damage. You could get arrested for that.

Especially if you did it in the public eye.

A cruel drunken light in Galloway's eye; companions, equally aroused, egged him on with grunts of encouragement.

Strong drink and a weak mind are bad company.

Galloway grinned like a rat and feinted to catch at her but before it was possible to see how far this confrontation might progress, a voice from the darkness moved into and across matters.

'Aye, Jean. Cutting back the weeds, eh?'

James McLevy stood in the semi-darkness on the fringe of the arc where the house lights expired, with Mulholland by his side.

Both men then moved forward unhurriedly; Mulholland's hornbeam stick hanging loose at his side as he loped forward, the inspector with the deceptively benign air of a man out for an evening constitutional.

The policemen had met up again at the station where the constable reported that he had got nowhere with the Grierson robbery enquiries, and were out on their usual evening saunter round the streets of Leith when word came that, amongst a few other incidents of note, Patrick Fraser had received a severe kicking that involved the bridge of his nose being squashed like a cowpat.

Retributive action was being sworn by his gang.

McLevy had planned to head this off should the vengeful crew have made for the Just Land but found instead another altercation.

Halloween often bred them.

'Inspector. Well on hand. This witch has attacked me!' Galloway blustered.

'Just a wee snip,' said Jean.

The jacket flapped dismal agreement as Galloway continued his litany of complaint.

'I have been most foully robbed in this woman's establishment. My wallet emptied!'

'While you danced the Reels o' Bogie?' McLevy enquired sardonically, this being the poet Robert Burn's allusion to copulation of a frenzied nature.

A shrewd shaft dismissed by the justified sinner.

'I deserve and demand satisfaction.'

'Demand away,' Jean muttered, wondering how the hell McLevy seemed to manifest all over Leith. Her people had reported him down by the docks the last she had heard and not that long since.

Mulholland had been silent so far but curled his lip at Galloway's protestations.

'You don't deserve a damned thing,' he pronounced. 'Look at the odds on hand. Three to one. That's shameful.'

'I was here!' said Jessie, who had reappeared at Jean's side now that matters were less turbulent.

This was ignored as the two policemen placed themselves directly in front of the sullen malcontents.

'What would your Aunt Katie say tae these specimens?' McLevy asked mildly of his constable. To a certain extent things had been a little strained between them and it was nice to get back into an old routine.

'Get out o' my sight, you'd give the dry boak to a dead badger,' was the uncompromising response.

'What a woman,' said McLevy admiringly.

He suddenly moved in very close to the young men.

'You heard the constable, Galloway, absent yourself while you have the chance. I catch you or your friends near these grounds again, I'll run you in for trespass.'

There was a mean glitter in the inspector's eyes; it had been a long day and he was in no mood to suffer fools.

The other two had piped down immediately at the sound of

his voice but as they slouched off towards the gates Galloway turned round to indicate he had some puff left.

'I shall complain to your Lieutenant Roach!' he cried.

'Do that,' replied McLevy. 'He could use some humour in his life. Now – honour us with your departure.'

Mulholland moved threateningly to the loitering Galloway who stepped away to splash his foot into the water in Jean's fish-pond, thus alarming the large piscine inhabitants and causing great amusement to the audience of magpies who hooted further as his fashionable shoe became entangled in some exotic fronds.

As he shook his leg unavailingly to clear it of the weed's fond embrace, Galloway strived for the last word.

'This is not finished, Jean Brash. I was robbed, I can assure you, and I will have lawful redress!'

'Fear grips me by the throat,' she called back, mockingly. However she was annoyed to find herself in the situation of arguing with a runty snab under McLevy's amused gaze. She shot Jessie a look to indicate that there would be words exchanged as soon as the chance presented itself.

The swankie boys finally quit the scene, slamming the iron gates shut to indicate their manhood was still intact, which left four survivors of the incident.

Jean became aware that McLevy was looking with interest at her hand and realised she was still holding the implement which had changed the shape of Galloway's jacket.

'That's a fine sharp knife you have,' he observed.

Jean had taken it out as a precaution, it fitting snugly into the reticule on her arm. In fact, if you discounted the fact that she kept a bawdy hoose and sliced folk up to the armpit, the woman cut an impressively respectable figure in her evening coat and elegant bonnet.

'It's for pruning the roses,' she answered. 'Anything that protrudes, in fact.'

McLevy extended his hand and she placed the knife carefully across the palm. He peered at it closely in the gloom, and then passed the weapon to Mulholland.

'What d'you make o' that, constable?' he asked.

Mulholland hefted the blade expertly in the manner of a man who had read *The Count of Monte Cristo*.

'Well balanced. Finest Italian steel.'

'It's from an admirer,' Jean offered.

'A cutpurse?' McLevy asked, retrieving the thing from Mulholland who was waving it around in deft circles.

'No. A surgeon.'

Her dry response provoked a whoop of laughter from the inspector. He was beginning to enjoy himself; life had been a bit quiet recently other than his outlandish dreams.

Now, to paraphrase the great John Milton, McLevy had a feeling that all hell was about to break loose and it cheered him up no end.

The inspector nevertheless wasted his breath in one more warning to the mistress of the Just Land, stepping in close so that the conversation between them was low, like lovers in the shadows.

'Ah Jean, Jean,' he murmured. 'The path you travel can have but one destination. A prison cell. I shall sweep it clean with my own hands.'

'Don't delude yourself,' she murmured also. 'And may I have my pruner returned?'

He handed it over with ceremony and then tipped back his low-brimmed bowler with one finger to a rakish angle.

'Well, constable,' he announced, loudly, 'best be on our way. Duty done. Fair maidens saved.'

'The fair maiden sings your praises,' Jean remarked ironically to his departing back.

He did not turn round, indeed the rest of the exchange was conducted with him marching off into the darkness, the lanky figure of Mulholland trailing behind.

They made an odd contrast but she had seen them both in action and the swankie boys didn't know how lucky they had been that the stramash had not spiralled into further violence.

Mulholland dealt it out dispassionately with that hornbeam stick like the hand of God, and McLevy? He was the most physically dangerous man she had ever witnessed and had a reservoir of fury profound as death itself.

She recalled him as a young constable lying on the tavern floor and a thug ready to bring his boot crashing down into the upturned face.

Jean was a nascent whore working in the Holy Land then, and

her pimp, Henry Preger, was the thug in question. A vicious bastard she hated with good reason.

In the moment before Preger brought his boot down, she had winked at the young policeman, to provoke, to encourage, who knows, but he came off that floor like a madman and battered Preger from one end of the tavern to the other.

The man died not long after and folk were inclined to put it down to the after-effects of that beating but Jean would have put her money on poison.

And she should know.

These were her thoughts as she watched McLevy walk away.

'By the by, Jean,' the inspector called over his shoulder, 'I hear that Patrick Fraser had a nasty accident.'

'He keeps bad company,' she shouted over.

A raucous laugh came in response.

'Oh, you and the Countess. . .' sounded his voice in the gloom. 'Well matched, the pair o' ye.'

As the policemen strode past the pond, Mulholland shook his head in disapproval.

'They want to put a net over that,' he announced gravely. 'Birds of prey will be queuing up for these fish.'

'I've tellt her,' said McLevy, who in fact had not done so, he had just thought it. However, it was nearly the same thing. 'When have you ever known a woman take a telling?'

'Not so far in my life,' was the solemn response, as the constable thought to the past where his beloved Emily had refused further communication on account of her father having hung himself high by the neck.

Mind you, it was a hard thing to get round right enough. Walk under, but not get round.

They had reached the gates, which were still reverberating from the previous abrupt closure and McLevy at last turned to survey the Just Land.

It was a strange sight, the place ablaze with light and a woman's face in every window.

Jean remained where he had left her, with Jessie's figure standing to the side like a rejected conspirator.

For a moment the inspector's face was thoughtful, then he grinned and bawled out a last piece of advice.

'Watch your back, Jean. . .gardyloo!'

McLevy then observed his constable's face to be somewhat overcast and guessed that memory had made an unwelcome intrusion.

Young men bruise easy.

'Come along, Mulholland,' he declared in hearty fashion to cover any trace of what would be an equally unwelcome show of compassion. 'We'll away tae the Auld Ship, chap at the back door, see if they can rustle up a twa-eyed steak.'

Mulholland shivered at that prospect, which was a strong smoked herring in Leith parlance.

'It'll repeat on me all through the night,' he said.

'All right then, my mannie,' rejoined McLevy. 'I'll tackle the fish and we'll scare you up some sheep's heid broth.'

And so melancholy was banished in favour of a stewed head of mutton but as they began to walk down the brae, a thought occurred to the constable.

'You didn't mention that knifing at the Rustie Nail?' he said. 'Sounds like the man she's after.'

'No, I didnae mention it,' replied McLevy, 'and neither did Jean Brash. I'll let her think she's got one over on me. When folk think that, is when they make mistakes.'

Mulholland shook his head at the sleekit depths of his inspector and McLevy began whistling an old Jacobite air.

'Charlie is my darling, the young Chevalier.'

The strains of the tune made its way back to the garden of the Just Land where Jean watched the two men disappear into the night.

For a moment she felt oddly moved, as if something that had been a fixed point was changing and would never be the same again. That melody she always associated with a side of James McLevy that no-one ever saw.

The fighter of lost causes.

Madness in his mind.

The law was his life. He had no other.

And as for love?

God knows what feeling existed between her and him, but it was deep.

A sensation of loss swept over her.

With an effort she shook herself free of premonition and then turned to Jessie.

Back to the real world. Burnt backs and drunken half-wits. She gestured to where Galloway had been ranting.

'How did this happen?'

The Paisley girl shrugged.

'They spent a' their money on champagne, or better he did. The other two were sookin' on his titties. Then he opened his pocketbook. His money was gone and then he got rambunctious. Then I pit him out the door. Then he started yallyhooing. Blood in his eye.'

A pithy enough summation but Jean was not impressed.

'Hardly through the door yourself, Jessie Nairn. How come you stuck your nose in?'

Jessie shrugged again. She was wearing her working assemblage; that is, a simple dress with a certain amount of décolletage but not overly so. Jean did not approve of too much vulgar show, despite the Countess's jibe about the flesher's slab and the contents thereon.

The dress was however somewhat skimpy and now that the furore had abated, Jessie felt the dank October night.

She shivered uncontrollably, her sharp feral little face screwing up. Jessie was no great beauty but there was an impudent gleam in her eye and a proud lift of the head that provided her own pert brand of desirability.

Her apparent discomfort was not intended to garner sympathy from Jean nor did it receive such.

'I asked,' said the mistress of the Just Land, 'how come you stuck your neb in?'

'Naebody else did. He was kicking up hell.'

'What about Big Annie Drummond?'

'She doesnae like a rammy.'

This was undeniably true, Annie was a motherly figure to all the magpies and could command a certain authority but, unlike Hannah Semple or Jean herself, she was a gentle soul. In fact if Jean was being fair she might acknowledge that Jessie had done her a favour of sorts but she was not in a rational frame of mind. Things were falling apart, inside and out – evil spirits abroad.

Therefore she behaved like a sour-faced scold and Jessie was confirmed in the way she had always been treated in life. Even if she had to create the circumstances for herself sometimes.

We are all complicit in our own persecution.

'I thought I had explained the rules of the house to you, Jessie Nairn,' said Jean with a sniff because the cold air was beginning to get to her as well. 'If a customer is too puggled to know what he's done with his money, humour him, sit a girl on his knee, coddle him like a wee baby.'

'*You* didnae do that,' Jessie quite reasonably pointed out.

'It was too late then!' Jean snapped grouchily, aware she was losing the exchange. 'He was beyond redemption.'

'That's whit I thought,' said Jessie.

Another reasonable remark.

This time, unanswered.

The Paisley girl shivered once more.

'Ye better get inside,' said Jean.

Jessie shrugged, a mannerism that could easily get on the nerves, and walked slowly back towards the house.

The windows began to empty of magpies as they caught the power of Jean's cold gaze. Annie Drummond, who filled a frame all by herself, looked shamefaced and bowed her head but two figures who remained in view were French.

Simone cut a frail portrait at the high window of the nursery room with Francine just behind, a proprietorial hand on the other's shoulder.

Jean shook her head. She could smell trouble a mile off in that configuration, and where was Lily Baxter?

Come to think of it, where were all the clients?

'Are there no gentlemen callers this evening?' she enquired of Jessie who had finally got to the door and was on the point of disappearing out of sight.

'Some early birds, but they pecked and ran,' Jessie called back. 'A quiet night. Except for the rammy.'

The door closed. Jean looked up again at the two figures. The French. Trouble and strife.

Down in the cellar of the Just Land, Lily Baxter sat astride the Berkley Horse. Dotted around the walls of the room were various implements for inflicting sought-after suffering to any given area.

Lily did not desire agony but she had it just the same.

She had deliberated long and hard before revealing that she had witnessed the man who had attacked Simone.

Finally she had passed the paper with the drawing to Hannah Semple because she could not bear to approach her lover Francine.

Lily rocked back and forwards on the horse. Eyes closed. Lost in another world.

16

'Tis witching night, the criminal's ally;
it comes accomplice-like, wolf-soft; the sky
slowly is closing every giant door,
and man the rebel turns a beast once more.

CHARLES BAUDELAIRE, *Le Crépuscule du Soir*

The hunched, bear-like figure moved silently across the damp slates of the rooftop with animal certainty. A black cloak billowed out behind it, with a scarlet lining that suggested some flayed internal organ.

The cloak had a hood, which obscured the head of the creature, but oddly the feet were bare, toes fastening onto the slimy, angled surface with prehensile skill.

For a moment the figure paused and sniffed the air as if picking up the scent of prey but it was the acrid smell of smoke coming from a nearby chimney-stack had attracted its attention.

This marked the spot. A sign. The stack was crooked as if it had been struck by lightning, unlike the adjoining roofs where the chimneypots and surrounds pointed straight at the sky.

The middle house of the terrace. The beast knew this was the mark.

But the smoke meant someone was awake. Still alive. Care must be taken. There was much to be done.

A low, coughing grunt emitted from its throat. A series of words burnt into the mind.

Find. Kill. Destroy.

It was only right. The good man lay dead. Like a dog. Nothing left. Bits of flesh. Not even a face.

Only right. Pay for the sin. Hell is hungry.

The beast moved sideways, lurching at speed, knuckles close to the slates as it moved with silent precision to a window set into the roof.

A skylight. Fast locked. Bolted at the inside. The hinges of heavy metal. Hasped. Strong.

To keep death out.

But the betrayed call for vengeance.

Nothing is stronger than that.

The frame of the window had a slight overlap. The creature hunched over, gloved fingers splayed, gripping round the wood and slowly levering upwards.

At first nothing happened, then with a muffled creak the whole top half of the frame began to lift up as the bolts inside were wrenched slowly out of their sockets by the immense power generating from the rigid arms and squatting form above. A metallic screech signalled the hinges parting from the wood, the screw nails ripped from their safe haven, and with a sudden jolt, the whole structure was lifted off its moorings like the sliced top of a boiled egg.

For a moment the beast froze with its prize clasped between the paws, the heavy black gauntlets anchoring the timber and glass in place against its thick torso though some small splinters of metal and wood fell onto the slates to skitter down and lodge in the guttering.

Had anyone heard that sound?

Had the sinner within been warned?

The beast waited for a voice to call and break the silence of the night.

Somewhere far off in the distance a cat yowled, a low menacing growl, but nothing answered.

And nothing sounded below in the house.

The buckled frame was laid carefully upon the sloping roof and wedged into the chimneystack to keep it in fast position.

Somewhere in the dark sky, a seagull let loose a doleful screech like a mourner at a funeral.

The figure then moved to the gaping hole it had created and swiftly dropped out of sight into the darkness below.

Meantime, in the safety of his house with solid walls and locked doors, Gilbert Morrison gazed into the dying flames of the fire and reflected with muted satisfaction upon his life.

Heat was his one indulgence; he had thin blood and felt the cold most bitterly, unlike his brother Walter who could be enclosed in an iceberg and not remark the situation.

Gilbert jabbed at the fire with a heavy poker and wondered to add some more coal but decided contra.

Coal cost money.

Not that he couldn't afford such but he had stayed up well beyond his usual bedtime and enough was enough.

And, to be strictly exact, he had one other indulgence which had been relished this night.

He replayed a scene in his mind from his visit to the establishment of the Countess and took great satisfaction.

The woman supplied had been too fleshy for his taste but she had white skin and marked up in rousing fashion.

The French girl had left the establishment and the little sensitive was beyond his grasp but he had kept her pale, veiled face in his memory while laying on the quirt.

A most fulfilling encounter.

The recollection would keep him warm in his cold bed and who knows what pleasant dreams might ensue?

Behind him, the door to his study opened and a massive figure slipped inside with astonishing speed and stealth.

The room was dark except for the glow of the fire and Gilbert was too absorbed in happy reminiscence to notice the addition to his company; also he suffered from wax in his hairy ears, thus tending to partial deafness.

So what followed came as a big surprise.

Two huge hands like bear's paws circled his neck and wrenched him bodily from his armchair up into empty space.

As he wriggled in agonised shock, feet kicking, eyes wide with fear, Gilbert was lifted higher until he must have been at least eight feet from the ground.

He had lifted his own hands to claw unavailingly at the leather gauntlets, the nails scraping hard at the stiff material. They made little impression.

Gilbert's ears popped and his hearing improved to the point

where he was able to distinguish the following words, coming from somewhere just beneath.

It was in a guttural animal growl but just enough remained of speech that a dangling man might comprehend.

'Betrayed. His sweet face. Nothing left.'

Having uttered these words to no response from the choking man, the creature then followed the three precepts embedded in its psyche.

Find.

This had been accomplished.

Kill.

The hood of the cloak fell back and for a moment Gilbert twisted round to see his nemesis. Eyes blinked in recognition at the contorted face staring up into his, and then the beast's hands jerked powerfully and the pinioned neck was snapped like a chicken.

Destroy.

Gilbert's body was lowered carefully to the carpet, which was thick and received the corpus with a certain amount of give.

For a moment the beast caught sight of itself in a mirror above the mantle of the fire, snarled in fear at its image and tore at its own hair.

Then it looked. And saw the heavy poker lying in the hearth.

As if it were a sign.

Destroy.

17

He who plays at dice with death must expect the dog's throw.

EDWARD BULWER-LYTTON, *The Last Days of Pompeii*

The candle flickered in a weak draught from the window and a hand was cupped round to shelter the flame. The writer laid his pen aside and peered closely at the heading on the page:

That was the constant. What followed was variable and deserved all the secrecy granted.

Private thoughts. Keep them so. But read on anyway.

When I observe humanity I am aye struck by the fact that every bugger wants to have their own way.

And takes it badly amiss when some other bugger, or life itself, does not correspond to requirements.

Then violence of one kind or another ensues, the obvious being physical, the more deadly when the mind warps like an old piece of shipwrecked timber left out in the hot sun. Since I'm the one that writes this diary and the only one who ever gets to read it, I will allow myself the luxury of overblown simile.

But it's true in any case.

A warped mind is the worst foe. It is not easy to see and as the Bard himself put it, 'There's no art to find the mind's construction in the face.'

Shakespeare would have made a great detective.

Or criminal.

When does an idea become so fixed that anything to oppose it is perceived as an attack? And furthermore, anything that does not lend its weight to the bone-crushing, grinding mill of this misplaced certainty is regarded as an enemy in waiting.

'Wha's no for me is against me.'

Not quite so poetic, but accurate enough.

I hold to justice. It is my rock. And the law is its chosen implement.

Yet the law itself can turn to persecution, thinking itself infallible, crushing all who dare question it.

As a politician will ignore the very folk who have elected him, thinking them beneath contempt. Or attention.

And here I am, stuck in the middle.

When I was younger I had no doubts but of late I am beset with nagging misgivings like a pack of dogs snapping at my heels.

I don't even like dogs.

Perhaps I am being unfair, perhaps rather than some canine coven, my hesitations are subtle messages from an organism that has charged through youth and enjoyed the fruits of prime manhood but now finds the going a bit heavy, like a Clydesdale horse lugging a coal cart up a hill.

And my body feels in its bones, in its cells, in the network of nerves dancing within and without my skeleton that a reckoning is being prepared.

Somewhere along the line.

Death is enough to give any man doubts.

I have digressed. Let us return to the warped mind that is not my own.

What is it protecting?

What is the secret that must not be let into the light of day?

Perhaps that secret is not even known. Or buried so deep that it cannot even be sensed.

But it must be protected.

At all costs.

McLevy closed his diary with a thud.

The trouble with writing is that often more questions are raised than can be decently answered by an author's limited intelligence.

He carefully stowed away the bulky tome; it was in fact an old office ledger, the cover once red in colour now faded with use, a gift from a grateful banker after the inspector had uncovered a case of embezzlement.

It went into a cupboard by his writing table which was ranged against the wall and contained relics of past crimes solved and unsolved; but he would not delve in there tonight.

A man has too many memories as it is.

The half-drunk mug of coffee lay on his desk and he picked it up before walking to the window.

As usual it was the dark, early hours of morning, the city not altered much from the night before, save perhaps that there was a brooding, heavy feel to the clouds as they almost sat upon the rooftops.

McLevy slurped the brew and pondered about what he had just committed to words.

He had no idea what it all meant but something was coming up from the depths, that was for sure.

A reckoning.

A warped mind.

A secret to be protected.

The inspector peered into his coffee cup as if he might divine this hidden matter or receive a message from a hidden universe but at that moment a coiled shape suddenly unfurled itself from a corner of the room and flew through the air to land with a screech of claws upon his table.

For a moment McLevy, as Mulholland's Aunt Katie would say, almost jumped out of his skin and left it lying there, but then the inspector realised the fiendish intruder was none other than Bathsheba.

He had let her in earlier to partake of some milk from one of his many chipped saucers and she had promptly lapped her fill then gone to sleep.

On awakening the cat had noticed a fat lazy fly that should have by rights been culled this late autumn but had survived in some cranny of the untidy attic room, lurking between Edgar Allan Poe's *The Fall of the House of Usher* and a journal of forensic science.

Thus fortified by literature and research it had droned through the air to descend upon some crumbs where a collection of ginger biscuits had once held sway.

The fly landed, then Bathsheba landed harder.

A quick snap of the jaws and only a fragment of gossamer wing was left to indicate that one of nature's marvels, evolving from egg to larva, pupa to adult, had once existed. The compound eyes now saw nothing unless the fly presently inhabited the spirit dimension and buzzed around annoying the spectres on their daily round.

McLevy opened the window and the cat, thus nourished, leapt from table to sill, thence to pad cautiously on the slates, disappearing without so much as a backward glance.

Nature has no time for losers.

Kill or be killed, thought McLevy. *No matter how much ye wrap it up, that's what it all comes down to now.*

He pulled the window back down and considered risking sleep. Perhaps tonight he would have no dreams, or perhaps a mermaid floating peacefully under water – though the last seamaiden he had summoned from the depths of slumber had turned out to be his dead mother with maggots and water eels crawling out of her head.

Up from the depths.

As long as it wasn't the figure in the cloak.

The naked females bouncing round the fire he could just about thole.

But that other put a hitherto unknown feeling into him, a misgiving of dread that had reappeared throughout this whole day.

What was it in the image that had stirred such fear?

Like a heavy weight. Dragging him down to the bottom.

McLevy could sense something out there in his city. A menace that would unleash its power. A deadly presence.

Would it be the death of him?

He softly whistled the Jacobite air of a king lost across the sea, who had carried so many desperate hopes and drowned under such a burden.

'Charlie is my darling, the young Chevalier.'

The window reflected back McLevy's face like a ghost.

Kill or be killed.

In another part of Leith, Alfred Binnie slept like a child, the razor-sharp knife close to his hand by the pillow. There was a secret entrance to the Countess's hotel from the back lane and he had used it to slip back inside and up the rear stairs to the room at the top where she had stationed him. Not long now. As he slumbered, his podgy little body twitched like a piglet in the sty. *Whee, whee, whee, all the way home.*

The Countess prepared for sleep, eyeing herself in the mirror. It was not, in fact, a very attractive face but she could live with that. She bared her teeth to reveal a pair of small incisors, pointed on each side of the mouth like a predatory animal. She had received from certain quarters this night information that she would put to good use. Or bad. The good for her. The bad for Jean Brash. Such thought was amusing. She laughed aloud. A pity about poor Patrick but his nose would still function and she had warned him to take no more action. It might spoil a plan that was forming in her mind. A sweet surprise. She could almost taste it.

All she had to do was convince a young fool that he could take revenge and be rewarded.

The sins of the flesh were useful to that end.

Jean Brash slept fitfully. Her bedroom was bedecked with delicate filmy curtains that rustled a little in a damp breeze coming through the part-opened window. An oil lamp burned by her bed that Hannah Semple forever worried might overturn and set the whole place aflame. The mistress of the Just Land, however, did not like the dark.

Bad things had happened to her in the absence of light. She had lost her childhood. Taken from her. No way back. She surrounded herself with beauty, pretty favours, pampered her body with oils and perfume, but there was no way back. Burn a light, but the dark is always waiting.

Sophia Adler loved the night. Lying in the pitch black, still as a corpse, eyes half closed, she listened to the voices take shape in her mind. Fragments of speech, echoes of disembodied plaintive cries, a force field of garbled sound that she floated through almost like a ghost herself. But never the voice she waited for. It would come. One day. And her life would have meaning. All would be at peace. One day. Or night.

In the Sweet By and By. On the boat to San Francisco, there had been a gospel choir who sang hymns. *For the Father waits over the way, to prepare us a dwelling place there.* Their simple faith had touched her. But that was not her fate.

Arthur Conan Doyle rarely knew serenity in sleep. His dreams were often peopled with malignant vampire women who sought to chain him to their bodies, and then twist the iron till they drained him of lifeblood. They bore no resemblance to the fair ladies of beauty and grace that he witnessed in daylight. His giant form twitched uneasily as dark tales unravelled in his mind. He feared a father's genetic demon in the blood and marshalled his mind to resist by holding logic like a sword before him. Raised high, crashed down.

But the dismembered monsters crawled back into his mind to burrow and feast upon the cells of sanity.

From the evidence presented, it would be safe to assume that there was a difference between the outer and inner man.

Conan Doyle's life would always be a struggle between what

he presented to the world and the intensity of an inner vision that would not let him rest in peace. Art in the blood gives no quarter.

Samuel and Muriel slumbered together as if children, she cuddled against his broad back. Her breath fluttered upon his neck and he marvelled that she put her trust in him. It made what he had committed all the more regrettable.

Magnus Bannerman's body smelled of soap and cologne. Sophia had bathed him like a baby then put him to bed. The blinding headache had gone and now he slept the sleep of the righteous.

And James McLevy still hadn't made it into the Arms of Morpheus. Too much on his plate.

The unconscious could wait its hurry.

18

One day Massa rode aroun' de farm,
De flies so numerous they did swarm;
One bit his pony on the thigh,
De devil take dat blue-tailed fly.

TRADITIONAL, 'The Blue-tailed Fly'

Glasgow, 1864.

My Dearest Melissa,

I feel as if I am embroiled in a world where nothing can be trusted and to be truthful I am not certain if this letter will ever reach you without being tampered with, opened, read, and perhaps destroyed.

In that case it will never accomplish its mission. But I must write as if it does, as if it will.

It is as if I have become a shadow, as if the life I have led up until now has no meaning, insubstantial, and I hunger for one moment that might give it significance.

As if my identity, what I call myself, Jonathen Sinclair, is losing shape. I am becoming. . .indistinct.

I fear that the fever which struck after Gettysburg is still hectic in my blood and I cannot trust my own thoughts, as if I am being manipulated by someone else who pulls the strings to make the puppet jump.

When I asked Secretary Mallory why he would delegate such an onerous responsibility to a soldier who lacks all experience for such a task, he answered, 'Because you are an honest man.'

I would have thought honesty to be the last attribute necessary for this damned business.

There is a deadly game of hide and seek being enacted in the docks of Glasgow. Lincoln's Federal agents know a messenger has arrived with bonded certificates to purchase ships for the South and run the blockade that strangles our Confederate forces. It is their intention, by fair means or foul, to stop me in my tracks.

The British Government is now turning against us and the local Emancipation Societies, no doubt whipped up by the Federals, are delivering petitions to the Foreign Office.

Liverpool and Birkenhead are closed to us now and this is one of our last ports of call.

Our own agents have contacted the shipping magnates but the usual conduits have been forestalled.

They are watched. Known. We must go further afield.

Meanwhile my men guard me like jealous bridegrooms, ring me round to protect that precious honesty.

One of our meetings was betrayed, by whom I cannot tell, and two of our men wounded in the ambush.

I myself shot at the assailants and believe I winged one, or perhaps even killed him, who knows?

Do you remember John Findhorn? I spoke of him when I rode day and night to lie by your side just before that bloody battle.

Remember? I left in the morning and you cried me to fight well for the South. I shouted back that John and I would whip them blind.

It was I who was blind. Blinded by glory.

He died of his wounds, the flies around him where he lay, with the cries of those in agony rising to the sky.

His last words to me were, 'I wish I was home.'

He was a good comrade and before death claimed him, bequeathed me his revolver, oiled, cleaned and true if the aim was such. His father was a gunsmith and had made it for John to keep him safe.

It was with that I fired in the Glasgow docks. I now have only three bullets left. I have been offered other weapons but I shall stay with my bequeathment. Three bullets should be enough.

I glimpsed my main adversary. He wears a black oilskin cape, a man *of sense given the unremitting rain, and goes by the name of William Mitchell.*

For a moment our eyes met. I saw belief in his and trust he saw the same in mine. Then I let fire but he ducked back out of sight, the man behind him fell and the rest of the night was spent on the run from our pursuers.

The Federals outman us and are well organised. We rely on our native wits.

It is like a small version of the war itself.

I will send this letter by our next departing messenger and ship. Arrangements have been made for me to move cities. I shall not be sorry to leave Glasgow.

A low place, to be sure.

When I wheeled my horse on the ridge, you were standing in front of the house in the early summer blossom.

I am sure I cut a romantic figure.

If you receive this, think of me kindly. That is all I would wish from you. It is all we can do until this carnage is over and we all come home.

Your husband,
Jonathen

19

> L'homme est, je vous l'avoue, un méchant animal.
> Man, I can assure you, is a nasty creature.
>
> MOLIÈRE, *Le Tartuffe*

Lieutenant Roach rubbed a furry tongue over his snaggled teeth and reviewed the events of the previous night in his mind. The onions had finally stopped repeating upon him at the hour of midnight with the aid of some powders but his wife unfortunately was not so easily neutralised.

She engaged him in an intense discussion – intense, that is, on her side – which ranged from some unexpected accidents that had befallen members of her family – ergo, was there some curse or evil spirit on her familial trail? – thence to the idea that the ether might be jam-packed with whirling ghosts jostling impatiently to get a word in edgeways and full of as many complaints as they had enjoyed in real life.

Mrs Roach had a somewhat sporadic, impulsive mind which, when activated, was capable of jumping from one subject to the other with no discernible link or lack of pace. For some reason her thoughts had ended up in a whist game where her partner Muriel Grierson, whom they had seen at the gathering and barely acknowledged, had played a card so bereft of intelligence that she cost their side the game.

A certain coolness had existed between the ladies since then but when Roach reluctantly vouchsafed the information that the woman had been burgled, he was subsumed in a welter of demand for details and a sudden gush of sympathy for the dear soul; not one of nature's brightest creations but undeserving of rapine and pillage or whatever had been visited upon the poor creature.

Though there had been certain rumours of her being seen with a mysterious man in out-of-the-way places, these were only stories and it was ever a widow's fate to have insinuations follow her, which Mrs Roach hoped would never be her own doom.

Roach agreed somewhat dryly and finally the woman ran out of steam. Just before they closed their eyes in the bed of matrimony, however, she had one more shaft of intuition.

'Robert,' she asked, in the merciful darkness. 'Have you anything you would wish to tell me?'

'About what?' Roach responded tersely.

'Anything. . .*shameful*. That might have been witnessed from above?'

The lieutenant was not sure whether his wife was referring to an all-seeing God or the swirling spirits and hoped sincerely that the balance came down on the Christian side. But then he had to consider the question.

Do we all not have something so petty and shameful hidden away as to make us cringe within?

Not a huge offence such as regicide or bank robbery and the like – these can be dealt with by the authorities – but something so small and so morally miserable that not even our worst enemy could conceive that we might sink so low as to commit this act.

And the one who cannot forgive us or forget is not the Almighty or a plaintive spectre but ourselves.

In Roach's case, inevitably, it had to do with the game of golf.

From an early age the prospect of a green fairway and a white ball curving in a graceful trajectory to land and then skip like a free man onwards to a destination marked by a red flag, only the top of which was visible waving in the breeze above the undulations of green hills – this vision had taken root in his soul.

Late spring in the President's Cup, however, while searching amidst the early morning heather for his chief constable's misdirected drive – a man who had distracted him the year before by jingling coins in his pocket while Roach contemplated then missed a tricky putt, a man who was a fellow Mason to boot and higher in the golden chain than his lowly lieutenant and therefore should know better, a man who puffed cigar smoke so that it drifted across the line of a complex mashie niblick shot – Roach rested his case there – but the memory of his own heinous offence against the gods of golf almost set off the onions once again.

He had stood on the man's ball while it nestled in the wiry gorse. Not only stood but with full weight bore down.

There was the excuse of a whipping east wind stinging at his eyes and fooling his feet, he not seeing the ball buried like a murder victim in the bonny blooming heather.

It was his heel however that did the damage. And having done so, Roach did not say a word until Sandy Grant, the aforementioned chief constable, stumbled upon the impacted body himself. Under Roach's watchful eye, of course, lest the ball in some miraculous fashion be resurrected into a decent lie.

It took Sandy three hacks to dislodge the thing and by that margin he lost the round.

Of course the man could have taken a drop. But that was not in his character.

And what of Roach's own persona?

What is the fine line between accidental mishap and a cognisance that refuses to cognise itself?

While the lieutenant had thus pondered he realised that his wife had fortunately gone to sleep.

And when he uncloaked his guilty eyes in his station office, these thoughts having flooded inappropriately into his mind, he found himself staring at Constable Ballantyne.

'I knocked the door, sir,' stammered the young man, his birthmark already a rising tide of red. 'Ye didnae answer.'

Ballantyne indeed, having tapped timidly to no response, had pushed gently at the door, which had to his dismay sprung open like a yawning pit.

He had received a summons at his desk and expected the worst even though he had avoided mirrors like the plague.

Roach frowned. It came easy to his countenance.

'Ballantyne,' he announced severely. 'I have decided to overlook that unfortunate happening in the uniform quarters and trust it will not be repeated.'

The constable nodded gratefully.

'We all make mistakes,' said Roach. 'Now, go away and make yourself useful somewhere.'

He closed his eyes but when he prised them apart once more, Ballantyne was still in the office.

'I was wondering, sir,' declared the constable, emboldened by reprieve. 'If I might have another try at the patrolling?'

The last venture on the streets had ended somewhat ignominiously; a female pocket delver had dipped his police whistle and when Ballantyne had raised hand to lip in order to signal alarm, he found it empty of purpose.

'I will consult the inspector,' said Roach, who felt an irrational anxiety suddenly seize him. 'Now, go away.'

This time when he shut his eyes the door closed with a satisfying thud but after a few moments it banged open once more. Roach was irritated beyond his usual level because the events of last night, not to mention the recalled *Incident of the Golf Ball in the Heather*, had set his nerves a-jangle.

'Whit do you damned well want now?' he snapped.

'Ye need tae get that door fixed, lieutenant,' said James McLevy. 'It runs the risk of unwarranted entry.'

Roach sighed and blinked open weary eyes to see his inspector, glowing with health and efficiency, standing at what even might have been claimed as attention before him.

Just behind McLevy on the wall, Queen Victoria also stood with her hand resting on the back of a chair.

It was said she had attended a séance at the Royal Palace to contact her beloved, deceased Albert. Sadly the departed consort had failed to put in an appearance, which might explain the disappointed look on her face as she gazed out of the portrait photograph, which Roach himself wiped clean every morning with averted eyes, lest her Majesty think him intrusive.

Intrusive, however, was exactly the word for McLevy.

'The morning had hardly started,' Roach declared, 'and I already received a complaint about you, inspector.'

'Logan Galloway?'

'The same. He claims you took Jean Brash's part against him, his wallet rifled at the Just Land, his own well-being insulted and physically threatened by the police who are for the protection of respectable citizens –'

'If he's all that winsome, whit's he doing at a bawdy-hoose?'

'Exactly the point I made before I sent him packing,' said Roach, surprising McLevy by a change of direction; now and again the lieutenant was capable of something that suggested his mind did not entirely run with the Masonic pack. Not often, but now and again.

'I don't like the stupid wee gomeril and I like his father even less,' Roach continued, 'but if you must side with a bawdy-hoose keeper can you do it in a way that doesn't threaten the bedrock of society?'

Now the lieutenant was back on track. He disapproved mightily of McLevy's close entanglement with Jean Brash, believing there might be more to it than a love of coffee.

But McLevy could deal with this in his sleep.

'Galloway was rantin' fou,' he replied. 'And I didnae lift a pinkie. It was Mulholland and some fish.'

Roach knew better than to follow that trail.

'What, I repeat, do you want in my presence?'

'Morning report, sir!'

McLevy straightened up in a parody of eager, soldier-like attention. In truth he was feeling spry as a mountain goat this day; he'd had five hours uninterrupted sleep and not one visitation from the weird sisters.

'Report away,' said Roach, also straightening up; business was business after all and he'd make a propitious offering to the gods of golf by deliberately missing a five yard putt the next time he played his chief constable.

'Two sharpers sliced deep in the Rustie Nail.'

'By the throat?'

'Belly. They'll live.'

'God's mercy knows no bounds,' said Roach, a trifle enigmatically.

'The perpetrator answers the description of the acid-pourer of Leith Market.'

'A busy man.'

'And elusive,' said McLevy. 'I may pay a visit to the Countess.'

'You seem at home in these establishments.'

McLevy ignored the caustic tone of his superior.

'Also we had a few rammies on the streets between the rival clans.'

Roach had been put in the picture as regards the conflict betwixt the Queens of Procurement, and nodded sagely. Then he put the knife in.

'If all this escalates to proven violence, will you be able to discharge your duties?'

The only indicator of a hit was that the slate-grey eyes darkened slightly.

'The guilty will not evade me.'

'Even Jean Brash?'

'Justice has no favourites.'

'I am glad to hear that. What about the Grierson robbery?'

'An inside job, I believe. The widow woman has a secret she keeps close.'

'I am sure you will find it out.'

Roach was content to leave it there, because he knew McLevy would have covered all other avenues such as domestic staff with lovers and flapping tongues. He had a prurient curiosity as regards Muriel Grierson; perhaps his wife was correct, widows excite a strange inquisitory bent.

In any case, let McLevy hunt it down.

And then tell him about it.

Roach folded his hands together indicating dismissal but the inspector had yet more to contribute.

'Ballantyne tells me ye want him out on patrol.'

The lieutenant was about to deny this indignantly when, on impulse, he decided to content himself with a nod of the head. If the constable was playing one off against the other then there was more to that boy than met the eye.

'I don't know if the parish is ready for Ballantyne,' McLevy muttered dubiously.

'How is the constable to develop else?'

Now it was McLevy's turn to leave it be. Far be it from him to mention that other than staring into cracked mirrors and waving his hands about, Ballantyne's other pastime was collecting live insects from the busy horde that crept around the station, carefully depositing them outside lest a hobnailed boot curtail their existence.

He nodded and turned to go but Roach had a question that suddenly popped into his mind.

It had been bothering him since yesterday morning; the passing reference to widows with things to hide and the memory of last night when a giant form rose to apprehend the two capering demons brought it back into his mind.

'Arthur Conan Doyle?'

'Uhuh?' McLevy stood by the open door, his face not easy to read.

'How did you know all that. . .medical boxing palaver about him?'

'Deduction.'

Not easy to read had now become sphinx-like.

'*Deduction?*' Roach shook his head, obscurely annoyed as he often was at the outcome of certain conversations with his inspector. 'I don't remember you indulging yourself in that particular pastime before.'

'Whit I do all the time. Scientific.'

'*You?*'

Here the lieutenant was being unfair because he knew fine well that McLevy kept surprisingly up to scratch with forensic developments, though he tended to hide that particular light under a large bushel basket.

It is ever the Scots trait not to flaunt learning and give aye the appearance of someone who has stumbled upon erudition by accident, if at all.

'Just got a fancy name, now.'

But Roach was not completely accepting this; he had never heard McLevy launch forth in such flowery style to such devastating effect.

'But how did you come upon all this *deduction?*'

McLevy frowned for a moment, then his face lit up.

'That's my secret,' he said.

In the silence following that unhelpful comment, a strangled scream came from the direction of the main station room outside.

McLevy wheeled; Roach, showing a surprising turn of speed, followed after, and when they emerged it was to find a macabre scene being re-enacted before them.

An old man staggered around in the main hall, his hands covered in blood, streaks of the same in his white hair that then ran down his face.

King Lear in Leith.

His mouth opened and closed without a sound, the previous shriek having drained his vocal cords.

The young constables who were just about to depart on the morning shift stood frozen at the sight. Sergeant Murdoch, who had not even noticed the man pass like a ghost beyond the reception counter, was also fixed in time and space; Ballantyne had risen from his untidy desk, a blotting paper that had held a large beetle falling limply from his hand to let the insect scuttle off towards its own fate.

Mulholland who had been gazing glumly at his face in the cracked mirror emerged from the cubby-hole and swiftly moved to catch the old man before he came to harm on one of the stone pillars that held the very building in place.

He helped the old fellow gently down onto one of the chairs as McLevy moved to join them.

Fergus MacLean was the old man's name. He was a servant who did not live in with his master but arrived each morning to light the fire and heat the house.

He was badly paid, his diligence unappreciated by his sovereign lord but, as is the manner of those who serve, regarded it as part of his drudgery.

No longer. No more. The kindling and the coal were in the bunker but they would not be utilised this day.

McLevy and Mulholland stood looking down at him till Fergus finally found some words.

'The maister. . .' he croaked. 'He lies. In blood. I could not raise him.'

So the streaks of gore were not his own, though the man's face was full of sorrow and fear as if life would never be the same.

Death is enough to give any man doubts.

20

The smyler with the knyf under the cloke.

GEOFFREY CHAUCER, *The Knight's Tale*

When Alfred Binnie was born there were no celebrations of fireworks or grateful peasants gathering under the castle windows to shower the newborn infant with gifts from the harvest table.

His mother dropped him like a crouching animal to grow as best he might manage and join the brood of children that swarmed onto the streets of Shoreditch like maggots.

Cholera had come and gone but the stench remained, safely ensconced in the dead bodies of the dogs, cats, and rats that littered the highways.

The mudlarks went to scour the mud of the Thames for coal dropped by the cargo boats but Binnie stayed in the crevices of alley and side-streets, his cunning round face disguising the predatory purpose within.

He was apprenticed by his kidsman to a pocket delver and learned the trade well. Alfred had swift, dexterous hands – lightning swift, despite his mole-like appearance.

He also learned the gift of invisibility, how to mingle with the crowd, become non-existent almost until the moment when he struck for the pocket or razor-slit the handbag.

The young Alfred developed apace but few found him appealing, girls especially; the little ladybirds who gave their favours with carefree abandon to other young keelies found him oddly repellent, part to do with his appearance which was, as one sharp dollymop accurately described, *like something crawled out of a rat's arse.*

The other part was not so easily defined and in fact puzzled Alfred himself.

It was as if he starved for something, a hunger that came out of his pores like a sweat and it put an aura around him that even the most hard-bitten of street dwellers found to provoke an uneasy feeling.

His hungry little heart could only suffer, not name its desire, only the empty yearning.

Then one day he found it.

Death.

His mobsman mentor, flushed with gin, a drink that encourages the careless rapture that no harm will befall a man soused and saturated with its cloying alcoholic charm, overreached himself in a flash house, a tavern where the cream of London's reprobates mixed with the lowest of the low. All equal under the blanket of crime.

It was a given rule that no pocket delving was done, no sharping, no find-the-lady. Not in this tavern.

Good behaviour between thieves.

However the tooler could not resist the temptation of a heavy pocketbook in the side coat of a quietly dressed mark at the bar.

He signalled Alfred to supply distraction, a clumsy trip and spilling of a beer glass that would fit in so well with the boy's oafish demeanour.

But Alfred hung back.

He had noticed that there was space around this man, no-one slapped him on the back or attempted familiarity. He had been drinking alone, steadily, the best rum, not making a show or unnecessary move.

Which was what the mobsman did.

Bumped in, fixed apologetic smile already upon his face, fingers upon the leather of the pocketbook, then a sharp pain under his ribcage as the knife punctured his skin and pierced the heart like a blackbird's beak.

The executioner then placed the tooler's hands upon the bar as if to steady him, laid down the empty glass of rum, then turned and walked unhurriedly out of the place.

Tom Partridge, for that was the mark's name, walked carefully through the dirty streets of Shoreditch until he became aware that someone was dogging his steps.

When he turned, he saw a strange lumpen creature neither man nor child.

'How did you do that?' asked Alfred Binnie.

'Practice,' said Tom.

'Will you teach me?'

Partridge looked into the boy's eyes and saw the same emptiness that met his own gaze in the mirror every morning.

The blank, dispassionate stare of an assassin.

He said nothing. A sudden uproar in the distance signalled the discovery of a dead man slumped over the bar with a smile fixed upon his face.

'Why did you stick him through?'

'He broke the rules.'

Alfred smiled. That made sense.

'What did you see?' asked Tom quietly.

'I saw your hand. The steel. But not where you kept it. That's a mystery.'

Partridge sighed. He had no wish to take on an acolyte but the alternative was to kill the witness.

Any witness runs that risk.

He turned and walked away, with Alfred taking this as acceptance, following like a dog its master.

The boy had learned and learned well.

Alfred Binnie allowed himself a smile of satisfaction as he thought of the pleasure in that sweep under the table when his knife cut through the thick material to find the soft flesh beneath.

The Countess, however, who was sitting opposite him, was anything but pleased.

She had been informed at first light as to the events in the Rustie Nail and it did not fit with her plans so carefully constructed while the city slept.

'How could you do this?' she asked.

Alfred laughed, a strange sound.

'My hand slipped,' he replied.

'You might have ruined everything.'

'I don't like being bilked.'

The Countess fixed him with a cold stare and the pleasure drained from his face.

'You were to stay here,' she said.

'I was confined to no purpose! This poky little room offends me and that woman you sent up was no such thing.'

'What?'

'All bones and elbows.'

His face was now like that of a sulky boy and her thin eyebrows rose in some surprise. Binnie's taste ran to large women and she had provided him with the fleshiest specimen in the hotel.

'Not many would describe her so,' she murmured.

He laughed scornfully.

'She wouldn't play any games. I like games. That's why I defenestrated.'

Indeed after realising that what he thought of as a bit of fun had produced a look of repugnance in the woman's eyes, Binnie had dismissed her and then suspecting that the Countess might have a watch kept on his door, swung out of the window and down the drainpipe.

It was no strain, either for him or the pipe. Binnie was surprisingly agile despite his appearance and though plump was small enough not to weigh a great deal.

The two large German Shepherds that the Countess kept as watchdogs had growled in their kennels but Binnie was silent in movement and possessed the odd attribute of having no body odour. His pores gave nothing away.

He returned by the back stairs, however, not the drainpipe. Alfred Binnie was no monkey.

His unattractive but unthreatening form had been a great boon to him in his chosen and beloved profession; many a body mouldering in the grave, if it ever got to such a resting place, bore witness to the fact that violent death can come from other sources than the belching mouth of cannon.

She watched him as his face smoothed out again till it resembled a nondescript little man, easily overlooked.

Binnie had come highly recommended, laid down a fierce price that would not be haggled over and the Countess, foreseeing the coming war as soon as Simone had deserted, indeed almost welcoming the opportunity, needed a secret card to play.

Needed him badly.

Though now that secret was somewhat compromised.

However, even that she could use to advantage.

The Countess took a thin, crumpled piece of paper from her pocket and placed it before Binnie.

'This was delivered to me this morning from a trusted source. You are discovered, Mister Binnie.'

He slowly unwrapped the paper to find a crude likeness of his own face staring back.

'When you poured the acid, you were witnessed,' she informed him, with a malicious edge. 'Tut, tut.'

Alfred said nothing but his professional pride was hurt. His speciality was the unseen strike. A witness; that was bad. The drawing was a complication but that proved nothing. The witness was another matter.

'Who saw me?' he said quietly.

'A deaf mute, I am told. Lily Baxter. One of Jean Brash's impaired whores.'

A slow nod, the eyes blank.

'She can't live.'

'That will be part of the plan. But from now on you must lie low, only out in cover of darkness, no cutting bellies in taverns, no defenestrating.'

A sudden glint of merriment once more in the dark beady eyes; she would keep this little monster close to hand like a dog on a lead.

But now it was time to grease the palm. Was that the phrase? English was such a slippery tongue.

'Put out your hand,' she commanded.

'Which one?'

'Which do you favour?'

'The left. Always.'

'Extend the same.'

An evil little grin spread across the face of Alfred.

'Are you going to punish me, Countess?'

She said nothing. He extended the hand, and she produced a small leather bag from which she extracted ten gold coins which she dropped one after the other into his upturned palm. A sensuous smile appeared on his face; next to death this was his best pleasure, large women came a poor third at the races.

'That much again awaits,' she promised, herself excited by the quickening in her own being. 'When we have executed what is in my mind. This night.'

Alfred caught her bloodlust, you could almost taste it; pity she was such a scrawny type.

'This seems acceptable,' he said chastely.

'You will be a good boy till then?'

'You have my word,' he replied, as he pocketed the coins, 'but tonight, I will be a very bad boy.'

They sat and stared at each other like two perfect embodiments of evil intent until the Countess smiled over a random thought of impending destruction.

'Do you enjoy long, slow suffering?' she remarked.

'If there's blood involved.'

That response brought a slight frown to her face and she was moved to more precise definition of their objective.

'The most exquisite torture is in the mind. We may throw in a bit of blood to keep you happy.'

'I like being happy,' he replied simply.

For a moment she gazed at him with a curious fondness.

'You are most valuable to me, Mister Binnie. I shall take *very* good care of you.'

'I don't like Scotch beer.'

'I shall find you another kind.'

'And I like *big* women. Something I can find in the dark.'

'I will search out such a magnitude.'

'Then we have an agreement, Countess,' said Binnie with solemn gravity.

'We have an agreement, Mister Binnie.'

They each then retreated to their thoughts, his of the victim's surprise and fear, hers of the delights to come.

21

I went out to Charing Cross, to see Major-general
Harrison hanged, drawn and quartered; which was
done there, he looking as cheerful as any man could
do in that condition.

SAMUEL PEPYS, *Diary* (13 October, 1660)

James McLevy had seen some messy corpses in his time but this
one took the biscuit.

Strangely enough the trunk and limbs were untouched save
for the fragments of gore and splinters of bone that had spat-
tered over the respectable garmentation.

The body encased and covered in a heavy suit as custom demanded, the shoes shiny, though dull red drops had given birth
to thin rivulets which trickled down until they had been arrested
by the edging sole of a solid brogue.

Everything was fine until you got above the neck.

Then it was as if someone had dropped a huge blancmange,
the flesh split, and the bones crushed to a pulp.

It was hardly recognisable as a human head and so far the inspector had hardly been able to find an eyeball that he could call
his own.

Constable Ballantyne, thrilled at being included in his first
murder investigation, though merely there to stand and watch,
stood, watched, and then bolted outside to boak his breakfast up
all over the street.

The other two young green-faced constables had been dismissed to join Ballantyne lest they spewed precipitously and obliterated evidence.

Mulholland, who had looked but not boaked, was in the higher reaches of the house in search of forcible entry because nothing indicated such below.

It was just how McLevy liked it.

Him and a corpse.

Plus the word.

Daubed in blood on the wall above the mantelpiece, the letters crude and misshapen but the word clear enough.

JUDAS.

How that applied to the dead Gilbert Morrison was a mystery to be solved. He had been thus identified by Fergus MacLean through his clothing and a scar across the palm of his hand, the result of an accident on board a ship when a sharp metal shackle had broken free from the chain cable and cut the maister's hand.

Long ago. But the mark remained.

Like that of Cain.

McLevy had known the man and hadn't liked him. Avaricious, cruel-eyed, thin-lipped, a dry stick of rectitude.

None of that left now.

Not a shred.

The inspector carefully skirted the huddle of fleshly remains and bent over what appeared to be the implement of destruction. A heavy iron poker, the lower third of which had the metal twisted round in a spiral so that when thrust it might worm itself into the coals.

The whirling indentation had retained fragments of tissue that might be useful, although there was enough to be going on with, scattered all around.

He peered at the weapon and produced a magnifier to squint through but there were no foreign substances and only smears of blood upon the handle.

McLevy had read recently in the scientific journal *Nature* an article by a physician – Scots of course – Henry Faulds, suggesting that fingerprints might one day be used to identify the perpetrators of crime. The inspector looked forward to that prospect though it was still a distance off. One day. Loops and whorls.

Though there was nothing on the handle of the poker but red smudges, whoever had wielded it with such ferocious purpose might well have worn a hand covering of some kind. A strange contradiction; the crime suggested mindless violence but was there an element of calculation involved?

He placed the poker aside neatly, to be wrapped up and scrutinised later at the station, then moved to the mantelpiece with his magnifier.

JUDAS. Very biblical. The betrayer of Jesus. That suggested vengeance. But who had been betrayed?

And who desired vengeance?

He bent down, and using the magnifier, carefully scanned the fireplace, grunting a little as his body did not take to folding over in such fashion. By the side of the grate, his painstaking search uncovered a thin strand of hair. He fished it out between finger and thumb then raised it up to the light.

Indeed it was human filament but not the servant's or Morrison's. Fergus was white haired and the deceased Gilbert, from McLevy's memory, had few hairs if any, a bald pate like a monk – it must have made a fine target.

But this was long, darkish in colour as far as he could tell and, under the magnifier, perhaps even a little wavy.

He sniffed at the hair and then his fingers. An acrid trace of ash from the fireplace but something else as well.

So faint as to be near unidentifiable. A pomade of sorts? Hard to tell. McLevy's eyes were not the best but his nose was infallible; possibly some oiling agent, some unguent? The odour though, what was it?

Honey? A sweet smell but fading even as he sniffed; he was lucky it had lasted this long. He would store it in his olfactory bank and hope for a similar waft someday.

McLevy diligently placed the hair into some thin paper and deposited it into the evidence bag.

Man or woman? Long enough for either but he would wager a man.

His little secret for the nonce.

Mulholland entered and McLevy turned; they spoke across the crushed cadaver as if it had no meaning or life, which latter indeed was true enough.

A necessary callousness becomes the good policeman; too much sensitivity and you'd never get anything done.

'Came in through the skylight, wrenched the thing right off its hinges. No mark of a tool. Bare hands.'

Having announced this, Mulholland demonstrated the action somewhat dramatically for he had been impressed by the mangled frame still propped against the chimneybreast.

'That takes a bit of doing,' muttered the inspector.

'You should see it.'

'I intend to.'

Both men then looked at the corpse as if it might contribute to the discussion.

'Find anything?' Mulholland asked.

'Looks like murder,' was the answer.

A glint of gallows humour but there was no gainsaying the fact that this was a crime with a strange supernatural bent as if some berserk elemental force had come in to wreak havoc and vengeance.

Mulholland looked at the name on the wall.

'Judas,' McLevy remarked. 'Gets the blame for everything.'

'Something from the past caught up with Mister Morrison?'

'Possible. We'll dig it up and see.'

Morrison had the reputation of a ruthless swine who would sell his granny for a profit, or at the very least put her on a tramp steamer.

This, however, was beyond natural retribution.

This was violent death, intense and savage.

The constable shivered slightly.

'Whatever did the deed, I wouldn't want to meet the same without a revolver to hand.'

'Not even your hornbeam stick?'

'Not even that.'

'Near Halloween. Maybe the devil paid a visit.'

While they had been almost idly discoursing both had been sweeping the room with their eyes to see if anything besides the fairly obvious carcass was awry, but nothing seemed out of place.

Just the dead body.

All the mayhem had been localised.

'The poker is the murder weapon.'

'I noticed that.'

'But did you observe the angle of the neck?'

'No. You sent me to skies above.'

'Observe it now.'

The constable collapsed his lanky frame somewhat like a giraffe getting to its knees and gazed at the columnar connection between the trunk and smithereens on top.

Oddly enough, though the head was smashed to bits the neck remained intact. Reasonably.

'Snapped clean,' he announced.

'Uhuh. I would wager before the attack upon the face.'

'He was dead already?'

'That's my contention.'

This put a different complexion on the event. A mixture of explosive ferocity and deliberate intent.

McLevy also knelt and then took out a flat leather pouch from which he extracted a thin metal rod with a delicate sharp point. One of a matching set of lock-picks that had mysteriously found its way into his possession and which he had put to many uses.

He used this one to scrape under the nails of the dead hand, finding imbedded beneath first and second fingerplates fragmentary scraps of a stiff, dark blue material.

Mulholland took one and held it up to the light while McLevy sniffed at the other, on guard lest it disappear up his nose.

'Tarry,' he opined.

'Scraped off – but from what?'

Then Mulholland had a sudden thought and answered his own question.

'Gauntlets, perhaps? To protect and leave no trace?'

'But they did,' said McLevy. 'And it's the protection that interests me.'

Again he was struck by the contrast of animal fury and careful planning.

Also something that had been nagging at him since the sighting of the body had just fallen into place; probably it possessed no relevance but the inspector was a great believer in random slices of the brain.

'I once saw a victim as bad smashed as this but it was a bullet had done the trick. Shot from close. Down by the docks. I was a constable then. Not my case.'

'That wouldn't be yesterday.'

'No. It was not. We never did find the killer.'

The inspector seemed lost in reverie and Mulholland knew better than to disturb him. Finally though McLevy shook his head and put the scraps away in his evidence bag.

'Let's hope we have better luck this time,' he said.

The door opened and an ashen-faced Ballantyne entered, holding something low down by his side.

'Ye're back,' acknowledged the inspector. 'Good. Now the investigation can begin in earnest.'

Ballantyne nodded guilelessly.

'I've been returned a bit, sir,' he said solemnly. 'I ran out of things tae bring up. I had a wee poke about in the other rooms.'

'Did ye now?'

McLevy shot a sidelong glance to Mulholland who kept his face straight; the boy had some sand to him then, from a dry boak to searching of premises in the one fell swoop.

'Aye, and I found this in the bottom of his wardrobe. Wrapped up in velvet.'

Ballantyne studiously avoided looking in the direction of the corpse and held up a pliant leather quirt.

In truth he was quaking inside because he had been on his way back, leaving the other two loitering in the street eyeing up some cheeky shopgirls, when he impulsively shot upstairs and through the first door, which turned out to be the one that led to the man's bedroom.

There he 'poked about', a phrase Ballantyne often heard his inspector use to describe apparent rootless snuffling that often had surprising results.

His fear was that he had done something out of turn, that he should have waited for his superiors, but he wanted to prove there was more to him than opinion warranted.

Anyway. He held the quirt up like a policeman stopping a runaway carriage. Hoping for the best.

'Whit colour was the velvet wrapping?' McLevy asked, while he took in the tableau of Ballantyne with a quirt to hand in a murder room.

'Red, sir.'

'Goes well wi' the rest of him then.'

Ballantyne's own strawberry birthmark pulsed upon his face and he forced himself to survey the crunched remains.

Nothing more to bring up, as he had said, so he took a deep breath and held firm.

'Were there any other horsey accoutrements?'

'Not that I could see, sir.'

Mulholland, observing that Ballantyne's arm was beginning to waver, took pity and reached over to pluck the quirt from him.

The tall constable swished it through the air and the slender rod cut a fine dash.

The Count of Monte Cristo.

He met McLevy's eyes.

'I have heard rumours,' the inspector remarked, 'that Mister Morrison was inclined in the way of chastisement.'

Jean Brash had dropped a hint to the effect when, in friendlier times, they had gossiped over the coffee cups.

'Inflicting, or taking on board?' asked Mulholland.

The question was never answered because at that moment the door to the room opened and a fat man, puffed up with his own importance and splendid living, burst in.

He did not at first see the corpse, which was partly hidden behind the three policemen ranged before him.

The rest of the room of course, was untouched by death.

'What is going on here?' he demanded loudly.

'Who are you when at home?' asked the inspector.

'Walter Morrison, no less,' replied the fat man huffily. 'Gilbert is my kith and kin. Your fellows had the impertinence to try to prevent me entering the premises.'

Indeed the constables had attempted to bar Walter's entry but on his insistent blustering, they let him pass, sniggering to themselves as policemen often will, at the thought of things that come to the unsuspecting public.

'What do you want with your brother?'

The fat man puffed up further at the inspector's brusque enquiry.

'We have a business appointment,' he replied loftily.

'I don't think he'll be keeping it.'

With this succinct statement McLevy stood aside to reveal the body.

Walter Morrison gasped in horror.

For a moment Ballantyne almost felt sorry for the man but he remembered what the inspector had once told him at the station when he found the constable on his hands and knees trying to catch a cockroach. The insect had shown no gratitude towards his would-be rescuer and had crawled into a narrow gap in the floorboards. Ballantyne was muttering over this event when he looked up to see the face of McLevy looming over like the dark side of the moon.

'Folk in the main are not grateful for kindness proffered, Ballantyne. So if in this life ye treat everyone you meet as a potential guilty party and deeply suspicion each individual's intentions, ye will not go far wrong.'

So Ballantyne held pity at bay.

Mulholland did not need to be told such. He lived by that edict as regards criminal activity.

The fat man's face was white, like the belly of a whale. A good colour for interrogation.

'My God. My poor brother. Who has done this?'

'That's what we intend to find out,' said McLevy.

Walter bowed his head and murmured brokenly to himself but McLevy was unmoved. Despite his opening question, he had recognised and placed the man as soon as seen.

If anything his reputation was of being even more merciless in business than his brother except that Walter had the jollier appearance.

The fat man's complexion recovered somewhat to that of a suet pudding.

In, before he regains full health.

'Did yer brother say anything?'

'What?'

'About someone on his trail. Death threats, murder in mind, any wee thing like that?'

'Not at all.'

'Any recent enemies? Folk he did down. Betrayed. Ruined. Swearing vengeance upon him?'

'My brother was a good man.'

'Uhuh. But in the world of commerce enemies abound.'

'We are respectable shipping merchants.'

McLevy looked hard into Walter's eyes. He knew for a fact that the brothers had swindled and destroyed two decent men of business. Owed them money then denied the contract. Watched them go bankrupt, one man indeed dying of the strain and shame.

Just the world of commerce.

'I need not remind you, sir,' he said sombrely. 'That you are accounted close to your deceased kith and kin. I would not wish your fate to mirror his.'

141

Walter's eyes flicked towards the bloody heap then jerked away convulsively.

'I would ask you once more, is there anything you can tell me, anything you know that might bear relevance to this hellish butchery?'

For a moment Walter hesitated then he shook his head.

'Might it not just be simple robbery?' he offered.

'Simple?'

'The thief disturbed in the act, lashes out?'

The fat man seemed to find some comfort in this notion and his terrible grief was perhaps assuaged by the thought that he would now be the sole owner of the shipping firm.

Just the world of commerce.

'What about this then?' said McLevy signalling the tall figure of Mulholland to stand aside and reveal upon the wall a word scrawled in blood.

JUDAS.

All comfort fled. Walter's eyeballs pitched up to the word on the wall, his mouth opened but no sound emerged.

Then he fainted forwards to thud onto the floor with a reverberation that paid homage to his avoirdupois.

For a second there was silence as the three policemen gazed down at the recumbent body.

McLevy finally addressed Ballantyne.

'That is whit we call in the trade, constable. . .a heavy dwam. Out for the count.'

22

Will you, won't you, will you, won't you, will you join
the dance?

LEWIS CARROLL, *Alice's Adventures in Wonderland*

Arthur Conan Doyle was three sheets to the wind.

A nautical term whose derivation he had discovered from experience and maritime lore to be a square sail out on the lash because its control ropes are flapping in the salty gusts.

The previous year in a quest for glorious adventure and some necessary financial gain, he had enlisted as a ship's surgeon aboard an Arctic whaler, the sailor's jacket and cap from which he still wore with pride.

He had come of age at 80 degrees north latitude, then days later watched and taken part in the grisly ritual of mother seals being shot, the little ones' brains being bludgeoned with spiked clubs; heigh-ho for a life on the ocean waves.

In perhaps unconscious expiation for this bloody slaughter he had managed to fall into the icy waters five times, surviving, however, in better condition than the seal cubs. Heigh-ho.

He had learned to hold his own with drink and hard brawling both at sea and in the Lerwick taverns, but this day had begun early with some fellow students to celebrate his friends attaining passes in their recent exams.

The revels had continued till he found himself strangely alone in the nether regions of Leith.

His companions had been scattered astray in the various taverns from the Royal Mile to the Shore in descending order of good vittles and beer but now only Arthur remained, full of beans and ready for anything.

Witness him swaying slightly in the gathering gloom of early evening in a most insalubrious part of the docks.

Doyle was large and tough enough in appearance that no-one would have marked him as easy prey, but from the side a few watched and wondered if he might be tempted by a nymph of the pavé into the wynds and there summarily relieved of the contents of his pocketbook.

However, any approach was held in suspense when the frail notes of a beautiful song sounded like a summons to love in the dank, dampening air.

Notes only, but Doyle's mind supplied the words.

> 'Flow gently, Sweet Afton
> Amang thy green braes.
> Flow gently, I'll sing thee
> A sang in thy praise.'

They floated in the mildewed firmament of the old harbour, an invocation to the kind of tenderness that was noticeably absent in the denizens lurking by the shadows.

143

The young man took a deep, steadying breath and licked his lips where the moustache curled.

Could he, by chance, have stumbled upon the most vital clue of all? Was the purloined music box calling to him for rescue as a fair maiden has every right to do?

The quavering melodic strain was issuing from a small weather-beaten tavern that crouched like a gnarled goblin at the end of a row of buildings.

The sign above proclaimed this to be the Foul Anchor and it more than lived up to the name.

Doyle walked with measured tread towards the dirty windows and peeped through, tipping his old naval cap back for better viewing.

It was a strange sight within. The tavern was almost empty, save for two men huddled close together at a back table with a barman behind the counter, but in front of them, on the bare boards in shabby finery, were three weird harpies dancing to the music, eyes half-shut, fingers trailing in the air.

Their gaudy clothes proclaimed them women of a certain profession or at least the two elder had been at one time and the other on the far cusp of whoredom.

And yet their faces were rapt and seraphic, lost in the dance as the melody played on.

> 'Thou stock dove whose echo resounds thro' the glen
> Ye wild whistly blackbirds in yon thorny den
> Thou green crested lapwing, thy screaming forbear
> I charge you, disturb not my slumbering fair.'

It is a tribute to the art of Robert Burns that he had produced such sweetness and dreams of forgotten innocence amongst these lost souls.

But it left Conan Doyle with a problem. The chances of two music boxes playing that particular tune were a thousand to one. If indeed it was Muriel's precious gift how could he reclaim it from the dragon's castle?

How would Sir Lancelot, or even the young Lochinvar, handle this situation?

Inside the Foul Anchor, Seth Moxey watched his ladies dance and smiled to see such fun.

'Are they no' beautiful?' he observed. 'I'll stick the man who says otherwise.'

Samuel Grant nodded assent but his guts were churning inside. The Moxey gang were cut-throats to a man and woman, dance or no dance. Life was cheap to them, and Samuel, if he played his cards wrongly, might pay the forfeit.

'Do you have the brooch?' he asked quietly.

Seth grinned, the wide gaps in his teeth in no way at odds with his lank scalloped hair and the scar that ran down the right side of his face.

'I sold on the rest but kept this as per requestit. But, it'll cost ye,' he replied, waving at his good lady, Agnes Devlin, who had supported him with her earnings these many years but now was more for skulduggery, being possessed of a sharp wit for the possible criminal chance. Of the other two, Sadie Shields could still turn a penny but Jennie Martin had also seen better days.

'How much?' asked Samuel with a dark frown.

Seth took the brooch out from his pocket and laid it carefully upon the table.

'Five pun', take or leave.'

'That's robbery!'

'Ye hae that correct, Silver Sam.'

Seth roared with laughter while Samuel boiled with indignation.

'If it hadnae been for me –' he began.

An evil smile from the man opposite stopped him in his tracks.

Indeed there was the bitter truth. If it had not been for Samuel trying to impress Seth Moxey, puffing himself up by telling of the cash discovery in the desk and how he might help himself one night while the mistress lay satiated by his virile charms. . .a cheap, stupid vaunt that had landed him in this mess of potage.

'I kennt you would never have the nerve,' said Seth, a scornful twist to his chapped lips. 'My Agnes said so and she never has it wrong.'

Samuel bowed his head. It was true. He was not a thief, or particularly violence-prone.

What he had not known was that Seth's gang had cased Muriel's house previously through an informant amongst the funeral catering staff, who had noted the jammed window but had not opportunity to copy out the keys in wax.

Seth had therefore not considered it worth the risk till Mister Grant opened his big trap-door.

'Is the cash not enough for you?' he asked mournfully.

'Naething satisfies,' said Seth. 'I have many mouths tae feed. It was ane of our own nephews that stood upon my shoulders tae get through the high window. A big family.'

He gestured to the dancing maidens and two villainous young keelies, twin offspring of himself and Agnes, who were sucking on their cheap cigarettes tucked away in one of the corners as they played at cards.

'Five pun'. Take or leave.'

Seth's eyes had narrowed, the tone flat, uninterested, and Samuel knew miserably that he did not possess such a sum so he might kiss goodbye to the mother's brooch.

At that moment the music box ran out of tune and Sadie Shields, herself puffing on a penny cigarette, darted forward to wind the spring once more; things had been quiet and this, for the women, was a sweet diversion.

It is an oddity how in the most estranged of hearts, some crevice of feeling can still maintain existence, and who knows what dreams had been conjured by the movement of their ransacked bodies to the melancholy strain?

But before her fingers touched the winding key, a voice rang through the tavern striking a different note.

'Hold your hand!'

Arthur Conan Doyle stood in the tavern doorway, a massive figure of due retribution.

'I have reason to believe that music box is not your property. I respectfully ask you to hand it over and we will find an authority that may pronounce upon this matter.'

A frozen silence followed this highfalutin assertion, for in truth Conan Doyle was not sure how a Knight Errant might address three dancing whores in a Leith tavern.

Seth Moxey rose slowly to his feet, hand sliding to a side pocket where a short thick stub of sharpened iron had its dwelling place. He preferred close quarters and often allowed his opponent to haul him tight before delivering a lethal blow.

The two keelies rose also, taking the parental cue, one fitting a set of knuckledusters, the other unveiling a lead cosh.

Doyle took note of all this and raised his hands in a pugilist's posture, left extended, right cocked under his chin. His slightly protruding eyes gave the misleading impression of fear but life for six months in a whaler is not a penny arcade and physical terror never would find purchase in his psyche.

He waited. The keelies split ranks so that they were on each side with Seth facing the target straight on.

All in silence.

But this was not a seal cub.

Finally Seth spat onto the floor just beside Doyle's stout walking shoes.

'Are you accusing me of theftuous activity?' he asked, in a parody of Doyle's high tone.

'If the cap fits,' replied Arthur.

Out of the blue, both keelies moving with practised stealth slid into action, attacking simultaneously while Seth weaved this way and that searching out an opening for the iron that had magically appeared in his hand.

The knuckleduster twin received a straight left that smashed him backwards, while the other, cosh upraised, benefited from an upwards right hook as recommended by that expert on pugilism, James McLevy.

This caught the keelie in the throat, sending him spluttering to the floor, and as Doyle whirled round he smacked Seth full in the mouth with a lashed blow that loosened one of the man's few remaining teeth.

Moxey let out a strangled roar of pain and fury ready to kill the man who had done this.

Doyle moved to grab the music box but as he did so, Agnes, who was wearing a long white crushed gown with a train almost like that that of a bride that trailed over the floor, threw her skirt up in the air and jammed it over Doyle's head, enveloping him in filmy gauze which smelled of far from exotic female secretions and effectively blinded him. In this state he was wrestled to the floor and when Agnes whisked away her bridal dress, Doyle found himself looking into the bleeding face of Seth Moxey.

It was not a pretty sight.

Moxey spat out some blood, then rested the point of the iron in the soft flesh under Doyle's chin.

Arthur's arms were pinioned one on each side by the twins, with Seth kneeling on his chest crushing the breath out of him. Not a promising situation.

'Where would ye like me tae begin?' asked Seth digging the point of his iron spike cruelly into the skin.

'It matters little to me,' choked Arthur.

'Mebbye I'll split your guts, pull them out like a washing line eh?'

'Go to hell,' was the defiant response.

A wild light came into Moxey's eyes; he lifted the spike till it hung directly above Conan Doyle's face.

Agnes was alarmed; she knew her man well and had no wish to see him kill without profit.

'Let him be, my bonny boy,' she advised. 'Take his money and kick his backside out of here.'

The barman opened his mouth to agree. He had watched all proceedings with a jaundiced eye but had no wish to see murder on his premises. Business was slack enough. Then he observed something behind the gathering that sent him back to wiping at the dirty glasses with an equally dirty cloth.

'Too late,' replied Seth, prising the loose molar out with his tongue and spitting it to the floor. 'I have incurred a loss. Tooth for a tooth.'

He gazed into Doyle's eyes and lifted the spike higher so that it hung as Excalibur in the tobacco smoke that swirled around like mist hanging over the Dozmary Pool.

But there was no Lady of the Lake on hand and Conan Doyle realised with a sickening thud that this was not some ebullient adventure. This was the real world.

For a moment the face of Sophia Adler flashed into his mind. Would he be a voice in her mind from the dead? Would she close her eyes in the shared experience of a departed soul? Would he reach out to her for comfort?

A trickle of blood ran from the corner of Seth's mouth, giving him the appearance of a Halloween vampire.

The whores had grouped behind him as if waiting to be fed. White-faced. Innocence fled.

'Kiss yer life goodbye.'

Whether Moxey intended to plunge downwards or merely meant to terrify the tethered Arthur must be left in the annals of unfinished actions because a hornbeam shaft cut through the fog of nicotine fumes and cracked upon Seth Moxey's wrist.

A howl of pain, then the circle of whores fell back to reveal behind them like a *coup de théâtre* the tall figure of Mulholland.

Beside him was James McLevy. Hands in his pockets, lips pursed, a cheery glint in his eyes.

'Aye, Seth. . .life's a bugger is it not?'

A somewhat cryptic statement that had its roots in the fact that he and Mulholland had spent all day in the station fielding increasingly urgent demands from Lieutenant Roach – himself a conduit for his own chief constable and many other Masonic worthies – regarding Gilbert Morrison, the murdered man, a member of one of the most powerful lodges in the city.

The demands were that the case be solved at once, the murderer found, order restored, God put back in his heaven and all the rest of it.

Walter Morrison had insisted that his faint was to do with a wave of grief and not the word *JUDAS*. The extant brother then took himself off, refusing to disclose any of their past commercial or personal activities, citing an unblemished life of respect for convention.

McLevy had contacted his reputable financial sources; it is amazing how many skeletons rattle around inside the cupboards of certain bankers of high standing.

The inspector was familiar with these restless bones and knew how to play an inviting tune upon them.

Only one thing emerged that he did not know already.

He was confirmed in the particulars of the brothers being ruthless, treacherous and duplicitous in dealings but that was only to be expected in business.

Now they were of a solid – well, perhaps the beheaded Gilbert lacked a certain density – financial standing, but some eighteen years previous, when they were cutting their teeth in the maritime market, there had been rumours of an overextension of capital.

However, a large amount of cash had of a sudden been brandished at all and sundry, putting paid to vile rumour.

Where this pecuniary injection had its origin no-one knew, but McLevy's informant was adamant that it had not come from any of the known Edinburgh financial institutions.

A long time ago. A distant mystery. But somewhere at the back of the inspector's mind, a vague pattern was forming.

When it would emerge at the front, however, was another matter.

In the meantime, on the seamier side of things, it had been confirmed through McLevy's street sources that Gilbert was indeed fond of the laying on of quirt as opposed to hands, and found his predilection indulged at the hotel of the Countess.

Might that be the reason for murder? A vengeful father, brother, lover? But what was that father, brother, lover doing letting the female cause for his reprisal suffer such a whipping in the first place?

McLevy's head had been birling with it all so he had hauled Mulholland out on the saunter round the docks, because he was mindful yet that the wee acid pourer was still on the loose and he desired to keep tabs on the streets, though also thus avoiding his lieutenant's reproachful presence.

He and the constable had discussed the case to and fro, up and down as they trawled the docks but could advance the investigation no further.

Ergo he was inwardly delighted when he heard clamour from the Foul Anchor, slid in unnoticed save by the barman through the door, crept up behind the backs of the watching whores and then signalled Mulholland to do his stuff.

Which he did.

As Moxey rolled cursing away to scrabble after the spike which had flown off to land at the foot of the bar counter, the policemen observed in some surprise that the gang's intended victim was none other than Big Arthur.

'This mannie gets around,' said McLevy.

'Like the plague,' was Mulholland's terse response.

They hauled the shaken Doyle to his feet just as two other members of the gang emerged from a side room, woken from their slumbers by the howls of Seth.

That left five against three, not counting the women.

A species, Conan Doyle might counsel from recent experience, you should never overlook.

A veil may be drawn over most of the consequent conflict save that it consisted of Mulholland's stick whirling like a dervish, Doyle's fists flying, the fear that had pumped through his system now a galvanising force, and McLevy's stalking of Seth Moxey, tripping one of the twins *en passant* so that he ran headlong into a beefy embrace from Conan Doyle that cracked his ribs.

Agnes tried to sneak up once more, skirts at the ready, but Mulholland, who had been raised in the school of hard knocks and disregard for the delicate female, poked her sharply in the breadbasket with the end of his stick and she fell back into a chair gasping for breath.

The other two women left well alone and in quick time the gang were a groaning heap upon the scabby floor.

Only Moxey remained, spike pointing towards McLevy in his weaker hand, the other hanging uselessly by his side.

'I'll have your wee pikey,' said McLevy.

'Come and get it,' replied Seth.

'As you will.'

Conan Doyle had sharp eyesight honed at sea but the movement that followed was so fast that it became a blur like a flying fish.

In one motion McLevy's hand shot out to grasp the wrist of Moxey just above the held spike and then jerked him off balance. The inspector, using himself as a fulcrum, heaved the man round in a circle, spinning faster and faster until Seth Moxey was a helpless victim of centrifugal force.

Finally McLevy stopped. Let go. And waited.

Seth managed one faltering step before vertigo took over and he pitched forward to join the heap upon the floor.

Miraculously the spike had transferred to McLevy's hand during this reel of unleashed criminality and he popped it into the inside pocket of his coat with a flourish.

'No need for violence,' he announced to one and all. 'I am a great believer in soft procedure.'

Mulholland sniffed dubiously, having witnessed the opposite behaviour many times from his inspector.

'If I may be so bold, Mister Doyle,' McLevy asked, benignly, 'what was the cause of this unseemly rammy?'

Doyle pointed towards the music box, which had been knocked off the table to lie somewhat mangled on the floor, Mulholland having stood upon it in pursuit of one of the twins.

'It plays "Sweet Afton",' Arthur declared solemnly.

McLevy nodded as if all made sense then picked up the damaged box. The workings had spilled out of its innards though the winding key was yet intact.

'I fear it may have warbled its last note,' he muttered, before stooping to haul Moxey up by the hair in spite of his avowed procedural moderation.

'Ye made a heavy lift frae Bonnington Road,' he growled. 'Where is your stash?'

'Right up my backside,' Seth replied, his face creased in agony. 'Welcome tae look.'

McLevy slammed him down again and bent his gaze upon the women.

'Where is it, Agnes? We'll find it anyhow but at least I can tell the judge ye showed willing.'

Her face was like stone but behind the woman in her faded wedding gown, Sadie Shields, hoping for leniency of sorts, jerked her head to indicate a door at the back where the gang had its quarters.

The inspector nodded and whistled to himself, then grinned happily at Conan Doyle.

'Ye brought me good fortune, Mister Doyle,' he said. 'I've been after this rabble for many a year and now we have the entirety.'

'Not all,' replied Doyle. 'There was one more man at the table, and he is gone.'

The barman felt it was time he made a contribution to affairs.

'He's no' of the family,' he offered. 'Ran out the back door.'

Moxey's head whipped painfully round and his lips parted in a snarl.

Silver Samuel was indeed gone.

And so was the mother's brooch.

23

The butcher looked for his knife,
when he had it in his mouth.

Roxburghe Ballads

Jean Brash hesitated for a moment, then having knocked at the
door to no response, pushed gently. It swung open. She took a
quick, almost guilty, glance up and down the street, then slipped
inside.

She found herself in a long gloomy hall with a sliver of light
coming from a door, slightly ajar, at the opposite end from where
she stood.

Deep breath. Her mind flipped back to the hand-delivered letter she had received that afternoon.

Mistress Brash,

*I apologise for my behaviour of last night but I was sore enraged at the
injustice. I know I am headstrong but I am also honest and I can assure you
that money was robbed from me in your establishment. I have made enquiries with some of your other clients, men of my own stamp, and I have irrefutable proof that some of your girls are operating behind your back. Money
has been taken and you stand to lose much because of it. Perhaps someone
is plotting against you? I do not know but if you will visit me at the hour of
six this evening, 32 Iona Street, I will show you the evidence and explain my
suspicions. Come alone, and tell no-one, for there is no-one you can trust.*

Yours in truth,

Logan Galloway

Hannah Semple, the only person Jean held in credence on this
earth was at the safe house by Leith Links, the giant Angus to
hand, making ready to scour the streets with their people once
more to find the acid-pourer.

Jean's reasoning was that the little swine would not show his
face during the day and she had decided to stay at the Just Land
to await results, part because she was too restless to sit on her

backside and part because she did not want another incident like the Galloway one.

Then lo and behold the man himself had sent a missive.

And it chimed with some uneasy feelings that had been nagging away at her since this war with the Countess had begun.

Who could she really trust at the bitter end?

Once before she had let slip the reins of the bawdy-hoose when her heart had been usurped by an unscrupulous man who had twisted her like a fool.

Never again.

She had betrayed herself.

But what if this time it was another agent?

Jessie Nairn, for instance? Or was that too obvious? She had taken in a bunch of new magpies recently, wear and tear the cause. What if the Countess had been plotting ahead, and put her own agents inside to burrow and destroy from inwards like a worm in the gut? To steal? To destroy?

A bawdy-hoose, not unlike a merchant bank, stands or falls by reputation.

Jean had been queen bee for a long time and now there was another on the scene.

Had she grown too indolent, soft, lost her edge?

So she now found herself walking down the shadowed hall to prove or disprove all the thoughts milling round in her mind.

She called out softly, one hand inside her reticule firmly grasped upon her surgeon's knife.

'Mister Galloway? If you are present, step forward. Let us make peace and parley.'

No answer. She was not afraid. The man was a pipsqueak. But did he have a tale to tell?

She pushed at the partly opened door and it swung inwards to disclose a form wedged against the window, facing away from her. The room was in semi-darkness and the figure barely outlined by the light from outside but it seemed to be Logan Galloway, hands pressed up against the sill as if to steady himself.

Jean stepped in. Hand with the knife now by her side. A girl can't be too careful.

'Mister Galloway? You're away in the wrong direction. I am here, sir. Ready to attend your proof.'

He made no response, stubbornly gazing out of the window as if deaf to her words.

'Are you in the huff, Mister Galloway?'

Having said this, Jean stepped up with the intention to swing him round by the shoulder.

As she did so, there was a sharp movement behind her and a sudden accurate blow, crisply delivered, separated her from consciousness.

She fell to the floor, the knife in her outflung hand.

A girl can't be too careful.

Not long after, Constable Ballantyne marched up Iona Street modestly aware that he was on time for his new beat, the previous constable having reported sick.

Ballantyne had jumped at the chance to take the man's place and Lieutenant Roach, in the absence of his inspector, an absence that galled the good man no end, had granted permission with the proviso that the young constable held on firmly to his whistle.

However, such mistakes were in the past.

A seasoned campaigner.

Had he not already seen a corpse and only boaked the once?

So far, little of consequence, his mere presence on the streets giving the potential lawbreakers something to fear.

He checked the timepiece his mother had given him to celebrate his joining the ranks of law and order some three years before.

Half past the evening hour of six, precisely correct for the patrol; he had been given the times that the other officer, now sick of some palsy but a man to whom punctuality was God, adhered to without fail.

Time now to turn and make his way back home, to the end of this street and then right down Leith Walk itself, a proud but not prideful representative of authority in action.

A missile of some sort struck his official helmet with enough force to make his ears ring and what sounded like a snigger disturbed the stately calm of his patrol.

Ballantyne whipped round but there was nothing to be seen except. . . Now his hawklike eyes fixed upon an open door which had escaped his earlier scrutiny.

It swung slightly as if a malefactor had perhaps just dashed inside.

Ballantyne noted the number. Thirty-two. It would be in his report.

He took a firm grip of his now-drawn truncheon and followed the path of another pilgrim who had taken the same route some time previous.

Down the same gloomy corridor, heart pumping, not daring to say a word lest it come out a wee bit squeaky.

Pushed at the same partly opened door and walked inside.

There was enough light from the moon to let Ballantyne come to certain conclusions.

For the moment it was an assumption to be verified but it forced a gasp of strange exultation from his lips. It was a policeman's dream.

A tableau arranged in tasteful fashion; no gobbets of gore to spoil the elegant lines, save for one outstretched hand bearing traces of what looked like blood.

'Dead bodies,' announced Constable Ballantyne in wonder to himself. 'A' over the place.'

24

Oh Lady! we receive but what we give,
And in our life alone does Nature live.
SAMUEL TAYLOR COLERIDGE, 'Dejection: an Ode'

Samuel Grant might cheerfully have strangled his beloved Muriel but true love has ever steered between the rocks of passion and exasperation.

The boat had navigated towards vexation at her reaction to his proffered gift.

He had expected little cries of delight translating into a sidelong glance towards the room where the bouncier mattress had its domain. However in his haste, Samuel had reckoned without his banging upon the door to be answered by a squat purposeful little maid who looked at his form as if a stray dog had fetched him up upon the doorstep.

Upon his insistence she had ferried him to her mistress who was sitting somewhat listlessly in the drawing room.

Her demeanour changed at the sight of him as if a bumblebee had shot up her skirts. Ellen the maid was shooed from the room and once Muriel was certain the coast was clear, she, in nothing that could be mistaken for loving tones, hissed, 'What in God's name are you doing here?'

Samuel caught sight of himself in a cunningly sited mirror and realised that his normal faultless presentation was a trifle compromised.

The silver hair was standing on end, his clothes dishevelled; the canary yellow neckerchief had worked loose from its moorings and was hanging limply over the lapels of his jacket as if signalling quarantine.

All this of course the result of his headlong rush after grabbing the prize while Seth and the giant sailor had got to grips and given Samuel the chance to prove a hero.

At a cost.

All he could hope for was that Moxey would somehow be debilitated by the giant and either die or lose his memory.

None such very likely.

But in the meantime he might raise the money, with a little contribution from his beloved Muriel, and offer Seth enough to avoid his vengeance.

Her reaction, however, after he had related a rather altered version of his daring deeds, was not hopeful.

'How much did you pay this man?'

'Five pounds, Moumou.'

'Please don't call me inappropriate endearments,' she hissed once again. 'The maid might listen by the door.'

Samuel could not have cared less. It was dawning on him that he had risked his neck for next to nothing.

'And where did you meet him?'

'In a tavern,' he muttered to her formal tones.

Muriel gazed at the brooch in her hand. It certainly appeared unscathed though she would give it a good clean.

'And you wish me to reimburse you, sir?'

'It is a matter of life and death,' Samuel replied loudly, growing heartily sick of the charade. 'And I might remind you, madam, that the life might be yours and the death mine.'

There was enough underlying truth in his tone that her face softened and she almost forgave him the intrusion that shrieked to a watching neighbour or any acquaintance of Ellen's who might be a confidante, that Mistress Grierson had entertained a man with a loose cravat.

Almost.

But it is a sad fact that just when a man thinks a woman has run out of foolish moves, she can always find another.

'What about the rest?' she asked.

'Whit?'

'The rest of my stolen valuables?'

'*Whit?*'

This came out in a strangled indignant yelp and might surely have warned Muriel that a limit had been reached but by now she had the bit between her teeth and perhaps earlier misgivings about the company Samuel kept had resurfaced.

'Ye said ye didnae care about such!'

Samuel glared at her and she glared back, forgetting that the imaginary maid might be pressing her avid ear against the keyhole.

'*Relatively*, I did not care,' she replied, proving the adage that to argue with women is to pass water in a howling gale. 'And what of the music box?'

'It was busy,' he retorted sullenly.

'Busy?'

Again they locked eyes and it is possible that given a passage of time, her lips may have quirked in humour at his wild hair and askew neckwear like a grumpy little boy at a birthday party; he may have, on seeing this, risked sweeping her into his arms, a breathless kiss, a tremor in the limbs, five pounds pressed in his hands along with softer rewards, a heroic action recognised, receiving due adulation.

All this was possible, but every moment has a wealth of possibilities only one of which is manifested in the given world. Unfortunately, what came was not romantic recompense.

Three loud bangs at the door. Samuel knew in his bones that the law was a-calling.

He suddenly grabbed Muriel close anyway and gave her a resounding buss full on the lips.

'Keep them occupied,' said he, and darted out into the garden through the French windows.

Samuel suddenly felt heroic again; that kiss had done wonders. He measured the wall that led to freedom with a cool eye. There was a garden table nearby and he hauled it across so that the edge crunched to the wall, clambered aboard and parked his belly on the top then lowered his legs over the other side, preparing to drop.

Two hands seized his ankles.

'Ye'll do yerself a mischief, Samuel,' said James McLevy. 'Let me lower ye down like a king in state.'

When the inspector hauled Samuel round the front and the door was hammered once again, the wee maid Ellen opened up with a frown to see more traffic passing through.

'Like Waverley Station,' she announced.

'Indeed you have it, Ellen,' said McLevy breezily. 'I cannot argue the point but where would we be without the trains?'

Ellen noted the firm grasp McLevy had on Samuel's arm just above the elbow.

'Ye'll know yer way,' she said dourly.

'Oh, lead me on,' the inspector replied. 'A guide, a buckler and example.'

This quote from Burns sailed over Ellen's head but as she marched grimly up the hall followed by the two, a few random memories from the visit she'd paid to her mother the night before came into her mind.

He lived with his Auntie Jean because his own mother had taken her life, said Ellen's ma, her eyes round with horror at the recollection.

Cut the throat across with her sharp scissors, she being a dressmaker by trade. The reason never known but madness hinted. The boy had found her slumped in her recess bed and sat there for hours, surrounded by blood and death.

Nae wonder he became whit he is, thought Ellen.

She led them into the drawing room where her mistress stood stiffly beside an equally uncomfortable Conan Doyle, made a brief curtsey and got to hell out of there.

Ellen was devoid of two character traits that make up a strong part of the Scots nature.

Nosiness and malice.

She was content to leave what was not her business to remain so on the principle of *whit ye don't know doesnae dae ye damage*, and as a consequence of that contentedness found herself free from envy and its malicious offshoots.

But she still did not get out the door untrammelled.

'Jist before ye depart, Ellen Girvan, have ye seen this man before?'

The maid turned slowly. So the bugger knew her all the time, otherwise why remember her given name?

In fact it had only come into McLevy's mind when she'd opened up the door; something in the cast of her features and the way she had glowered at him brought to mind a similar face from childhood.

Looking across the cobbled square at him one day when he had just kicked hell out of a thug who had persecuted him for a deal of his young life.

So he had taken a flyer and was gratified to see the hit; a reputation for omniscience does a policeman no harm.

'Aye, I've seen him,' Ellen said, staring more at the inspector than Samuel. 'A wee time ago at the door.'

'Never before that?'

Ellen could *almost* swear she had observed the man loitering in the street when she left on her weekly visit to her mother but she only operated on conviction. She had also noted a twinkle in Muriel's eye of late and a loose vivacity in her movements. *But whit ye don't know...*

'Not to my decent knowledge,' she responded carefully.

McLevy thought to push it but there was a flinty cast to Ellen's face that dissuaded him from the effort.

'Are ye going to make us any hot beverage?' he asked instead.

'It wisnae in my mind.'

Ellen looked at her mistress who gazed downwards and the maid took that for a negative.

She left.

Samuel had not said a word.

Conan Doyle for once had nothing to deduct.

McLevy had sent him on to batter at the door and sneaked off round the side with productive results but Arthur had the feeling he had been used as a decoy of sorts.

A disgruntled Constable Mulholland, who was beginning to regard Conan Doyle with jaundiced eye, had been dispatched to the station with a pack of summoned helpers to transport the Moxey gang.

But Seth had lost no time in pointing a dislocated finger towards a certain direction; there being no honour amongst thieves and he being foul indignant at someone stealing his hard-earned lift.

The constable was not best pleased at being left out of the action but McLevy persuaded him that he was essential for safe transport of the gang. Besides Doyle might be useful because of his local knowledge.

It amused McLevy to see the giant so discomfited by personal relationships. That's why McLevy, in the main, tried very hard not to have them.

Deduction has its drawbacks.

'Mistress Grierson, can you enlighten us as to your dealings with this fellow?'

A simple enough question, but a nest of vipers. Silver Samuel, according to Seth, had supplied the knowledge for the lift and danced the Reels o' Bogie with the lusty widow.

Muriel swallowed hard but before she might formulate a response Samuel burst into speech.

'Easy enough,' he declared. 'Moxey made vaunt tae me where he had thieved a brooch.'

Samuel waved his free hand in Doyle's direction.

'When that big hooligan started a rammy, I took my chance, thieved it in turn and came here to sell it back.'

'Is this true?' asked the inspector.

Muriel closed her eyes and nodded.

'Where is the brooch now?'

She brought her hand slowly from a pocket in her dress and displayed the cause of all these shenanigans.

'Did you pay for such?'

'We were interrupted,' said Samuel quickly.

McLevy carried on looking at Muriel and was rewarded by a shake of the head.

'Then why leave it?' he asked Samuel with a mean glint in his eye. The inspector didn't need much in the way of deduction to smell a rat up a drainpipe somewhere.

'As I tellt ye,' Samuel offered defiantly. 'We were interrupted. I ran for my life.'

'And this is the first and only time you have seen this man, Mistress Grierson? You have never met him previous?'

To this query of the inspector's Muriel, after gazing into the eyes of a person who had hazarded his very existence to preserve her name, shook her head much after the manner of St Peter in the garden.

Conan Doyle, who had been still as a statue during all this, prayed inwardly that McLevy would not repeat what the young man earnestly hoped were the calumnies that Moxey had disgorged.

'And you, Silver Sam, this is your first visit here?'

'Aye. And I wish I'd never set foot.'

The inspector let out a sudden bark of laughter.

'So be it. But ye surprise me, Samuel. You're more in the mode of turning some daft woman's head wi' your charms then living free and easy. This is not your style.'

Samuel flushed and bit his lip.

Muriel's face drained of colour.

McLevy fished in his pocket and produced the crumpled music box.

'We found the Moxey gang's stash but no trace of your other belongings,' he remarked genially to Muriel, 'save this wounded soldier.'

He twisted the key and the melody began to play brokenly, notes missing like Moxey's teeth, the melancholy tune rendered even more heartbreaking by the failure to sustain its rightful pitch.

The inspector put it on a nearby table and stepped back to delve in his pocket for the restrainers that he planned to fit around Samuel's wrists.

The other three figures, in a strange repeat of the hell-hags in the tavern, shifted slightly while the music traced a crippled path around them, then Conan Doyle stood back and it was only Muriel and Silver Samuel who remained in the dance.

Her eyes were shining with a feeling within and his were full of pain.

Late-discovered love. What a bugger it can be.

'My Mary's asleep by thy murmuring stream
Flow gently, sweet Afton, disturb not her dream.'

25

Weep no more, lady, weep no more,
thy sorrow is in vain;
For violets plucked, the sweetest showers
Will ne'er make grow again.

ANONYMOUS, 'The Friar of Orders Gray'

Sophia Adler sat across the room from the two men and wondered why a memory from long ago had flashed a picture into her mind.

Her Uncle Bartholomew, smelling of strong tobacco, lifted her up into his arms and thrust her face into the magnolia blossom of a young tree. It was the middle of April, not long before her eighth birthday and she was giddy with excitement.

The sweet smell of the flowers, safely ensconced in their leathery green leaves, filled her very soul with a wild longing for something far beyond this existence.

'Higher! *Higher!*' she commanded and, grinning like a racoon, cigar clenched between his teeth, he thrust her up to the very limit of his powerful arms.

And there she lost herself.

Exultant.

That was before the mother's betrayal of honour. Seven years later. In front of her daughter's eyes.

Now, in an Edinburgh hotel room, with subdued pale pastels unlike the vivid colours of childhood, and a leaden sky outside which signalled clear blue was a distant recollection along with a yellow sun, she found herself gazing at Inspector James McLevy, wondering at the many paths that must have led the two of them into each other's orbit.

For make no mistake, this was a dangerous man. The eyes slate-grey and wolf-like stared back into hers without the usual evasions of protocol.

He just. . .*looked*. Dispassionate. Observing. Perfectly still within. Nothing to prove.

Not unlike herself.

For McLevy's part he, behind the deadpan exterior, was in the not uncommon state of having the voice of reason and authority blethering in one ear, and a slice of intuition that had no basis in East of Scotland pragmatism whispering in the other about some strange force field where unseen lines, like some sort of invisible web, connect all events, murderous and otherwise.

A sort of forensic mesmerism perhaps.

While taking Silver Samuel back to the station he had run into Sergeant Murdoch in the street, on his way back from a colleague's funeral.

A fellow sergeant. All the more to be mourned.

But Murdoch did not partake of the demon drink. So while the rest of the mourners, in the main from Haymarket where the dead man had his station, got lashed into the funeral meats and decent whisky, Murdoch pressed the widow's hand in sympathy and left.

McLevy took it as an omen. Murdoch in motion was like the sighting of a rare comet blazing through the heavens.

He shovelled the manacled Samuel onto the solemn-faced sergeant and bade him escort the prisoner to the cells where the inspector, on his return, would fill in the paperwork and all would be well with the known world.

What he did not mention was that Lieutenant Roach, already no doubt unimpressed by the detritus of the Moxey gang, would be likewise indifferent to Samuel's arrival; small fry while more murderous and bigger fish swam free.

He would also be tired of receiving various delegations from his inspector like some sort of offering from a papal legate.

There would be hell to pay when he showed his face.

'Tell him I'm on the case!' McLevy bawled as he and Conan Doyle left the statuesque figures of sergeant and prisoner. 'On the case!'

But was he? Or did he just, like many a married man, not want to find his way back home? Roach taking the part of the wife on the doorstep, rolling pin to hand?

Doyle had been pressing, as they marched down the street with the withdrawn Samuel in tow, attracting many passing curious glances which young Arthur rather revelled in, for an opportunity to accompany McLevy on a more demanding challenge – he, the great deductor having helped solve this one in the twinkling of an eye.

The inspector, his mind full of the problem of how to unravel *The Riddle of the Battered Mason*, muttered out a few details of the homicide investigation including at a final stroke the name of the murder victim.

No great confidentiality breached here; this would be in the newspaper soon enough, though Roach would try to keep it all under the carpet as long as he could in the hope that crime and solution appear on the same page.

McLevy doubted that. Such only occurred in cheap fiction. Easy in an armchair.

Doyle, after his initial shock, was thrilled by the gory details and fired questions right, left and centre.

His medical enthusiasm for the bloody entrails of the crime amused McLevy and lifted his spirits a little, for in truth he, at this juncture, had no route that opened out onto the killer. He needed something to break for cover.

The inspector teased the young man by withholding the name of Gilbert Morrison, revealing it at the end with a flourish as if he had accomplished some triumph, but Doyle, not for the first time, provided a surprise.

And what he said, face lit up with an infectious grin, was what had brought McLevy, after the felicitous dumping of Samuel, to the George Hotel.

To request an audience with Sophie Adler in his guise of investigating officer.

A slice of intuition.

Or just catching at a straw?

Conan Doyle, on the other hand, was counting his good fortune to be in her presence so unexpectedly soon for the favourable reply had come straight back. She had no audience that night and, even better, when they arrived at her door, Magnus Bannerman was notable by his absence.

The man had been pleasant enough but the younger man sensed a rival and a certain veiled contempt.

Many people took Doyle's boisterous personality at face value and that was their mistake.

Sophia looked wan but composed. Some of the white-blonde hair escaped in wisps that clung to her delicate neck. Pretty as a picture.

She was once again wearing a simple gown, pale lilac in colour, which accentuated her youthful appearance and tenuous fragility.

Introductions made, politesse observed, all parties seated, McLevy got stuck in.

'In your wee soirée last night, Mister Doyle here tells me you picked out a member of the audience and near choked at the sight of him.'

'These were not my words,' protested Doyle.

She smiled reassuringly at him but said nothing.

'Ye pointed at him. A shilpit individual.'

'Ah yes. I remember now.' Sophia nodded slowly.

She rose from her chair and walked to the window to stare out at the back of the hotel building where the laundry rooms, kitchens and servant's quarters lay.

Sophia had made it her business to spy out the lie of the land down there for her own reasons.

Magnus had the better view of the street but she enjoyed listening to the murmur of activity below, the occasional clatter of a plate and hastily stifled laughter.

Voices everywhere.

'Do you believe in other worlds, inspector? A supra-normal plane where other forces exist and the spirits of the dead wander like lost children?'

She spoke formally, as if laying an injunction upon the policeman.

Now it was McLevy's turn for silence. His face betrayed nothing. Doyle kept his eyes fixed upon Sophia as if at any moment a great mystery was about to be revealed.

'An existence beyond ours,' she continued more simply. 'After death. Yet connected. A force like magnetism. Flows like blood around us all. We bathe in the same stream.'

McLevy surprised Doyle by nodding slowly, his face grave and thoughtful.

'I know that dreams would indicate there's more tae life than meets the eye. My mind is open.'

This seemed to satisfy her that she would not be casting her pearls before the swinish embodiment of a legal system that believed most spirits were in a brandy bottle.

'The man last night. I remember him well. His face. It was not one of my voices but now and then, a vision comes. A dark visitation. It shakes me to the very core.'

McLevy had sudden recall of the figure ahead of him in the tunnel and felt a weird tremor.

He shook it off and got to business.

'Whit did you see?'

'A skull. I looked at his face and saw a skull.'

'Surely a portent of death?' Doyle interjected, a little miffed that these two had almost excluded him from the exchange and eager to embrace the idea that Sophia had, in some way, foreseen the future.

The inspector shot the young man a warning glance. The murder was his to reveal and in his own good time.

'Anything else?' asked McLevy.

'Such as?' Sophia responded.

They now, despite Doyle's effortful intervention, were locked into each other's gaze as if some unseen battle were taking place. Perhaps a battle of wills, of mental force, or even attraction, as one subtle psyche probed into the other.

'A word, say. Written in blood.'

McLevy observed her violet eyes to darken the merest touch then she slowly shook her head.

'I saw a skull. No flesh. Just bone.'

'No word upon a wall?'

'Words are cheap.'

This cryptic reply would seem to signal conclusion to that line of questioning, so he shifted ground slightly.

'According to Mister Doyle, you screamed aloud?'

'I did.'

'Why?'

'As I said, I was shaken.'

'Surely you have seen such visions before? Skull and crossbones?'

'No. Never. Not of that kind.'

'Where did you meet this man?'

'I had never met him. Until last night.'

To the watching Doyle it seemed that the tenor of the exchange had almost become that of interrogation but he supposed that must be the nature of a policeman.

Let nothing lie at peace.

'And whit do ye conclude from this bony apparition?'

A faint smile came to her lips at the deliberate obtuseness of his question.

'As Mister Doyle remarked. Death, I suppose.'

Arthur was beginning to feel like some sort of reference point on the map of Edinburgh.

'And you saw nothing else?'

Sophia raised her hands for a moment then let them fall to clasp each other in a graceful enfolding.

'My gift is both a blessing and a curse, inspector. It is not clarity but confusion. When I am in a state of such. . .invasion, my mind is almost overcome.'

For a moment her voice trembled and she looked towards Doyle whose heart lifted in response. Then she turned back to the obdurate figure still attending answer.

'As I say, it was a confusion but behind the skull, in a terrible darkness – though this may not be part, it may be from some other force that was present – I saw a man, far away, lying in a pool of blood.'

Doyle stiffened. McLevy's face was unchanged.

'Did ye see the face?'

'No. Only the body. And the blood.'

'In a room? A fireplace to hand?'

'No. In the open. At night. On the street. On stone.'

No-one ever tells *all* of the truth, we hold back a little as an obedient child, in some cultures, will keep a morsel of food aside on their plate for God.

But the inspector reckoned that Sophia had put enough in to get a little back.

'The man you saw was called Gilbert Morrison. He was murdered late last night, his head smashed by a heavy iron poker.'

A sardonic smile came to McLevy's lips.

'He is in fragments of blood and bone. The poker is still intact. The nature of iron.'

Sophia did not respond at first to the bleak statement.

'That is a cruel fate,' she murmured finally.

'Aye. There's nae justice.'

'It would seem so.'

For a moment her face seemed troubled and she glanced over at Doyle whose heart lifted once more at the vulnerable creature before him. McLevy, on the other hand, didn't give a damn. There was something about her containment...an almost sensual invitation.

He had been close quarters with many attractive and dangerous women but this one was in a class of her own.

Back to business.

'It's a pity your vision didnae include a wee keek at the murderer, save me a deal o' time and trouble.'

'I saw nothing more than what I have told you. A skeleton face.'

'Uhuh?'

For a moment they stood in silence then a sudden screech from outside the window made them all jump.

A seagull had swooped down to grab a piece of crust thrown from the kitchen below. It rose triumphantly into the air, white bread clutched in its orange talons, and flapped away into the dull sky.

Sophia shook her head as if trying to break free from her inward thoughts. She saw the anxious look on Doyle's face and spoke directly to him.

'You are a kind person, Mister Doyle,' she said, quite out of the blue.

'I try to be,' he said in some confusion, the tips of his large ears becoming tinged with colour.

'It is a rare quality,' Sophia smiled.

Then she turned once more to McLevy, who in no way qualified for similar approbation.

'I am sorry I cannot help you further, inspector. I have nothing more to add. Fate is cruel.'

McLevy accepted this implicit dismissal with a cheerful nod, and banged his hands together.

'Ach well, never mind. I will bring the killer tae justice and watch the judge pit on the black cap.'

He let out a harsh whoop of laughter.

'Then I'll watch him dance the Perth two-step on the hangman's rope. The rewards of my chosen profession.'

Doyle recognised the technique employed.

An apparent mercurial shift of behaviour at times verging on direct brutality; all to disguise the fact that behind all this was a probing intelligence of intent.

Designed to keep the suspect on the hop.

Doyle would keep that in mind for future reference.

But surely Sophia was not under suspicion?

Or was everyone so in James McLevy's eyes?

The man himself turned as if to go and then shot out a sudden question at Sophia.

'Whit does Judas mean tae you?'

She took a breath and for the first time seemed a little flustered.

'I suppose. . .the betrayer of a good man. Lord Jesus.'

'Aye, the Bible tells us so. That was the word on the wall. In blood. Why would it be written there, d'ye think?'

'Those who are betrayed seek vengeance,' she answered slowly.

'My thought precisely!'

The inspector beamed at Conan Doyle as if he was also in agreement.

'Somewhere in Gilbert Morrison's past lies the reason for his present condition, which is in smithereens.'

McLevy was the only one who seemed to find relish at this prospect. He nodded goodbye to Sophia and jerked his head at Doyle as a sign to leave.

As the young man replaced his sailor's cap – McLevy as usual had kept on his low-brimmed bowler – Sophia noticed something which set her to a frown of concern.

'You have a mark, Mister Doyle,' she said.

Indeed, where Seth Moxey had dug his iron spike into the neck, the flesh was raw and inflamed with a trickle of dried blood, which had come to a discreet stop just short of his collar.

'It is nothing,' said Doyle in heroic mode. 'A small altercation.'

'He was for the chop,' offered McLevy. 'But we pulled him out. Jist as well. We have enough corpses to hand.'

Sophia paid no heed to this strange humour. She took out a small handkerchief, reached forward and dabbed at his neck. It was a curiously intimate gesture and McLevy wished suddenly that he had a wound to heal.

She ended her ministration under which the young man had not dared move lest it break the spell.

'You must take care, Mister Doyle.'

'I will try my best, Miss Adler.'

Arthur bowed over the hand she extended, like a braw gallant. He wished tremendously to ask her for a rendezvous with a more pleasant subject matter but found McLevy's presence inhibiting to a marked degree.

He would return.

Conan Doyle thought of signalling this with a glance but fearing he might resemble an idiot, and seeing a glint of humour in her eyes, contented himself with backing away.

The space he left was filled with James McLevy who had an odd smile upon his lips as if he and Sophia would also meet again.

'When is your next soirée?' he asked.

'Two nights hence. At the Tanfield Hall, I believe.'

McLevy, who had already seen the posters and knew this well, affected surprise.

'Tanfield Hall? That's a space tae fill.'

'It is already sold out.'

'I have my ticket in advance,' Conan Doyle said proudly.

'Not me,' said McLevy. 'I never know the future.'

'I may leave you one, if you wish,' Sophia offered.

'A future?'

'A ticket. At the box office.'

'That's very nice,' was the reply. 'Put it under *James McLevy – Inspector of Police.*'

Something in his tone brought her eyes to focus on his. A level stare. Violet to slate-grey. Unflinching both.

'I was just thinking,' said he. 'If Gilbert Morrison is now in the ultramundane. Maybe you could have a wee word with him. On the quiet. In case he has a name in mind. Speir amongst the sprits, eh?'

This notion seemed to bring Sophia no pleasure.

'I have little control over what comes and goes.'

The inspector gave her one more look, then left abruptly without saying goodbye, as was sometimes his custom.

Doyle followed hastily, bidding his adieus before stopping at the door to gaze back at Sophia who had turned once more to the window.

A beautiful princess.

Waiting for a valiant knight.

By the time Doyle caught up with McLevy the inspector was half way down the stairs, whistling a snatch of 'Charlie is my Darling'.

'How old d'ye think the hizzie might be?' he asked suddenly.

Doyle frowned to hear Sophia so described.

'I would imagine. . .some twenty years. Perhaps less.'

'I would say less. Whit d'ye think of her?'

'She is. . .impressive.'

'Uhuh? So was Delilah.'

By this time they had reached the ground floor of the hotel and before Doyle could ask McLevy to explain the remark, the young man was greeted by a voice booming through the foyer.

'Mister Doyle. What brings you to these parts?'

Magnus Bannerman, large as life, resplendent in a heavy evening cape, walking stick to hand, swept off his felt hat and shook Edinburgh's misty dampness out of his hair much as a dog would after a run in the park.

His teeth flashed in a friendly grin but the eyes did not reflect such. They were watchfully appraising Conan Doyle, as one animal might another that wanders into his territory.

McLevy, for a man who took up so much room by dint of his noisy personality, had the gift of self-effacement and used it to melt aside and measure Mister Bannerman.

No doubt as to the man's power and magnetism. A few women in the foyer had already turned to register his presence. Of equal height to Doyle but seemed larger, more expansive as he shook the young man's hand in a bone-crushing grip that was returned with interest.

The inspector would put him down as a showman, a flashy Dan, a high-class version of someone who would sell fake health elixirs in the Leith Market.

But what was behind that erected façade? Often people with such a constructed personality made it so to disguise a weakness within.

McLevy was introduced and the purpose of their visit explained to Magnus who shook his head worriedly.

'Sophia lives in many worlds and needs her rest. I would be obliged next time gentlemen if you might channel any requests for an interview through my good self.'

Doyle expected McLevy to show his teeth at that statement, as in *this is a criminal investigation and you can go and whistle* but the inspector nodded docilely enough.

'Did you also see the dead man?'

'Alive. And only for a moment.'

'Recognise him – from the past, say?'

'We have no past here. Not long arrived in your fair city, sir.'

Magnus's face was open and friendly with no shadow in his eyes. His teeth flashed in a winning smile, shining like moonlit tombstones.

'I have just been to your Tanfield Hall to arrange for Sophia's mesmeric demonstration. Facilities are excellent. A splendid establishment.'

'Aye. It'll do her proud,' said McLevy dryly. 'It's where the Great Schism took place.'

'Schism?'

'The Church divided. A long story.'

'Then I must leave it with you.'

'Aye,' said McLevy dryly. 'Ye have your own religion.'

'Indeed we do. This will be the last demonstration, and the day after we will sadly take our leave from your Bonnie Scotland.'

Conan Doyle's face fell. Sophia had made no mention of such.

'Where do you travel, sir?' he asked.

'A short tour of Europe and then. . .America calls! We must spread the gospel in our own land.'

'Have ye no' spread it already?' McLevy asked.

'The seeds have been scattered. Now we must reap the harvest.'

Having divested himself of this arable metaphor and noted Doyle's crestfallen air, Bannerman shook his mane of hair with added vigour.

'Well, you must excuse me, gentlemen. Supper calls, and Miss Adler has a keen appetite which must be satisfied.'

For a moment there was the slightest hint of earthy satisfaction in his eyes and then he bounded up the hotel stairs without a backward glance, leaving a trace of the damp evening air like a spoor of sorts.

'Did ye notice aught about Mister Bannerman?' McLevy asked almost idly, while part of his senses concentrated on something else.

'I noticed many things,' replied Conan Doyle somewhat stiffly.

'I'm talking about murder.'

Doyle thought for a moment, recalling the whole exchange in every detail.

'The killing,' he said slowly. 'It hardly seemed to register with him.'

'Uhuh. Most folk, even at second or third hand, are impacted by murder, even a medicinal ghoul like yourself, but Mister Bannerman sailed on past. Unaffected. As if he'd just wiped it off the slate.'

McLevy sniffed and seemed in no hurry to move.

'What do you conclude?' asked Doyle.

'Some folk avoid death like the pestilence. Could be as simple as that.'

This cryptic statement made, McLevy began to go but Doyle had a question of his own which had been niggling at him for a length of time; but he was almost afraid of the answer and so had long delayed the query.

'What Seth Moxey implied about Mistress Grierson. Do you believe it to have credence?'

'Seth had no reason to lie. Silver Sam did. He was shielding her.'

McLevy took a last sniff.

'It's aye a mistake tae protect women. They're perfectly capable of fending for themselves.'

By this time they were out in the street and both men fell silent for different reasons.

Conan Doyle because, if what the inspector said was true, then Mister Grant had performed a gallant act, though perhaps the circumstances were a little on the sordid side. Also it meant that Muriel Grierson was part of that seamy situation.

Being around the inspector seemed to provoke complexity of motive and behaviour. Nothing could be trusted but by God it was fascinating stuff.

McLevy meantime was processing the faint odour that Magnus Bannerman had left behind with the evening damp.

A pomade with a sweet smell, though so faded it was like an impression rather than reality.

But it might possibly match the aroma he remembered from the murder scene.

And Bannerman's hair was dark in colour. That matched also. And long. You could even say wavy.

Nothing you might lay before a judge, and the faintest of indicators; most likely a figment of wishful imagination.

A straw in the wind.

But he began to whistle nevertheless as he and Big Arthur walked down the street together.

Who knows? This large lump beside him might yet be a lucky charm.

'Charlie is my darling, the young Chevalier.'

26

A strong nor-easter's blowing, Bill;
Hark! Don't ye hear it blow now!
Lord help 'em, how I pities them
Unhappy folks on shore now!

WILLIAM PITT, 'The Sailor's Consolation'

Lieutenant Roach was waiting like a lighthouse keeper when McLevy walked slowly into the station.

The inspector had much on his mind. Fragments of thought, half-remembered scraps of conversation, an odd nagging feeling that he had missed something somewhere, some connection. But his mind was cloudy, possibly to do with the fact that he had forgotten to eat since his breakfast cup of coffee. The inspector had been tempted to call in at his favourite tavern the Auld Ship for a bowl of sheep's heid broth but denied himself the relief because he felt he had prevaricated long enough.

Accordingly he ignored his rumbling belly, bade goodbye to Conan Doyle, promising the great deductor that he would keep him in mind for future developments or if he ran out of inspiration, and trudged back to face the music.

The tune was not as expected.

Roach being often dragged to the opera by his culture fanatic of a wife, McLevy had braced himself for a full-blooded aria of remonstrance backed up by a wailing chorus of constables.

But no such thing.

In fact a wintry smile of sorts, which immediately alerted the inspector that something was lurking.

Something up the sleeve.

'Well, well,' Roach announced to the world at large. 'The native returns. Wandering Willie.'

A reference to Willie Steenson, the blind fiddler who narrates the tale in *Redgauntlet*. A story of abject failure; Bonnie Prince Charlie and the Jacobites scarcely covering themselves in glory.

'It aye amazes me how familiar you are wi' the works of Wattie Scott, sir. I bow before such erudition.'

'Sir Walter Scott paid his debts and did his bounden duty,' replied Roach to the other's sally. 'Would that we all performed so.'

Out of the corner of his eye, McLevy saw Mulholland emerge from the direction of the cells and almost leap in the air at the sight of his inspector.

Was it a jump for joy? Or a guilty start?

'I take it all the prisoners I sent are locked away safe and sound?' he asked, trying to decipher the enigmatic smile on his lieutenant's physiognomy.

Whatever was up the sleeve was tickling the bugger pink.

'All safe and sound,' replied Roach. 'With a few additions.'

McLevy ignored the invitation to bite at that trailing hook. Mulholland had busied himself at the front desk with Sergeant Murdoch, which was an act suspicious in itself.

'Ye didnae lodge Samuel Grant wi' the Moxey gang, I trust?'

'Not at all. Constable Mulholland and I, in consultation with Ballantyne, have arranged the cells to what I am sure will be your satisfaction.'

'Full tae the brim, I'm sure,' muttered McLevy.

'Oh. . .always room for one more.'

Another hook unbitten.

'Well, well,' said Roach, almost hugging his thin arms about his immaculately uniformed self. 'Have you made progress with the Morrison crime?'

'Things are on the move,' McLevy said, hoping he didn't have to go into too much detail. 'Shifting.'

'I hope so,' replied Roach. 'Ballantyne!'

The lieutenant, having bawled out the name as if to draw the attention of everyone in the station, carried on talking as the constable rose above his midden of a desk like Venus from the waves and came eagerly in response, his mark of birth pulsing with excitement.

'Because inspector,' Roach continued. 'We have another murder on hand but, unlike yourself, Constable Ballantyne has brought in the guilty party.'

Ballantyne caught the tail end of that remark and didn't know where to put himself.

'Another murder?'

'The body lies in the cold room.'

Roach waved a hand at the constable as if inviting contribution.

'I was on patrol,' said Ballantyne, in what he hoped was a formal tone of report. 'I found him dead. On the floor. Wi' a knife stuck in him, inspector. Stuck right in.'

'Did you touch it?'

'Aye. I pulled it out.'

'Why?'

'In case he was still alive. Ye never know.'

McLevy closed his eyes for a moment.

'Did ye do anything else, Ballantyne?'

'Aye, I blew my whistle. Naebody stole it this time.'

Ballantyne stood proudly and the inspector just didn't have the heart to tell him that he should have left the damned knife in the damned body.

McLevy marched away from both lieutenant and constable to the cold room door which he wrenched open.

Then he stopped.

A body indeed lay on the slab.

Logan Galloway had not been handsome in life and death marked no improvement.

His long horsey countenance faced mournfully towards the ceiling, the eyes shut, the mouth closed and his thin corpse made little impression under the covering as if shrinking already into oblivion.

McLevy twitched the sheet aside to reveal a neat wound on the right hand side of the waxy body.

'Between the third and fourth back rib,' Roach announced from behind, having followed with Ballantyne tagging along. 'Straight into the heart. We await Doctor Jarvis for further elucidation.'

Jarvis was the police surgeon, a man McLevy did not admire and who more than returned the compliment.

The good doctor had examined the Morrison cadaver and come to the profound conclusion that the murder weapon was the poker and the force used excessive.

'He'll be on his second bottle of claret by this time,' McLevy rejoined, bending over the cadaver, which, other than the wound, seemed remarkably untouched.

'Drunk or sober,' Roach said grimly, his face changing to reflect an inner resolution. 'He does his job. What more can you ask of a man?'

The murder weapon lay on a shelf, also waiting for the doctor's visit. McLevy picked it up and slid the blade gently into the wound. Fitted well enough. Slid in, slid out.

Professionally executed.

As the inspector put the knife back and replaced the sheet, Roach finished his train of thought.

'And now inspector, you must do yours.'

'My job?'

'Indeed.'

'That's no great exertion. Whit I'm paid for.'

McLevy caught a glimpse of ironic amusement in his lieutenant's eyes, plus a keen curiosity as to how his inspector would play out the hand.

'Ballantyne,' said Roach, quietly, 'you have acquitted yourself well, so far as becomes an officer of the law. Now show the inspector the fruits of your labour.'

'The guilty party?' asked McLevy.

'Red-handed,' Roach replied with a lopsided smile.

McLevy followed the embarrassed Ballantyne who found the idea of leading his inspector anywhere excruciating, especially through the station where it seemed every eye was upon them.

As they passed Mulholland he murmured, 'I have the interview room entirely prepared, sir.'

The inspector grunted in annoyance. All this secrecy was getting on his nerves; who did they have in there, Pope Leo the Eighth?

He followed Ballantyne, not to the main cell quarter but to a door which led to a smaller, more secluded part of the jail for the more delicate, highborn prisoners.

Perhaps it *was* the Pope.

Ballantyne went ahead inside and then pointed vaguely at someone who rested behind bars.

'There ye are, sir,' he announced. 'Found on the scene. Recumbent.'

But unless the supreme pontiff had red hair, green eyes and female form, McLevy had guessed wrong.

'Jean Brash,' he said softly.

She had been lying down on a hard bunk, sleeping or pretending so.

The Mistress of the Just Land behind bars.

A sight to behold.

No wonder the lieutenant was laughing up his sleeve.

27

Assuredly we bring not innocence into the world, we bring impurity much rather; that which purifies us is trial, and trial is by what is contrary.

JOHN MILTON, *Aereopagetica*

McLevy and Mulholland had broken many suspects in the interview room.

It was a cold, bare chamber with incriminating smears on the walls; the only furniture was a single unsteady table, which had been hammered on so many times by the inspector's fist that the legs splayed and were almost coming off their mastic moorings.

Two chairs of the same ilk faced each other under and across the table. Jean Brash, composed enough but a little shaken from events so far, sat in one of them.

McLevy was in the other with Mulholland occupying the usual place, leaning against the wall by the door.

He and the inspector swapped positions, depending on the suspect. This time there had been a tacit assumption that McLevy would be a close, if not intimate, interrogator.

For this was no normal interrogation.

It was a well known fact that McLevy and Jean Brash were companions in coffee and rumour had it more than that in past times, though Mulholland had never seen evidence of such. But there was an undeniable connection.

She was queen bee of Leith and McLevy was king of the streets. A compromised royalty between them.

Whether love or congress had ever taken place, was no business of anyone's save the two who faced each other.

So far the interview had been conducted in a civilised manner; Jean had calmly explained the circumstances right up until, according to her version, the lights went out.

'I was hit on the head, that's all I know,' she ended the tale. Then I woke up and saw that boy's face staring down at me. Poor soul.'

'Poor soul?' asked the inspector.

'Wi' that mark on him.'

'We all have them. Some show, some don't.'

Jean made no response to that portentous statement but unconsciously her hand massaged at the nape of the neck.

'Aye, you've a wee bruise on the back belfry,' said McLevy brusquely. 'But nothing that would contradict the known facts.'

Mulholland altered position at the door as if he had received a hidden signal.

'And what are these facts?' Jean asked quietly.

'You and Galloway quarrelled, the knife was drawn, he turned to flee —'

'You stuck him in the rear side, direct into the vital organs,' Mulholland chimed in, coming away from the wall, while McLevy stood up from his chair.

A well-worn routine but no less effective for all that.

'Your hand was smeared with blood,' McLevy stated.

'Galloway's blood,' from Mulholland.

'With his dying breath he lashed out.'

180

'Knocked you over. You hit your head. Down and out.'

'Until Ballantyne found you. Lucky that,' said the inspector.

'Lucky? I don't see how,' Jean muttered. She was beginning to develop a savage neck ache and these two big baw-faced policemen looming over her did not help.

'Lucky for us, Mistress Brash. The unconscious part,' answered Mulholland.

'Otherwise you'd have retrieved the knife and made off, free as a bird,' the inspector added.

'But not this time,' Mulholland ventured.

McLevy put his hands on the table and leaned in towards Jean to emphasise the words.

'This time, you've come to earth.'

Jean clasped her own hands in front of her like a pious churchgoer and looked coolly into McLevy's grim face.

'I deny everything you say.'

He swung away as if in disbelief at her bare-faced repudiation and Mulholland took over the frame.

'We checked the house. Belonged to a crony of Galloway's. For their wild rants and suchlike. Why were you there, Mistress Brash?'

'I told you. He wrote me a letter. To meet together.'

'Why?'

'Perhaps he wished. . .to apologise.'

'Where is this letter?'

Jean closed her eyes for a moment trying to concentrate her very being; the ground was sliding beneath her feet.

'In my. . .travelling bag.'

McLevy spoke, examining one of the smears on the wall, back turned as if he had lost interest.

'I took the liberty of examining the contents of your reticule. There is no such thing.'

'You rifled my belongings?'

'You are in custody now. You belong tae us.'

'Anyone else see this disappearing letter?' asked Mulholland sceptically.

Jean sighed. 'No.'

'And you went tae meet this man on your own?' McLevy said to the smear. 'No Hannah Semple? No Angus?'

'They were busy, and I can look after myself.'

'That's what it looks like,' Mulholland commented. 'What with your knife planted in his corpse.'

'Things are not always what they seem. He may well have been dead when I arrived.'

'You couldn't see?'

'The room was dark.'

Jean sighed again. It wasn't so much a matter of how she had got into the mess; there had been time to think on the hard bunk and she had a deep suspicion about who was behind all this. The problem was how to get out of it.

There was nothing she could do stuck in jail and Hannah Semple, redoubtable though she might be, did not have the wherewithal to untangle this web of deceit.

And her lawyers could do nothing. Not with the given facts. She was stuck like a cow in the mire.

No. There was only one hope.

And he was returning from the stained wall to stand before her.

'*Not whit they seem*? Is that the best you have to offer?' McLevy declared.

'I could say more. But it's a waste of time. I'll content myself wi' this: I am innocent.'

'That's not much in the way of proof, Mistress Brash,' Mulholland said remonstratively.

Jean shrugged. She had not taken her eyes off McLevy.

'It leaves us with the facts as witnessed,' he uttered soberly. 'And I think they're strong enough to seal your death warrant. Or if not execution, a long slow miserable demise rotting away in the Perth penitentiary.'

This was not music to her ears.

Not at all hopeful.

McLevy leaned in tight again and whispered the words, softly, as if he might utilise the mesmeric influences floating around Edinburgh.

'Confess, Jean. Gang easy. Throw yourself on the mercy of the court; admit your guilt. It may work in mitigation. But you must confess.'

They were eye to eye now and she could not tell if he were

challenging from what he truly believed or trying to push her to the limit of self-credence.

'I'll see you in hell first,' she replied equally softly. 'And answer me this: why would I want to kill him?'

'Ye'd had a rammy the night before. He threatened you, perhaps. Self-defence, eh?'

'Defence or no, I never touched the man.'

'His blood on your hand, your knife in his rearward side. It's more than enough.'

She shivered, not from any residual guilt but from a shaft of pain that had clamped around her neck.

Surely the inspector would believe her?

As if in answer, McLevy moved ever closer. His white parchment face filled her vision and, for the inspector's part, he gazed into her green eyes and caught the delicate scent of French perfume.

They say that you should only smell a woman's fragrance when in the act of love.

But there are other times.

'Look in my eyes, Jean, he murmured. 'Tell me you are innocent.'

There was a long moment as she held his gaze, her own regard unwavering.

'I am innocent,' she finally answered.

From Mulholland's point of view all he could see was two heads together, like horses whispering in a field.

Then the silence was broken by a soft cruel laugh.

'What a pity,' said the inspector of police to the bawdy-hoose keeper, 'your whole life contradicts that wee notion.'

Jean still did not waver.

'You are a bastard, James McLevy,' she said calmly.

Then, under her breath, as if she did not even want to hear the words herself she added, '*Help me.*'

'*Only if you confess.*'

'*Never.*'

His eyes searched hers then he jerked his head back and spoke loudly as if to a listening audience.

'You will hang or end in prison. An old toothless crone. Either way, ye'll die like a dog.'

'And you'll go to your grave knowing that I am an innocent

woman. And you did nothing to assist me,' she almost spat into his face, green eyes filled with a baffled fury. 'Go to hell.'

That was that, then.

After Jean had been taken back to the cells by one of the female helpers at the station, McLevy and Mulholland stood in the main hall, pondering in their different ways upon what had passed in the interrogation room.

'What do you think, sir?'

'I think,' said McLevy, 'justice will prevail.'

He shot a look sideways at Mulholland. The gap between himself and the constable was partly mended but McLevy could not rid himself of the suspicion that the details of the interrogation would find their way back to Roach. He had modulated his reactions accordingly but this was probably an unfair assessment of his constable and more to do with his own odd feeling of guilt that he had sidelined Mulholland because he found Conan Doyle's company more bracing.

One thing for sure, things were hotting up. Murders right, left and centre, sliced sharpers in the taverns, acid-pourers in the markets and the only crime solved, that of burglary with a wee bit of hanky-panky perhaps thrown in.

As regards Jean Brash, he had warned her of the dangers of starting a war with the Countess and now it looked as if she had suffered the consequences.

And if the Countess was behind this, then it bore the marks of long-term planning.

Jean may have met her match.

How the hell could he get her out of this pickle?

Or was she guilty in any case?

She had a fierce temper and the knife to hand.

McLevy became aware that he was under scrutiny.

'Your stomach's kicking up a blue storm,' Mulholland observed. 'You need some fuel in the boiler, sir.'

Ratiocination pays little heed to animal needs, and McLevy had been oblivious to the organic growling noise that lamented a lack of sustenance.

'Do you think the woman's culpable?' he asked suddenly.

But before Mulholland could answer, Lieutenant Roach emerged from his office and approached at a rate of knots.

'Well?' He demanded.

'Guilty as hell. Dead to rights. Open and shut case. Hang her the morrow morning.'

Roach sighed at his obdurate subordinate.

'I can exist without the sarcastic recitation, inspector. What is your *professional* opinion?'

'It looks bad.'

'Or good. Depending on the point of view.'

Having corrected the potentially skewed approach of his inspector, Roach glanced back to his office. In truth, though he derived a deal of satisfaction at the thought of McLevy putting Jean Brash though the wringer of the law and would keep an eagle eye on the process, he had other matters on his mind. Pressure building everywhere he looked.

The newspapers had got wind of the Morrison murder, possibly Doctor Jarvis had been talking in his club, and it was only a matter of time before the story broke. This he told McLevy before going on to a more immediate matter.

'Mister Galloway is sitting in my office,' he said.

'Is he now?'

'I still don't like the fellow,' muttered Roach. 'But a father's grief must be respected.'

Indeed the man had broken down in unexpected floods of tears at the sight of his son's dead body. While his horses were slaughtered and gourmandised all over France, a carcass nearer to home had unleashed the water of wretchedness.

Roach had planked him down in his office to recover and was not looking forward to more dolour on return.

Sympathy came in short supply for the lieutenant. One of the few characteristics he shared with his inspector.

He did not like his heart disturbed because it brought great unease and he did not wish to delve into the reasons why. Men find emotions an alarming prospect.

'I offered the poor man consolation that the killer of his son was under lock and key.'

'That's nice,' replied McLevy.

Not an enthusiastic response and Roach was provoked enough to needle the inert responder.

'Oh, come along, McLevy, you can surely allow yourself a wee gloat. The Queen of Crime dethroned, eh?'

Roach smiled at Mulholland who was po-faced as his inspector.

'You should be rejoicing, James. Your greatest ambition realised. Jean Brash behind bars!'

'But is she the killer?' muttered McLevy.

Roach almost hopped in the air with delight that he had provoked this reaction.

'Of course she is.'

'Innocent till proven guilty, sir,' Mulholland hazarded.

'Yes, yes, but look at the evidence, man! Who else could it be – a Halloween ghost?'

Having made this, to his mind, unanswerable point, Roach prepared to return to his office.

'Aye, well, Galloway should have pulled himself together by now,' he announced as he departed the scene. 'I hope so. But as I say, his consolation is the guilty party. In the cells where she belongs.'

As his lieutenant passed by, Ballantyne looked up shyly from his desk, hand over to hide a wiry insect he had found crawling around inside. The creepy-crawly bush telegraph had obviously passed on word that succour was to be found in the Leith Station at a certain outpost.

Roach gave him an approving glance then turned to almost strike a pose like a man addressing his golf ball.

'The evidence is inconvertible, McLevy,' he declared roundly. 'Tie up the case and hammer in the nails. Then get on to the Morrison matter. Crime never sleeps!'

With that admonitory assertion, he opened the door to his office and disappeared inside.

He had managed to annoy McLevy no end.

'With any luck Mister Galloway will assuage his grief by swiping the good lieutenant over his head wi' the jawbone of an ass,' he muttered.

'Or even a horse,' Mulholland said.

McLevy went back to something he had observed when viewing the corpse.

'Did ye examine the death wound?' he asked.

'I did.'

'We'll hae to wait for Doctor Jarvis in the morning but – it would appear to me that it was a *sinister* blow.'

'My opinion also. From the left.'

'Jean Brash is right-handed. And a stab frae the back. That's not her style. She would face you.'

Mulholland nodded. That made sense of sorts but nothing you might prove.

'She would strike from the front,' McLevy surmised.

'Into the stomach and up.'

'Or down,' added the inspector, a grim smile upon his face. 'One thing for certain sure, constable. There's too many knives in this city.'

And too many dead bodies.

28

De poney run, he jump an' pitch,
An' tumble massa in de ditch;
He died, an' de jury wonder'd why
De verdic was de blue-tailed fly.

Traditional, 'The Blue-tailed Fly'

Edinburgh, 1864

My Dearest Melissa,

Now it is almost over. The hounds of hell are still on my trail but I will fox them yet!

This city is a contrast to the other but underneath the fine buildings and straight lines of the streets the same poverty exists, only Edinburgh hides it better. Beneath its skirts, as it were. Glasgow makes no secret of its privation.

East and West. North and South. Nothing changes.

I find I am beginning to be affected by the strange ways of the people here and the even stranger part I have been asked to play in this war.

The news I receive is not good. The steamer Juno ran the blockade all the way from Greenock into Galveston as you no doubt have heard, but we lost the Emma Henry and the Iona was in offshore collision with another steamer whose captain was drunk as a skunk, and while his own ship survived ours went to the bottom.

Not much justice there, I am afraid.

The Iona now lies in the deep waters of the Clyde with fish swimming all around the great load of coal that she had shipped on board for the Atlantic crossing.

It is as if the Fates have lined up against us, and I know there are those who pour scorn on such superstitious nonsense, but I have seen grotesque events on the field of battle that have made me sometimes doubt my Christian reason.

For instance a bullet that was headed straight for me beside a river was intercepted by the poor unwitting body of one of my own men who had stepped up to return me a newly filled flask of water.

It was my fate to live and his to die. The chance was on my side that moment.

The single shot marksman who had climbed up on a bluff by the water was himself brought down by John Findhorn with a buffalo rifle that had been, so he told me, in his family for generations.

He lost it on the retreat from Gettysburg, along with his life.

But I repeat myself, do I not? I have surely told of John's death before.

And Fate? What does it mean? A force beyond us that works its will despite our puny efforts to dictate otherwise.

Like God without the beard.

I have been spared. But for what cause?

Ever since I arrived in this dank country, this Scotland that the natives hold in such great esteem that they leave the place in droves while lamenting their lost heritage, I have felt as if it was meant to be.

That every move I made was predestined, ordained, as if there is no other place on earth for me to arrive at and exist.

Is this not a kind of madness?

My mind is fragile. Like a shipwreck that water snakes swim in and out of, through the skeleton bones that once held the hull in place now with great gaps between them.

Between one thought, one action and another, lies eternity.

I am almost ashamed to say how lonely I have become, how desperate my need for solace and warmth; like a starving man. My very hand trembles as I write these words.

Again I have been billeted down by the docks, a rabbit warren of 'wynds' as they call the narrow little lanes. At dark they become alive with the creatures of the night that would sell both body and soul for a silver coin.

Tomorrow I meet with the two merchants who have promised ships in return for the cash bonds I have guarded with my life since I arrived on these shores.

I will not hand them over till I am satisfied that the papers are in order and then an exchange will be arranged.

Soon. It will all be over. Soon.

The Federal spies are never far from my trail. I caught a glimpse of my adversary in his long black oilskin cape.

Like myself he wears a wide-brimmed hat; my reason is to conceal the colour of my hair, which howls my name as if a finger were pointing from the sky.

I could dye it, of course, but I'll be damned if I will.

William Mitchell. My enemy. I wonder what his reason is? Disguise, perhaps. To hide the face of death?

I shall give this letter to Bartholomew Jones. One of my best agents. Wily and wild. They say he is a devil with the ladies.

If anyone survives this, he will. I have charged him to put this letter in your hand but God knows when that will be. It is all in doubt.

I write and yet I feel as if I have nothing much to say that might have meaning for you.

This whole venture is like a dream and I a shadow that moves within. The air of Edinburgh, the very air I breathe, has mixed in with my blood to create strange thoughts and fancies that bewilder me.

As if I am being seduced into a world where nothing is certain. Everything is in suspense. Especially myself.

I must stop now.

If we do not break this blockade, we lose the war.

Another thing I have said before.

I have heard that the ports of Wilmington and Charleston are now closed to our ships. We may have lost it already.

Be brave. I'll do my best.

Your husband,

Jonathen

29

And before the throne there was a sea of glass like
unto crystal: and in the midst of the throne, and
round about the throne, were four beasts full of eyes
before and behind.

THE BIBLE, Revelation

As he sat drinking his coffee in the attic room, James McLevy reflected that he might well have done a foolish thing this night. More than one in fact. Two at least recognisable. God knows what others had slipped past the sleeping sentries.

Mulholland had gone home and McLevy, having finally arrived at the Auld Ship and found to his despair that the last of the sheep's heid broth had been scoffed by some swine from Kilmarnock, had drowned his sorrows with a hooker of whisky and hairy tatties.

Unfortunately a side effect of the mashed potatoes and flaked dried saltfish was a raging thirst.

He called for water, remarked it lacking in gusto, and called for more whisky.

And it was in this state of unaccustomed inebriation that he had found himself sitting before the amused gaze of the Countess while a delicate tune from a piano traced a passage in the air around them, coming from some other room in the bawdy-hoose.

McLevy had knocked upon the door in peremptory fashion and demanded to see the *Madame* of the 'hotel' on official business. To his surprise, after a moment's wait, he found himself ushered politely inside by a tall cadaverous fellow dressed up to the nines as a butler.

'I don't recognise your features,' he declared as he followed the fellow down a long narrow hall with tasteful landscape paintings on the wall, most unlike the Just Land where Jean Brash's favourite picture was an octopus dragging a scantily clad woman under the sea.

'I am not from these parts, sir,' the man answered in rounded tones. 'My previous employer was the Earl of Essex.'

'Oh?' said McLevy. 'Come down in the world, eh?'

'The remuneration,' replied the butler, smoothly opening a door to deposit the inspector within, 'is far superior. And regular to boot.'

The Countess was sitting at a large mahogany desk with a spread of papers before her.

'You may remove your hat, sir,' she remarked. 'No-one will steal it from you.'

While McLevy did so, with a somewhat befuddled air, the Countess beckoned towards a small table set by the window where, as if ordained, a crystal decanter of whisky with two large equally crystal glasses had their pride of place.

'I welcome the distraction,' she smiled, throwing one of the papers back onto the desk as she rose. 'There is too much paper-work in this world.'

'I would concur. But I didnae know a bawdy-keeper and police-man shared the same predicament.'

The Countess raised a thin eyebrow to signal otherwise and motioned him to the table where she poured out two large slugs of whisky without asking.

It was not their first meeting. He had dropped in a time before with Mulholland to inform her that Leith was his parish and she had best be discreet. The woman had nodded polite assent and did not attempt to offer a free sample of the wares within.

Then they had met again when someone had tried to break in by her back garden and the German Shepherds she kept had near torn the man to pieces.

The Countess declined to press charges; the animals had earned their keep and the word would get round.

Beware of the dogs.

So, this was their third meeting.

They drank. It was good whisky.

'Business or pleasure, inspector?' she asked with a modest smile.

McLevy tried a flanker.

'A respectable man has been murdered. You know him well. He has been seen in your company.'

She registered this remark calmly enough, dabbing at her mouth with a lace handkerchief lest the whisky linger.

'Who is this man?'

'Witnesses link him to your establishment. Artefacts found on the premises point in your direction.'

Her gaze was steady but he noticed the faintest tremor just above the lip; the lips of women sometimes give them away. Looking in their eyes is just a waste of time.

'A brutal murder. The head smashed into a thousand pieces. As if a monster had broken it for vengeance.'

'But surely –'

'But surely, what?'

The inspector put on his *daftie* face, easy enough with the amount of blood alcohol.

'A thousand pieces?'

'Bones and flesh under your feet. Whit a mess!'

Now the Countess was blinking her small eyes as if her thoughts were speeding too fast.

That had not been the description given to her.

'How is this to do with me?'

'He visits you. In your company. Witnessed.'

'That's not possible.'

'Definite.'

'Who *is* this man?'

'You already know the name.'

'I do not.'

'Gilbert Morrison!'

Try as she might, the Countess was unable to suppress the fleeting stab of relief which left a mark on the heart-shaped face, the visage changing from cloudy confusion to a sharp focus of concentration.

'Mister Morrison. I know nothing of his death.'

'Whit about Logan Galloway?'

McLevy shot out the other name like a bullet into her face and despite herself, she almost blinked recognition.

Then recovered.

And he knew he would get little more for his pains.

But he also knew that she was complicit, if not the *fons et origo* of events surrounding Jean Brash.

How to prove it was another matter.

'Who might that be?' she queried finally.

'Another deid body. Jist thought tae throw it in.'

The inspector grinned somewhat foolishly as if the drink was leading him by the nose, but although she had smelled the whisky as soon as he walked in and sought to augment the effect, the Countess bore in mind that every member of the fraternity she had so far encountered had described McLevy by various detrimental adjectives, but *stupid* was not one of them.

'I have not heard or met with this. . .Mister Galloways,' said the Countess carefully.

'Galloway.'

'Yet Mister Morrison, how sad. A good client.'

'Dead as a doornail,' said McLevy cheerfully. 'Oh, here. . .' He hauled from the deep poacher's pouch in his coat the quirt Ballantyne had unearthed and which he had stuffed in his pocket before parting from the station.

An act which might indicate that, whisky or not, he had intended to come a-visiting.

'Ye recognise this artefact?'

Her eyes, narrow at best, became slits.

'It is for horses,' she said.

'And other beasts of burden.'

The Countess shrugged as if the matter had nothing to recommend further discussion.

'I respect the privacy of my clients. Especially when dead. Let us leave them in peace.'

'Not if they're murdered. No-one gets any peace if there's a murder in Leith.'

McLevy slugged back his drink and noticed that the Countess did not rush to replenish the libation.

'Then how can I help you?' she asked with a hint of frost in the tone.

'I'm looking for a motive,' said McLevy artlessly. 'In my opinion, murder always has a motive. Revenge often.'

'Revenge?'

'Aye.'

The inspector scratched his head absent-mindedly with the tip of the quirt. 'Someone suffers loss or pain, they wish the downfall of the one they blame for that. Next thing ye know, death on the carpet!'

This all-embracing concept found little favour with the Countess.

'Morrison liked to leather hell out of women, perhaps someone took exception?' the inspector continued.

'Not in this house. You pay for your pleasure. A business transaction.'

'Whit about wee Simone? Did she not flee the nest because of such transaction?'

'Simone had her own reasons,' the Countess responded cautiously; as was common with McLevy the conversation was veering all over like a coach with a headless driver.

'And then she ends up wi' acid poured down her back, does that not suggest revenge to you, Countess?'

She waited with ready answer should he accuse her but he sniffed appreciatively at his whisky and tilted the dregs down his gullet. It was not an elegant gesture and for some reason annoyed her.

'What has this to do with Mister Morrison?' she questioned abruptly.

'Who knows? I'm jist asking round the doors.'

McLevy held his empty glass up to the light and squinted through it. The Countess sighed and poured again but only half way, and then the inspector rocked back in his chair as if settling in for the night.

'My head is fair birlin' with the events of the last few days,' he remarked equably.

She made no reply. They sat in silence. Her drink was almost untouched and she glanced back to her pile of papers, which had suddenly assumed a revitalised importance.

The music wafted over them once more and McLevy bobbed his head rather foolishly to the notes.

'Is that Chopin?' he asked.

'Yes,' she answered a little surprised. 'The *Etudes*. Most nights I have a classical pianist in the main salon. It adds quality.'

'I like Chopin,' remarked McLevy. 'He has never to my knowledge murdered anybody.'

She once more made no response and for a moment it seemed

oddly peaceful in the room as they both appreciated the beauty of a fragile melody.

The Countess looked into the inspector's eyes and was disturbed by the depth of understanding in his gaze.

'Gilbert Morrison died because past action called for a retribution that has only now surfaced in the present,' he said quietly. 'I will find it out. Do you know this man?'

He held out the rough likeness of Alfred Binnie, the very fellow to whom the Countess had recently paid further gold coin as a mark of appreciation for a task accomplished.

Binnie had followed her plan to the letter, killed Galloway, left the man's blood on Jean Brash and had one more deed to perform before he would vanish back to London.

Meanwhile he perched in a room three storeys above.

This she knew, but discretion was paramount. What was good for clients was surely good enough for Binnie.

'No,' she answered. 'I have never seen him.'

So be it. One crime spills into another and the lies mount up.

McLevy thought such, put away the drawn likeness with the quirt then slugged back the rest of his whisky.

The Countess relaxed a little thinking this strange and contradictory fellow was about to take his leave, but not quite yet.

Not quite.

'Ye didnae ask,' he stated, thumping down the heavy tumbler.

'What?'

'Why I showed you that portrait. Ye didnae ask the reason.'

'Because I assumed you would tell me.'

'Uhuh?'

A good answer, but not *sufficient* good.

'He's the one who poured the acid down Simone's back. Bad wee bugger, eh?'

McLevy had still made no mention of the obvious correlation between the war waged and events unfolding so the Countess thought she might beat him to the punch.

'I hope you don't connect me with this dreadful act?'

'Not at all. Ye don't look anything like the mannie.'

He laughed loudly at his own joke and she managed a small twitch of a smile.

'She screamed like a witch on the bonfire. The French girl. So they say. I wisnae there.'

McLevy stood up, low-brimmed bowler hanging loose in his hand.

'Jist as well Simone had Jean Brash tae fall back on, eh?' he muttered. 'Be in a fine state else.'

The Countess hesitated and then nodded in a non-committal fashion. Binnie had inveigled the young policeman to enter the house in Iona Street and heard a whistle blow.

After that, he'd made himself scarce. Left it in the lap of the gods.

'Except that Jean is in the police cells now.'

The inspector having dropped this bombshell put on his hat as if to go but a newly enlivened Countess forestalled the anticipated departure.

'Jean Brash. But how is that?'

'She stands accused of murder; all the rage and she likes tae be in fashion,' he remarked dryly.

'My God. But who was the victim?'

'Your Mister Galloways.'

'He is not mine!' she cried.

Indeed the Countess was struggling to control a feeling of exultation. The gods were most definitely upon her side.

But as mankind has so often experienced, the gods are on no-one's side but their own.

'What a terrible thing!'

'Not for you,' McLevy noted, his face blank and impassive. 'She is your sworn enemy.'

'But I would not wish. . .even an enemy.'

'Wouldn't you? You're nicer that me. I would. Every time. Anyway she stands accused. Her knife in his body.'

McLevy made sudden stabbing movement with his hand towards the Countess who flinched for a moment.

His face registered an evil, murderous smile then returned to a soggy repose.

'That's what it looks like, anyway,' he said.

'Do you believe her guilty?'

A shrewd question. Worth a decent response.

For a moment it seemed as if the inspector's body was charged with a strange energy that vibrated in the very air of the room. The study itself was dark, with pools of light from various table lamps, but he had stepped back so that the white face hung in the gloom like a Halloween ghost.

He rendered then with great formality, a statement of intent.

'I believe I will find out the truth,' said James McLevy. 'No matter how many lies I am told, how many misdirections, how many secrets kept. If you have broken the law, I will find you out. It is my profession, my life's work, and I am good at my job.'

Then he eructated softly as the whisky came back to haunt him, and grinned like a wolf.

'So, Countess, if you have told truth ye have nothing to worry about.'

'My conscience is clear,' she replied demurely.

The music next door came to an end with a final subtle chord and as if taking cue, he let out a roar of laughter.

'Whit a merry-go-round it all is, eh? But the best way not tae get dizzy, is to stand in the middle and watch the wheel go round. Stand in the middle.'

A curt nod and he was gone.

The Countess pulled at a bell rope to signal the butler, returned to her desk and thought for a moment. Then a sly, malicious smile came to her lips and she pulled a sheet of paper towards her and began to write.

The inspector observed her through the keyhole; it always amazed him how many folk never thought to keek in by this aperture.

He straightened up just in time as the servant came out from a side room to escort him back towards the door.

'Whit is your name?' he asked in friendly fashion.

'James Feeney,' the other answered.

'Feeney? That's Irish.'

'I am of that extraction, sir.'

'Ye'd never guess,' said McLevy as they walked down the long corridor, staggering a little as if losing his bearings. 'But the Irish, they're everywhere, eh?'

As they passed the door to the main salon, the inspector suddenly lurched and sprung open the portal with a thump. Only a momentary glimpse before the butler rushed to close it again, but enough for McLevy to see some women in décolletage fussing around two bald heads that mercifully were facing away lest they be Masonic panjandrums that the inspector might have seen in Roach's company.

That, however, was not what held his interest. One of the girls he recognised, Maisie Powers; he winked at her and she scowled when she saw his face; a hefty specimen and one that he might try to intercept on another occasion.

He turned from the newly closed door with an affable smile.

'Night night, Mister Feeney,' he said cheerily. 'Don't let the bugs bite.'

And with that, he stepped out into the night.

A scratching at the glass brought McLevy back to the present of a hungry cat at his attic window.

He let Bathsheba in to snash at the scraps he had deposited in the chipped saucer and walked back to the frame, which he had left open.

The dank October air made him shiver, but he enjoyed the dampness on his face.

The inspector decided he might have been a bit hard on himself. Normally it was not a good idea to see suspects with drink taken but perhaps that may have worked in his favour. Had he been bristling with sobriety, perhaps the Countess would have been even more defensive.

Perhaps it was not such a foolish move. But the second action was definitely daft.

On his way home, the weight of the world upon his shoulders, he had chanced to run into three young hoydens, out late on the streets, dressed as Halloween hell-hags, one a besom rider with broom, the others ripe for mischief.

Something in his demeanour set them to caper; they were masked and much mischief can be done behind the visor.

They linked hands to surround him and demanded a golden apple or he must pay forfeit.

McLevy had been put in mind of Paris with the three goddesses and see what happened to him.

The Trojan War.

He had no apple to hand in any case and demanded to know the forfeit.

And thus he could be witnessed in Constitution Street, a fine respectable thoroughfare, dancing a highland fling, arms aloft, in the middle of three giggling females.

The inspector shook his head at the attic window, while the lights of Edinburgh blinked in admonition.

Like many a man before him, he blamed the whisky for this wild cantrip; the resemblance to his dream of some nights ago did not escape his notice.

And like the dream, it had a strange aftermath.

No tunnels or spectres in a red cloak, just the glimpsed sight of a face looking out of a passing carriage.

A moment only, but surely it was the visage of Sophia Adler?

Or was it hallucination brought on by whisky, the highland fling and unaccustomed exertion?

The face jerked back inside, the carriage flung round a corner and was gone, the muffled figure of the coachman no help to identification.

McLevy stood frozen with raised arms until a sharp pain in his side caused them to lower. He broke through the chain of witches with a muttered excuse and walked swiftly home without once looking back.

And now he was. Home.

He mused upon these strange events. This mesmerism was catching – was the dream a premonition and if so, was there more to follow?

All his life he had balanced the gut instinct of a policeman with sudden shafts of intuition.

Earth and heaven.

He valued both.

Somewhere in the dark night there was a high-pitched squealing noise along the rooftops. A breaking hinge or a dying animal.

Take your pick.

McLevy thought back to that face in the carriage. Was it Sophia Adler and if so, what did it signify?

And what would she have observed? A man with his arms in the air. Surrender or the highland fling?

Take your pick.

A foolish move indeed. He had exposed himself to some unknown forces but what did it all signify?

Bathsheba jumped up onto the table and out of the window to terrorise the rodent population and McLevy was suddenly overcome by a feeling of utter helplessness.

Four cups of strong coffee had raised him to a plateau from which there was only one way to go.

Down.

A crash. As if he had lost control of everything. A feeling of dark panic, not unlike the death dream but this was waking consciousness.

His diary lay open on the table but what could he write?

Two murders, one burnt body, two cut bellies, one assaulted music box, a jail full of slinkers, Silver Samuel, and Jean Brash, well-known bawdy-hoose keeper; a madman on the loose, mesmerism, pools of blood, dead spirits talking in your lughole, Big Arthur, wee Muriel, the Countess and Roach laughing up their sleeves, strawberry birthmarks and hornbeam sticks. A cross-segment of the lunatic planet. Yours truly, James McLevy, Inspector of Police.

'That takes the biscuit,' he declared aloud. 'That is quite sufficient!'

Oddly enough, it was.

The recitation of these bizarre events had calmed him down.

His mind began to work again, sifting through it all and coming to certain conclusions.

The key to the Morrison murder was Sophia Adler.

How, he did not yet surmise and her connection might even be innocent and tenuous but she *contained* something.

Spirits or earthbound, she was a key.

Something she had said, in his litany he had named it. A pool of blood. Not on the carpet but on the street, she had said. On the stones.

On the slab?

He had mentioned it to Mulholland, a random slice of the brain but now it had returned with a vengeance.

A case some eighteen years ago, he had been a young constable only fit for investigation of minor criminality but his sergeant George Cameron had brought him into the cold room.

A body on the slab.

'I'm doing this for your own good, Jamie,' he said and pulled the sheet aside.

The young constable looked and said nothing.

'This is violent death,' Cameron declared. 'Ye don't get much worse. We found him down by the docks.'

Where the man's face should have been was a bloody mess. As if a giant fist had smashed down to obliterate all traces of self.

Just like Gilbert Morrison's.

The case was never solved and he was a lowly constable only fit for day patrol then with a sergeant who, despite his rough ways, looked after him like a son.

The cold room was as near as he got to that particular investigation.

But he seemed to remember they discovered the man to be American. Was that the body she had seen in her vision?

Was there a connection?

A constable then but now he was inspector. He would examine the records of the case. Might yield nothing but he would look anyway.

On the financial side, a banker, who owed him his son's reputation, had promised to move heaven and earth to delve deeper into the monetary affairs of the Morrison Brothers.

Hopefully the man would deliver soon.

Walter was the surviving brother, but how long would he last?

McLevy had stationed a watch on the man's house; part protection, part surveillance. So far there was nothing to report. Walter was lying low.

As regards Jean Brash, he had no doubt now that she had walked into a trap.

The knife. A professional job.

The barman in the pub where the sharpers were sliced remembered the little man complaining about the beer. The London ale was better, he had said. Shoreditch stout put the Scots beer to shame.

McLevy had sent a cable to a good police friend in that dungeon of a city, describing in as much detail as possible the wee acid-pourer and mentioning the Shoreditch connection.

A pity he could not send the sketch itself by wire but science had not yet moved on that far. One day.

The answer should arrive tomorrow, with any luck.

He would also make it his business to catch up with Maisie Powers, who worked for the Countess but might possibly be persuaded despite her profound dislike of McLevy to divulge some titbits. The persuading was the problem.

Oh, and he'd nearly forgot the faint lingering smell of that pomade from Magnus Bannnerman.

He had sniffed at the single filament from the murder scene but the odour had disappeared.

Even if he yanked a hair out of the man's head and put both under the microscope to find some similarity it would still prove nothing.

But it was something.

A pattern was beginning to form.

Somewhere.

And then his mind shifted back to Conan Doyle. The way the big lump had been gawking at Sophia Adler did not bode well. Where the eyes gaze the heart follows.

Yet there were depths to this fellow that intrigued McLevy.

Arthur was also a talisman in this case; how, the inspector did not precisely know but he was certain that Doyle had a part to play.

Tomorrow.

It was going to be a busy day.

30

Out of the crooked timber of humanity no straight thing can ever be made.

IMMANUEL KANT, *Proposition 6*

Hannah Semple gazed through the cell bars at Jean Brash. The mistress was tired, bags under the eyes, missing her morning jolt of coffee no doubt.

'This doesnae look good,' the old woman announced.

Jean sighed. Hannah would have made a great Job's comforter all those years ago.

'Whit did the lawyers say?' she asked the visage before her, which resembled a bloodhound that had lost the trail.

'They're not hopeful.'

Neither was Hannah. She had just spent two hours at the offices of Duncan Paterson, Jean's expensive and knabbie-faced advocate who had circumlocuted his way round the legal houses before admitting that, as the facts stood, there was not a cat's chance in hell of Jean getting out before trial.

And after the trial, perhaps even less chance.

'It would not have been so bad,' pronounced the supercilious wee runt, who possessed a huge head that made him look as if he had been wrenched out of the womb by pair of cow pliers, 'if Mistress Brash had not been found with her own knife impaled into the corpse and his blood upon her person.'

'She was unconscious!' Hannah had retorted.

'Unfortunately,' Paterson had responded with a sideways sniff of a nose that could smell money at least three miles away, 'the legal process does not recognise that particular condition as valid mitigation.'

Paterson had promised Hannah that he would arrive at the station later to see Jean but for the moment his time would be best served by going through the preliminary evidence with a fine toothcomb.

Give the wee puddock his due, he would accomplish this. He was one of the best advocates in the city, but the message the lawyer sent was not a cheerful one.

'Ye're stuck here till hell freezes,' was Hannah's pithy summing up, minus the legal jargon.

Jean sighed once more.

'I would kill for a cup of coffee.'

'Ye already have,' said Hannah with graveyard humour, 'and I tried tae bring ye in a stone flask o' the stuff but they widnae let me.'

'How come not?' Jean sat up a bit straighter, green eyes flashing with indignation.

'That big stupit bastard of a sergeant at the desk. Murdoch. He said there might be poison in it. Tae help ye escape from justice.'

Jean shook her head. Hannah hesitated, not wanting to pile it, on but events could not be undone.

'I've mair bad news. If it's no' one thing it's the other. Never rains but it pours.'

'Go ahead,' said Jean. 'Me and catastrophe are well acquainted these days.'

'Simone and Francine have flown the coop. Left a note this early morning. Awa' tae gay Paree or wherever. Wee Lily Baxter's in a hellish state, the whole house is in uproar.'

Indeed Lily's distress had been a pitiful sight to behold and the only person able to comfort her had been, surprisingly enough, Jessie Nairn.

But then the news about Jean had arrived in addition to the mayhem and Hannah was off on her travels.

'God knows whit the Just Land is like this very moment. You're no' there, I'm no' there, big Annie's there but she's a soft touch; these magpies will be up tae high doh. Hingin' frae the rafters.'

Jean made a quick decision.

'We will close the place for a week at least.'

'Whit?'

'The girls can find their own way home, they're big enough. Back to their families or wherever. We have too much on our plate. One less thing to worry about.'

Hannah thought for a moment. It made sense. With a few reservations.

'Whit about the clients?'

'They can whistle.'

'What about wee Lily?'

'She can stay. Feed the fish.'

Indeed Lily was often to be found by the ornamental pond, staring into the water with rapt concentration as the piscine layabouts swam around.

Perhaps she had been looking for better days.

'She'll need company.'

'Who do you suggest?'

'Jessie Nairn,' replied Hannah surprisingly. 'She's kind tae Lily and Jessie tellt me when we were hingin' oot the washing that if she ever goes back to her family in Paisley, she'll get her throat cut.'

'Who by?'

'Her family.'

'Then she can stay with Lily.'

'Whit about me?' It had suddenly dawned on Hannah that she had no wish to share a bawdy-hoose with a doleful deaf-mute and a snippet from Paisley.

'You will bide in the safe house in Laurie Street and continue to organise the search for this acid man.'

'But Simone's run away and left us in the lurch!'

Jean straightened up a bit more to resemble the proud mistress of the Just Land.

'It is a matter of principle,' she said firmly.

Besides, she had a hidden hope that should they find this slimy wee bastard and stick some lighted Halloween splinters under his fingernails, he might well provide some much-needed answers.

Somebody had plunged a knife into Logan Galloway and it wouldn't be the Countess, too refined by half.

The outside door to the cells creaked open, with a noise that made Jean wince, and Ballantyne entered.

'I've been sent to inform you, madam,' he said to Hannah, 'that your visiting time is up. Regulations.'

'Have I no' seen you before, my mannie?' speired Hannah, a wicked glint in her eye. 'Inside the Just Land wi' two big hizzies hingin' on your arm?'

'I don't believe so,' replied the constable, his birth-mark flaming at the thought. 'That's not on my patrol.'

'I could've sworn otherwise,' said Hannah. Then she turned to Jean Brash who was smiling a little at the byplay, any humour being welcome in this situation. 'I'll do what you've tellt me, mistress. Your wish. My command.'

With that ironic statement to hide the worry in her mind, Hannah looked Jean straight in the face, nodded her head in determined fashion and then left.

Ballantyne did not follow but fished in his pocket and produced a slightly creased, sealed envelope.

'This was handed in for you,' he said to Jean.

As he motioned to give it over, Jean held up her hand.

'Are you not concerned there may be poison within, or perhaps even a dagger to help me evade your clutches?'

'No,' replied Ballantyne with serious mien. 'Sergeant Murdoch held it up to the light. Jist paper inside.'

He inserted it carefully through the bars, bowed his head respectfully and left.

Jean sniffed the envelope. It was scented. She did not recognise the writing, which was small and somewhat crabbed.

But as soon as she read the opening words, it was like a stab in the heart.

Indeed, it was meant to be so.

She could almost hear the gloating voice.

My dear Jean,

I am so sorry to hear of your misfortune. It must be terrible to feel that the whole world has turned against you and that everything you worked so hard to build up can be of no consequence when you are behind a prison wall.

I shall attend the trial and each time you look up, there will be my eyes fixed upon you. I know it will be hard when they strip off your fine clothes and I hope they do not cut off your beautiful hair lest it suffer infestation.

But here I am, taken with the vanity of outward show when it must be inner suffering that concerns you.

An agony twisting like a knife, more painful with each passing year, which will only cease with your own cessation.

I wish you the strength to bear such suffering.

They say that in prison each day is like a year, each year an eternity. What a dreadful prospect!

I would think that nothing can comfort you now but I offer you what love and affection lies within my breast.

Yours,
A friend

Jean Brash closed her eyes and crumpled up the letter in her two hands.

The words she spoke were like an incantation or prayer of malediction.

'I'll see you buried yet, Countess,' she muttered. 'And I'll spit in your grave when they lower you down.'

'Dearie me. That's no' very nice,' said a voice.

She had heard the door creak while reading and assumed it to be Ballantyne keeking in to check she wasn't trying to choke herself to death on the paper.

But it was McLevy, with a tin mug in his hand inside which an evil-looking brew was slopping up against the sides like a muddy black tide.

The brew smelt strong and acrid with a sense that it might once have been coffee.

'It's the station special,' he said. 'Made by Sergeant Murdoch's own fair hands.'

He passed it carefully through the bars, the mug being just wide enough for the gap.

She passed him the letter in return. Tit for tat.

While Jean sipped, nose screwed up, mouth pursed at the awful taste, McLevy squinted at the letter, holding it at arm's length for deciphering.

'You need ocular assistance,' she remarked.

'I have the drift,' he replied.

Jean took another hungry gulp at the coffee and nearly spat it back into the mug.

'That sergeant of yours is worried I might poison myself but he's near beat me to it.'

McLevy handed back the letter without immediate comment on the contents.

'Ye best keep that safe. Evidence at trial.'

'Whit good will it do?'

'Depends on the accused.'

The inspector had a big smile on his face and Jean was at once wary.

A policeman's smile is second only to a politician's in terms of potential treachery.

'Alfred Binnie,' he announced. 'That's his name as I am told by cable from London town this morning.'

'Who might that be?'

'The acid-pourer. Handy wi' a knife as well.'

Jean had a feeling that she was being manoeuvred in the mind; was McLevy holding out some hope?

'And I think I know where tae find him.'

She said nothing. It would come. McLevy chuckled annoyingly to himself.

'How mony occasions have we twa sat together?'

'Every time there's misery in the land,' she replied grimly as he chortled away, as if at some private joke.

'How's your neck?' he asked.

'What?'

'Ye had an ache there.'

'It's better now.'

'It'll be worse after trial.'

His face was serious all of a sudden.

'The Countess. She is too clever for you, Jean.'

'I wouldnae say that.'

'She set a trap and in you walked like a blind fool.'

Jean threw the dregs of coffee from the tin mug onto the cell floor and McLevy frowned to see such desecration, but she had used the displacement for her own calculation.

'That means you believe me innocent.'

'It is of no matter.'

'Why?'

'Because I can provide no proof.'

McLevy leant in close to the bars so that his big white face filled up the space like a huge balloon.

'She has you beaten, Jean, every way you turn – admit the fact.'

'I'll never admit it.'

'Then help me prove otherwise.'

'How?'

This was the second time in days that the inspector had glimpsed a look of naked entreaty in her eyes and he wondered at the feelings it provoked in his heart.

A cruel affection. One fights the other.

Love like a trail of blood.

He ignored any depth of thought and returned to facts.

'Maisie Powers. She left your establishment.'

'I caught her jinking on the side. That's against the rules of the house. They all know the rules.'

'Yet ye dealt with her kindly?'

Jean nodded.

The girl's brother had been a hopeless opium addict and the reason for Maisie selling her wares outside of the Just Land was to clear his debts with the suppliers.

By supplying them with her stock in trade.

But then you ran a high risk of the pox and it was instant dismissal for that reason. Jean ran a clean house; it could not be otherwise.

She had felt sorry for Maisie and given her a small sum of money to cushion the blow.

The girl had been grateful for small mercies.

The brother had died not long after, so it was all for nothing.

And Maisie?

'She sells her body for the Countess now,' McLevy offered, as Jean's silence had stretched.

'That's one way of putting it.'

'She may have inside knowledge. I need tae tap upon it. She will not talk to me.'

'No wonder. You threw her mother in jail.'

'I caught her shoplifting.'

'For her own daughter's wedding!'

Maisie's older sister, rendering McLevy somewhat unwelcome in the family circle.

He glared at Jean.

This was developing into an unseemly fracas despite the deadly situation.

'The law is the law.'

'Aye. Kiss my backside, said the rich man.'

McLevy took a deep breath. He'd be damned if this woman would distract him from his bounden duty.

'You must get word to her that I am to be trusted.'

'How can I do that? I am in the jail.'

'And liable to stay there!'

He bawled this into her face from short distance, eyes almost popping in fury.

Jean took thought. This was her only hope at present, pop-eyes or not.

It went against the grain having to provide a policeman with her official approval and if word spread, she would lose face amongst the fraternity, but needs must when Satan holds the reins.

'Calm yourself down, James,' she said primly. 'You'll give your body a seizure.'

She removed a thin gold ring with a tiny inset gem from her little finger.

'Show Maisie this. She aye admired it. Say it's hers with my blessing for the right information.'

Jean dropped it into his hand.

The tiny circlet of gold glinted against the hard skin of his palm. Resting where the line of life crossed over.

31

It's a damned, long, dark, boggy, dirty, dangerous way.
OLIVER GOLDSMITH, *She Stoops to Conquer*

Maisie Powers looked at the ring as it lay in McLevy's hand and near spat on it. The hand that is, not the circlet.

He had tracked her down to one of the smaller taverns by the dockside, the Green Lady, a respectable enough place where they at least washed the floor now and then, where she was in the habit of treating her aged mother, Molly, to a mid-morning dram before starting the day's labour.

Luckily the old harridan had not yet arrived and the inspector was in a hurry to get out before Molly got in.

'I dae this for Jean,' said Maisie. 'No' for you. Give back the ring. This is for free.'

Jean Brash is dead meat unless you help me, had been his opening remark.

It got her attention and he still had it, no matter how grudging.

'I'm looking for a man. Small, plump, nasty piece o' work. Maybe has a London cant,' he murmured, re-pocketing the ring.

Maisie hesitated. She had heard what had happened to Simone. This could be dangerous for the health.

'Whit's he to do wi' Jean?'

'She is in the frame for murder. I think he hung the picture round her neck. Him and the Countess.'

Now it was a shiver. The Countess ruled by fear. One glance from the eye was enough. She paid well and looked after the herd of whores like prime cattle. But you did what you were told. You took your licks.

He noted the hesitation as this thought passed through her mind and resisted the temptation to push further.

Finally Maisie spoke slowly, softly, unlike her usual strident tone; so quietly that he had to lean in at the table where they sat.

'The top room. A man stays up there. Since a wee while ago. We never see. He comes and goes by the back.'

'Whit about the dogs?'

'They must like him.'

'Ye *never* see? Tell me a wee bit more.'

She took a breath.

'Thank God it wisnae myself.'

'Tell me, if you please.'

'Lizzie Jessock. Big lump o' a girl. She didnae last.'

McLevy raised his eyebrows enquiringly; not another murder surely?

'She was sent up. Tae service him. Keep her mouth shut. But she tellt me only. Frae the same street ye know?'

'Uhuh.'

The door to the tavern swung open and McLevy cursed under his breath lest it might be Molly, the once-arrested shoplifter, but it was just a chimney-sweep, covered in soot and thirsty for beer.

For a laugh to celebrate the Halloween, which had finally arrived, he had gouged off the soot round his eyes and the white skin made him look like a daylight demon.

'A horrible wee pot-belly man,' Maisie continued. 'Wi' a whiney kind of voice and he –'

Her voice almost trailed away. The inspector waited, trying to make himself inconspicuous as if she might be talking to herself.

'– he pits a knife against her bare breast.'

'Whit happened?'

'She started tae howl tears and he kicked her out.'

'Top room, you say?'

'Ye cannae get higher.'

McLevy fumbled in his pocket.

'I have a likeness of this man, I want Lizzie to –'

'No!'

The word came out with enough vehemence to turn the sweep back from the bar and he wondered for a moment what the man had said to cause the woman such distress.

His white-rimmed eyes blinked comically at them for a second before he went back to his beer.

'No,' Maisie repeated less loudly, but with gritty resolve. 'I've taken my life in my hands enough and if my mother sees me sitting wi' you, she'll hae a convulsion.'

She pointed to the door.

'You get tae hell out of here, McLevy. I don't wish to be seen in your company. I have a reputation tae keep.'

And so he took her advice, nodding politely to the sweep, who grinned, broken teeth in the black face.

'It's my birthday,' the man announced. 'Born on Halloween. Whit a nonsense, eh?'

But he was talking to a closed door. The man had vanished. So he turned back and smiled at the woman.

A fine big specimen. *Happy Birthday.*

Meantime, Constable Ballantyne sat in the records room and counted the number of dead beetles he had found inside the folder pages like so many bookmarks. He had arranged the insects in a neat echelon all along the dusty surface.

Fourteen. Most the same kind as far as he could see, with a little yellowish marking on their back shell.

A tribe perhaps on their way to the Promised Land when they got sidetracked into the annals of crime.

Larder or Bacon Beetle – *Dermestes lardarius* – unless Ballantyne missed his guess. He had been reading up on the targets of his merciful interventions and these fitted the book description.

Very destructive to paper. But one bite of Leith's past criminality seemed to have put paid to the whole clan.

Ballantyne sighed. He had found it oddly peaceful in the records room, no-one to bother him, a line-up of dead insects for company and he, like the curator of a museum, lost in the dusty tomes of ancient homicidal lore.

To wit, approximately eighteen years ago when a brutally shot body was discovered in the Leith Docks.

Inspector McLevy had set him the task of finding the relevant dossier and this had taken most of the morning.

But here it was. The gist of it anyway.

The writing was in large block capitals by a certain Inspector

Brunswick who had retired not long after and returned to his native Stirling.

Name of corpse: Jonathen Sinclair, identified from papers as American citizen. No trace of address in Edinburgh.

Cause of death: Two bullets. One to the body. The other from close range to the face, causing great damage.

Motive for killing: Undiscovered. Lack of evidence.

Case closed: Three months later. Lack of evidence.

Further notes: the American Consul in Glasgow, Warner L. Underwood, disclaims all knowledge of the man save that he was suspected of being a Confederate agent who may have been attempting to buy ships for the South and who deserved what he got. We have enough troubles in Leith without other folk bringing their mess here.

On that somewhat personal note, Inspector Brunswick ended his report.

There were a few other additions but Ballantyne reckoned he had absorbed the substance and anyway it was for McLevy to peruse and cogitate upon.

Accordingly he swept the defunct insects into a small piece of paper, which he wrapped around neatly to be shaken out with due ceremony from the back window of the station at a later juncture, tucked the folder under his triumphant arm, and walked off with mission accomplished.

In Roach's office, however, little was consummated and tempers were rising.

The lieutenant was sitting at his desk, McLevy leaning over, Mulholland at the door; again not unlike their usual automatically assumed interrogation positions but this was more the other way round.

McLevy had laid out his whole case but his superior was unconvinced.

'It is not enough,' Roach remarked. 'Not by a long swipe, McLevy. You are at least two clubs lengths short.'

This golfing reference sailed over the inspector's head as he tried to rein in his frustration.

He took a deep breath and drove in again to restate the case for the defence.

'Doctor Jarvis agreed wi' me, sir –'

'A wonder in itself, I know, but still not enough –'

'A professional job, atween the third and fourth ribs, straight into the heart, one thrust.'

'Scientific, almost,' Mulholland offered.

'A practised killer. *Too professional*. Even for Jean Brash.'

'You think so?' Roach looked across at Queen Victoria who seemed doubtful as well.

The monarch had been on that wall for a while. Stasis breeds doubt, no denying that.

'Jarvis remarked the wound to be a touch wider than Jean's blade.'

'She may have sawed it back and forth to extract the weapon she had just used for murder. Not very professional, of course, which destroys your previous argument.'

Roach was pleased with this and glanced to see if Mulholland had appreciated the subtle riposte but for some reason the constable's face registered a blank.

'Again,' McLevy hammered out, undeterred, 'Jarvis agreed with what both Mulholland and I had previously noted; Galloway was stabbed from the left. "*Sinister*", said he.'

'Jean Brash is right-handed,' Mulholland added.

'Her only orthodoxy,' said Roach dryly, however it did make some impression on him; left-handers were the bane of his life, he had lost in the President's Cup to one not two months ago.

However it was still not enough.

'All very circumstantial and does not justify an official search warrant to enter the property.'

This was the rub.

To apply successfully for such a warrant through official channels needed a lieutenant's approval.

Of course McLevy could barge in unofficially and rampage through the Countess's hotel but if resisted, if there were problems, he would need a force of men.

Without endorsement he could only rely on Mulholland at best and even that was not sure; and if by any chance the raid was unsuccessful the inspector ran the risk of the instant discipline of demotion.

McLevy had too many black marks on his record as it stood. A series of heavy scores. He had once got across the present prime minister, Gladstone, and was only rescued by the fact that he saved the man's life.

The inspector indicated the cable that lay on Roach's desk, read by the lieutenant but not, McLevy was certain, appreciated to full extent.

'The knifeman frae the Rustie Nail, the acid-pourer at the market –'

The likeness of Lily's was beside the cable and McLevy gestured again to make sure Roach realised the burgeoning significance of it all.

'I sent the description to a colleague of mine in London. . .a *professional killer, plump, left-handed, looks like a squashed toad,* and he came back with a name. Alfred Binnie. A hired assassin. Apprentice at one time to Tom Partridge of Shoreditch, who was top of his trade. Binnie took over the mantle. Some say he killed his master to be the only one on hand.'

'This colleague has done you proud,' Roach muttered, skimming the contents once more.

'Binnie has not been seen around his usual haunts in Shoreditch for a wee while. I believe he is in Edinburgh.'

'And where does that get us exactly?'

This from Roach was quite hopeful in that he had not dismissed the cable out of hand.

Mulholland had been well briefed by McLevy before they entered and though he may have had lingering doubts himself, he took a deep breath as they went for broke.

'Jean Brash may have walked into a trap, sir,' he opined, moving off the door to the side so that they flanked Roach as if he indeed were a suspect.

'Binnie made the kill. Laid it on Jean,' McLevy said.

'The Countess is behind it. A war between them, sir.'

'I have a witness who has seen Binnie in the lair of the Countess,' McLevy added, his eyes gleaming with hunting fever. 'I know his hiding place. Take him and we crack the case but I need to get in the front door!'

'We'll cover the back with a few men,' Mulholland said hopefully. 'Diversion and deception, sir.'

Which might well describe what the two were about with their own superior officer.

'Who is this witness?' asked Roach, unmoved by all this diversification.

'Her identity must be secret. For the moment. But I guarantee her veracity.'

The lieutenant sniffed at that unsatisfactory reply from his inspector and then asked the question that had been in his mind since the two had entered his office.

'Inspector. Are you sure your feelings are not personally involved and that you are therefore indulging in what I can only describe as. . .wishful thinking?'

McLevy froze like a statue and Mulholland tensed, wondering if, as his Aunt Katie would have put it, *the fox has bit the hen and watch the feathers flying.*

'I have no personal feeling where justice is concerned,' the inspector said quietly. 'But I believe there is a danger we may fail innocence in this case no matter how unlikely the accused is to deserve such designation.'

'*Belief?*' said Roach seizing on the word. 'I need more than that. I need proof. Facts. Indisputable facts.'

'Then you may have to take my word for it, sir. That we will find proof. Behind the door of the Countess.'

Roach said nothing.

Over the years he had borne witness to the fact that McLevy's instincts had their own truth to tell. But they also invariably got the lieutenant into hot water.

Scalding, on occasions.

This could be one of those times.

Mulholland thought to say something more but a slight movement of his inspector's hand stilled the voice within.

In the stretched silence there was a timid knock at the door and it sprang open, breaking the tension, to reveal the figure of Ballantyne who held out a dusty folder like some sort of sacrificial offering.

'I found it, sir,' he said. 'It was gey well hidden.'

'My thanks, Ballantyne,' replied McLevy accepting the folder with due gravity. 'We are lost without you.'

He turned to the questioning look of his lieutenant.

'The Morrison case,' he said. 'Key information.'

'Oh? You haven't forgotten it then?'

To this waspish retort the inspector inclined a dignified nod. Dignity, as a poet had once told him, is a good way to keep your hat on your head in a howling gale.

'My mind is full of many things, sir. Many of them awaiting action.'

Back to Roach.

His long jaw twitched from side to side, a sign of intense cogitation.

McLevy, a man who was rarely still, once more resembled a statue.

Ballantyne looked at Mulholland, who was taller than everyone else and could therefore stare off into space without being interrupted.

The young constable apprehended something was going on but he was buggered if he knew how it was constituted.

Then he saw to his dismay that just past Mulholland's lanky figure, on the wall, a small insect was making its way up the portrait of Queen Victoria.

It looked like a churchyard beetle, which had the habit, when disturbed, of squirting a smelly, yellowish-brown fluid from the raised tip of the abdomen.

What if it did so over Queen Victoria?

However if Ballantyne raised the alarm, either one of these three merciless men, in defence of the realm, would spatter the insect where it strived.

But could he stand by and let such a creature crawl over the face of the monarch?

Decision, decisions.

32

Three merry boys, and three merry boys,
And three merry boys are we,
As ever did sing in a hempen string
Under the Gallows-Tree.

JOHN FLETCHER, *The Bloody Brother*

The Countess read the search warrant, seemingly unperturbed as police prepared to file past her into the crevices of her bawdy-hoose.

'This appears to be in order,' she observed. 'And it is such a pleasure to meet you in the flesh, lieutenant.'

The only part of his anatomy Roach could see was the hand holding the warrant and he wondered, not for the first time, if he had made a mistake by insisting that he come along to keep an eye on proceedings since it was his name on the warrant just under the sheriff officer's.

'You have been pointed out to me at the opera,' the Countess continued serenely. 'I believe it was *La Traviata*. Such a sad story. *The Wayward One*.'

Verdi's tale of a noble-hearted courtesan rang too many bells for Roach at this moment so he contented himself by taking back the search warrant, and signalling his men to move past into the bowels of the house.

'Don't break anything,' he ordered, with a warning glance to Ballantyne who sped past, eager to take part in his first official raid.

McLevy had been chafing at the bit behind and now the courtesies had been observed, trampled them underfoot.

'Alfred Binnie – where is he?' he demanded, almost shoving in front of his lieutenant.

'I beg your pardon?' she replied but in the beat before this, he noted her eyes flick for a moment to the flight of stairs that led to the upper rooms.

'The object of our search, madam,' said Roach.

'A hired assassin and acid-pourer, his speciality is the knife,' McLevy threw at her.

It worried him slightly how calm the Countess was being; hopefully all that would change.

'I do not know who you might mean, inspector –'

'Then let me find him for you!'

Rudely interrupting her measured tones, he pushed past and moved with surprising speed up the stairs, his old black revolver in his coat pocket bumping reassuringly against his leg as he thrust upwards.

'Bring some men with you!' Roach called unavailingly, but then an uproar from the main salon distracted him.

An irate voice, one that the lieutenant found disturbingly familiar, rang out into the hall.

'Take your hands from me, ye illiterate extraction!'

Then there was a roar of indignation and outrage before Ballantyne emerged with what looked like a brown wig in his possession.

'I'm sorry, sir,' he explained in some confusion. 'The man resisted being moved and this came away in my hands.'

Another roar of outrage and Roach, to his horror, finally placed the voice. At the same time the butler who had admitted them at the door, then retreated out of sight, suddenly reappeared from the door of the salon, snatched the wig from Ballantyne and darted back inside to restore it to the rightful owner.

Another bellow resembling something that might have greeted Perseus from the middle of the Labyrinth came from the unseen presence, followed by some alarmed female shrieks a little further away.

Roach's face was ashen.

Ballantyne's strawberry red.

The sonorous baritone of the butler sounded, trying to calm the situation.

More shrieks in chorus.

The high tenor of outraged authority.

The Countess laughed softly.

'Just like the opera,' she murmured.

Meanwhile James McLevy had a sick feeling in the pit of his

stomach. He had found the room, he was certain of that. It bore the marks of sequestered occupation – a single mattress bed jammed into a corner, a glass with dregs of stale beer, biscuit crumbs, a cheap case with a few items of male clothing – but nothing else.

The bird had flown.

He hauled up the window and looked down into the back garden where the snarling yelps of dogs could be heard.

Mulholland plus a few men were milling around in uncertain fashion and the constable looked up at McLevy with annoyance on his face,

'That was the very devil!' he shouted up. 'Getting these dogs back in their kennel. Two of the men got bit.'

'Never mind that,' the inspector bawled back. 'Did ye corner him?'

'Binnie? No – do you not have him?'

'No. Are ye sure?'

'Of course I'm sure!'

'Bugger!'

McLevy slammed the window shut again and scrabbled in the suitcase to see if there might be some clue as to where the fellow had gone.

But there was nothing but dirty underpants and smelly socks. The man was not house-proud.

And this was not proceeding according to plan.

Ballantyne came though the open door, which bore the mark of a hefty boot that McLevy had dealt the lock before charging in to find nothing behind it.

'The lieutenant wishes your presence downstairs, sir.'

McLevy thought to ask why but decided to find out for himself; one thing for sure, it would not be congratulations on a job well done.

In fact he met Roach part way up the stairs, the lieutenant trying to put some distance between himself and looming catastrophe.

Just before they began talking there was the crash of china and a muffled cry from the Countess.

Roach was hissing like an angry alligator.

'McLevy! I have just left a senior high court official in the downstairs salon, half-dressed, at least his wig restored, and not a happy man. Please tell me there is a successful conclusion to all this.'

'Not so far,' responded McLevy cheerily.

The lieutenant fixed him with a cold, saurian eye.

'I authorised this raid against my better judgement and I now –'

'Lieutenant Roach!' a voice was calling angrily.

'– regret it bitterly.'

The Countess suddenly appeared on the scene, eyes bright with fury.

'Your men have just upset a most valuable antique!' she cried in piercing tone.

'Is it the court official?' asked McLevy, just for devilment. When things were at their worst the imp of mischief often took a bow in his psyche and life became a sight more adventurous.

'It is a Persian vase!'

'An unfortunate accident,' said Roach.

'I demand compensation!' she wailed, all calmness fled at the broken artefact or perhaps just using it as an excuse to let rip at the law.

McLevy meanwhile had been searching in the melee for a face he knew and thought to glimpse it in the main salon.

Mulholland came through the back door to join the burgeoning kerfuffle and the inspector saw his chance.

'Ah, constable, no doubt you have important tidings!' he boomed, crossing past the other two and heading for Mulholland.

McLevy beckoned the constable close as if they were exchanging significant news.

'You know my tidings,' muttered Mulholland. 'They're not worth a damn.'

'I must search out someone,' McLevy said urgently. 'You must assuage the Countess.'

'Assuage?'

While Mulholland puzzled out the exact shade of meaning to this word, McLevy turned towards the others.

'Constable Mulholland is an expert on Persian crockery,' he announced grandly. 'He is your man!'

With that he shoved Mulholland towards the Countess and slid past her and the baleful glare of Roach into the main salon, followed by Ballantyne, who had sense enough not to want to stay where he had been which was stuck part way up the stairs and an easy target.

Inside the main salon some of the younger policemen were trying not to stare too obviously at the presented décolletage of the assembled *belles de nuit* while they asked after the whereabouts of a wee plump man.

The court official and his wig had removed to another room. McLevy looked around in vain for his objective yet saw nothing.

Then he noticed that one of the curtains by the window was swaying gently as if someone had slipped behind.

He moved over to stand in front.

'Ballantyne,' he whispered. 'Put your body atwixt me and the rest of the room.'

'Whit for, sir?'

'Do as you're damned well told!'

The constable hopped to it and stood rather awkwardly but served as a barrier between the others and McLevy.

A voice sounded behind. Low enough just to hear.

'You're too late, inspector.'

'I gathered that.'

'A while before ye arrived. The Countess got a letter. Hand-delivered. Upstairs she went like a shot frae a gun.'

McLevy frowned. Had they been betrayed? But how? Surely not. Unless someone at the station or sheriff's office had tipped the nod?

That was not possible. Surely.

Yet it would seem as if Binnie might have left because of that delivery.

Or was it all just bad timing?

'Where is this letter?' he asked under his breath.

'In her dress. I saw her stash it there. A hidden pocket just under the bosom.'

The inspector was momentarily disquieted.

'*The bosom?*'

'Aye.' There was a hint of laughter in the hidden tones. 'Ye surely know where such has its position.'

McLevy nodded.

'I owe you for this, Maisie.'

'I tellt ye. I do it for Jean, not you. Besides, the Countess is an auld bitch.'

McLevy moved away abruptly, followed again by the bewildered Ballantyne who had witnessed his inspector talking to himself and being answered from the ether in the best traditions of mesmerism.

As Maisie emerged from the curtain she caught the eye of Feeney the butler who was standing across, having emerged from the side room.

The woman had no idea whether he had twigged the exchange or not but better safe than sorry.

And anyway she had now nailed her colours to the mast.

She walked over to stare him straight in the eye.

'If you so much as open your mouth, you will find your means of manhood bouncing before your very eyes. And after that my good friend, Mister McLevy, will throw you in jail for the rest of your life. This is Leith.'

Feeney made a silent resolve to quit the place as soon as possible.

Back to the Earl of Essex. The man was a wastrel and paid badly but castration was low on the agenda.

Mulholland had been discounted as a Middle Eastern specialist by the time McLevy and Ballantyne rejoined the fray, and Roach was getting an earful of condemnation from the Countess to which he had little defence.

'You have upset my establishment,' she almost spat at him, 'destroyed my possessions, and for what? The stupid idea of a stupid man!'

'And here I am!'

McLevy appeared suddenly with a face like fury, then went on the attack, grand opera style.

'In the room at the top of your house is a suitcase with clothes of a male persuasion. Who is their master?'

'They have been so for a good long time. A client left them,' replied the Countess quickly.

'Liked tae dress up in smelly socks, did he?'

'All sorts make the world.'

'For a good long time, eh?' McLevy came towards her with what seemed violent intent. 'And whit about the dregs o' beer and bits o' biscuit, are they from long ago as well?'

'One of the girls perhaps. They are wilful creatures.'

This insouciant response angered the inspector even more, it seemed, and he moved as if to confront the Countess face to face. But as he did so, he caught his foot on one of Mulholland's large policeman's boots and tripped headlong to send himself and the Countess crashing to the floor in a tangle of limbs and rustle of garments.

Her modest dress, by appearance more suited for a sewing circle than a bawdy-hoose, was jerked at rudely by McLevy's digits as he scrabbled for purchase.

She let out a violated squeak.

'Remove your hands, sir!'

'No' my fault,' replied McLevy. 'Mulholland's feet.'

'I was nowhere near,' protested the constable, which in fact was the truth of the matter.

Roach was horrified at the apparent ravishment beneath as McLevy slid on top of the woman.

The hidden bosom-pocket was very well hidden.

'McLevy. What in God's name are you doing?'

A high-pitched scream from the Countess came in answer, and then the inspector wrenched back with a folded letter in his hands.

'Extrication only, sir,' he explained, and then clambered to his feet as the gallant Ballantyne helped the Countess to hers. Her eyes widened when she saw what McLevy held.

'Give that back –'

'Why so?'

'It belongs to me!'

'Does it? Let me see.'

He stood at a distance away and stepped back from the tiny hands of the Countess, which were stretching out like talons to reclaim her property.

'Oh aye. Right enough. Here's your name at the top.'

The writing was in a bold, childlike fist and when he saw a name at the bottom, the whole thing fell into place.

And a death was surely on the cards.

'Now I know where Binnie is,' he muttered. 'Come on Mulholland, and pray that we're not too late –'

As the inspector made for the door followed by his two constables, Ballantyne not wanting to be left out and having the time of his young life, Roach gave voice.

'Where are you going, McLevy?'

'Tae find you proof, sir,' the response came as the party disappeared through the door. 'Hold that harlot till then. All will be clear. All will be well!'

Then there was the sound from outside of one of the police wagons being whipped into motion and clattering off into the night.

In for a penny, in for a pound, Roach thought grimly.

He smiled at the Countess who looked as if she would like to bite out someone's throat.

'Let us sit down somewhere, madam,' he said in an eerily tranquil tone. 'And discuss the opera. To tell you the truth, it is more my wife's passion. I often find the stories rather dismal.'

He looked around at the chaos, closed his mind to consequences for the moment and continued to think through his theme with some words that he decided to keep to himself lest they prove an unfortunate augury.

The reason why dismal?

They rarely have a happy ending.

33

The long habit of living indisposeth us for dying.

SIR THOMAS BROWNE, *Urn Burial*

The body at his feet still had a vestige of life left, but that soon would disappear in flames. And who knows, he might have a little fun just before the main event?

Alfred Binnie pulled down the gauze curtains and threw them to join the pile he had gathered in the middle of the room. He liked this house. From what he could see with the furnishings and such, a few broken oil lamps thrown in, the Just Land would go up like a tinder-box.

And Jean Brash's boudoir was the perfect place to start the conflagration.

This was not his speciality but he was adroit enough in the mechanics of fire-raising; it was a matter of draught and fierce combustion. Luckily he had opened the windows to find a breeze of sorts blowing in.

Indeed he had already seen some Halloween bonfires dotted at points over the city.

But this would top them all.

He giggled a little at that thought. A fitting way to leave his mark on Edinburgh.

A scorched trail.

He had kept to the shadows on the way here, conscious that the night had many eyes, but with the streets alive with Halloween-garbed figures had availed himself of Satan's image in the form of a livid red mask.

The Countess supplied it. She thought of everything.

The woman on the floor groaned and he wondered about a momentary diversion but decided against. No time.

He could of course put her out of misery but decided to let the flames have their way. In any case Alfred always disliked a second plunge of the knife. Sloppy. Once should always be enough.

Should have been.

Yet the woman had caught his movement out of the corner of her eye and twisted away.

Not far or fast enough, however.

She deserved what she got. Should have known better.

He surveyed the scene with proud satisfaction; Alfred was a craftsman after all, even if it was in death.

His bowler hat lay on a table neatly to the side and he must remember to reclaim it as the flames leapt up.

A neighbouring church clock began to toll the hour and he took that as a good omen.

On the ninth bell, then.

But as he put his hand inside his coat to find the lucifers, the door burst open and two policemen appeared.

One tall and lanky, the other with a red mark on his face. Young. Easy meat.

Mulholland took a firm grasp of his hornbeam stick and motioned Ballantyne to stay in place behind him.

'You will come with us, Mister Binnie.'

Alfred smiled disarmingly, at the same time slipping the knife out of its sheath pocket of his coat and holding it low to his side.

'You know my name? That's good.'

'You will come with us accordingly and release your weapon. At once, if it please you, sir.'

Mulholland's accent had thickened with the tension and Binnie frowned in displeasure.

'Oh. . .a stinking Irish, eh? Right out of the bog.'

As Mulholland moved slowly in, the woman whimpered once more and Alfred kicked at her.

'These sluts. Noisy bitches, eh?'

Another whimper and Mulholland's face tightened in anger, which was Alfred's intention.

Angry people make mistakes.

'Come and get me, bogman.'

The constable raised his stick in response and Alfred grinned like a cesspit rodent.

'Come on, bogman. I'll slice up your potatoes.'

Mulholland was angry but he had channelled the feeling into his right arm. He knew the man would be fast but backed his reflexes against some sewer rat from Shoreditch.

However Fate and Ballantyne took a hand.

All the inexperienced young fellow saw was a slimy, corpulent man, slow-moving, eyes twitching. Easy meat.

He made a rash move from the side and while Mulholland's attention was distracted by alarm for his colleague, Alfred moved with blinding speed.

His knife shot out at Mulholland like a snake's tongue.

The constable was alert too late to the danger but managed to wrench away; the blade cut deep into his side and he gasped in pain to fall stunned to the floor, the stick falling to land a distance away.

Ballantyne was stricken, Alfred grinned some more and James McLevy burst finally upon the scene.

As he had been about to follow the constables up the stairs to the top of the house, the other rooms found empty, McLevy heard a noise from below in the cellars.

The inspector hesitated a moment then decided his men were big enough to look after themselves.

He moved swiftly down the stone steps to the cellar and stepped cautiously inside.

Was the killer here?

It was dark, but enough light from the hall above the stairs was coming down to show the implements for inflicting a piercing pleasure hung neatly in rows on the wall.

The noise was coming from a closed door at the other end, where the Berkley Horse stood.

A muffled thudding came from this portal, a large iron key in the lock.

Mindful it might be a trap, McLevy grasped his heavy revolver in one hand, turned the key with the other and sprang the door.

A frightened Lily Baxter almost fell into his arms.

She took a deep breath, mimed someone pushing her in, then pointed urgently upwards.

McLevy cursed to himself. This was the wrong place to be for a policeman searching out a murderer.

Now, moments later, after heaving himself up the stairs, he was in the right place. At the wrong time.

Two bodies lay on the floor. One Mulholland, the other Jessie Nairn.

A cold light came into his eyes and he raised the revolver to point at Binnie.

'Give me an excuse,' said the inspector of police.

But the little man had one more trick up his sleeve, darting to the side behind the paralysed Ballantyne and putting the sharp edge of his knife against the red patch that signalled a beginning to the birthmark.

'I'll cut his throat,' he said softly. 'No problem.'

McLevy sighted down the barrel but Binnie ducked behind Ballantyne and started edging towards the door using the other as cover, dragging the young constable like a dumb animal to slaughter.

'Keep well back,' he warned. 'Or his head falls off. That'd be fun.'

The inspector performed as bidden. The little man's calmness was oddly unnerving but that was not the reason.

McLevy had noted, as they shuffled past Mulholland, that the constable's hand had wrapped itself once more around his stick. Good that the man wasn't entirely dead.

Now what he needed was a chance.

McLevy suddenly let out a tremendous roar and pointed to the window as if Satan had just flown in.

An old trick for sure. But old are often best.

Alfred's turn to be distracted. For a second his head turned and the knife came away a fraction from Ballantyne's neck.

Not much, but enough.

Mulholland's arm swept up in an arc and the hard tip of hornbeam crunched against Binnie's left elbow, numbing the arm like a bolt from the blue and enabling Ballantyne to pull himself free while McLevy stepped forward to confront the cursing Binnie.

The little man flipped the knife over to his other hand.

'I'm just as good with the right,' he said.

'That's nice,' replied McLevy.

He stepped up so that there was hardly arm's length between them, and before Binnie could make his move, the inspector's hand was a blur in the air as the barrel of his gun crashed against the side of the killer's head.

As Binnie slumped downwards, McLevy adroitly relieved him of his knife, turned him, slapped on the restrainers to pinion his hands behind the back, and then threw the man bodily into the corner like a sack of coal.

In almost the same motion he moved to kneel by Mulholland who was wincing in pain, supporting himself on the one elbow.

'How are ye, Martin?' McLevy questioned anxiously.

'Terrible, if that's you on my Christian name,' gasped the constable.

'Jist asking.'

They both looked down to where the blood was oozing slowly through the thick serge of Mulholland's uniform.

'I think only a flesh wound,' muttered the constable, 'but it's a deal of flesh.'

'I can help,' said Ballantyne, suddenly pulling a pure Egyptian cotton sheet from the bed of Jean Brash and ripping it in pieces.

He knelt down and gently undid the buttons of the uniform and pulled up the shirt to uncover a nasty looking gash mercifully not near any vital organs, which he neatly wiped clean and then began to wrap round with the makeshift bandage.

'My mother's a nurse,' he explained.

Then he looked up for a second at Mulholland.

'I am sorry, sir,' he said. 'I brought this on.'

In spite of it all, Mulholland was oddly pleased to be called 'sir'.

'Just don't do it again, constable,' he replied with a grimace of pain. 'Lest the luck run out.'

A low moan from Jessie brought McLevy over to her side. This wound was not so hopeful.

The death sheen was already on her face. It was something the inspector had observed before and he could see in her eyes that Jessie knew she was going into darkness.

'Are you of the faith, McLevy?' she murmured faintly.

'No. Jist a policeman.'

She managed a crooked smile at the answer.

'I need tae confess.'

'Consider it so.'

He motioned the other two over to listen in as evidential proof; Mulholland had to inch along, wound or no wound. Every dying testimony needs a living witness. That's the law.

Her eyes closed and McLevy knew there was little time.

'You were planted, were you not, Jessie?'

'Aye. The Countess had doubts on Simone. I was to go with her. Wherever. Spy the land.'

'And Galloway?'

'That jist happened by accident. But I sent word tae her that he might be an enemy of Jean's. And the Countess made a plan.'

'What would he get out of it?'

'Promised him free rein. The Countess. A' the women in the world.'

She coughed and a little smear of blood fell out of the corner of her mouth. Ballantyne leant forward and wiped it clean with a rag of Egyptian cotton.

'Good looking boy,' said Jessie.

Ballantyne retreated in confusion.

McLevy considered it time to help the girl along.

'So Galloway was a dupe. He thought Jean was to be enticed, then kidnapped, stuck on a boat tae South America, lost at sea, whatever. Disappeared, at all counts. He didnae realise he was to be the corpse, and she get the blame.'

Jessie nodded slowly.

'Aye. No flies on you, inspector.'

Jessie tried to laugh but the effort was too painful.

'That's whit I thought as well. That she'd be stuck away some-where. But when the killing happened. Too late. *No going back*, the Countess said.'

'Why did ye do it all, Jessie?'

'I'm jist pure evil.'

'No, you're not.'

For a moment she looked into his eyes.

'Sure you're no' a priest?'

He smiled bleakly. Shook his head. She sighed.

'The Countess. Promised me my own place. I'd be queen bee. Never had anything. Of my own. Ever.'

For a moment he looked into her eyes and saw a lonely child who had never known love or anything close to it.

'And I'll wager ye locked wee Lily in the cellar to keep her safe? Once the fire had started, let her out, say it was all an accident. No Mistress Brash tae worry you?'

Jessie nodded.

'Jean was fair. I felt bad. But I did it anyway.'

An epitaph for humankind.

I felt bad, but I did it anyway.

McLevy assumed official tones.

'Jessie Nairn, do you swear in the presence of these witnesses that what you have told is the mortal truth?'

'I swear.'

He took the letter he had filched from the bosom of the Coun-tess and waved it in front of her dying eyes.

No mercy. Not while there's breath.

'And this is in your own hand to the Countess?'

'I do so swear,' said Jessie. 'Bless me Father, for I have sinned.' Her eyelids closed then her head fell back.

Lily Baxter had stood in the doorway watching events unfold.

She recognised the inert form in the corner as the wicked man from the market, saw the policemen crouching over Jessie and then her friend crumple like a leaf.

Lily darted forward; the men stood up to give room as she knelt beside Jessie and reached out her hand to caress the cold face of death.

Jessie's last words were in a broken undertone, from the childhood game that she and Lily had been playing in the Just Land to while away the time of occupation.

Indeed it was the ruse that had enabled her to lock Lily away in safety.

Hide and seek.

In the darkness.

It had been great fun.

'Peeky-boo,' Jessie murmured. 'Here I come. Ready or no'. It's not my fault.'

Lily bowed her head.

The policemen did also, McLevy removing his low-brimmed bowler while Binnie moaned softly in the corner.

Hide and seek.

Here I come.

Ready or not.

34

Now I lay me down to sleep,
I pray the Lord my soul to keep;
And if I die before I wake,
I pray the Lord my soul to take.

Child's bedtime verse

Lieutenant Robert Roach was a much-relieved man as he waited for the changing of the guard at the station.

He had an injured constable to consider but the wound had been dressed by Doctor Jarvis and Mulholland was no doubt at his lodgings now, sitting with his feet up in front of the fire, regaling his landlady with tales of bravery.

Roach did not know Mulholland's landlady from Eve but imagined her to be a buxom lady of Irish extraction who doted upon her lodger's every word and plied him with sweet tea and homemade ginger biscuits.

The lieutenant was content enough with this image; a man needs as much comfort as he can garner these days.

In his hand he held the letter from Jessie that had set McLevy off and running.

Just to make sure, he read it once again. Roach had been brought up to date with all the events so far but it never did any harm to re-examine the evidence.

Countess,

The coast is now clear. Only Lily Baxter and me, the house empty. I can deal with her. Hannah Semple is gone. I will let your man in by the gate. You must keep your promise to me. A murder has been done. Logan Galloway. It has all been to your plan and my reward must be soon.

Jessie Nairn

'Poor lassie. She signed her death warrant.'

McLevy had ghosted up at his elbow in a manner Roach always found disconcerting; the man would have made a fine footpad.

'Indeed,' Roach observed. 'Blackmail implicit. Not a good idea.'

'I don't doubt the Countess would have got rid of her anyway,' said McLevy. 'Once Binnie was safely back in London the only person who had knowledge of it all was Jessie. The threat in that letter just. . .hurried things on.'

McLevy pursed his lips as he remembered the pain in Jessie's eyes.

I felt bad but I did it anyway.

'It is also possible that when it came to the point of Jean being put away for the rest of her life, Jessie may have recanted.'

'I doubt it.'

'Ye never know. And the Countess wouldnae take that chance either.'

'It was a clever plan she laid.'

'Very strategic.'

Roach handed the letter back to McLevy and reflected once

more how his inspector could manage to land in a clump full of thistles and emerge unscathed.

As if he could mesmerically read his superior's mind McLevy suddenly ventured, 'Whit about the court official with the wig that jumped?'

'He has decided to forgive and forget.'

'In case his wife finds out?'

'Exactly.'

McLevy's lips quirked in amusement. They were standing in the middle of the station but the place seemed oddly empty and calm as if a great storm had just passed over.

'In all this excitement,' Roach remarked almost casually, 'it rather slipped my mind. Samuel Grant? I assume we are to charge him with attempting to sell back stolen goods to the rightful owner?'

'Aye. Providing Mistress Grierson attests to such.'

'I assume she will. After all, what other explanation could there be? A respectable widow. . .'

In fact the lieutenant had been unwise enough to mention a hint of the happening to his wife; she had thrown her horrified arms in the air at the invasion into Muriel Grierson's decency but also pressed him to keep her abreast of additional developments.

Thus widows attract curiosity by dint of standing alone in the field of matrimony.

An exception to the rule.

He glanced at McLevy who seemed to have forgotten the last question, so the lieutenant returned to the present crime.

When McLevy had sent word back to the lair of the Countess that he had taken Binnie to uncover proof on the murder of Galloway and the plot hatched by this woman, Roach had not hesitated to have her hauled in.

But the case was not yet nailed down to his satisfaction.

'We may not have enough on the Countess,' said Roach thoughtfully. 'Even with this letter and Jessie's witnessed confession, a good lawyer and she might wriggle free.'

'That was before Mister Binnie offered to turn Queen's evidence,' replied McLevy with a certain inner glee. 'I have just been in close conference with the wee toad and he is anxious to save his neck. He is at this moment writing out a formal confession naming the Countess as the Machiavelli behind these wicked deeds and he a mere tool in her hands.'

'Machiavelli was a man.'

'I am aware of that, sir.'

'And what does Binnie wish in return?'

'Some clemency from the judge.'

'A word in His Honour's ear?'

'That sort of thing.'

'The fellow has committed two murders, plus attempted arson and an acid assault to boot. Not a great deal of leeway, inspector.'

'I know that. But I didnae want to hurt his feelings.'

This sardonic exchange had been conducted as they watched the Countess emerge from a side room with two of the female helpers at the station. The procession was led by a bashfully triumphant Ballantyne.

'More to that boy than vision would indicate,' Roach allowed.

'His mother's a nurse,' came the cryptic response.

McLevy and Mulholland had decided not to acquaint Roach or the world at large with Ballantyne's error as regards the stab in Jean's boudoir.

Anyone can make a mistake. Anytime. Anywhere.

As the Countess spied Roach she made one more effort to reassert a somewhat shrunken authority.

'You make a misjudgement, Lieutenant Roach,' she averred. 'And I shall write to the highest in the land.'

'Her Majesty may be a trifle occupied,' Roach replied dryly. 'Please avail yourself, however, of our facilities of pen and paper but you must purchase your own postage.'

As she turned away in contempt at this trifle, thus avoiding the stare of a stone-faced McLevy, the Countess found herself on a collision course with Jean Brash – who had just been released from the cells.

Hannah Semple at the side of her mistress. Patterson the lawyer with his large head made up the rear.

And so it came to pass that the *War of the Bawdy-hoose Keepers* had its final act in the Leith station.

'Ships that pass in the night, eh McLevy?' Roach uttered without moving his lips.

'Uhuh.'

Silence as the two women appraised each other, then Jean stepped up to the mark.

'Countess – you take my place, it would seem,' she slid in sweetly. 'One for the other.'

The older woman spat out her rejoinder.

'I am worth twenty of you. You are nothing more than a common slut.'

Jean nodded as if in complete agreement.

'What was it you said?' She screwed up her eyes as if remembering the words. '*In prison. . .each day is like a year, each year like an eternity.* Very nicely put.'

For a moment it appeared as if the Countess would launch herself tooth and nail at Jean, then she gathered herself together for the last word.

'May your future be as diseased as your body,' she announced before turning with dignity to Ballantyne and linking her arm through his in a proprietorial fashion.

'Lead me on, young man,' she announced, as if he the consort and she the royal quality.

Ballantyne nodded, did not attempt to disengage his arm and led her off to the very cell that Jean had just vacated, the door still open, the lumpy mattress waiting like a sullen lover.

'I'll write ye a letter,' Mistress Brash called after, but the Countess did not look back.

Jean watched her go then turned to Roach. She was conscious of all eyes in the station upon her, the various young constables in various corners and even Murdoch rooted at his desk, all ears aquiver.

Was she now a legend?

Imprisoned and released.

The queen bee.

'I thank you for the hospitality, lieutenant,' she said solemnly. 'You must sample mine some day.'

Roach was not inclined to indulge in mythical exchange.

'I would have left you to rot in jail, Mistress Brash,' he retorted bluntly. 'You may thank McLevy here.'

The inspector's face was part hidden in the shadows into which he had stepped back as soon as Jean's entourage had appeared.

She did not thank him. McLevy did not wish it so.

'How is Constable Mulholland?' she asked him formally.

'Still alive.'

'I am sorry for his wound.'

'I'll pass it on.'

Then McLevy hesitated a moment before a request.

'Jessie Nairn. Make sure she gets a decent burial. She wisnae all bad.'

Jean thought about that for a moment before nodding acceptance; she owed the inspector that much at least.

Patterson stepped forward importantly to lead her from the station. As Hannah Semple passed, she winked at McLevy.

'Ye're a bloody menace,' she whispered. 'I don't know your equal.'

'Oh, one thing?' the inspector could not resist calling just as Jean reached the station door. 'Your wee boudoir nearly went up in flames.'

'That's happened before,' she replied a trifle enigmatically.

McLevy felt a sudden onrush of anger and let her have it with both barrels.

'This is your fault, Jean. Your black pride was the cause of all this. Carry that with you to your bawdy-hoose.'

For a moment it was as if everyone else receded and it was just the two of them.

A spark of equal anger appeared in her eyes.

And then she was gone.

A few moments passed and a low murmur rose from the assembled constabulary. Whit a night.

The Countess had also left the scene.

Roach let out a huge exhalation of relief.

'Would you care to join me in a wee libation in the office, James?'

'No, thank you, sir,' said McLevy, surprisingly.

He was on his way to the station door and turned, conscious that his part in these events might also be rendered into legend.

'My work is not done and Halloween is not yet over.'

'The Morrison case?'

'None other.'

Roach thought to ask further then contented himself with a nod. The man was solving things right, left and centre; best let him get on with it.

As the inspector disappeared, Ballantyne came out of the cells and Roach crooked a finger at him.

Over walked the young constable.

'Do you drink malt whisky?' asked his lieutenant.

35

> I beheld the wretch – the miserable monster whom I had created.
>
> Mary Shelley, *Frankenstein*

Arthur Conan Doyle shivered in the dampness of Halloween night and gazed across at his companion, who seemed totally impervious to the clammy moist air that wraithed around them like a witch's spell.

Midnight had come and gone; some snatches of smoke from a distant bonfire that had not yet expired also swirled at their feet; and Doyle was reminded of a scene from *Hamlet* when the ghost appears on the battlements. It had been at the Lyceum in London, he was fifteen years of age and staying a most glorious three weeks over Christmas with his uncles and their families.

The great Henry Irving had played the Dane.

Tall, slim, a handsome brooding presence with a shock of dark hair, quietly spoken but with the impression of a superb intelligence, black glittering eyes and a long nose that sniffed out corruption in the state of Denmark.

And when his father's ghost appeared, it seemed the prince's very soul was split in twain.

It had been the happiest time Conan Doyle had enjoyed in England since being sent at the age of nine to the tender mercies of the Jesuits at Stonyhurst College.

His wild, adventurous spirit had collided head-on with the spartan discipline hammered down upon him and though there had been moments of gratification and scholastic success, he had felt, not unlike Prince Hamlet, suffocated and beaten down by an authority he did not at times recognise or respect.

Arthur had felt almost betrayed by his mother but now realised that she had sent him away to protect the young boy from the worsening state of his own father.

An alcoholic ghost.

Still residing in the institution where he moved between sweet clarity and dangerous fits of violence. A madness to be feared lest it travel in the blood.

All this had passed through Doyle's mind; there was little else to do huddled in a doorway, watching the roof-tops for a murderous beast to take its bow.

A bang on the door of his mother's house.

Doyle had thought one of the lodgers had forgotten his key but there on the threshold was James McLevy.

'I'm going hunting, Mister Doyle,' he said, face white in the dark outside. 'You were on my way.'

No more needed to be said. Arthur had bolted for his old sailor's coat, stuck on the cap, shouted upstairs to his puzzled mother that he would be a time or so, and then was off into the misty night for adventure.

Though it did not seem much of an exploit so far.

They had relieved the shivering constables stationed on watch outside the house of Walter Morrison and then McLevy had hunkered down like an animal settling into its den, tipped his hat over his eyes and not uttered a word or moved a muscle since that moment.

Arthur was restless. He took out one of his pipes and thought to light up and puff some comfort but then worried that it might signal occupation and so replaced it.

Once more he scanned the rooftops where he had been instructed to fix his eagle eye.

Nothing. A few seagulls wheeling despondently, pale shapes in the leaden sky.

'Ye see any fiendish ogres?' asked the inspector from under the brim.

'Nary a one,' replied Doyle.

'Ah well. Time yet.'

Anxious that McLevy might disappear once more into the land of Nod, Doyle threw a question at him.

"What makes you think this killer will appear tonight, inspector?'

'Jist a wee intuition.'

And in fact, it was no more than that. But on the way to Doyle's he had stopped off at the banker's house. The man, in the midst of Halloween celebrations, a bonfire in the back garden, festooned with overexcited grandchildren, had not welcomed the intrusion but supplied what information he had gleaned on the Morrisons' finances.

An interesting harvest. It chimed with a picture that was beginning to build up at the back of McLevy's mind.

And if he was correct, this might be the last night possible for murderous excursion.

If he was wrong, a watch had still been kept according to plan. Though, as opposed to obvious constabulary on the street, he and Doyle were well tucked out of sight.

So to enquiring eyes, it might appear as if the castle were unguarded and the drawbridge down.

Both men were hidden in the crevice of a small wynd running off Henderson Row, a stately street of terraced-houses where fine respectable folk had their dwelling.

McLevy had made himself comfortable against the wall, leaving Doyle to stand guard. Now the inspector, refreshed after a catnap of sorts, levered himself up and glanced at the large form beside him.

Had Mulholland not been indisposed, the man might not be here but McLevy had a feeling that this medical colossus had yet a part to play in the drama.

Time would tell and though Roach would have a blue fit at a member of the public being involved at a potential crime scene, what the lieutenant didn't know would not hurt.

From Conan Doyle's point of view, this was the perfect opportunity to delve into the mind of a successful detective.

A character was taking shape in his imagination that he had explored in rough-and-ready fashion in a story delivered by his own hand to *Blackwood's Magazine* in Edinburgh and never heard about again.

Perhaps it had been murdered and the body buried in a file marked 'Too Many Ghosts?'

Doyle frowned. That title wasn't any better than the original tale.

The Haunted Grange at Goresthorpe. Not good enough by a long shot, and he had one published in an Edinburgh weekly that he had set in South Africa. *The Mystery of Sassassa Valley.* Another cumbersome title. Rough efforts.

But there was more to come.

Writing is like a fever in the blood cells.

'D'ye peruse Edgar Allan Poe?' McLevy asked, as if he knew which way Arthur's mind was running.

'I consider him to be a supremely original writer of the short story,' Doyle replied somewhat stiffly, because the thought of Poe's genius only threw his own efforts into an unflattering relief.

'Aye. Every one like an open wound.'

McLevy, having summed up the master of the macabre with this pithy phrase, whistled softly under his breath as he risked a quick glance up and down the thoroughfare.

In the distance he could hear the faint sound of carriage wheels but other than a few bedraggled Halloween revellers making their way home, the streets were empty.

'How did you know I was thinking of literary matters?' asked Doyle suddenly.

'Your fingers were twitching.'

The inspector let out a short bark of laughter and Doyle took this as a sign that communication was in order.

'At our first meeting, sir,' he began, as if making formal examination, 'you deduced certain facts about me that were not noticeable to the untrained eye. What is your method of procedure, if I may so ask?'

McLevy thought to make more mischief in Doyle's mind but decided that Big Arthur deserved a bit more – at the moment the young man's intelligence was somewhat tramlined, but the policeman could sense what he would term *activity at the back of the hoose.* Intuition. The acumen of nerve ends.

However as regards his 'deduction' in the station, it had only too mundane a source.

'I saw ye,' he said simply.

'What?'

'I like the boxing. I was informed there might be a good contest up at the university. I saw you in the ring.'

Indeed it had been a fine contest. McLevy stood well to the back as the students cheered on one side against another. The final bout had been Conan Doyle contra the squat form of a burly Welshman, the visiting college being St David's from the land of leeks.

Doyle at first had found it hard to lay a glove on the man who was built like a small bull, had a low centre of gravity, and was crafty withal according to the popular conception of his race.

Arthur had hurt his hand punching down and a roundhouse swing from his opponent had hit him flush under the eye. The second round was more even but in the third, as the Welshman ran out of steam, Doyle finally landed a straight right that put the man on the floor and ended proceedings.

The winner was cheered on especially by the medical students, an unruly lot and more so by dint of some being recently qualified.

All this McLevy had observed, so when Doyle came charging into Leith station the next morning, his card was already marked and accounted.

The purveyor of the straight right had his guard down and jaw dropped.

'So your deduction was completely false?'

'Not at all. Completely true. I jist knew the facts before. Not after.'

Doyle gave the unperturbed inspector what could only be described as an old-fashioned look.

'I might beg to differ with you on the matter of truth here.'

'Differ away.'

'You deceived me.'

'Not at all. Had ye asked I would have told you. Ye didnae think tae ask. You were too caught up in the process tae consider otherwise. The mind is full of such traps.'

They had been speaking softly enough for such a potentially barbed exchange and McLevy hung his head out again to scan the street and rooftops.

Nothing. Silence. Back to Big Arthur. He had a disappointed expression; a dog lost its bone.

'And your deductions of the Grierson burglary?

'Based on experience. I told you.'

James McLevy rarely explained himself; the way he saw things, the more folk knew about you the more they jumped to erroneous conclusions.

However something about this young man dictated McLevy ignore his usual practice.

And nothing was stirring out there. Not even a mouse.

'There are three intelligences we must bring to a crime, Mister Doyle. Forensic, intuitive and experiential.'

'Which is most important?'

'That depends on the crime. Mostly they go hand in hand.'

Doyle mulled that over. He had his own ideas. 'Have you heard of Joseph Bell?' he asked.

'Uhuh. Even attended one his lectures. He's a wee bit gabby but not daft.'

This description of the brilliant lecturer and forensic surgeon that Doyle worshipped and admired above all men came up a little short in his estimation but he now knew enough about McLevy not to rise to the bait.

'I serve as his clerk at the Edinburgh Royal,' Arthur said quietly. 'He is certainly not daft.'

The lecture McLevy had attended by sneaking in at the back, having brandished his warrant card at a university porter, had been a bravura performance.

Bell was a compelling orator and the students hung on his every word. His deductive forensic qualities were striking but, to the inspector's jaundiced eye, it was all theory. Murder is not theoretical. It involves passion and blood.

He could see how Bell would appeal to a hungry intelligence like Doyle's and wondered if his niggling feeling of annoyance was jealousy of sorts.

Bell was famous. Admired. McLevy was a policeman.

He suddenly stiffened and put his hand warningly on Conan Doyle's sleeve.

For a moment the young man thought the inspector was trying to distract from an argument he might lose, then he heard what McLevy's sharp ears had picked up a moment ago.

A scraping noise, high above.

They both peeped out like two boys hiding away in a child's game.

In the blackness, on the slates opposite, a dark shape was moving across the rooftops. Difficult to see in the mirk of this late October night but there was a moment when a shaft of pale moonlight pierced the sullen clouds and the shrouded figure of something showed for a second before the dark descended once more.

'Come on!'

McLevy darted across the road and rapped sharply three times upon one of the doors opposite. A moment later, the frightened face of Walter Morrison peeped out.

The inspector signalled and a small horse and trap that had been parked out of sight, in fact a contrivance that Doyle had known nothing about, trotted up with a stolid driver who wore a cloth cap pulled over his eyes.

'Take the gentleman to your mother's abode, Murdo,' said McLevy, urgently, 'and wait till you hear from me.'

He virtually bundled Morrison into the trap and just before Murdo set the horse in motion, McLevy fixed the scared Walter with a cold implacable stare.

'Eighteen years ago,' he declared. 'I know the story. When I see you next, I want the truth.'

Morrison's face went a shade of sickly white as Murdo flicked the horse with a whip being used for proper purpose, and off they went.

As McLevy and Doyle went through the house and up the stairs, the inspector explained events so far.

'Murdo is slow-witted but trustworthy. He was once accused over the murder of a bairn, but I cleared him. His mother is forever grateful and runs a respectable lodging house.'

They conversed breathlessly as they hurried to the top of the stairs where another small flight led upwards to the attic room.

'I spoke tae Morrison some days ago and warned him that if he didnae wish to be slaughtered under his own roof, he should open the door instant to my signalled knock.'

'You anticipated all this?'

'It was a possibility. That's the fourth intelligence I forgot tae tell you as regards crime. Predetermination.'

They now entered the attic room with the skylight window

letting in faint light from above; McLevy signed Doyle to a corner in the gloom, and stood back so that he had a clear view of the window above.

He produced his old black revolver and took a deep breath.

'You will observe only, Mister Doyle,' he said softly. 'With luck, the killer will be taken. Clean and simple.'

That wasn't, however, the feeling he had in his bones.

They waited in silence. Doyle thrilled to be a part of the murder investigation, McLevy as if carved out of stone.

A creak on the roof above.

Wait.

Silence.

Then the skylight began to buckle as if some force were pressing it out of shape. A slow protest of hinges being wrenched and suddenly the window was hauled bodily off its moorings and a rush of damp evening air announced that the room was now at the mercy of the elements.

A grunting animal noise and then strangely a voice that was unlike any human sound but made words like an axe would splinter shards out of stone.

'*Find. Kill. Destroy.*'

The hairs on the back of Doyle's neck prickled and he felt a primitive fear that urged him to run. Do not meddle with the beast. Run. Run for your life.

McLevy was an immovable, shapeless mass in the opposite corner; his hand hung by the side with the dark metal of the revolver outlining the white skin where he gripped.

Then a huge shape suddenly appeared, towering above, visible through the empty window frame; it was backlit by the dull sky and enveloped in a black cloak with the hood pulled over so that the face was obscured.

For a moment it stood there and then jumped through the created aperture to land barefooted like a cat in the centre of the attic room.

As it did so the inspector stepped forward, revolver rock-steady in his hand, raised and levelled.

'I am James McLevy, inspector of police. I must ask you to come to the station with me, my mannie. You have murder on your mind and I must forestall that intention.'

For a moment the beast was motionless under the muzzle of the revolver, the metal orifice ready to spit flame at the pressure of a finger. It had registered the sound of the words but not any kind of meaning; like any animal, however, it sensed danger and death at close quarters.

'Turn yourself round, if you please. Extend your hands backwards towards me.'

The monster suddenly grabbed at Conan Doyle, who could not resist a venture nearer to the action, and whirled him by the arm to crash into the inspector.

As they both tumbled to the floor it leapt with incredible agility to hook its gauntlet hands like claws over the edge of the skylight window, haul itself up and then off into the darkness above.

McLevy cursed to himself as Doyle muttered his apologies. Damned fool. Himself. To bring an amateur along.

'Give me a lift up!' he commanded.

Doyle knew at least the mechanics of such; he had given many hikes to the sailors on the whaler.

Up the mast goes the jolly Jack Tar.

He bent over to make a cradle of his hands and as McLevy lifted a stubby leg to place his foot on top, Doyle took a deep breath and thrust the policeman upwards with all the force he could muster.

McLevy shot up towards the skylight and banged his head against the frame. Another muttered curse and then he scrambled out and for a moment stopped down on hands and knees to get his bearings.

'What shall I do?' Doyle called from below.

The inspector fought back the temptation to say enough damage had been done. Besides the man might still have a part to play.

'Get out on the street,' he called back softly. 'I shall keep my eyes peeled for you. If you see him, signal.'

'Good luck,' came in answer then Doyle bolted for the door and was gone.

McLevy took stock. It was not luck he needed, just a primitive instinct to survive.

The roofs were shrouded in darkness, some pale light coming upwards from the street lamps but dying long before it might become a messenger of hope.

He must assume that the beast would return the way it had come so began to inch along in that direction, holding on to the crown of the roof with one hand, revolver in the other, trying to find purchase on the damp slates with his shoes, the soles of which slid alarmingly. The inspector had noted the beast was barefooted, another natural advantage.

McLevy had also noted the heavy gauntlets on its hands, both to protect and leave no evidence. The feet were for grip, the hands did the killing.

As he began to gain confidence and move more quickly, McLevy glanced down to see Doyle's figure far below on the opposite side of the street. The young man pointed further on to indicate he had spotted something, so at least the inspector was on the right track.

Towards getting his neck broken, no doubt.

The chimneystacks stuck up into the night like assassins waiting to pounce. Behind any one of them the creature might lurk.

McLevy sniffed the air. Acrid smoke and dank industrial dew. Auld Reekie.

He sent a prayer up to the gods of the city.

I am your favourite son. Do not forsake me.

He glanced down at Doyle again but the young man spread his arms to signal that he had lost sight of whatever had been observed earlier.

A large chimneystack loomed up. McLevy rested for a moment against the brickwork, heart in his chest like a hammer, a clammy combination of sweat and damp trickling down his face.

Then as he started to cautiously find his way along past the stack, the beast struck.

It had waited patiently, sensing the approach of the prey from the smell of a damp heavy overcoat, the scrape of leather sole on slate. Then as McLevy stepped into view it emerged from cover and smashed its arm into his face, sending him sprawling along the roof, the revolver skittering off to wedge itself in a piece of guttering.

The inspector could feel blood spattering from his nose; he was dazed and winded from the precipitous thud of his belly and chest on the triangular coping stone of the rooftop.

As he scrambled round on hands and knees once more, he

looked up to see the massive hooded form, hands clenched above its head, about to deliver the killer blow.

This was not hopeful.

Down below Conan Doyle watched helplessly as the beast stood for a moment, outlined against the sky. Now a perfect target if he had only a gun to hand.

He beat his hands against his sides in frustration and then felt a hard round object in his pocket.

The cricket ball. A projectile of sorts. Better than nothing. Better than nothing, Arthur Conan.

He hauled it out, took aim, sent a message to the gods of chivalry and good purpose, and then let fly.

Conan Doyle had a mighty arm. He fielded on the boundary of life and his motto was *steel true, blade straight.*

The cricket ball is a hard, dangerous object and has killed more men than might be supposed by those who see only fellows dressed in white upon green grass.

It flew through the night air of Edinburgh like an arrow and smashed into the head of the beast as it prepared to crash down its clasped fists in a deadly strike.

The monster staggered to the side and in that moment James McLevy, himself like an animal on all fours, scrabbled over to where the Edinburgh gods had seen fit to lodge his revolver, grabbed it, wedged himself against the nearest brickwork and aimed.

'I ask you once more, my mannie,' he gasped, the blood running down into his mouth causing the words to thicken. 'Will ye come in peace or rest in the grave?'

The beast paid no heed; the fugue that played within its mind was only set for killing. It charged. Bare feet certain on the slates, body powerful and full of fury, it came full tilt with intent to murder the sitting man.

McLevy had no choice.

He shot twice. The first impact to the chest slowed the beast a moment but still it hurtled on. The second hit near to the same spot and halted the onrush.

The creature let out a strangled cry of almost pathetic surprise and then toppled slowly over to roll down the slates, off the edge of the roof and down into the back green below on the other side of the terraces from the road beneath.

The cricket ball had come back down the slates and jumped the guttering to fall and bounce on the road then to be caught neatly by Doyle as if fielding at long-on.

McLevy stood and signalled below to show all was well though the blood pouring down from his nose might detail otherwise. Doyle waved exuberantly in response before heading off to see if he might gain entrance to the back of the terrace.

The inspector was in no hurry. The beast would not be leaving the scene. Not for a while.

A sudden dizzy spell near overcame him and he grasped at the stack to maintain his balance.

As he gazed down over the back streets, his eye was caught by a movement. A small figure in red, also cloaked, darted up a side alley then was gone.

Or was it a figment of imagination? For a moment he had the wild notion to hurl himself off and swoop down like a bird of prey, snatch the woman up in his claws.

Was it a woman? Was it anything at all?

The figure from his dream came in his mind and he felt a short stabbing pain in his chest. A cold sweat ran down his face and he gasped for breath.

Hold on. Hold on.

After some time, the pain passed.

He reassured himself. It was nothing. Running about on rooftops, all this exertion, thrown on his belly, proximity to violent death, no wonder he felt a wee bit of pain.

Any sensible man would.

It was nothing.

Though it was as if the dream were coming true and the case not yet solved.

By a long haul.

So. . .by the time McLevy had clambered down from the roof and got to the back green, Conan Doyle was already on hand looking down at the crumpled body, which lay face down upon the muddy earth and grass, the one arm outflung.

'I'll need that cricket ball as evidence,' said McLevy, who by this instance had mopped up the blood with a large white hankie which he held against his nose.

Doyle nodded, not sure if this was a joke, both men's adrenalin still pumping hard.

'Have ye touched the corpus?'

'I took the pulse. That is all.'

'Good man. I take it death has occurred?'

Again Doyle nodded.

'Nothing could survive that fall.'

McLevy took away the hankie and touched under his nose somewhat gingerly.

'Whit's that fancy word when the blood stops?'

'Coagulation?'

'It has occurred.'

The inspector looked at young Arthur.

'I thank you, Mister Doyle,' he said.

Doyle knew he was being thanked for more than just a fancy word, and said nothing.

They both gazed down at the body.

As well as not wanting to disturb the scene of the crime, Arthur had a strange dread of turning over the corpse where it lay.

Had he not partly caused the death?

'Aye well,' McLevy muttered. 'Halloween is over now.'

He grasped the inert mass by the shoulder and pulled the body round with no great finesse; mind you, the beast had tried in its turn to end the inspector's life.

An eye for an eye.

And there he was finally.

Facing up to heaven the handsome countenance distorted by impacted death and animal rage.

Magnus Bannerman.

McLevy bent down and sniffed the hair. Yes, and now he thought he might place the aroma. Sweet magnolia.

As the inspector came back up, Conan Doyle sighed.

'Miss Adler will be devastated,' he remarked in shock.

McLevy said nothing. One thing he knew. There would be hell to pay for this.

And a sore nose is a terrible thing.

36

Among the sheep set me a place and separate me
from the goats, standing me on the right-hand side.

Order of Mass for the Dead

Sophia Adler indeed seemed devastated at first, the violet eyes
glittering with incipient tears that she kept at bay while the
watchful McLevy stood in her hotel room.

Just the two of them. He had arranged for the body of Bannerman to be transported back to the station in the carry wagon, and
sent a somewhat shaken Conan Doyle home.

No doubt Big Arthur would have wished to be on hand with
a manly arm for the delicate maiden, but as a civilian he had no
place in the investigation at all, and Roach, when he discovered
these events in the morning, would not be pleased that Doyle
had even taken the part he did, without the young man being further embroiled.

Mind you, if it hadn't been for that cricket ball. . .

However, Mister Doyle had a soft spot for Miss Adler and soft
spots were not a requirement here.

So the inspector had kept his intentions away from Arthur and
to himself, which was that despite the hour, having wrapped up
the formalities as best he could and sent Doyle on his way with
an admonition to leave things to the proper authorities at the
proper time, McLevy had headed at once for the George Hotel.

He had been tempted to make detour to the lodging house
and haul Walter Morrison from his uneasy bed, but that might
come later.

No. First port of call was Sophia Adler.

The night porter had been most reluctant, given the unearth-
ly hour, but a combination of the words *murder investigation* and
McLevy's lupine stare augmented by the smear of blood still hanging round the inspector's nostrils convinced the man sufficiently

to tap upon Sophia's door and announce a policeman to be pending.

It did not take long for her to answer.

And it would seem she had not been asleep, the dressing gown and slippers already donned, blonde hair scraped back with a white headband to match her pale complexion.

McLevy was also parchment white, his pallor worse than usual from the painful proceedings of the night.

Accordingly they were like two ghosts as he entered, closed the door in the curious night porter's face and then told her of the macabre series of events which had led to the death of Magnus Bannerman.

He left out the cricket ball and Conan Doyle in case it proved a distraction.

No gentle recitation. He wanted to hit her early and hard. This was murder and he himself had killed a man. It would haunt him for a long time and his mind would hold the vision of that body jolting with the impact of the bullets like the stuff of nightmare.

She was the key. He was now certain of that.

Yet he had never met someone so perfectly enclosed within themselves. So apparently untouchable.

And therefore he told her. Laid it on the slab.

Brutal rendition.

Her hand went to her throat and the aforementioned eyes glistened while he watched like a hawk.

The story so far.

'Poor Magnus,' she murmured. 'I cannot quite believe –'

'Oh it's true enough. He fell like Icarus onto the back green. Broke every bone in his body.'

She went to the windows and pulled back the curtains to let the pallid light of early morning seep into the room.

'And I have some questions I need to ask you, Miss Adler,' McLevy continued.

'Ask away.'

She turned from the window, he gestured to a chair; she refused with a shake of the head and so they stood like two survivors on a battlefield.

No quarter. Given or requested.

'Whit do you know of these events?'

'Nothing at all.'

'A man you share a deal of your waking life with has turned from human form into a murderous beast, and you know nothing about it?'

'Murderous?'

'He most certainly killed Gilbert Morrison, was after his brother Walter and then deviated tae me. I'd call that murderous.'

'I saw no sign of this.'

'You with all your sensitive ways? Voices? Visions?'

The sardonic streak that underlay his tone struck home and her face tightened the merest fraction.

'Magnus was a. . .hidden soul. Secretive.'

'Surely not tae one of your abilities?'

'We are all hidden from each other, inspector.'

He acknowledged the truth of that with a nod of sorts then returned to his theme.

'You saw no sign of the beast he became?'

Into Sophia's mind flashed an image of Magnus, his face contorted in pain.

Afterwards.

'One thing. Of late, he. . .he endured the most terrible agony in his head. A blinding torment. Perhaps he was being split in two.'

'Whit would cause that?'

'The past. Everything comes from the past.'

'I would agree. And you had no influence in all this?'

'In what way?'

'To engender this split?'

'How should I accomplish such a thing?'

'You talk of the powerful forces that surround you. Could Bannerman have been. . .distorted by them somehow?'

'If so, it escaped me.'

McLevy wondered a moment whether to throw a name in her face but decided to hold fire.

Later. Wait for occasion.

'What were your movements this night?' he asked instead.

She showed no surprise at the question, almost as if she had been expecting such.

'In the hotel. Resting. I had early supper sent to my room.'

He would check with the night porter but the man had been half-asleep when McLevy arrived and was no sentinel.

She could have left easily without scrutiny. Front or back. The kitchens below might well have an entrance onto the street. Hotels were like rabbit warrens.

'Whit about Magnus? Did you see him leave?'

'He makes – made – his own arrangements. We were not in each other's pockets. He often went out at night with his own objectives in mind.'

'Women? Murder? Rapine? Any ideas?'

For a moment the slightest trace of a smile showed on her lips; this man was not predictable.

A pity he suspected her so deeply.

'It was his concern.'

'Now it is mine.'

She frowned at something.

'You have hurt your nose.'

McLevy wiped the damaged organ with the back of his hand, like a child in the playground.

'Whit's going tae happen tomorrow night?' he asked suddenly.

'I beg your pardon?'

'Oh, I'm not searching out prediction. The Tanfield Hall. How can you mesmerise without your right-hand man?'

'I shall think. And make my decision tomorrow.'

'Thought's a good thing, right enough.'

But he had a feeling that she had already made up her mind. She would go through with it. The woman had steel.

'So – you allege not to have been out guising for Halloween?'

'It is a fact. I have not left this place.'

The inspector began to wander around the room in an idle fashion, whistling a Jacobite tune under his breath; any member of the fraternity would have warned that a wolf was on the prowl.

'D'ye have such a thing as a red cloak?' he asked out of the blue.

Her eyes widened a touch but that may have been to do with the random quality of the query.

'I am afraid I do not. Sorry.'

His eyes switched towards the clothes stand, which stood by

the door. It held no cloak, just some scarves and bonnets. Then he looked at the closed wardrobe in a corner of the room.

As if reading his thought, she smiled thinly.

'Be my guest, inspector.'

As he rummaged through the garments, conscious of her amused eyes on his back, McLevy found of course that there was no sign of such clothing, nor did any of the other coats show any sign of evening damp. So much for that.

He popped out again like a clockwork toy.

'Whit about Magnus Bannerman – did he have a black cloak of sorts?'

'Yes. I believe he did. Won it in a poker game. He used to wear it for fun.'

'Fun?'

That wasn't McLevy's recollection of events.

And what Sophia did not add was that the wearing of such apparel and experiencing of such fun was within their bedroom walls.

Poor Magnus.

'Did he. . .suffer much?' she murmured.

'Two bullets in the chest. As I said. Every bone broken. Blood from his ears. I'd say he suffered.'

She made no reply but nodded gravely as if his bleak description had not touched her. Just words.

McLevy had noted that Sophia had made no question about why he was interested in cloaks and the like.

A lack of curiosity in a suspect betokens many things; one of them is that they're as guilty as hell and concealing the fact.

For the first time since entering, he walked up and stood close to her, face to face.

Her visage was clear, unlined, composed, and you could drown yourself in those violet eyes.

'Forgive me for saying,' he remarked, softly, 'but ye don't seem overly grief-stricken by the news I bring.'

'I regard death as a bridge from life not the end of it,' she replied succinctly.

'If so, then Magnus Bannerman has much to answer for in the world of spirits.'

'That is his doom.'

'Nothing to do with you?'

'Nothing at all.'

By now they were near enough that their breaths almost commingled, hers sweet, his fraught with blood.

Her eyes were fixed deep on his, and out of the blue she near knocked him into a sideways shock.

'Your mother haunts you,' she said.

'Whit?'

'She haunts you. A memory.'

'My mother cut her throat. I found her. In the room I sat with her. And waited.'

He had blurted out a truth concealed for fear of the dark shame. A gang of children following Jamie McLevy through the wynds, sniggering, calling names of madness and contamination.

Why had he told this woman?

What was happening?

'I feel such sorrow. In you.'

'Is she out there wi' the voices?' he asked.

'I am sure. Somewhere.'

'Did you hear her?'

Sophia shook her head and he was suddenly like a bewildered child caught between belief and experience.

'It came into my mind. I have no control over these forces. At times, they invade me. Body and soul.'

She gazed at him as if in supplication and a charge passed between them.

The child became a man. Priapic to boot.

Her lip trembled and the upright man wondered what it would be like to sink his teeth into that flesh.

As if in reflex, Sophia's tongue passed along the upper lip leaving a glistening trail before disappearing inside her mouth.

It was as if everything had magnified, her lower lip sensual and pink.

Full and inviting.

The Valley of Venus.

And what would be the harm of delving in?

Only compromising the whole investigation by a kiss. And what followed. There would be no stopping what followed.

There was nothing in his vision but that face; the eyes, unmoving, fixed upon his own.

Those eyes began to lose focus, turn inwards towards each other and the effect was curiously erotic.

McLevy felt a force of such power drawing him to her, a psychic envelopment augmented by a jolt in the nether regions that had little to do with deductive faculties.

Passion. Pure and simple.

Neither pure nor simple.

Dangerous as hell and he was bent upon it.

Where would be the harm?

Then he had a vision of Magnus Bannerman sliding from the slates off the edge of the known world.

That's where passion got you.

'Aye well,' he near whispered. 'As you say. Everything in the past.'

He let out a mirthless laugh and drew back his head to shake it like someone emerging from a spell. His eyes swept once more around the room as if seeing it anew and something he had noticed from his earlier perambulation came to mind.

All the doors to the various rooms were ajar, save one. He had glimpsed into her bedroom and then a wee vanity recess of sorts, no doubt leading to the bathroom.

But there was a small room to the side with the door firm shut and a lock that he had no doubt was fast secure.

He spoke edgily, passion still lurking disappointed and frustrated. The flames not drowned.

'Whit's behind that wee door, eh?'

She looked to where he indicated, herself feeling an emptiness, cheated of fusion.

And fusion is a powerful weapon.

'That is for my privacy,' she replied tersely.

'Where ye keep your secrets?'

'Where I am private.'

To forestall further portal enquiries, she closed her eyes as if overwhelmed by events and sighed deeply.

'I must ask you to leave me now, inspector. I have answered your questions as best I can. It is already morning and I have much to consider.'

'No doubt ye have, no doubt.'

McLevy as usual had forgotten to remove his hat and tapped the crown as if to make sure the thing remained still on his head.

The Valley of Venus had been a close call and who knows but that the low-brimmed bowler had kept him safe.

He took one more jaunty tour round the room as if signalling a farewell voyage.

'A messenger will be sent at some time to bring you to the station to identify the body of Mister Bannerman and make formal statement.'

He grinned like a wolf.

'Clean him up, best we can, he will be recognisable.'

Sophia said nothing. He had by now reached the outside door and she would be glad to see the back of him.

His hand touched the knob to throw it open and then he hesitated.

'Jonathen Sinclair,' he shot the words out suddenly. 'Whit does the name mean to you?'

For a moment it was as if her whole body froze and then an instant later, she had recovered.

'It means nothing at all.'

'Ye sure?'

'I am certain.'

But he had seen the shock and aftermath.

She knew. Bugger your certainty. She knew.

Like the cricket ball of Conan Doyle, a long shot had hit the mark.

'A pool of blood,' he said.

'I beg your pardon?'

'When ye had a wee confab with Mister Doyle and myself, you mentioned the sight of a man in such a state.'

'I did. A vision. But I know nothing more.'

'In a street, not a room. You said.'

'I did.'

'Eighteen years ago. In the Leith Docks. A man was shot, his head obliterated, bones and flesh. I believe that to be your pool of blood.'

'Anything is possible.'

'He was a Confederate Officer. Jonathen Sinclair.'

Sophia's face was like a mask now. 'What was he doing here?'

'Buying ships for the South, I believe. You hail from the South, do you not Miss Adler?'

'I am not alone in that.'

He nodded acceptance of this point and opened the door as if to finally leave, then turned to stare back at her.

'The case was never solved. Now we have another. Twa pools of blood.'

'If true. If it. . .was this man. Sinclair. I do not see the connection. To Mister Bannerman. Or his actions.'

McLevy smiled.

'Neither do I. Quite. Yet. But I will find it. That's my job.'

As he moved out through the doorway he threw some words casually over his shoulder.

'Find, kill, destroy,' he remarked cheerily.

'What?'

'The beast that was once Magnus Bannerman. He said these words. Do you recollect them?'

He wanted her to know that however she twisted and turned, spirits, visions be damned. He was on her trail.

She registered that but shook her head anyway.

'It is all a mystery to me.'

'That's my meat and drink,' said McLevy, 'mystery.'

He closed the door but just as she breathed a sigh of relief, it popped open again and he stuck his head in like an ogre from some fairy tale, the gaps in his teeth showing from a troll-like grin.

'Don't forget my ticket.'

'What?'

'The box office. At the Tanfield Hall. Wouldnae want to miss your last show.'

'I have not yet decided.'

'Oh, you'll be there,' said James McLevy. 'I feel it in my bones.'

The door finally closed and Sophia moved swiftly to turn the key in the lock lest another visitation occur.

Then she leant her back against it and let the hot scalding tears flow down her face.

The vision she had seen. The pool of blood, the body in the street – had it been the good man?

Grief and rage.

One dead, one still alive.

37

There's nothing of so infinite vexation
As man's own thoughts.

JOHN WEBSTER, *The White Devil*

The Diary of James McLevy

It is a rare event for me to feel tired but I am driven to that conclusion this hour of four in the morning.

No wonder, however, I am exhausted.

In one day I have been near brained to death by ravening beast, watched a young woman breathe her last, shot the aforesaid beastie, rescued a bawdy-hoose keeper from a doom she brought upon herself, stuck another in jail for much the same thing, hammered a knifeman, been delivered by a projected cricket ball, near disgraced myself by passion inappropriate and forgot to feed the cat.

Indeed McLevy had returned, heated up a pot of coffee as best he could on the embers of the big late-night fire his landlady had left burning in the grate, then opened the attic window to scan the rooftops for Bathsheba.

But she was not to be seen. In the huff, probably. The inspector had then commenced to sit at his table and write.

A good way to get things out of the system.

The birdies are beginning to chirp away at the dawn chorus and I am too tired to go to bed.

Sophia Adler is a powerful creature and you may only wonder what would happen if such power were used for malevolent ends. As I believe it has been.

I have read a deal about mesmerism in my scientific journals and though there is great debate over the merits, there seems little doubt over its capacity to influence others through the medium of such power. Whether this triggers a kind of auto-suggestion or is imposed from without, one of its striking offshoots is the ability to control the minds of others.

Hypnotic trance. Witchcraft by any other name, according to the good Christian folk who burnt those accused of sorcery right, left and centre to preserve the faith.

There is no doubt Sophia Adler has that power, I could have lost my very essence in her violet eyes.

Luckily, as in my dream, I was able to wrench myself to safety.

But what if you did not have the strength?

What if she was able to control Magnus Bannerman and then unleash a primitive anger and violence such as we all have lurking in the depths of our being?

It's never far away. See what happens in war.

Civilisation. Skin deep.

I believe Magnus Bannerman to have been her instrument of destruction so she didnae get her hands dirty.

A perfect crime.

How do I therefore find her out?

She is like an amphibian that slips from one world to another. I am on dry land, she in the waters. By the time I get the boat launched, she's back on shore.

And underneath it all I sense the Imp of Vengeance. A livid presence, an opposite figure to the Christian God with his white hair or saintly son, crowned in thorns.

Another primitive, dark force that dwells in the deep fissures of the psyche and cuts a swathe through any concept of morality or structured law.

It will have blood.

I am only too aware of this force in myself that I keep contained within the boundaries of justice.

Without them I too might be a beast on the prowl.

Seeking vengeance from the world for a wee boy who watched the blood drip from his mother's throat onto the pillow where she laid her head.

We all seek reparation for past wrongs.

Or even present ones.

But it must be done within the bounds of law, otherwise the world is mad and the savage beast within holds sway.

Sophia Adler is such a beast. No matter how beautiful her face, how justified her cause – she has caused death for her own dark ends.

And I must bring her down.

But how?

McLevy slowly shut his diary and let his mind drift this way and that with the current of his unconscious.

What had she said?

I do not see the connection.

Was there a challenge in these words? A part of the wrongdoer seeks to be discovered. To sabotage the guilty self.

For some reason Poe's story of *The Tell-Tale Heart* came into his mind.

A man kills another then buries his victim beneath the dead man's own floorboards. The thud of the murdered heart haunts the killer, growing louder by the second until he screams out a confession to the police who are sitting in the very room come to investigate the disappearance but, in the main, probably just hoping for a cup of tea somewhere.

McLevy could see little sign of weakness in Sophia save for the smallest crack when the name of Jonathen Sinclair was thrown in her face.

But was something within working against her? A truth she refused to recognise, or perhaps did not even yet know?

For instance, had she not mentioned the pool of blood in her vision being in the street, not the room, perhaps he might not have made – yes – made *connection*?

Had she betrayed herself?

And if you were to believe in her world of spirits and voices and God alone knows what whirling around in the ether – how would they feel about being party to murder?

Because if she, using her 'gift', had split off or unearthed the beast in Magnus Bannerman, would that not perturb the spirit world?

Power misused and abused.

This was getting too deep for the inspector and he decided he'd better go to his bed no matter the hour.

That deathly figure from his dream of some time ago still worried, however. And the pain he had felt on the rooftop didn't make him feel too cheerful either.

He patted his chest to feel the reassuring flesh and his own heart beat steadily under his fingers.

Telling no tales.

All was well.

And he would have a decent breakfast for a change this day. At the Auld Ship.

Drappit egg, his favourite, being an egg poached in gravy from the liver of a fowl. With a slab of pan bread and maybe a blood sausage on the side.

Perhaps a kidney or two? Lamb, preferably.

Little Bo Peep has lost her sheep.

McLevy might need sustenance because he would catch a reasonable amount of hell from Lieutenant Roach on account of Conan Doyle's presence at the attempted murder of one Walter Morrison.

And that's another reason he was tired.

Because after leaving the George Hotel, he had stopped off at the lodging house, hauled Walter Morrison from his bed and got some of the truth from the terrified merchant.

At least as much as the man knew, for he claimed Gilbert to be the main protagonist, he being a good-natured type and his younger brother a grasping, treacherous fellow.

For sure greed and treachery were in the story.

A decent man betrayed and murdered.

Some might say a casualty of war, but McLevy saw it differently. Just a cold-blooded killing.

Betrayed for gain.

For the filthy lucre.

JUDAS. The name on the wall. It made some sense now.

But what was the connection?

McLevy decided that, after all, he would not go to his slumbers.

If he closed his eyes, he might miss something.

38

Remember thee?
Ay, thou poor ghost, while memory holds a seat
In this distracted globe. Remember thee?

WILLIAM SHAKESPEARE, *Hamlet*

The day had been long but now Sophia had found peace, the demons no longer plagued her.

She sat before his picture, the uniform grey, the tasselled hat at a rakish angle, blond hair curling out under the rim, teeth white in a smile of life and love as he stood under the full blossom of a sweet magnolia tree.

The trip to the police station had been uneventful; she had made a formal statement as the inspector had warned would be necessary.

The body she had identified also, its face carved by death into harsh lines, the bullet holes, two, just like before, but not one to the face to smash the bones to bits and pieces. No. To the chest, hidden under the sheet, to leave the face above a death mask, eyes closed, mouth twisted, soul departed, the form that had once been Magnus Bannerman now an empty ruin for winds to blow through.

She had sat in the lieutenant's office with a portrait of their gloomy English queen staring out at something no-one else could see and answered the questions quietly, the same, some of them, as had been asked by the inspector on their last meeting.

Most of her answers were lies but she told the truth wherever possible.

She knew nothing of the why of the crime, had rested all night at the hotel, was astonished by Bannerman's actions, and cognised of no reason why he had ascended the rooftops to bring down murder.

Those were the lies.

She intended to leave the country as soon as possible, would give her last mesmeric demonstration at the Tanfield Hall despite the loss of her audience-conductor as she did not wish to disappoint her loyal followers, and trusted that the spirit voices would not forsake her in the hour of need.

This was the truth.

McLevy asked the questions in a dull, uninterested monotone; they were conveyed to paper by a station scribe and at the end she signed her name.

The police lieutenant, Roach, was a dry-skinned creature with eyes that seemed bloodshot but not from dissipation. He was tall and bore the imprint of someone whose expectations were confined to a limited horizon.

A photo on the wall showed him dressed in golfing apparel with a club in his hand and a ball at his feet.

The other photo was a collection of solemn-faced men in strange regalia, sitting in a row.

The inscription below announced 'The Grand Masonic Lodge of Leith'.

The lieutenant sat at the end of the row.

A narrow life.

Between him and the inspector, a strange relationship existed. Both wore uniform, one buckled in by authority, the other bursting at the seams.

A palpable tension.

After signing and just before she left, Roach, who had been mostly silent save for formal greetings and expressions of sympathy, asked her a question that must have been annoying his mind during the whole interview.

'If Mister Bannerman is in the world of spirits, will he not make contact with you?'

'That is beyond my governance.'

'Ah yes,' Roach muttered. 'These voices come and go, you are merely the meeting point.'

'Like Waverley Station,' McLevy suddenly piped up.

Roach paid no attention to this. They were all sitting at a table, which doubled as an official desk of sorts.

The lieutenant leant forward and Sophia became aware that there was a hard intelligence in his eyes. It might be a narrow mind but this was not a stupid one.

'I must inform you, Miss Adler,' he remarked stonily, 'that I find no accordance with your belief, which I think to be a dangerous delusion – no matter how sincerely felt. In my opinion it appeals only to the simple-minded amongst us.'

Sophia said nothing but she remembered the woman sitting beside him in the audience who drank up every word when Magnus addressed the assembly.

The lieutenant's wife, perhaps.

A husband and wife do not always believe in the same things.

'However,' Roach continued, grimly, 'I can do little to stop the flight of the gullible towards manifestations outwith the proper bounds of the Christian Church. It is a free country.'

'I am glad to hear it,' she replied quietly.

'It would appear that your Mister Bannerman was a profoundly split person. One part human, one part monster, if what the inspector tells me is true.'

'It would appear so.'

'And yet someone with your – if I am to believe you – mystic abilities saw no sign of this?'

'My point entirely!' McLevy chimed in.

'Great minds,' said Roach, 'coincide.'

He gave his inspector a sharp look and McLevy sat a little back into his chair. Sophia had never seen the man so subdued and wondered for a moment at the cause.

But then she had a response to find.

'To be split is to be separated from the other. There is no connection. No trace between. Inside the one entity is another. Neither knows of the other's existence.'

'That is all you have to say?'

'That is all I *can* say.'

Then it was over. McLevy stayed slumped in his seat as if drained of pith, the lieutenant escorted her to the door where a gawky young constable saw her to the station exit.

The constable had a livid red birthmark spreading up his face from the side of his neck and kept rubbing at it as they crossed the station floor.

She was aware of all eyes upon her and a babble of noise coming from the outside.

The young man kept his gaze averted till they got to the door then just before he opened, blurted out a question.

'Can you cure people, like Jesus?'

His eyes were innocent. Like a child's. And it pierced her to the heart.

'No,' she answered softly. 'I cannot perform miracles. It is not my gift. I am sorry.'

For a second she almost reached out to touch the mark that lay upon his face but touching a policeman can often be misconstrued.

He released the door and delivered her to the waiting journalists who were milling around in the street; the news had been at last officially broken to them of the murder of Gilbert Morrison and the death of a murderous American, and the Edinburgh press were hungry for blood.

She stood helpless, pinned at the threshold as the questions rained in upon her; like stones thrown, sharp, cutting, insinuating, wheedling, each seeking to slice a headline from her body.

Sophia knew a moment of panic as if she had been cast out, abandoned, then the door behind opened and a hand grasped her elbow.

James McLevy, his face set in grim lines, steered her through the jostling horde and into her waiting carriage.

He slammed the carriage door shut and leaned in with the voices calling like seagulls in the background.

Her words of gratitude were beaten to the punch.

'Don't thank me too soon,' he said.

Then it was a race back to the hotel where more of the press waited, back to her rooms past the curious glances of the good citizens in the foyer, then close the door and pull the curtains.

All that was past.

Everything is in the past.

Now she sat at the shrine. Safely locked away. No-one could touch her in this place. The small precious leather suitcase lay empty, the contents arranged as they were in every hotel, every lodging place. A secure room must be laid aside and there she had her peace.

Where he watched over her.

The good man.

Tonight she would sit in front of an audience of hungry souls and inhabit the terrifying emptiness inside her mind before the voices began to announce themselves.

Not unlike a railway station. . . There was some truth in what the inspector had remarked.

For a moment there was a tug of humour at her lips and then she surveyed everything laid out like an altar: a white linen cloth, the candles lit for purification, a smell of scented honey, a shaving brush and closed razor, a leather belt stained with travel, two silver uniform buttons that she polished every day.

And the letters. Inside the mother-of-pearl box and tied with her own silk ribbon, red as if love tokens.

Sophia had just perused and replaced inside the last. It filled her with the same terrible anger as always.

Betrayal. On every side.

She closed her eyes and let the past wash over her like the sea.

Sweet magnolia trees.

Sophia was riding hard. Just turned fifteen, her blood racing with the horse; she rode bareback, legs astride, *like a nigra heathen*, said Uncle Bart.

Though he was not really her uncle, just. . .a friend of the family.

They had lost the plantation to the carpetbaggers but kept a small farm, enough to eke out a decent living, though not enough for her mother who lamented a lost life.

The Glorious South.

Melissa Sinclair mourned that loss, her airs and graces wasted on a hard life of toil.

Sophia did not think it so hard. They had enough to eat, some horses, cows and chickens, two men, ex-Johnny Rebs who worked the place and that Uncle Bart kept in line on his frequent visits.

She was a strange child, so said her mother. Left by the faeries perhaps. Or by a dead soldier. Lived in a world of her own.

And Sophia did. An intense, secret world where her father rode over the hill to wave his hat in the air before sweeping down to hoist her on to the saddle and off to ride the wild winds.

The father she had never seen.

He had died in the war. Melissa told stories of his bravery and noble ways but her daughter felt that the mother blamed him somehow for the lost battles.

The more she praised, the more something did not ring true but Sophia loved him with a fierce pride.

He was a good man. She could see it in the photograph that Melissa had kept along with a pitifully few mementoes of his last and hasty visit.

His death was a mystery. Her mother would not let her see the letters that she guarded so jealously and when she questioned Uncle Bart he merely said, *Died for his country, little girl.*

Now she was a big girl. Fifteen. Bart looked at her different. Made her feel hot. Strange. Flattered.

Men change when women do.

Her mother looked at her oddly as well, and then sang praises of the father as if the memory might keep Sophia still a worshipping child.

That day when she left the horse to cool down in the stable, why did she do things differently?

No shout through the house to announce her arrival, no slam of the front door which she delighted to do because it made the whole house shake to the rafters.

No. Walk quietly up the stairs, led by the sounds to the mother's bedroom.

Did she already know what she would find?

A strange chorus like a bullfrog and a mocking bird. Low grunts, high stifled shrieks.

Open the door softly to see her supposed uncle but no such thing, his hairy naked back, her mother's legs splayed around him, mouth contorted, the Glorious South.

And Sophia had screamed. Lord, how she had screamed.

Betrayed. Her father. Herself.

Ran to her mother's den, grabbed a small leather case that was lying there, swept all the precious remnants of her father, letters, photographs, official papers, all she could find into that willing receptacle, downstairs without pause, back onto that sweating horse and – disappeared.

Right out of sight.

Never to be seen again.

Just as well, because if she ever came across them again she would shoot the pair where they stood.

Sophia came out of the reverie to find her face wet with tears. Not of grief or rage, just – tears.

Sometimes they fall. All of their own accord.

She took a deep breath of the honey-scented air in the shrine, dried her eyes and then frowned.

The framed picture she had fixed upon the wall, so that it looked down upon her sitting form, had slanted.

While she had closed her eyes.

How was that possible?

Sophia reached up to straighten it. Good. The Glorious South.

She had wanted to die but that had not happened. Fell in with some wild river-men who used her like a toy but she didn't mind. Life was not important.

Then the voices began. In her mind. In the dark of the night, whispering of things unseen.

She *knew* things and the river-men left her alone. A voodoo woman. She had power. Pure and simple.

Wherever she went she followed that power. It led her to San Francisco by the waterfront, to Magnus Bannerman.

The chosen one.

When she saw him, deep into him, to see the weakness inside, she knew that part of her search was over.

And the other part just beginning.

They became lovers almost at once. That was good. Fusion was power.

He was her public face, with his charm, energy and sharp gambler's brain. She became known in certain circles.

Her name was changed to make her sound more mysterious. Sophia Adler. As if from distant Europe. His mother's maiden name, Adler. Magnus found great amusement in that and she accepted it without fuss.

Sophia had many secrets to keep and now could hold her father's name to herself. Hidden. For her alone.

The Spiritualists took her under their wing, her fragile quality offset by Bannerman's brash salesman's pitch, and she began to do private meetings, then the larger halls, all the time her reputation growing.

A grand tour of Europe was proposed. Last port of call, Edinburgh. She had insisted upon that.

Vengeance at last.

It had been simple to slip out, hire a coachman and find out where the Morrison brothers lived. To see their greedy, pitiless faces. To identify how a beast might break through to kill.

Not just kill but mirror another death.

Amongst the papers Sophia ripped that day from her mother was a report forwarded to Melissa about her husband's demise. From an unsympathetic consul in Glasgow, Warner L. Underwood. In it was a factual description of the body, its head blown to unrecognisable shreds. Lying in the gutter.

The good man.

In the report those responsible for the crime were not found. But from her father's letters Sophia knew the guilty ones. As if a finger pointed. The betrayers.

And when she saw Gilbert Morrison that night, sitting in the audience, a face that she had seen not days before, that was the sign. *The spirits had led him there.* Her scream had not been fear but exultation.

Isolating the beast in Magnus had not been difficult; he had a dark, primitive, superstitious being and a mind that was infinitely suggestible.

Especially after the act of love.

She might put him easily into a mesmeric trance; it came naturally to her, and after a time used three key words to bring about an instant effect.

Find.

Kill.

Destroy.

The murder night they had walked the street cloaked to mingle with the Halloween revellers, thence to the Morrison house where she pointed him the way, bade him remove his socks and shoes for balance, gave him gauntlets to protect his hands from evidence of blood then set the beast loose.

Find.

Kill.

Destroy.

In the aftermath she brought him back through a rear entrance she had discovered in the hotel, unseen since the kitchens were now closed, and then bathed him like a child.

When he woke in the morning he remembered nothing of being an instrument of vengeance.

As it should be.

But now he was dead. Poor Magnus.

He had suffered from these evil headaches after each *possession* and died to serve her.

Sophia had watched from the shadows as McLevy's two shots rang out in the still night and Bannerman plunged to his death from the rooftop. But she was certain that in his heart he would rejoice and wish her to live on in glory.

And therefore she had a duty to perform. The spirits would wish it so. This was the largest audience she had ever faced and would be her biggest challenge.

For her father. She would do it for him. Perhaps at last, she might hear his voice.

The voice she had waited for all her life.

Walter Morrison, unfortunately, was now safe from anything except her curse.

And she had to hope that one wasn't heading her own way because her voices had been silent these last days.

Did they disapprove of what she had done?

Or were they just saving themselves for the challenge?

39

They buried him 'neath the sycamore tree
His epitaph there for to see
'Beneath this stone I'm forced to lie
The victim of a blue-tailed Fly.'

TRADITIONAL, 'The Blue-tailed Fly'

Ballantyne was worried, his innocent eyes perplexed as McLevy fiddled with the lock-picks.

'D'ye think this a good idea, sir?' he asked.

'Sssh!'

The inspector's face was a mask of concentration. This lock was of the latest manufacture, as would suit a newly refitted hotel such as the George, and was proving resistant to his charms so far.

All day McLevy had played the penitent, accepting meekly Roach's severe admonition as regards using a cricket-ball-throwing medical man for support rather than the proper officers; the inspector forbore to mention that, in fact, the killer had been stopped in his murderous act and justice triumphant, well, mostly triumphant.

There was a bit to do yet, which was why he was wielding the lock-pick.

Mulholland was still indisposed, and might well have had the good sense to refuse in any case, so McLevy had mildly suggested to Roach that since a newspaperman from the *Edinburgh Herald* was coming in to interview the lieutenant this very afternoon, the inspector might take a wee turn on the saunter with Ballantyne for company, so as not to get in the way. He had no wish to detract by individual presence from the glowing reports that were certain to be written about the Leith Police, his lieutenant in particular.

Earlier he had brought Roach up to date, as you were supposed to do with a superior officer, as regards what he had discovered from the banker and wrung out of Walter Morrison.

The wretched man had confessed that eighteen years ago they had had a cash flow predicament, which was threatening to bankrupt the firm of Morrison Brothers.

They had been approached by one Jonathen Sinclair, an agent for the Confederate forces, to purchase two ships in order to run the Federal blockade.

Sinclair had cash bonds that he would make over to them. This they agreed though they knew there to be considerable official disapproval of taking sides in the Civil War, especially with the South since it seemed to be the losing party.

Always back a winner.

They were then approached by the Federal agents, in the person of a man named William Mitchell, to warn that they were under scrutiny.

The Federals had been searching for Sinclair and their pursuit had driven him from Glasgow. He was a wanted man. Badly wanted.

Then devious brother Gilbert, as opposed to honest brother Walter, offered Mitchell a deal.

If they could keep the money, they would deliver Sinclair into his hands.

And hold onto their ships as well.

Just good business.

The deal was struck.

Sinclair was told that the bonds must be signed over for an interim contract and once the certificates had been cashed in and verified, the Confederate officer was then to attend the Morrison offices at the Leith Docks on the stroke of midnight to collect the full ships' papers.

The Federals were informed, Sinclair intercepted.

Walter protested that neither brother expected the man to be so brutally executed. Imprisonment perhaps, sent back to America in a fish barrel, but not the firing squad.

Why he had fainted at the word *JUDAS* on the wall was that it had always been on his conscience and Sinclair had warned the brothers that if they played Judas, he would kill them both.

For that reason the word stuck in his mind.

When McLevy had finished, Roach sighed.

'A motive of sorts and the similarity in death not to be ignored, but what is the connection to Bannerman?'

Connection. That word again.

'Other than America,' continued Roach. 'And America is a very big country. How do we proceed?'

'Best foot forward, sir. That's all we can offer.'

These muted, obedient tones brought a narrowing to Roach's eyes.

'Are you up to something, James?' he asked.

'I'm a wee bit fatigued and I had a big breakfast,' came the oblique response. Then Sophia Adler arrived and left, the journalists were waiting outside, the man from the *Herald* was imminent, so Roach waved McLevy off to the streets before the inspector grabbed unauthorised acclaim.

The saunter with Ballantyne had, oddly enough, taken McLevy out of his parish up to George Street, where they had waited a deal of time till early evening when Sophia Adler left for the Tanfield Hall, followed by a hungry pack of journalists.

While everyone was looking one way, McLevy and a slightly reluctant Ballantyne slipped in the other.

Her hotel door yielded easily to his lock-pick but the other was not so accommodating. Until now.

A click as the tiny hook at the end of the instrument caught hold, a twist and –

'Open Sesame,' muttered James McLevy.

The private door was sprung but Ballantyne was still in a fret of sorts.

'Is this not against the law?' he queried.

'We *are* the law, constable.'

'Do we not need a search warrant?'

'We'll get one later, now come on!'

In truth, McLevy was not sure why he had brought Ballantyne along other than if things went wrong it was nice to share the blame with someone.

But the boy had brought luck so far. He stumbled over things. Bodies and suchlike.

They entered a narrow recess, McLevy leading the way to where a curtain, pinned up, and not, he was certain, part of the hotel furnishings, barred their way.

This he pushed gently aside to reveal a small room with an alcove of sorts. There was no window so the shapes within were shrouded in mirk.

McLevy sniffed through his still tender nose.

'I can smell a candle,' he announced. 'Recent burnt. Honey, I'll be bound.'

Ballantyne whose eyes were attuned to spotting minute insects and therefore sharp as a tack, pointed to what might be two yellow blobs set on a white covering of sorts.

'There,' he indicated with a certain reserve, for a saying of Mulholland's had come into his mind from a time they had sat together, he with a dislocated shoulder and Mulholland with the blame of a suicide on his hands.

Both the results of being associated with McLevy.

Trouble follows the inspector like a black dog.

That's what Mulholland had said and that's what Ballantyne was thinking as he watched McLevy light up a lucifer and pass that fire to the candles.

The man himself waited till the flickering flame steadied itself and then scanned the scene.

'Well, well,' he remarked, softly. 'The things ye find.'

Before them in the alcove was what looked like an altar, where various items had been laid carefully in place.

A worn leather belt curled up like a sleeping snake, two equally worn silver buttons, a shaving brush standing on its end, the dry hairs brushed to attention, and what looked like a curved, folded, shaving razor, the yellow surface of its handle shining like beeswax.

On the other side was what appeared to be a cord with two acorn tassels attached. A spare perhaps. And destined to fit round the hat of a Confederate Army Officer.

Such as McLevy saw in the picture that faced him on the wall.

Hanging beside it on a nail was a red cloak.

Female to the male, for the man in the picture also wore a cloak: grey, falling round his shoulders, a riding cape of some sort, which gave him a winter look even through the summer blossoms hung ripe above.

And though his teeth were bared in a smile, the light hazel eyes glinting, to McLevy's gaze there was evidence of tension in the taut cheekbones and hooked nose.

Below, written across the photograph in a firm slanting hand was. . .

My Father, Jonathen Sinclair. His last visit. Just before Gettysburg. Nine months later I was born.

'Sir?' While McLevy had been peering closely to read the writing, Ballantyne, who in fact was almost as nosy as his inspector, had delicately lifted the lid of a mother-of-pearl box, which lay behind the cord and tassels.

It disclosed a pile of letters tied in red silk, with one loose upon the top.

McLevy bowed his head solemnly and Ballantyne's long tapering fingers, more suited to acolyte priest than practising policeman, lifted the letter and passed it over.

The inspector held it at arm's length and as words fell into focus so did the last pieces of the Morrison case.

Edinburgh, 1864

My Dear Wife Melissa,

I write this as your husband with what seems eternity between us. I have lost my way. I have lost my way.

I can find no sense in all of this but I blunder on, as if, as if it will make a difference. But it all seems like shadows on the wall as if my existence is not myself, just a shape, a shadow.

I have fallen into an abyss and don't know how to retrieve myself or if I even wish to do so.

Well, let it all be so. I put one foot, one action in front of the other and grasp at what comfort the moment can bring.

'He disnae seem very happy,' observed Ballantyne, who was reading over McLevy's shoulder.

'No,' replied McLevy, re-ordering his eyes for better vision. 'And whit does he mean by comfort?'

They scanned further.

Let that be so. When death is on our trail, we ride that poor horse so hard to escape that it would shake loose the bridle and saddle to run wild and free, to separate from us.

It is not the target. We are.

Let that be so.

I give you two names.

Gilbert and Walter Morrison. These are men I am forced to now have dealings with and I do not trust them.

I have lost all my agents in the field except Bartholomew, who leaves this very afternoon on a cargo ship with some important papers for Secretary Mallory and will carry this letter along with him.

It will join my earlier communication, which is still in his possession because we have been unable to find a safe ship for him to travel in. It will have to be a roundabout route because traffic between here and the Southern states is now more and more difficult. This is a rare chance for him to make the journey.

He will have to land in Union territory and make his way by horse to the South.

With luck he will deliver both letters to you at the same time. In your hands.

Two, as they say, for the price of one.

I have had no response from you to my previous letters nor would I expect such. I do not know if you have even received them. Let us hope so.

I must wait till midnight.

I have already been persuaded to hand over the cash bonds in order to guarantee delivery of two blockade ships and will receive the final papers this night.

I have warned the Morrisons that should they fail me I will have no compunction but to shoot them dead.

There are three bullets left in John Findhorn's revolver. That should be enough.

This cannot sound to your ears like a gallant Southern officer but I am not so gallant these days.

I fear betrayal. Judas. But I must go on.

I have no option.

As a shadow has no option but to follow the body to which it is attached.

If I succeed I shall follow Bartholomew as soon as possible.

If I do not win through then it means that I have fallen. I will not be coming after.

I have fallen. I have fallen.

Please forgive me.

Your husband,

Jonathen

McLevy pondered. Something in the letter did not ring true. Something not expressed. Hidden. A secret.

'It's very sad,' said Ballantyne.

'It's the cause of homicide,' replied McLevy. 'Let us depart this murderous sanctuary.'

He grabbed the other missives, closed the empty box, and stuffed them into the recesses of the poacher's pocket in his coat to smuggle past any watchers.

These he would examine later at his leisure.

But for now he had an appointment to keep.

40

Vengeance is mine; I will repay, saith the Lord.

THE BIBLE, Romans

As the hansom cab clattered to a halt outside the Tanfield Hall, McLevy handed the bound letters to Ballantyne.

'You carry on towards the station,' he commanded. 'Put them in a safe place.'

'In the records office, naebody ever gangs there,' Ballantyne said, looking at the crowds outside flocking in through the doors. 'But whit do I tell the lieutenant?'

'What I have instructed you.'

'It's no' exactly the truth.'

'It's near enough.'

He gave Ballantyne some money for the cab, knowing well the remuneration of a constable did not extend to such sums, waved goodbye to the worried face, took a deep breath and joined the throng.

'Aye. Turn your face from the rightful path, walk the way of Satan!'

Jupiter Carlisle's distorted visage thrust itself into McLevy's, while those around him scattered to avoid blanket condemnation. The placard held in his hand like a holy sword still read, *This is against God!*

The inspector was unimpressed; he had moved the man on many a time when his vituperation threatened to get out of control. This might be one of them but McLevy had too much on his plate as it was.

'Aye, Jupiter,' he acknowledged. 'Halloween's over. I thought you'd be having a rest. Now, behave yourself.'

The man's pale blue eyes burned with fierce indignation and he raised the placard as if to strike the infidel where he stood, but McLevy shoved past because he could hear a bell ringing inside the hall to announce that proceedings were about to begin.

Jupiter, white hair gleaming in the streetlights, called after McLevy and anyone else within range who had not yet lost their soul, a slight speck of froth at the edge of his thin lips indicating a man at the end of his Christian tether.

'Where is your shame? You should be on your knees in church not crawling on your belly like a snake to feast upon this woman.'

For a moment his zealous gaze met with Sophia Adler's, as her image on one of the posters to advertise the venue swam into his view.

'Whore of Babylon!' he howled at her. 'The Lord will smite you down! You will not escape his wrath!'

To this somewhat apocalyptic statement she made no response; the last straggle of crowd had disappeared inside and Jupiter cut a pathetic figure as he stood there like an Old Testament prophet whose flock had gone astray.

Meanwhile the inspector collected his ticket inside an envelope with his name written in full, *James McLevy, Inspector of Police*, and a handwritten note inside that said, *I always keep my promises.*

He thought about the varied meanings of these words as he searched for his place, finding it to be an excellent vantage in the centre of the stalls.

As he pushed his way in towards the empty seat in the row, he saw that it was set beside a giant of a man who sat with his eyes fixed on the empty stage.

Arthur Conan Doyle.

Either Sophia had arranged this or the Fates were at work. Take your pick.

Doyle, who was on his own, his mother Mary considering that she had had a surfeit of the spirits for the moment, gazed at McLevy with slightly bulging eyes as if the inspector might trail some more murderous events after him.

'I have been out of the city all day,' he said.

'Where?' grunted McLevy, as he sat down heavily.

'A fishing trip.'

'Fishing?' The inspector had wondered about Doyle's whereabouts; a note had been sent requesting his presence at the station but to no avail.

So that was the reason.

'Fishing?' he repeated.

'I needed to calm my mind.'

Indeed, Doyle had awoken with a welter of confused thoughts, grabbed his angling rod and spent an unsuccessful day attempting to lure a trout onto the fly.

It had eased his perturbation but reading some lurid headlines in the newspapers on his late afternoon return had set it off again.

'How is Miss Adler?' he asked, turning his eyes back to the empty stage. 'I tried to contact her at the hotel on my arrival back but she was not available. Hiding from the press, no doubt.'

'She has much to conceal.'

'It is a dreadful business.'

'And not over yet,' said McLevy bleakly.

While they were talking he had been scanning the audience. Unless he was mistaken he glimpsed Jean Brash and Hannah Semple further back in the hall, no doubt celebrating Jean's release while investigating the possibility of establishing a bawdy-hoose beyond the grave.

And was that not Lieutenant Roach ducking his head down, Mrs Roach beside him like a hungry chick waiting to be fed?

It would seem most of the players in this drama had gathered and McLevy wondered about the outcome.

He had retained the one letter from Sinclair, which rested in his pocket, naming the Morrison brothers.

But what did he hope to accomplish? Show it to Sophia and extract a confession of sorts?

Certainly it gave link and motive to her part in murder but provided no real proof.

He could just hear Roach's voice.

Circumstantial, McLevy. It will not hold.

Especially when you considered how he came by the letters.

He had risked a great deal and gained what?

He might hammer in at Sophia but would she crack?

McLevy became aware that Conan Doyle was gazing at him with a perplexed look upon his face.

'Did you not hear what I said, sir?' Arthur queried.

'I did not. Miles away.'

'I asked what you implied by *not over yet*. Surely the ghastly business has run its course?'

'No,' said McLevy. 'Miss Adler has yet a part to play.'

'In what fashion?'

There was a pugilistic set to Doyle's face, suddenly, as if he suspected McLevy of dark designs towards his sweet Sophia, and the inspector sighed.

'Has she not suffered enough?' declared the young man, and as McLevy thought best how to answer he was saved from what would undoubtedly have been an extremely fraught exchange of differing points of view by the stage lights dimming and an earnest member of the Edinburgh Spiritualist Society stepping forth.

In halting, dry tones, the man welcomed them, spoke briefly of the tenets of the Society's beliefs, made no mention of the unfortunate fate of Magnus Bannerman, spoke the name of Sophia Adler as one summoning up a presence from the deep, and then quit the stage.

She walked on. Veiled as usual, bride of the spirits, a circlet of silver round her head, arms bare, wearing a flowing dress, pale grey in colour.

The large honey candles were already in place and lit, the chair in position.

She sat. Silence. A held breath. Waiting.

For Sophia it was as if she was fixed in eternity. No audience, no outside trappings, completely held within her own being as she floated in the air, in darkness, her eyes closed, a nothingness, a void where the seeds of everything were held in suspension.

She waited for her father's voice. To bless her.

And in the silence, a voice sounded.

'Whore of Babylon!'

A scream of hatred from a mind that had festered for long years, nurtured on the image of a nailed Redeemer and no longer able to separate his own agony from that of the crucified Nazarene.

Jupiter Carlisle burst into the hall past the feeble efforts of the gatemen; in place of the discarded placard he held an ancient pistol, dusty and rust-clogged that he had stumbled on that very morning, a remnant of hunting days when he was a young man and had his own wits.

His eyes were rheumy and badly impaired so he saw only a

dim wavering image of grey on the stage, aimed the pistol wildly in that direction and pressed the trigger.

It was a miracle the gun did not explode, the barrel blocked with dust and dead insects, but it fired.

And the bullet could have gone anywhere, hit anyone in front of that pistol.

Even James McLevy.

Yet it somehow found a path straight into the heart of Sophia Adler as she waited for a blessing.

On the impact she slumped forward and fell slowly to the side as she had done once before, but this time there was no steadying hand from Magnus Bannerman.

This time she toppled straight to the floor and lay there. Unmoving. Unblessed. Alone.

With a muttered curse McLevy was out of his seat and trampling over the legs and feet of others as he struggled to get to the lunatic figure of Carlisle.

Screams and shouts rang out from the audience. Roach was also moving with surprising speed out of his row down towards the frail, deadly figure holding a gun that by all known science should have blown up in his hand.

As Carlisle waved the pistol round in a threatening arc, McLevy thudded in and brought the deranged man to the floor. As he hauled out the restrainers a hand pulled them from his grasp.

'I'll see to this,' said Roach grimly. 'You deal with the woman. She has the more need.'

McLevy ran for the stage and scrambled up onto the bare boards. Conan Doyle had already got there in one leap and leant over the still form of Sophia. The inspector was about to push the young man aside when he remembered that he was in fact a doctor.

Doyle by now had ripped a portion of the dress away to reveal the wound in her pale flesh.

One look in the man's eyes and McLevy had his own dark suspicions confirmed.

It was a death wound.

Deid strake.

Both men inclined over the veiled figure from either side and McLevy gently eased off the silver circlet to reveal the wan face below.

'You are late, inspector,' she murmured. 'I thought better of you.'

'I am here now,' he replied.

She signalled him close while Doyle tried in vain to stem a wound that would never cease.

'*You should have kissed me,*' she whispered, the ghost of a smile on her lips.

'Too risky,' McLevy muttered.

She laughed and the convulsion brought some blood up into her mouth.

The inspector was reminded that this was the second young woman he had watched die in a few days.

A bad habit.

Her eyes were focused on something over his shoulder.

'A black shape,' she said.

The inspector glanced upwards. He could see nothing.

'It was terrible luck,' he said. 'Jupiter couldnae hit a barn door.

'Jupiter?'

'That's his name.'

She smiled, then a look of pain came into her eyes.

'Not luck. Just. . .fate.'

He hesitated, she being on the point of death; but once a policeman, always so. He spoke quietly.

'Is there aught upon your conscience, Miss Sinclair?'

Sophia registered his deliberate use of the name but made no more of it.

'Should there be?'

'As regards, say, the murder of Gilbert Morrison?'

'He deserved it.'

'What did you do to Magnus Bannerman?'

'Whispered in his ear.'

With that she turned away to Conan Doyle who had heard nothing of their talk, being concerned to stanch the flow of blood even though he knew his efforts to be in vain.

Sophia reached up a hand to touch his face; Doyle held back his tears in the approved manly fashion, but his lip trembled and his eyes showed the feeling in his heart.

Perhaps a chivalric delusion.

Perhaps the love of his life.

Take your pick.

'You are a good man, Mister Doyle,' she said quietly. 'You must always. . .be on guard.'

He bent his great head over her hand and kissed it with his lips in the manner of a gallant knight.

She closed her eyes and saw a vision of her father riding over the hill, ready to sweep her up in his arms.

'You are a good man,' she said.

Then she died.

Slipped from one world to another. Or Heaven. Or Hell. Or nowhere. Depending upon the point of view.

Doyle took her pulse as a medical man should, then laid the veil softly once more over her white face.

McLevy stood up. The members of the Spiritualist Society had restrained the audience from crowding round the stage and the shouts and screams had become low murmurs.

Then strangely, as if a hand had been laid across them, they stilled the noise and the place once more fell silent.

All eyes were upon him.

The inspector stood like an actor who has forgotten his lines.

His mind was full of thoughts he could not share.

Was it just bad luck or had the spirits taken revenge for the misuse of power?

McLevy would never know.

He bowed his head to signal death and the whole audience followed suit.

One voice broke that terrible silence. It came from a man face down on the floor, hands cuffed behind his back.

Jupiter Carlisle chanted to himself in a cracked harsh croak, like a frog in the night.

'The Lord anoints. The Lord provides. He will weigh you in the balance. The Lord provides. The Lord anoints.'

41

Times go by turns, and chances change by course,
From foul to fair, from better hap to worse.

ROBERT SOUTHWELL, 'Times Go by Turns'

When McLevy entered the station next day, the first person to meet his eyes was Muriel Grierson.

In truth so much had happened in the interim that he almost did not recognise the woman. Also she had somewhat changed in appearance and attitude.

Her eyes gazed at him with level strength as opposed to their usual bird-like distraction, and she was dressed in a style more befitting to her age.

As if she had come to terms with something.

As if she meant business.

She was sitting on the little bench at the station desk, ignored by Sergeant Murdoch, who was laboriously filling out some official forms, and seemed content to be there, hands quiet and still upon her lap.

'Can I assist you, Mistress Grierson?' asked James McLevy.

'No. I am being dealt with, thank you.'

She did not rise or particularly acknowledge him and so he went on his merry way. One problem less to solve.

Ballantyne looked up from his desk and shook his head warningly; was it the inspector's imagination or did that birthmark seem not so livid this morning?

In any case for a moment he was reminded of Mulholland, who often shook his head in similar manner, and wondered how the constable was faring. He was missing the reservations that Mulholland often brought to bear on their activities.

But on to present times. McLevy took a deep breath and rapped upon the object of Ballantyne's caution and his own reckoning-to-be.

The door of Lieutenant Robert Roach.

'Enter,' said a voice within, and that he did.

Ballantyne pondered a little at his desk; the insects could fend for themselves this moment.

He had already been hauled over the coals by his lieutenant for unauthorised entry of a hotel room and given a severe flea in his ear as regards being party to any such events in the future. To his relief he was not going to be taken off the patrolling but partnered with a more sober, older constable to guide his wayward footsteps.

And yet. And yet. Ballantyne bent low so that no-one could see the grin upon his face.

He had stuck to the story McLevy had instructed in the hansom cab.

A fabrication, but he had stuck to it under Roach's questioning. In a way it undermined authority but he had found an odd delight in doing so.

What a time it had been.

Now he knew what it felt like to be a criminal.

Worth its weight in gold.

Meanwhile in Roach's office, strangely enough, other than official stricture, things weren't going too badly.

McLevy, the previous night, as the raving Carlisle was shoved into the cells to sing hymns from then on for the salvation of the Moxey gang and Silver Samuel, had brought the lieutenant up to date with his doings.

In his version, however, he had merely *pressed* upon the hotel door, having a few more questions to ask Miss Adler, only to find it spring open not unlike the lieutenant's own portal, thence into the room to find the door to the alcove wide open and so on and so on.

Roach did not believe a word of it but Ballantyne had backed the inspector up and, in truth, the lieutenant was not inclined to push too far.

The morning papers were full of the shooting of Sophia Adler and great play had been made of Roach's capture of the madman. He was assuming heroic status and so was inclined to magnanimity as befits that assumption.

In any case, as he was forever saying to the inspector, *where is your proof?*

In fact the last exchange between him and McLevy the previous night encapsulated the matter.

'You entered that room without approval,' he had accused his man.

'The woman's dead. Murdered to boot. We'd have been in there sooner or later. It was jist sooner.'

Unanswerable, if flawed, logic.

Roach now looked thoughtfully at McLevy who sat opposite, hair combed neatly, hat placed primly on Roach's table.

Indeed the lieutenant had now had a chance to reflect on all the facts of the case and had something up his sleeve for his all-knowing inspector from this very morning.

After delivering an expected and formal admonition, he sat back, while Queen Victoria still looked out sideways.

'How do you think we should proceed with the Morrison case?' he asked quietly.

McLevy blinked. The reprimand had been like water off a duck's back but he had been anticipating more of the same.

'Bannerman committed the killing and can be officially held culpable but that's all,' he answered. 'We cannot prove Sophia Adler's influence over him one way or the other. The father's betrayal and the letters provide a motive, but with her own death we have nothing to offer a judge.'

'My thought also,' said Roach, who liked things neat, tidy, and filed away. 'We have Binnie and the Countess coming up on trial for murder and the Moxey gang in the dock for aggravated assault and theft. Let sleeping dogs lie.'

He twitched his jaw to the side thoughtfully.

'I am assuming that Walter Morrison will not make a fuss either?'

'He was complicit in an earlier crime. Hard tae prove in court, mind you, but enough to keep his mouth shut.'

They nodded agreement on all of that.

The lieutenant had a strange expression on his face as if he were waiting for McLevy to ask something, and one item did come to the inspector's mind.

'I saw Mistress Grierson. Does she want her music box repaired?'

'No. She does not.'

Roach had something between a smile and scowl upon his

face. The smile on account that he was for once one up on his inspector; the scowl was because what he knew did not please him. Yet it would be a fine morsel for his wife, who was still trying to recover from events of last night, so back to the smile, though the scowl suited his face better.

Thus he continued with fractured delivery.

'She will not press charges against Samuel Grant.'

'Whit?'

'She has admitted to a relationship between them and confirmed that he was acting on her behalf by trying to recover the brooch.'

'Ye mean he confessed to save her name?'

'It would seem so.'

'And she's confessing to save his bacon?'

'Indeed.'

'Wonders will never cease.'

While McLevy ruminated upon such, Roach admitted to himself at being impressed by the steadfastness of Muriel Grierson as she sat in his office and virtually ruined her reputation. She would have to testify at the Moxey trial and admit her liaison in open court.

Yet, after confounding him by dropping the charges against Samuel Grant, she had answered all his questioning succinctly and ended with a simple yet telling statement.

'I believe Samuel to be an honourable man; it is not right that he should suffer and I do not care what the world thinks of me. That includes your spouse, sir.'

One in the eye for Roach, and he was tempted not to act as expected but then word would get round in any case and it would cheer Mrs Roach up no end; sudden death such as last night always depressed her, running as it did in the family.

While all this passed in a jumble through the lieutenant's normally ordered mind, McLevy's thoughts had been proceeding much the same minus the gossip.

She had a bit of ballast, this wifie.

Ye can never tell with human beings.

Especially women.

'I saw her at the desk. Would ye believe it, eh?'

'She will be waiting for Sergeant Murdoch to complete the papers of release.'

'I'll away and hurry him up; he'll take forever.'

McLevy rose. In fact he was nosy to see the couple before they left, Silver Sam and wee Muriel. . .what a prospect.

Wonder what Big Arthur would think of that?

Roach knew full well what was on McLevy's mind.

'Oh, inspector?'

McLevy stopped, one hand on the door.

'When will your Mister Doyle honour us with a visit?'

'I'm sure he'll arrive to make statement this day, sir.'

'Let us hope so. He has much to state,' said Roach dryly. Then something else came to mind.

'I received a note from Constable Mulholland. He has recovered somewhat and will report for duty shortly.'

'We have missed his reassuring presence, sir.'

'Uhuh?' said Roach dryly. 'But you managed to lead Ballantyne astray quick enough – and James?'

By now McLevy was three-quarters through the door, only one leg left to go.

'Try not to lean against any hotel doors in the foreseeable future, eh?'

'Your servant aye, lieutenant.'

Roach let out a caustic laugh at that idea and for a moment their eyes met.

'Eventful days, James. Even for Leith.'

'More to come, no doubt,' replied the inspector, not realising the truth of that remark.

He vanished out the door.

Roach looked up at Queen Victoria.

No matter what angle, she never did quite meet his eye.

When McLevy strode through the station, he found someone heading his way.

Silver Sam. A bit ragged from his sojourn in the cells but looking well enough. Over his shoulder McLevy could see Muriel waiting at the station door, a sheaf of papers in her hand.

Murdoch must have put a bit of speed on.

'I have something tae tell you,' said Samuel.

'Tell away.'

'I heard your constable talking.'

'Which one?'

'Wi' the red face.'

'Continue, if you please.'

In fact Ballantyne had been gossiping to one of the other constables as they fed the prisoners their breakfast.

The Countess and Binnie had been moved to the main Edinburgh jail to await trial, so it was just the Moxey gang and Silver Samuel; mercifully Jupiter Carlisle had fallen into a deep sleep and no-one wanted to wake him.

The breakfast was not much of a repast, being a handsel of grey-bread with a smear of butter, passed carefully through the bars with a tin mug of water.

The constable was especially careful because he had once, due to his kind heart and a prisoner pretending that his own was under attack, ventured in the cell to help.

He was then rendered unconscious and by the time he woke up, the prisoner was long gone.

However, Ballantyne was more experienced now – had he not accompanied the great McLevy on patrol?

The young man could not help but revel in the envy and admiration of his colleagues, nor resist the revelation of some juicy details.

'Such as that – and here's your bread, Mister Grant – the motive for murder would seem to be the death all these years ago of one Jonathen Sinclair in the Leith Docks.'

Samuel heard this and had his own thoughts, which he intended to keep to himself, but the glorious advent of Muriel had come just in time before he cracked and admitted that Seth Moxey's allegations of entanglement and disclosure were in fact true, though much good it might have done him because the police would aye take the word of a winsome widow over a jumped-up street keelie; anyway she had come *for his sake*.

It was the first act of unselfish love Samuel had ever witnessed on his behalf, and he was fierce proud of his wee Moumou.

His woman. When he came out of the cell, she looked at him and said, 'From this moment on, Samuel Grant, you will walk a straight line and I will walk it with you.'

He could have kissed her right there and then but didn't want to get her a bad name in a police station.

But then when they emerged and she went to get the papers,

Samuel saw McLevy on the prowl and decided to display his new credentials of respectability.

So, he continued his declaration.

'Jonathen Sinclair. The murder. I saw it.'

'Whit?'

McLevy's jaw dropped for real this time.

'I was sleeping rough. By the water. I saw it happen.'

The Leith Docks, 1864

Young Samuel Grant, having had a coin pushed between his teeth, looked into the cold eyes of the American and ran for his life.

But not far.

The boy was curious. Why would the man pay him to go away? Was there more money to be found?

So he crept back to the head of the wynd in time to see the blond hair shining in the dim radiance from the jostling ships as the man headed for the cluster of boatyard offices in the distance.

One window was illuminated, shining like a lighthouse in the dark.

Samuel watched.

The man he now knew as Jonathen Sinclair walked on, whistling a jaunty air, a tune the boy had never heard before. American probably.

Then another man stepped out from the shadows ahead, lifted a pistol and fired.

Samuel saw the impact of the bullet striking the body before Sinclair went down like a felled tree.

He did not move.

The other man, who wore a long oilskin coat and wide brimmed black hat, moved towards the fallen man, confident in his aim.

The boy could not breathe, such was his terror. This was a deadly business.

Then it got deadlier.

As the man bent over the still body another shot sounded and the killer was jolted back from short range.

His hat flew off to reveal a similar shock of fair hair while he staggered back then fell in his turn.

For a moment both bodies were still, then Jonathen Sinclair slowly rose to his feet, a long pistol gun held in his hand, the barrel still smoking.

For a long instance he looked down at the corpse, then he came to a decision.

He removed the man's oilskin coat and fitted his own coat in its place. Then he emptied all the pockets of the dead man, working swiftly while glancing around. He took a sheaf of papers from his pocket and put them in place to be in the other's possession.

Then he took a ring from his finger and put it on the stiff hand lying there.

That done, he sighted down the long pistol, put the nozzle in close and then blew the dead man's head clean off his shoulders.

The boy took to his heels this time and did not stop.

McLevy absorbed all this as Samuel brought his rendition to a close.

'Ye didnae think to tell the police?'

'I was a wee boy. Who would believe me?'

'Ye could have tried.'

'I'm no' that enamoured of the police.'

But Samuel hastily qualified the remark with a glance back to Muriel who was waiting with some impatience at the station door.

The bouncy mattress was calling. If she was going to lose her reputation, it might as well be worth her while.

Her mind flipped back to the time yesterday when, miserably going through her dead husband's desk for the want of anything better to do, she had opened the secret drawer again and stuck her hand to the back. There she found a small embossed knob which when she pulled, produced another aperture.

Undertakers have many boxes.

Inside this one was a letter addressed to her husband at his business address from a woman who signed herself *your loving creature and playmate, Beth Ryder*. The hand was not uneducated and the words to the point.

They promised further amatory adventures and were fairly graphic as to how this would be achieved.

They also thanked him for his generous offerings both in love and cash.

Which is when Muriel realised that a scamp who would go to jail for you was worth a hundred respectable men who keep a mistress to give them pleasure and a sour face to give their wife.

She had told the maid of her decision and Ellen's only comment was that she'd have the tea ready for them when they got back. And turn the bed down.

Muriel winked at Sam. Most unladylike.

'I'm better disposed now,' said the bold Samuel to the inspector.

And to prove the truth of that, he volunteered further endorsement of his new qualities.

'I'd seen him before. Sinclair.'

'Whereabouts?' asked McLevy, quickly.

'The Happy Land. He had a wee magpie there. My cousin Mamie worked the place, God rest her soul. She'd pass me a bite to eat and I'd watch them a' arrive frae the upstairs window. I saw him twice.'

The Happy Land had been a notorious bawdy-hoose, run and owned by one Henry Preger. A villainous type who had died in mysterious circumstances and was mourned by no-one.

'Sinclair was mad keen on that wee lassie. And she on him. Lovey-dovey. She was aye playing wi' his hair.'

'What was her name?'

'I don't know, and Mamie's dead now, but I can tell you one that does.'

McLevy did not need to be told. The woman who had plied her trade there was suspected of helping Henry shuffle off this mortal coil and who then opened her own place, the Holy Land, followed after a fire and insurance money by that quintessence of bordellos, the Just Land, was none other than Jean Brash.

And she owed him her sweet existence.

'I'll be in touch,' he said to Samuel.

'You know where tae find me,' replied Samuel, proudly, then turned and walked to the door where Muriel put her arm through his and off they walked to another life.

Silver Sam and Moumou.

No hidden drawers.

As they did so Constable Mulholland walked in, favouring his side slightly but telling himself he was fit for duty and ready for action.

Possibly after his landlady fussing around him – Roach's guess was right, she was Irish but not buxom, in fact thin as a rake – Mulholland was hoping for a hero's welcome at the station. No bunting, no pipe bands but the odd handshake or a clenched-fist salute.

What he received instead was his inspector coming up with a possessed look in his eye.

'How fit are ye, constable?' he demanded.

'I'll live till I die,' said Mulholland.

'Good,' came the response, 'for we have work to do.'

With that McLevy, who was luckily still in his outdoor clothes, hustled Mulholland out before he even managed to get a foot inside.

Ballantyne watched them go and sighed.

For the moment his days of glory were over. Back to the insects and a quiet life.

But what a time it had been.

42

Lead, kindly light, amid the encircling gloom,
lead thou me on;
The night is dark, and I am far from home.

JOHN HENRY NEWMAN, 'Lead, Kindly Light'

He watched the two figures approach in the gloom of the afternoon, walking slowly up the crooked road that wound its way through the bare fields.

They were city folk, or at least dressed so, the tall one leaning slightly to the side, the other a burly figure with a low-brimmed bowler, battling against the wind that always blew at this time of year.

Down towards Loch Leven lay the more fertile land but up here in the Braes of Orwell was a harsher proposition; a few cattle and sheep, with a tough grind to grow crops of any great matter save what the poor soil would allow.

The farm fed and housed them; it was a hard taskmaster and took its toll but he was content enough.

More than that, sometimes.

He had watched his wife and twin boys, their fair hair flopping to the ungainly sway of the ramshackle cart, leave some time earlier after a bite to eat.

Kirstie calling encouragement to Auld Bob, their stubborn and slow horse, who knew the road down was easy compared to the one back up when they would be loaded with provisions from the market town.

So the horse was saving his strength.

Age teaches you such wisdom.

Usually the farmer would have gone with them but this day had decided to remain at home.

There was always something to do: a fence to mend, a dyke to restore, the henhouse to repair, but that was not the reason he had stayed.

A dream last night.

Cannon fire, bodies piled on wagons, no clean straw, no springs to cushion against the jolts on a road the savage rains had washed back to sharp stone. Whips cracking, profanities shouted at the broken horses, the storm beating down, almost drowning the cries of agony.

Will no-one have mercy upon me?

My God – why cannot you let me die?

My poor wife, my dear children – what will become of you?

Some moaned, some prayed, some cursed their fate and some, like John Findhorn, held their peace.

His last words,

I wish I was home.

The farmer had awoken drenched in sweat, his wife sleeping peacefully beside him.

These dreams used to haunt him but then had faded with the years.

Now this one had returned, and so he stayed at home. Stayed to see the men approach. This had been his dread for a long, long time but like the dreams the fear had faded.

However, it too had now returned.

He walked away from the window into their bedroom where a locked, strong-ribbed chest had its place and opened it with a large key that was hidden high on the shelves.

These boys got in everywhere; they had arrived late, not six years before, and were making up for lost time.

He and Kirstie had almost given up hope but then they had been twice blessed.

The farmer had a lot to lose.

He reached into the chest and took out a dark piece of oil-cloth, which he unwrapped to reveal a long revolver. It shone in the light for he had taken good care of it over the years but the gun contained only the one bullet.

As he replaced the cloth, he saw buried deep in the chest the white piece of linen that held his grandfather's watch. A fine thick timepiece shattered all these years ago when a bullet smashed into its body at the Leith docks.

Saved his life. No denying that. The bullet still in place. Buried in broken time.

Below that was a hint of uniform grey.

He closed the chest, locked it, carefully replaced the key, for he was a careful man, and returned to the main room and kitchen where the family lived and ate. The revolver he placed inside a drawer in an old sideboard that butted up against the wall. It would be easy to reach under pretext.

Just as he did so, there was a knock at the door.

When he opened, a man stood there.

'I am James McLevy, inspector of police,' he said. 'My parish is Leith in the city of Edinburgh. May we come in, if you please, sir?'

The farmer without a word let Mulholland and McLevy make entrance. He showed no curiosity but poured out two glasses of water from a large jug on the table.

'Hospitality costs little,' he said at last.

They saw a tall whipcord man, with fair hair that was thinning a touch, hazel-eyed and hook-nosed. His face was craggy and lined like the land he tilled and a beard trimmed neatly enough with a darker colour than the hair, flecks of grey here and there.

There was a resemblance of sorts to the soldier in the picture McLevy had seen on the wall, but time changes us all.

The man still said nothing so the inspector gulped the water thirstily then started in.

It had been a long road via Jean Brash who had reluctantly

supplied the requested details, when reminded that if it were not for McLevy she would still be drinking Sergeant Murdoch's vile brew and looking forward to a slow death in the Perth penitentiary.

Armed with a name and geographical location she gave out, they had travelled by coach towards the town of Kinross to check the local records, and there come up lucky.

Kirstie Donnachie, a native of these parts, had left for a while then come back with a new husband and taken over the family farm; her widowed father had died of a lingering illness some time after her return.

The farm was registered in her name; the husband's coincidentally was the same appellation.

John Donnachie.

The policemen had then hired a pony and trap to take them to the farm but the driver had flatly refused to bring his precious cart up the heavily rutted road.

So, after agreeing a time for him to come back, they had walked the rest.

While Mulholland nursed his partially healed wound through all these different journeys, McLevy had brought him fully up to date with the twists and turns of the bizarre events. Bullets flying everywhere, bodies left and right.

'Whit would your Aunt Katie say tae all that?' he had asked, as they jolted in the coach to Kinross.

A dead dog breeds many a maggot was the obscure rejoinder.

The farmer had not made a single unnecessary move since allowing them entry and his very stillness was a sign for caution. He did not sit nor ask them to do the same.

Mulholland eased aside his policeman's cape to give better access to his hornbeam stick should the need arise, as his inspector began the tale.

'You are here known as John Donnachie,' McLevy said to the man. 'But I believe you to be Jonathen Sinclair, an officer in the Confederate Army sent tae buy ships for to run the blockade. Eighteen years ago.

'You were in fact betrayed to the Federal agents and shot at in the Leith Docks. The bullet hit and down ye went, yet by some miracle you survived, eh?'

John Donnachie was seemingly unsurprised by the details at McLevy's fingertips. He thought once more of his grandfather's watch that he always had worn high, over the heart, and finally spoke.

'Miracles can happen, sir.'

In his words it might be possible to catch some cadence of the South but the man had assimilated the local accent well enough.

Protective colouration. A shape-changer. Proteus.

'Right enough,' said McLevy. 'As the killer stooped over tae finish the job no doubt, you quite rightly shot him in your turn. Self-defence, no argument there, though the letter of the law might argue otherwise.'

The inspector poured out another glass of water and slugged it back. Thirsty work.

'But it's what ye did next that more catches at my concern. You were witnessed to change clothing with this man then blow his face tae buggery. I trust he was dead first.'

The farmer inclined his head slightly, but no more than that.

'Now I have read all your letters, sir. And I believe I can fathom the cause behind your actions.'

'My letters?'

'To your wife. I'll get tae that later.'

For the first time the man seemed taken aback and his eyes shifted to Mulholland.

'Don't look at me,' said the constable. 'I'm just along for the ride.'

For a moment a glance passed between him and the inspector; no matter how uncanny the circumstance it was good to be in tandem once more.

'I believe your soul was sick of war. Death. All that made you what you were and held you fast. You saw this as an opportunity to find another life. To leave it all behind.'

John Donnachie closed his eyes.

This man who had come from out of the blue, with his white parchment face and slate grey eyes, would seem to know the depth of his very being.

It was the truth. He had indeed been sick in his soul to the point where he no longer cared, no longer felt that life had any meaning. Only death. In that fine state, he had strayed, fallen, gone to a bawdy-hoose, a low-class place to further abase himself and there met a girl new arrived from the country.

Kirstie Donnachie.

A small girl, bright-eyed, dark-haired, with a low centre of gravity. *Near to the earth* she liked to joke.

In anger she had left a demanding father and come to the city for excitement. Instead she had found whoredom.

And then she had found him.

When he sighted down the pistol at William Mitchell, it was indeed himself he was destroying.

Even the hair colour was the same. Only the face was different. And then there was no face to worry over.

He left his papers on the body along with his wedding ring jammed upon the dead finger and returned to his lodging to collect some pitifully few belongings, one of which was his old Confederate uniform.

To honour John Findhorn if nothing more.

As for his wife, Melissa?

That was a dream. A dream he no longer believed in. She would manage. The South would lose but her family were rich – she'd make a pretty widow and would find someone else.

They had no children. Nothing to hold them together.

So he had grabbed Kirstie from the Happy Land and they had run like two children far, far away from the city, back to where she was born and raised.

They had married and John had taken her name.

Old man Donnachie had been suspicious at first but then when he saw how the man worked day and night, broke his nails, scarred his fine delicate fingers with hard labour, the old man, as is the way of Scots, took him to his heart.

Then the father died, Kirstie was left the farm and she and her man settled for a life that was hard but had its own rewards. Nature is cruel, but she is also generous.

The twins arrived and life was full.

The farmer had much to lose.

The policemen watched as Donnachie walked away and leant upon a sideboard, close to the wall.

'What do you want from me?' he asked softly.

Not for the first time McLevy surprised his constable.

'Confession would be nice but I doubt you're in the mood,' he replied. 'In fact without that, I have little proof. A wee boy eighteen years ago on a dark night, the compromised testimony of a bawdy-hoose keeper, a photo that gets near you but not enough. No, you're in the clear unless you sing like a lintie. And as I have said, I doubt that to happen.'

Donnachie slid the sideboard drawer back into place and turned to face them.

'Then what do you want here?'

McLevy seemed to have become stone, Mulholland though tilting a little was also immobile.

They waited. The farmer took a deep breath.

'How did you get the letters?'

'Your daughter brought them,' said McLevy. 'All the way from America.'

He suddenly let out a whoop of discordant laughter while Donnachie took his turn to freeze.

'Ye spent a night wi' your lawful wife, your bride Melissa, before – by the way, does wee Kirstie know she might be bigamously betrothed?'

'We have no secrets,' Donnachie replied tightly.

'That's nice. Well, before the battle of Gettysburg you went home to kiss the bride. Nine months later, she bore you a daughter. No way she could inform you of such because she didnae know where you were biding.'

'It's a tricky business,' said Mulholland.

'It is, constable,' rejoined McLevy, not taking his eyes from those of the farmer. 'Your daughter, sir, arrived in this country under the name of Sophia Adler. She carried your letters, a photograph and vengeance in her heart.'

Donnachie closed his eyes once more. Sophia. Wisdom. The name stood for wisdom. He and Melissa when love's young dream was holding true, had chosen that name.

For a child to be. One day. When the war was over.

'She had changed the surname tae Adler. Who knows why? Like yourself. In disguise. Must run in the family.'

McLevy now stepped in close and Mulholland moved discreetly to the side, gripping at his stick in case things got out of hand.

The inspector could see traces of Sophia in the man's face; not much but it was there.

'For your sake, for your betrayal and supposed death, she caused a man called Gilbert Morrison to be murdered. He wisnae much and he had indeed betrayed you like Judas, but he had some right to live.

'I myself put two bullets into the murderer, Magnus Bannerman, who was persuaded to the act by your daughter.'

McLevy's face became sombre as he prepared to deliver the last rites for Sophia Adler.

'What has happened to her?' asked Donnachie, with a dry rasp to his voice.

'She is dead, sir. Shot. A stray bullet. A fateful accident. She died in delusion.'

Donnachie's face was set and showed no emotion.

'Is there anything you would care to contribute?'

To this request of the inspector's, the man shook his head. 'I have nothing more to say.'

McLevy snapped upright, jerked his head towards the door and Mulholland realised again to his surprise that the inspector did not intend to stay much longer.

Donnachie stood in the centre of the room, an isolated figure in rough farming clothes.

Something in his stillness irritated McLevy beyond measure as if the man had absorbed all but not felt it.

The inspector spat out the words like bullets.

'Two days from now she'll be buried in Dean Cemetery wi' a crowd of folk who did not know her standing around the grave. Perhaps she would have taken the same road anyway, but your decision eighteen years ago has caused the death of three people, one of whom was your own flesh and blood. Stick that in your pipe and smoke it!'

With that he was out of the door.

Mulholland paused before following. He had noticed some home-made toys in a box to the side.

'You have children of your own now, sir?' he queried.

The man made no response.

'Let's hope you take good care of them,' said the constable, and followed his inspector out of sight.

After a long moment, John Donnachie moved over to the side-board and opened up the drawer.

He took out the long black revolver and hefted it in his hand. How many men had it killed in its time?

How many?

Mulholland had to put on a bit of speed to catch up with McLevy, anger putting wings on the inspector's feet.

'It's a long way to come to go all the way back again,' observed the constable.

'True enough,' grunted the inspector, noting that the pony and trap had put in an appearance at the bottom of the road as arranged.

Timing was everything.

'So we're just going to let him free?' muttered Mulholland, whose wound was giving him gyp and all for nothing.

'Our only hope was confession, and I knew as soon as I saw the man he would not crack. Too much to lose – wait!'

McLevy lifted his head and turned back towards the farm.

'Did you hear something?'

'Not a dicky-bird.'

'A crack? Gunshot?'

'You've got them on the brain.'

'Aye. Right enough,' said McLevy and they walked on down.

'So, we're just letting him go?'

'Will you stop saying that!'

Things were getting back to normal between them.

'It just seems a long way,' said Mulholland, like a dog with a bone.

'All right, all right. I came out here because – because – aghhh.'

McLevy threw his arms up in the air and sighed.

'It's all very Greek. Revenge. Retribution. I felt – I felt I owed it to Sophia Adler and don't ask me why, because I don't know. It is beyond my comprehension. But – I have told him tae his face. Now, he knows. Though she does not.'

'Unless she's floating around with the spirits?'

The constable's remark stopped McLevy in his tracks for a moment.

'Indeed. Unless that highly unlikely eventuality has occurred. Now, come on. The case is closed!'

McLevy hammered his low-brimmed bowler firmly on to his head as the wind was beginning to rise.

Timing is everything.

43

On doit des égards aux vivants: on ne doit aux morts que la vérité.

We owe respect to the living; to the dead we owe only truth.

VOLTAIRE

Arthur Conan Doyle stood like a ruined castle as the rain fell upon his shoulders. No more sailor's cap and jacket, though he would use those soon enough; he was dressed for a funeral. Sombre. Black.

The service had been long, despite the driving rain, with some folk there purely out of curiosity and a great many Spiritualist followers come to pay respects.

The minister had done his best to combine Christianity with mesmeric forces and had got into a rare tangle, which had taken a fair time to unravel.

Then the head of the Edinburgh Spiritualists, a tall, ascetic man who might well have been an undertaker in another life, spoke at great length of the comfort Sophia would find in the other regions of being.

Doyle's mind had drifted. He'd hoped his mother might accompany him but Mary Doyle was inclining towards the Anglicans these days and preferred to rest at home.

She was also a sensible woman and did not enjoy funerals. Plus the fact that anything to do with this whole business seemed fraught with danger and she would be pleased when her son was safely removed to sea for a while.

None of this was of any comfort to Conan Doyle as he brooded upon a lost love. A gentle, sensitive creature who had become the innocent victim of a madman.

McLevy could have told him differently but hadn't the heart, and besides, as the lieutenant had put in summation, *let sleeping dogs lie.*

Roach in fact had been in attendance with the wife hanging on his arm. Indeed there were quite a few wifies clustered around the lieutenant's gloomy form, possibly the whist club had doubled up with the ethereal forces.

Ballantyne had also put in an appearance, a home-knitted scarf knotted round his neck which both guarded against influenza and kept his birthmark concealed.

When at last the Head Spiritualist had concluded his sincere if overlong tribute, all the erstwhile mourners quit the scene and McLevy noticed that after solemn nods in his direction from both, Roach and Ballantyne walked down together with the gaggle of wifies chirping at the back, no doubt discussing the morals of Muriel Grierson and murder upon the stage in the same breath.

The inspector was intrigued by this odd pairing. Roach had no offspring. Perhaps he saw Ballantyne as a son of sorts? Or more likely was intent on keeping him away from McLevy's baleful influence.

Anyway, they deserved each other.

Mulholland had found shelter under a tree, his wound aching in the damp, so the inspector and Doyle had the mournful scene to themselves.

They looked down at the tombstone, which bore the name of Sophia Adler and the one quote:

They that are after the flesh do mind the things of the flesh; but they that are after the Spirit, the things of the Spirit.

'For to be carnally minded is death,' said McLevy.

Doyle was jolted out of his chivalric melancholy.

'What?'

'That's the rest of the saying. The Bible. Romans.'

Arthur sighed and looked at this strange man who had come into his life and brought its opposite. Death.

'I am bound for Liverpool,' he said.

'Guard your wallet, they're a shifty bunch down there.'

'I shall not stay long. I am to be ship's surgeon. On a steamship, the *Mayumba*. Cargo and passengers to and from Madeira and West Africa.'

'Will ye see any flying fish?'

'Undoubtedly.'

'I've aye wanted to see a fish fly.'

For a moment they both looked once more at the tombstone and in unison removed their hats.

McLevy's silent thought was that it was for the best that he had decided not to tell Conan Doyle about the resurrected father, the letters, plus the suspicion he had of Magnus Bannerman being possessed and used for murder. The young man had enough buzzing around in his head.

Perhaps some day. In the future.

For Doyle, he thought that he would never forget this woman. She was burnt into his heart.

He would recreate her one day though. Change the name a little but honour the essential memory.

In silence they both made goodbye in their own fashion to Sophia Adler and then walked slowly away.

Doyle suddenly stopped.

'One day I will write,' he said, 'a detective to rival any in fiction. He is much in my mind.'

'Will he be anything like me?' asked McLevy, curious that he might have bred a doppelganger.

'Not too much,' replied Doyle. 'Save in one attribute.'

'And whit is that?'

'A capacity for the unexpected.'

The young man grinned suddenly and McLevy let out a sharp bark of laughter before sticking out his hand.

'Goodbye Arthur Conan Doyle,' he said in formal tones.

'Ignatius.'

'Whit?'

'My other name. Between the Arthur and the Conan.'

McLevy, who was only James, whistled.

'An English king, martyred saint and Irish hero. A load tae carry.'

'I have broad shoulders.'

Having said this, Doyle almost stood to attention.

'Goodbye James McLevy, Inspector of Police.'

He took the proffered hand in his huge paw and the two men

gazed at each other as the Edinburgh rain fell upon their bare heads.

Then they banged on their hats and parted company.

McLevy watched the giant figure wend its way down a sinuous path, into the trees and out of sight.

Was it his imagination or did the young man already walk with a sailor's rolling gait?

McLevy stepped back to the disconsolate Mulholland who was feeling out of sorts.

'Didn't even say goodbye,' he complained, as regards the departed Doyle.

'Hardly knows ye,' was the unsympathetic response.

Mulholland snuffled into a hankie.

'I think I'm catching my death here.'

'You're gey feeble these days.'

'I've had a knife stuck in my ribs,' rejoined the constable indignantly. 'It tends to lower the resistance.'

McLevy nodded but made no move to go.

The rain suddenly stopped and a shaft of sun burst through the dark clouds.

A mist began to rise from the damp vegetation below and through it came the figure of a man in uniform. A grey outline that matched the haze and might even have been created out of it, so ghostly did the effigy seem.

McLevy saw it first and drew Mulholland further back into the shelter of the dripping trees. They watched as the figure approached from the opposite direction to that which the mourners had taken.

The man walked slowly, as if the incline caused him difficulty, but as he got closer they could see that his uniform was that of a Confederate officer, the slouch hat obscuring the face as his boots thudded dully into the damp earth.

He wore a cape of sorts over his shoulders and the mist seemed to cling as if attracted to the material.

At last he reached the grave of Sophia Adler and knelt down, again with difficulty as if his bones were creaking.

The sun vanished and mist swirled around to veil him once more as he swept off his hat.

Then after a long silence when Mulholland crammed the

hankie over his nose so as not to let out a snorting wheeze, the strains of a song were heard. The voice was in tune enough but harsh as if unused to melody.

> *'O Polly, O Polly,*
> *It's for your sake alone,*
> *I've left my old father,*
> *My country, my home.*
> *I've left my old mother*
> *To weep and to mourn,*
> *I am a Rebel soldier*
> *And far from my home.'*

Then there was a creak of leather boots as for a moment they glimpsed the figure rise and bring up something in his hand. Then the figure was concealed once more and after some time, a single shot was fired, the sound absorbed in the muffled damp, but unmistakable enough.

'Has he killed himself?' whispered Mulholland.

'Anything is possible,' the inspector whispered back. 'Let us investigate further.'

Mulholland took out his hornbeam stick as they walked cautiously towards the grave; bullets were no respecter of persons and he had scar tissue enough already.

But when they arrived, there was nothing to be seen.

'Was it a ghostie, d'ye think?' asked Mulholland, coming over a little Irish in the cemetery atmosphere.

'I doubt it,' responded McLevy, bending down to pick up something lying on the newly dug grave.

It was a revolver. Black. Shiny. He spun the chambers.

'Empty,' he said. 'Perhaps he shot at the sky or maybe even God – ye never know.'

The east wind made an appearance and the mist lifted. They could now see clearly in all directions but there was no trace of the uniformed figure.

'Like something in a dream,' said Mulholland quietly.

'Just so,' replied the inspector. 'Just so.'

Later on, a blackbird flew overhead and chattered indignantly at the two figures far below as Jean Brash and McLevy sipped their delicious brew.

Why the bird was in such a bate was not for them to know but it had just narrowly missed being impaled on the claws of a cat and considered the human beings in this garden to be partways responsible.

'What a business, eh?' said Jean Brash.

'Uhuh.'

Having packed the snuffling Mulholland back to his lodgings, the inspector had found himself at a loose end and, as often happened in such circumstance, his feet had led him to the Just Land.

It was late afternoon, and the girls just getting used to being back in the house after their banishment, so things were quiet and Jean, it seemed, happy to see him.

They sat companionably enough in a little gazebo in the garden sheltered from the drizzle, and enjoyed a rare moment of peace together.

McLevy sniffed at his coffee with relish.

'Whit d'ye cry this?'

'*Mountain Breeze*. A Lebanese blend. Aromatic.'

He took a delicate mouthful and Jean watched with some approval because he had a tendency to gulp at things.

She shook her head at the story he had just told of events stretching from eighteen years ago till now.

One event he had not covered, however, was Henry Preger's sudden death and her purchasing arsenic powder for the rats at an apothecary's far away geographically from the Holy Land. But no more of that, safer ground in holding to where the inspector had led her.

'More sugar biscuits?' she offered.

Hannah Semple had brought out a large plate of the same and although warning McLevy *no tae guzzle the whole lot doon at one snash*, indicated her gratitude for his pulling certain irons out of the fire by absent-mindedly tapping the crown of his low-brimmed bowler as if to make sure his head was still inside.

McLevy took two of the proffered biscuits, dipped one in his coffee and sucked at the soggy mixture with pleasure.

'And there's no charge you can lay at his door?' Jean asked, with a certain satisfaction, because she had been fond of Kirstie Donnachie and not happy about having to dole out the information to a policeman. It went against the grain.

'No. I put it all before the lieutenant and he felt the same. Too long ago, unreliable witnessing, and a'body deid but one. Not a hope in hell.'

He tackled the second sugar biscuit in the same manner as the first.

'John Donnachie, Jonathen Sinclair, is free. All he has to do is live with his own conscience.'

'From what you say at the grave, he might seem to be settling accounts as best he could.'

'If it was him. May have been a ghost.'

They laughed quietly and then saw two female figures come towards them.

'We've covered that fish pond,' said Maisie Powers. 'Wire netting; that'll keep the bugger out.'

Lily Baxter, who had linked arms with the bigger woman, grinned and mimed some creature with sharp claws trying to get through to the fish.

Maisie burst out laughing.

'She's a daft wee devil,' she announced; then, after a ritual scowl at McLevy, faced Lily and pronounced slowly.

'C'mon. I'll race ye tae the door.'

Off they went, Lily leading the way by a mile, the shrieks sounding like two children on the loose.

'I have invited Maisie to come and join us,' said Jean, as if it were a Masonic Lodge proposal. 'She will take over from Francine. What she lacks in finesse she will make up for in vigour and Lily can guide her.'

She caught a look in McLevy's eye and said firmly.

'At the moment they are just friends.'

'That's nice.'

'Maisie tells me that when she leathers the clients she will imagine your face upon their backside.'

'Very kind.'

Then Jean's face became serious.

'I've meant to tell you. Jessie Nairn was buried with due dignity. All the girls were on hand.'

McLevy wasn't sure how much dignity a tiding of magpies would bring, but contented himself with a nod.

'What'll happen tae the Countess's place?'

'Oh, someone will buy it,' said Jean airily. 'It's well enough equipped.'

He shot her a look but decided not to pursue this conversational bearing.

A low-pitched yowl came from the direction of the garden wall.

'That bloody cat!' Jean exclaimed.

'Whit?'

'The reason we had tae cover over the pool. It had one of the big fish out flopping on the grass!'

An offended black shape sat on the wall, just missed aim upon a fat bird and now the pond was out of reach.

'Bathsheba!' McLevy spluttered. 'Whit's she doing here?'

'Who?'

'Bathsheba. My cat. Well, comes tae visit. Whit's she doing up here?'

'Hunting,' said Jean grimly.

McLevy called out to the animal, which promptly jumped off the wall and disappeared.

'Seems to know you well enough,' Jean commented dryly.

The inspector shook his head. It was a long haul from his attic to this garden; feline ways are mysterious indeed.

He reached for another sugar biscuit.

'I have to thank you, James,' said Jean suddenly. 'The Countess. She had me down and out.'

'Ye'd have thought of something,' he grunted.

'I'm not so sure. Are you all right?'

She noticed that he had stopped in mid-stream, the sugar biscuit dipped into the coffee but not withdrawn.

A twinge of pain had hit him in the chest and he'd had another flash of that damned figure from the dream.

'I'm fine,' he replied.

And he was. Indigestion can take many forms and he had been eating haphazardly too much of late.

Unfortunately the sugar biscuit had now dissolved in the coffee. He tried to fish it out but things just got worse as the remnants swirled around.

'James McLevy, what a mucky creature you are,' scolded Jean, throwing away the dregs and giving him a clean cup into which she poured a fresh brew. 'Here!'

He accepted this, doled in his usual four spoons of sugar, and sat back meekly enough as if he and Jean were an old married couple, she tutting at his incapacity.

But in fact she was a bawdy-hoose keeper and he was a man knee deep in murders.

This last adventure would keep him going for a while, though.

'That poor girl,' said Jean as if she had read his mind. 'No matter what she did. To be shot like that. And die not knowing.'

'Well, she knows now,' he muttered.

The inspector keeked out of the gazebo and looked at the dull sky, wondering what might be going on in the spirit world; it would be busy up there.

He caught a trace of concern in Jean's gaze and smiled at her as he prepared to drink his coffee.

'Whit a caper, eh?' said James McLevy.